WEIRD THEATRE

An anthology of strange tales to tantalize the mind

First edition: 2014 (Published by Xlibris)
Second edition: 2018 (Upgraded and Unexpurgated, and includes previously-unpublished material—*Reality Check*, *Shades of the Underground* and *Daubers of Dark Dreams*)

A copy of this work is available through the British Library.

ISBN: 978-1-912601-54-7

Mirador Publishing
10 Greenbrook Terrace
Taunton
Somerset
UK
TA1 1UT

Weird Theatre

IXIDORR HACK

Contents

Introduction by the Author

I welcome back the Hack Pack. I hope life finds you in good stead.

This collection of short stories delves predominantly into science-fiction/fantasy concepts rather than anything else but retains my usual trademark approach. This book is more of a sideline for me. You see, I like a bit of science fiction and consider myself something of a Sci-fi geek and a Rock freak. I religiously watched *Doctor Who* throughout my formative years to wit end my school chums nicknamed me 'the Doctor'. At University, they used to call me 'Weird Hack' because of my constant fascination with *The X-Files*. So I thought it only fitting that I should take a stab at writing science fiction. Maybe not so much traditional science fiction but 'concept' fiction. I have a thing for concepts—it's become something of an obsession with me—and I try to base each story on a particular concept. Maybe by reading this anthology you can distinguish the concept from the 'idea' or the 'premise' or the 'theme'. Also, there is a reason for everything in life, hence the work has to make sense, which can sometimes become remarkably difficult when you are dealing with fantastical themes, but at least you don't want the Gentle Reader to suspend their disbelief to the point they can do so no more. And there's me, a Rationalist trying to write about the Irrational. Still, stranger things have happened.

Again, let me know what you think of my humble side-project, as honestly as you can, for we all remain Students of Life—

including Yours Truly—from our Birth to our Grave, questing for knowledge in our eternal desire to learn and better ourselves.

From android technology to psychokinetic powers to the Doomsday Virus, let me transport you to strange, uncharted worlds and the very fringes of the Universe—and *beyond*—with my concept tales, to either delude you or make you think. For that is my ultimate goal: to make you *think* about Identity and Humanity and the Nature of Time and Reality.

And you, as the Audience, can judge the merits of the work and decide with your coolest, constructive critique if your Author is up to scratch.

So pull aside the ancient, cobwebbed theatre drapes and come into my parlour . . .

From one eccentric to another—

Enjoy the show.

Ixidorr Hack
November 2013

Acknowledgments

Sometimes you just have to thank someone for something.

My sincerest thanks to Rod for discussing and devising the perfect virus in **Infection Will Travel** and for kindly consulting me on his journal article.

Archly Amused Pan is for the benefit of my Beautiful Wife. Do you trust me, my darling?

With regards **Reality Check**, I knew my philosophy degree would come in useful one day.

Shades of the Underground: For all those people who worked on our troublesome bathroom . . . The work still isn't finished, you know!

List of Tales

Point of Origin: A whacked-out hippie is chased by a shadowy organization after writing an article that hits far too close to the truth.

The Tryp: An Oxford professor tests out the brain-enhancing properties of a new hallucinogen and records his experiences.

Strange Meridians: Xander Hubley's exploration of weird Internet sites yields something he could never have conceived of.

Perfection on Demand: Marisa's second shot at a relationship with her boyfriend, Hector, reveals he has learned a lot more since last time and is made of much stronger stuff.

Love of a Machine: Upon waking, Zane Harglow cannot believe what's become of the world, and most of all, *him*.

A Question of Empathy: The hostess of a dinner party does not believe her guest is whom she claims she is.

The Janus Factor: A ride in his newly-purchased classic car takes Charlie Hammond to a place undreamed-of in his philosophy.

Mindforce: Edgar Byers is a severely autistic teenage boy. First come the dreams, then the powers . . .

Encounters of the Liminal Kind: Johnny Harding one day witnesses strange men conducting even stranger experiments on the unsuspecting members of the public.

The Litter Patrol: Woods End has a radical way of managing street pollution. Because anybody who drops litter never goes home . . .

Shades of the Underground: While doing routine building work on a private property, two handymen soon discover why the previous tradesmen left in such a hurry.

Tales from Space: A female journalist investigates a UFO sighting and the mysterious Men in Black.

Archly Amused Pan: A GP uses unconventional means to treat his sister-in-law of her vomit phobia.

The Operators: Straight out of medical school, Hitcham Gale begins to hear voices which grow more intense and malicious, leading him on a frightening journey and a revelation of mind-blowing proportions.

Horns of a Cornute: A patient reveals to his hypnotherapist more than he could possibly know.

Reality Check: A patient gets into a philosophical sparring contest with his psychiatrist as he tries to ascertain whether there is any truth to his delusions.

Daubers of Dark Dreams: A couple takes a detour and winds up at an art exhibition—with a difference.

All Our Yesterdays: When her daughter disappears, possibly kidnapped, Carolyn Hayden's world seems to dismantle, piece by piece. Literally.

Infection Will Travel: It is a case of survival of the fittest for a group of schoolfriends during the aftermath of a plague that has wiped out most of mankind.

Opening Narration

"*Please take your seats . . .*

"*Ixidorr Hack welcomes you to WEIRD THEATRE, where the stage is set and the curtain slowly raised to usher in these strange tales. Please allow the scene to gradually unfold before your eyes so you can fully appreciate the weirdness contained therein. You are about to enter an arena, unlike none you have ever witnessed before, where time does not exist and imagination calls the shots. Beware your nerves are about to be tested to their utmost limits. Your mind will have the power to see all, and beyond, even into the cracks between reality, glimpsing impenetrable dimensions, a journey stretching from artificial intelligence to distant alien shores, from the dawn of civilization to its slow, untimely destruction . . .*

"*Please take your roles . . .*

"*Now step onto the stage of Weird Theatre and be part of this mind-bending, immersive experience where weird is as weird gets and from where you might never return . . ."*

Point of Origin

"The most effective way to destroy people is to deny and obliterate their own understanding of their history."

George Orwell

They were coming for him.

It was always the same dream. There were men after him, except they were *not* men. He didn't know who or what they were—government agents, Men in Black, aliens, interdimensional beings or the next step in human evolution—but they were coming. *For him.* Haldane Radley may not have yet figured out whether they were human or not, with their short stature, bald craniums and identical dark suits, or where they hailed from, but he'd given them a name: the Outsiders. And they were apparently telepaths with the ability to probe your mind with their own, extract information that wasn't entirely forthcoming and do terrible things to your sanity. They had already dispatched his closest friend, Waylan Jackson, in their pursuit of him—not killed him outright but driven him permanently insane so as to be committed to the booby hatch for a long, long time. The doctors in their scholarly ignorance had put Waylan's madness down to a drug-induced psychosis on account of all the many different illicit substances in his system.

So why were these Outsiders tracking Haldane down? What could they possibly want with someone like him, a recycled hippie who was constantly whacked-out on drugs?

Before the Outsiders paid Waylan Jackson a visit and took his mind, he had rumoured that it might have something to do with an obscure magazine article that Haldane had published in 1969 called *The Invention of History*. In one of his trippy, paranoidy episodes, Haldane had alleged that all History was One Big Lie and that we were all slaves to a Master Race of Beings, who ultimately ruled over us for some dread purpose, keeping us complacent while faking our past. The editor at the time had loved the article and published it. It was just an article, of course, and Haldane went on to greater things, modestly-speaking, in underground, conspiracy-theory circles: the Apollo moon landings were staged, the Bilderberg Group was less a highly influential, philanthropic organization, discussing the absolute far-reaching politics of the world, but rather more a sub-rosa committee motivated only with serving the selfish interests of the elite, one-percent of the population at the expense of everyone else. All Haldane's later articles were well-received, enough to maintain a respectable income over the years, in the form of charitable donations, but it was only when he stumbled upon that original article lying dormant in a desk drawer and he revisited what he wrote back in the drug-hazed days of the late '60s about the fabrication of our entire history that he first became aware that the Outsiders were on his case through his nightly dreams and later learned of the psychic torture endured by his best friend.

Haldane had only been in his late teens, high on acid, hooked on Jefferson Airplane and constantly begging for free love, during that revolutionary Summer of Love, which kicked off in San Francisco and spread like wildfire throughout the Western world, with Britain's attempt nowhere near as awesome, and it was tragic to know all those credited with the Flower Power generation had, like himself, reached retirement age and were presently cruising through their golden years. Those vintage Jesus values of peace, love and free will still resonated with today's liberal-minded youth. The drugs had taken their toll on a lot of his contemporaries, but not him. His mind had been his stronghold, built to last. Or perhaps he was flakier than he thought and he didn't even know it. Could drugs be a rational response to insanity?

Hiding in his digs, a former disused underground bunker in the middle of Epping Forest, he lived, with no National Insurance number on record or home address or taxes owed to the Inland Revenue, so as far as the government was concerned, he did not exist. Just as well as he might get busted for the cornucopia of cannabis plants he grew for his own consumption in a section of the bunker he had converted into an artificial greenhouse. He enjoyed writing subversive literature, in the gonzo-style of Hunter S. Thompson, publishing it on his website, *Haldane's Beef*, consolidating his status as a minor celebrity among the conspiracy nuts, generating a lot of discussion, some vacuous, some serious, some hilarious. He had installed quite unique security software which could scramble the signal of anybody trying to locate him, making his presence somewhat undetectable to the Man.

But not undetectable enough, it seemed. For he knew today the Outsiders were nearby. Haldane could sense them approach over a five-mile radius, so powerful was their psychic radar, and he had already followed their progress within the safety of his dreams. He had evaded them so far, but with the net closing in around him, it wouldn't be too long before they discovered his secret hideaway, a remarkable feat that not even successive governments had achieved in half-a-century. Haldane decided to stop running, so to speak, and face the Outsiders like a man. He unscrewed the hatch, camouflaged by autumn leaves, and climbed down the rung ladder back into his operations' room, occupied by computer screens and tall, standing databanks, spilling a multi-coloured profusion of wires. He dumped himself in his swivel-chair, dropped some acid, sat back and waited . . .

The Outsiders descended the rungs of the metal ladder, their stomp of footsteps loud and echoey in the submarine-like confines of the operations' room. Even though Haldane could hear thunder reverberate in the sky outside and the noise of a torrential downpour, the men who stepped through the hatch of his World War II bunker—if men is what they were—appeared as dry as bone.

The three of them confronted Haldane, as he swivelled lackadaisically back and forth in his chair, knowing his hour was finally upon him, and he saw them in all their sinister glory.

They were all rather short, around five-foot-four in height, and slightly stocky, their skin hairless and as pale as alabaster. Above their crisp white shirts, they wore identical black suits and ties. A black fedora rested atop their bald pates, completing the appearance of them having dropped straight out of a 1950s comic strip. They could have been mistaken for clones, so similar were their pasty-white faces, unless you spotted the subtle differences between them: slightly narrower and longer nose or less rounded chin or pupils that were a shade darker than those of their colleagues.

"What is the meaning of this noise?" the foremost of the Outsiders inquired irritably, referring to the soft strains of *Journey to the Centre of the Mind* by the Amboy Dukes flowing out of the speakers of the ghetto-blaster. With a quick snap of his fingers, he telekinetically switched off the beatbox and, with it, the music, plunging the room into silence, broken only by the faint sound of the September storm carried through the open hatch. He spoke as though his mouth were filled with water. "Now we can talk . . ."

"Hey there, dudes," Haldane greeted them coolly. "Been seriously expecting you to drop by for some time."

"Mr. Radley, you are an extremely difficult man to track down," continued Outsider # 1 in his dull, watery voice. "Do you know who we are?"

"Hell, yeah, you're the dudes who keep haunting my dreams."

The first Outsider made the introductions, gesturing to his colleagues. "To my left is the Proctor, whose supervisory role includes Chief Administrator, and to my right is the Executive, whose executive functions also oversee operational procedure. I am the Director, who manages the Project. Together with the remaining four members of my team assigned to attend to the administrative duties of this planet, we are the Management, a subdivision of the Authority."

Assigned to this planet? "You're aliens . . ." There, Haldane said it.

"We do not use that phrase, as it carries certain prejudiced connotations."

"I didn't mean to be racist . . ." Haldane apologized.

"In fact, it may be you and your people who *are* the aliens on this planet . . ." the Director left his unexpected statement hanging in the air, but Haldane did not ask him to elaborate. "Have you any comprehension as to why we are here?"

"Let me guess . . . something to do with an article."

"You are correct."

"Why so hell-bent on hunting me down, dudes? It's only a piece of nonsense philosophy I once wrote in my heyday. I can't see any relevance to it."

"It is a very revealing publication easily disseminated in today's age of communication technology."

Haldane was understandably confused, curious. "How so?"

The Director continued in strange, hypersalivating tones: "Inadvertently written or not, you suggest that the entire history of the world is a falsehood."

Realization dawned on Haldane's face. He stared at the Outsiders, their pale faces waxy and expressionless in the eerie blue glow of the fluorescent light and computer monitors. "Are you telling me what I wrote is all true?"

"What you implied is an accurate depiction," the Director admitted.

"But I alleged that all history is bullshit!"

"Far from elegantly phrased, but you have alleged correctly."

"That's impossible! What about the evidence, carbon-dating and all that?"

"Using *our* technology," the Director stated, and went on to explain when he received a blank look from Haldane. "Evidence can be falsified. How do you know the Ancient Egyptians lived three thousand years ago? Or, with the advent of Christianity, the Dark Ages flourished? Or the Elizabethan era ever existed? Or the Duke of Wellington triumphed during the Napoleonic Wars?" The Director answered for Haldane. "Presumably because of artifacts in the earth, archaic relics uncovered at archaeological digs? Paintings and statues in museums purportedly proving the time of the Renaissance? Knowledge passed down generations by word of mouth or recorded on parchment?"

"I suppose . . ."

"None of it is authentic," the Director announced. "Every relic is a hard-light composite constructed by the Authority's Engineers. The Authority's Architects designed your cities. Our Historians furnished your species with the history we felt you deserved. Even your technology is a primitive variant of our own."

"You're shitting me?" Haldane exclaimed incredulously.

History Itself: The Greatest Cover-up of All. "But why do all this?"

"We have been the secret rulers of your world before the first proto-human even walked upright. We control every police department, every government office, every president or prime minister, using the media to implant subliminal messages into every human mind on the planet, thus maintaining the deception. Your species *is* the Project." The Director paused for a moment before continuing. "We experimented with human evolution, accelerated it. We got your species to where you are in the space of a hundred years, not six thousand years as your Bible claims or one-hundred-and-fifty-thousand years as your scientists postulate. From the point of origin, your history is less than a century old. Only the history of your so-called Twentieth Century constitutes the history of your human race."

The information overwhelmed Haldane. "This is getting way too crazy..."

"We want you to enjoy a rich and varied ancestry, a history that makes sense, has continuity, a past that you can identify with, helps you belong. Humans need to understand where they came from and where they are going. Otherwise your species will gradually go insane and die out."

This was stupefying, incredible, shocking. The past had never happened. Everything Haldane had been led to believe in history class, everything that defined his fellow man, was a fabrication, a product of a small cabal of manipulators. He didn't even know if his great-grandfather had ever lived or was just a fake memory.

Had Haldane lived through the '60s or had he received a message through the TV set to make him believe he'd lived through the '60s? Maybe the whole world—the sky, the sea, even the ground—was an illusion, a magic trick, a super-hologram conjured up by the Authority which humans were plugged into. What the Management had just divulged went beyond even the crackpot theories about Secret World Histories from the likes of Jonathan Black and Helena Blavatsky. He thought of that quote from Kafka: *The history of mankind is the instant between two strides taken by a traveller.* "So Churchill, Machiavelli and Orwell weren't kidding. History is written by the victors? Napoleon claimed History was a set of lies agreed upon."

"Some of those people never existed. At least not in this world."

Haldane inferred something. Alternate realities, perhaps? But Haldane didn't want to go there. "If you regulate the world, why keep it a messed-up place?"

"Your species is deeply flawed," the Director proclaimed critically. "We may have granted you greater intelligence, but your emotions make you irrational, dangerous. In those hundred years, your species has caused two World Wars, a Cold War that nearly brought you to the brink of extinction, two global financial collapses as well as wreaking ecological havoc: despoiling the planet, entirely eradicating two hundred lower species of life daily and stretching the homeostatic mechanisms of its climate to breaking point. No, we have you where we want you. Subdued, oblivious of your real purpose in life which is to serve us."

"So what exactly is our purpose? What is this elaborate charade in aid of? I'm sure most of my fellow human beings would be happy to co-exist with you, worship you as their gods, which is basically what you're telling me you are."

"We have no intention of co-existing or being worshipped. You are nothing but expendable to us. We only bred you because we need your minds."

"Minds, for what?"

"The Authority has been locked in a Psychic War against the Menos Grex for millions of your earth years," the Director explained. "The Menos are a disembodied race whose consciousnesses outlived their physical forms. Having ravaged other planets and destroyed countless carbon-based sentient species, they consider the human mind to be fertile ground where the battle is now fought. We have finally gained the advantage over the Menos after moulding your mental terrains to our favour."

Was there no end to these outrageous revelations? Could the human race really be an experiment, created to be battleground between two warring species? "In answer to your earlier criticism, emotions are what differentiates humans from animals or machines," Haldane said, beginning to get annoyed. "Otherwise we'd be nothing more than automatons in organic flesh. *Like you.*"

"That is very impertinent of you," replied the Director, equally irritably. "We created your species, ergo we are the superior race."

"There are so many conspiracy theorists out there. Why am I so different?"

"You wrote this literature. You have seen the men behind the curtain of reality. Protocol dictates that those memories be expunged."

"Just like you did with Waylan Jackson?"

"That is correct."

"That was very unhumanlike of you. Very *ignoble*." Haldane tried to reason with them. "I don't know how it solves anything and why the fault should be levied at me just because I rumbled you. The article's already in the public domain."

"A minor fluctuation in the plan," the Director responded implacably. "We have the resources to tinker with the minds of the public and rectify the deviation."

Haldane was *not* going to pay any penalty to these dudes even if they claimed they created the human race, forged its past and shaped its cities, laying the foundations to resume a million-year war, using the minds of man as the battlefield. "Nobody's wiping my mind clean or performing any psychic lobotomy on me, and I certainly won't let you suppress the truth. Gods or no gods, dare you dudes come near me and I will *blow* your minds."

"You cannot threaten us," the Director reminded him ominously, his mouthful-of-water tones rising a notch. "We are the superior species. We made you. We own you. The locus of control lies with *us*."

There was something Haldane knew that the others didn't. Whereas a lot of his contemporaries—those who hadn't gone straight during the Thatcher-Reagan era—had fallen by the wayside, unable to come back from wherever their bad trip took them, Haldane had, over the years, grown only resistant to any form of mental collapse, despite constantly labouring under the weight of psychoactive substances. He lived by the motto that you could turn your back on a person, but you could never turn your back on a drug. He was an absolute antiestablishmentarian—not even the government knew of his existence. Perhaps the Revolution didn't start in the days first advocated by Timothy Leary but would begin from this point on. *You heard it here first, dudes.* "I don't much care for this cloak-and-dagger crap. You think you can take me down? *Try me . . .*"

His undisguised confidence and the downright challenge in his voice caused the Outsiders to hesitate for a moment. He had touched a nerve, and they studied this creature again, in case they were missing something. This drug-addled, wrinkly, white-haired specimen of a man. The man was obviously bluffing. The Proctor and the Executive advanced, while the Director looked on impassively. The two Outsiders grabbed Haldane on either shoulder and connected their minds with his in the same way they had projected themselves into his dreams.

Haldane had held it together so far. Now he decided to let himself go. No need to resist. Let them explore his mind and taste its very interesting contents.

Within minutes, the Outsiders began to suffer. They physically released him, their faces twisted in a grimace of sheer excruciating agony. They collapsed on the floor, clutching their heads frenziedly, mumbling nonsensically. Haldane had mind-fucked them, driven the alien psychics insane, and he knew they would never recover. He had consumed every drug known to man in his lifetime and, being a long-established veteran like Keith

Richards, and for those minds not broken by their repeated trippy experiences, he had adapted to and learned to function within his shifting psychedelic state, the ego firmly anchored in the distorted, warped, unstable mindscape, but the Outsiders, with their over-precise, predictable routine and disciplined but narrowed way of thinking, were mere novices on the subject. They had latched on to the chaos in his mind, the kaleidoscopic swirl of confusion, the muddle of visuals, the impossible shapes and surrealistic patterns within a *horror vacui* that would have made Crumb and Gilliam smile, the explosions of colour streaking out of the phosphene storms, to engulf, seize, infect, *derail* the invading minds, and Haldane wouldn't let them go until they had partaken of and drowned in his unique internal LSD-frescoed landscape, contaminated, corrupted. Wholly, *irreparably*. There was nothing else they could do. The Authority could not afford to get rid of him because if this interstellar war was fought in the human psyche, he made a powerful weapon.

"Told you I'd blow your minds," Haldane wisecracked, understandably smug. "Only seven members of the Management wing of the Authority posted on this planet? Should be a doddle, dude." The Director stared, agape, at his fallen generals rolling around mindlessly on the floor and looked back up at Haldane with genuine wide-eyed fear on his face. "Care for a blowback?" Haldane offered, lighting up another joint, adding to the copious amounts of pot he smoked regularly, to help him come down... come down from the acid blotter he had taken earlier. "I guess the locus of control lies with me, after all." He waved the Director away with his hand. "This meeting is over . . . Drop by any time. I prefer to meet the Authority, those your Management report to, next time." Taking another couple of puffs from his joint, he gave a token victory sign and, whether the '60s had happened or not, the usual hippie jingle. "Peace out."

August 2013

The Tryp

"If the doors of perception were cleansed every thing would appear to man as it is, infinite. For man has closed himself up, till he sees all things through narrow chinks of his cavern."

The Marriage of Heaven and Hell (1793)
William Blake

I often ponder the meaning of life and deliberate whether or not there is a God. And every time my cogitations lead me to the same irrefutable conclusion.

What God in His right mind gives us Spina bifida, Mongoloid babies and Siamese twins? What God allows murderers and rapists and paedophiles to walk freely among our innocent children? What God predetermines our lives, then punishes us for our sins?

He could cure all the ills of the world with a click of His fingers if He so chooses, but instead He prefers to watch over us like a cruel kid with a magnifying glass over an ant farm.

Time for a reality check, methinks.

In this Age of Reason, how can we still put our faith in this cosmic High Pooh-Bah when no priest from any era has ever come close to providing us with the slightest shred of proof that God even exists?

Blind faith is not enough. Looking at the Eternal Question from another angle lends a different picture. It is not as insoluble as it would seem and may only be down to a matter of interpretation.

Could it not be that God is merely a metaphor for our moral conscience, as a hospital chaplain from my early days of Housemanship once admitted despondently? And Heaven and Hell are actually on this earth? If we do right by God's word and lead a good, clean, productive life, then won't we reap the rewards for our lifetime's work in a neighbourhood of our dreams? If, on the other hand, we choose a life of crime, then isn't prison the hell we'll find ourselves in, to be sodomized by a knuckle-dragging Neanderthal?

We are born, we live, we die. There is nothing beyond death—that's what I believe. When people talk of streets of gold, a land of milk and honey, angels with harps and haloes, I always wonder what they're smoking in their pipe.

Was it not George Bernard Shaw who said that all great truths begin as blasphemies? Did not Thomas Paine claim that all the tales of miracles, with which the Old and New Testament are filled, were fit only for impostors to preach and fools to believe in? You see, citing God as your absolute authority means you can 'prove' anything you set out to prove, and no-one can prove that you are wrong despite the absence of evidence. The idea of an Afterlife sounds like fantasy to the informed thinker; maybe Shakespeare was right all along when a dying Hamlet whispers: *The rest is silence* . . . Or should we accept Pascal's Wager? Pascal advised that people should act as though God exists because believing in the small probability of God's existence could mean the difference between infinite gains, such as eternity in Heaven, or infinite loss, like burning in Hell.

Schizophrenics commonly complain of a higher power controlling their thoughts and actions, let it be God, the Devil, Beings from Outer Space or Elvis. Isn't it therefore conceivable that the likes of Jesus, Moses or Mohammed were in fact zealous hysterians, no different from Joan of Arc, able to manipulate the masses through their incomparable oratorical skills? Perhaps, Jesus was just too charismatic and empathic a person for his word to be doubted. Real thinkers generally categorize him as nothing more than a moral reformist, re-establishing the 'truths' of the theological belief systems that had been altered, corrupted or lost in the tides of time. That is, if he existed in the first place and wasn't the product of myth. And haven't scientists recently discovered the presence of the 'God Module' hard-wired into all human brains which, when sufficiently stimulated by electrodes or certain psychoactive substances, leads to visions of Heaven and a sensation of apparent contact with an omnipotent power? Likewise, the 'God Helmet' apparatus allows you to sense a divine presence and explore these mystical experiences and altered states of consciousness by disruption of the temporal lobes by a low-intensity electromagnetic field, producing hallucinations, in the same manner that the piezoelectric effect in high granite areas generates neural correlates of ghosts and UFOs in those highly-suggestible individuals. Furthermore, if you were to argue that the holy prophets really do have a direct channel to God, then by the same token aren't you saying that all psychotics are blessed or cursed? So I ask you again: is there a God? I think you might just know the answer to that one by now.

The clip-on microphone is in place, so I shall start rolling . . .

Permit me to introduce myself. I—Professor Artemis Higham, Chair of Clinical Psychiatry, accomplished writer and philosopher with the Royal College—intend to unlock the potential of the human mind—my mind to be exact. I have in the last quarter-of-an-hour, at exactly seven in the evening, Greenwich Mean Time, used a pipette to squeeze a drop of XZ-99 on my tongue, a hallucinogen developed by our research chemists here at Oxford University. I make regular contributions to various scientific journals and have served as author of two critically-acclaimed books, *Mental Illness and the Arts* and *R.O.T: Reality Orientation 2000*. From my credentials you can guess I have a purely biological and humanistic viewpoint on human existence and the mind. To me, science serves humanity. Religious faith and prayer serve a fiction called God, lacking any credibility or insight, a delusion. *Where is the evidence?* Professor Dawkins frequently poses. In my opinion, our libido is sexual in nature and we are all sophisticated animals, here on this earth to procreate and pass on our genes and leave a decent legacy for our future generations. Madness is the result of an infinitesimally-small neurochemical imbalance, behaviour the product of the early interaction between nature and nurture. Qualifications aside, it is always important for an old-timer like me to be open to new possibilities. It minimizes bias whilst keeping a clinician like myself perpetually on his toes in his continued quest to find what the human mind is truly capable of.

My first foray into the scientific research on drugs was in the company of the common house spider. Every spider's web is as unique as every snowflake. The experiment provided a physical visualization, measurable and quantifiable, of the effects of different psychotropic drugs on the web-building skills of the spider. The pattern of the web deviated spectacularly, depending on the type of drug administered, rather than the time it was built which somehow remarkably, inherently remained between 2am and 5am. A drop of Cannabis gave the spider a reasonable stab at spinning its web, but it quickly appeared to get bored, losing interest and concentration, leaving it half-finished. The spider on Speed worked with great, zigzagging gusto, but constructed a flimsy, alien-looking web, apparently without much planning, leaving gaping great holes in its framework. Dosed on Caffeine, the spider seemed unable to weave anything better than a few threads strung together at random. Low doses of LSD led to a more orderly web, which went to pot at higher doses.

The purpose of today's experiment is to test out the effects of one particular drug, XZ-99. Depending on the success of this experiment, the plan would be to conduct a few clinical trials and ultimately market XZ-99 as a cognitive enhancer—a nootrope, to be exact—the generic properties of which consist of improving mood, intelligence, memory, creativity and concentration. What is allegedly unique about this particular nootropic drug, according to our 'cooks', is that it's supposed to grant the person access to 100% of their mental capacity an incredible 100% of the time. So you can imagine how valuable its brain-enhancing applications would be in conditions such as Alzheimer's or Parkinson's disease and in some cases of head injury, bringing hope to the damaged brain by, without getting too technical, adjusting its level of neurotransmitters, increasing blood perfusion, strengthening synaptic connections and even inducing neurogenesis. For those uncompromised by disease, XY99 should help the undamaged brain stay young by increasing its neuroplasticity, the brain's innate ability to change, renew and reprogram itself throughout our lifetime.

I have been asked to assess the actions of the drug on the human brain and record my findings for transcribing and later evaluation.

First, a little something about the drug. XZ-99 or 'the Tryp' as it's become known to my colleagues, is from the tryptamine family and a chemical derivative of DMT, Dimethyltryptamine, analogous to serotonin (our 'happiness' molecule), melatonin (our natural sleep hormone) and psilocybin (the psychoactive component of magic mushrooms). With the essential amino acid, tryptophan as its basic substrate, XZ-99 binds to the [serotonergic] 5HT2A receptors agonistically and therefore has antidepressant properties. DMT itself or its relatives are found widely in Nature: licking hallucinogenic toads, within the pineal glands of many animals and as messenger molecules in most plants. Just as the North American shamans have for centuries embraced ceremonial peyote (main ingredient being mescaline, in this instance) in order to enter a trance and communicate with the spirit world, anthropological studies have shown certain indigenous Amazonian tribes concocting a similar sacred ethnobotanical [DMT-rich] brew they call 'ayahuasca' for divination purposes and ritual healing and contacting their dead ancestors. These native users of ayahuasca report collective hallucinations of jaguars, snakes and jewelled birds accompanied by a perceived ability to see into the future and alleged telepathic communication amongst tribal members. Although a controlled substance throughout most of Western society, its mind-bending effects are well-documented: DMT has been able to induce profound mystical states, out-of-the-body experiences, even perceived alien contact. It never stops to amaze me the way the human brain is circuited and sensitive enough to receive or summon up these experiences. But that is purely academic. I am hoping for a qualitatively different experience with XZ-99.

The Beat Generation, personified by Kerouac and Ginsberg, set the wheels in motion for the Love Generation that flourished a decade later, one of the key pioneers of that age, Timothy Leary, recommending the consumption of vast quantities of recreational drugs while creating an illusion of peace and understanding. Lysergic acid, or LSD, was the psychedelic drug of choice. Surprisingly, it had first been synthesized well before, accidentally discovered in 1938 by Albert Hofmann, a Swiss chemist. The CIA began using LSD in their MK-ULTRA Mind Control Project. The soon-dismissed Anti-psychiatric movement, founded by R.D. Laing, himself a qualified psychiatrist, condemned the practice of conventional psychiatry as a means of coercing, oppressing and locking up people under the label of 'mental illness', adding in his own crazy, drug-fuelled state that 'madness' should not be medicalized since there was no such thing as mental illness, just a state of mind.

LSD allows you to mimic psychosis. There's an old saying in psychiatric circles: if you want to feel like a schizophrenic for a day, drop some acid. John Dryden once declared: *There is a certain pleasure in being mad which none but madmen know.* Perhaps, psychotomimetic drugs might explain the Eleusinian Mysteries of Antiquity, just as ergot poisoning (the culprit being an ergoline derivative similar to LSD,) led to the Salem Witch Trials—how hallucinating women were misconstrued as consorting with the Devil. Then there're those prophets again, what with their radio communications to God—keep in mind there were no enforceable drug laws in those ancient times. It's a known fact that our cave-dwelling ancestors attributed the magical effects of cacti, mushrooms, coca and marijuana to the gods, if you ever get the chance to see some Neolithic rock paintings.

Our governments constantly tell us that illicit drugs damage our minds. Perhaps they do . . . sometimes. I remember a patient I followed-up in clinic, a case in point, I suppose. Intelligent, articulate, knowledgeable, a former Law student. But so thought-disordered, unable to hold a single sentence in logical, sequential order. He had become psychotic after taking a single tab of acid at a Freshers' party. Went on to develop chronic, treatment-resistant schizophrenia, only partially responsive to clozapine. Never returned to his premorbid functioning. Tragic, very tragic, but also an exception in many respects. You see more people die from simple analgesia than all illicit drugs combined. Scientists are now suggesting psychedelic therapy be integrated into the medical model. There is evidence that suggests that magic mushrooms can treat the emotional distress and existential anxiety of those terminally-ill. MDMA is being studied in the treatment of severe PTSD, allowing the numbed individual to revisit the trauma in a more therapeutic way. Medical marijuana has been already used in the management of glaucoma, multiple sclerosis and significant anxiety-laden, self-injurious forms of ASD. LSD has been cited in the treatment of chronic alcohol addiction. Of course, these drugs should be regulated and controlled and only administered, if clinically indicated, under close supervision.

Modern society, however, has banned most mind-altering drugs probably because expanding the mind does not conform with the consumerist ideal, like the production and acquisition of material goods . . . unless, of course, the government can get a hefty cut of the profits.

The truth can get you into trouble. The world politicians shape our control systems. The more upfront, liberal Presidents, like Carter and Clinton, in conjunction with the World Drug Policy Committee, have officially admitted that the War on Drugs is unwinnable, but it is the Republican office, headed by Nixon and Reagan, who have wasted billions campaigning against the 'evils' of drugs for their own sinister political agenda. There is nothing wrong with being conservative and upholding family values, but the Republican Crooks-in-Power have always harboured an ulterior motive when they've declared war on anything . . . and Money has something to do with it. The only thing their nonsense has achieved is making the drug barons of Latin America some of the richest and most powerful people on the planet, alongside rumours that the CIA have tried to get in on some of the action. Banning drugs has taken them underground, creating a black market, thus providing the [Republican] government with a 'legitimate' means to marginalize the ethnic minorities and make money off the misery of the booming prison populations. Indeed, privatizing the prison system generates big business. But this is old hat. Social commentators will remind you that the Chinese immigrants suffered discrimination under the excuse of their opium addiction once they were no longer needed in the construction of the railroads. Then, the Irish and Italian immigrants were targeted during the Prohibition era. Again, drugs were declared illegal, as a method of social control, when the Environment, Women's Rights and Civil Rights were entering the public conscience, alongside the Anti-war Movement stepping up its protests against the truly-immoral—and truly-illegal—Vietnam War during the social upheaval of the 1960s. And we all know what became of Nixon.

The sanctimonious government rarely funds any meaningful scientific testing or research into the benefits of these more natural drugs because these drugs work better than pharmaceutical drugs, which are always an artificial way of treating someone. Our paranoid, insecure society of Orwellian control demands we medicate ourselves with corporate drugs to find happiness, yet all they do is dampen our identity and keep us docile, while the pharmaceutical companies chase their own moronic addiction to money. Natural drugs can change us forever, maybe even cure us, opening a partial window to freedom and an empathic connection with our fellow man.

But I won't discuss polemics. Suffice it to say, nobody can deny the appeal of drugs and the enjoyable escape they provide in today's depressing economic climate. Why waste your dollars at the cinema or the restaurant when you can practically get the same buzz—and more—without going anywhere, just lounging around on the couch, smoking dope? Hell, even I've picked magic mushrooms in the October woods in my heyday. Magic mushrooms manifest a subtler, more natural high than LSD, which tends to be a harsher assault on the senses. And what of all those celebrities and cult icons who have delivered the same message? Philip K. Dick was to science fiction what William S.

Burroughs was to fantasy what Hunter S. Thompson was to journalism. Get the picture? Psychedelic explorers in the name of their craft and in search of enlightenment. What I loved about Terry Gilliam's nostalgic road trip to Las Vegas, besides being based on Thompson's own personal experiences and indeed coming across as a labour of love on the part of both the director and the scriptwriter, was the idea of the two characters taking turns to get trashed while the other sobers up, relatively-speaking, and keeps his buddy safe.

Alas, here in this dark, empty lecture hall, I sit alone. In a chair on stage a few yards from the lectern on the left under the muted glow of a couple of recessed spotlights. Like floating in a Sensory Deprivation Tank, this is meant to be a subjective experience.

No EEG, no monitoring equipment, no technicians. Maybe no actual intention of approaching this with the scientific method. It's the Tryp that counts, with a 'y'—or a why?

As a highly-decorated psychonaut, I always fly solo.

Digression aside, I hope I have managed to distil the salient points for my less-than-brief introduction and can now safely move on to the main event.

Because things are now starting to happen . . .

7:32 PM. In terms of pharmacokinetics, I can vouch for its impressive rate of absorption.

Aldous Huxley postulated in his famous experiment with mescaline that psychedelic drugs reduce the effectiveness of the brain's filtering mechanism to selectively suppress certain unnecessary thoughts, emotions, perceptions and memories from ever reaching the conscious mind. Mind expansion prevents both the suppression of such irrelevant mental activity as well as widening the arena of actual external stimuli available to conscious awareness. In other words, this loosening of or complete erasure of the normal filters between the conscious mind and outside world means more information rushes in. You sense more, think more and feel more. In neurophysiological terms, the thalamus can no longer function as the selective, discerning gatekeeper, admitting everything up to the executive cerebral cortex once a psychedelic drug has been introduced. And no two trips are ever the same because everybody is unique.

Back to the present, I feel relaxed. I giggle, like I'm stoned. My head feels light, full of expectation. My senses begin to take in more stimuli. More sound: footsteps and laughter from somewhere else that impinge on the gloomy silence of the lecture theatre. I study the intricate details on familiar surfaces, experience the richness of sound, the brightness of colour, the complexity of my mental processes. Plato once said that everything that we see is just a shade, an imitation of how things truly are. I'm seeing things how they truly are. The puddled circles of illumination overhead glare luridly with a distinctly audible fluorescent buzz, as though someone has turned the juice up to eleven. Pattern recognition is greatly enhanced. Colours take on a more active vibrancy, a brilliance, spilling out kaleidoscopic hues of neon-pinks and xenon-blues. The angles of the walls seem to slant and warp as though they are made of some soft, pliant material, in the process of losing molecular cohesion, or perhaps straining under the weight of something behemoth and unseen.

I stare in fascination at my hands. One second they are tiny and far away and the next they are huge, as if belonging to a fairytale giant. These microspic/macropsic experiences are nothing compared to the way the creases of my hands squiggle around or how my fingers writhe like snakes. I can even create eerie misty trails with my fingers, tracers, lingering afterimages, visual echoes.

I seem to have acquired an unlimited wealth of energy and a sense of urgency. I experience different feelings all at once, contradictory emotions that smooth out into one whole. Moments of reflection and distracting thoughts. Flashes of insight into myself and the world. My introspective world is throwing up all manner of creative urges, ambitious designs, fantastical possibilities.

The perceptual distortions continue to intensify. I am actively hallucinating. A powerful experience that continues to take me beyond normal perception. Objects morphing into other objects, the gradual dissolution of symmetry. The lecture hall is another landscape altogether, shaped by suggestibility, bathed in hypervivid colours, its spatial dimensions in constant flux, as it pulses and shimmers and undulates and breathes like animated flesh. The murk, which feels like a solid thing, slowly retreats against the deliberate advance of light, the latter variegated and seemingly alive.

I want to be part of that light.

I know my pupils must be enormous, black pools, waxing to the dimensions of my irises, like cat's eyes in the dark. My body temperature rises, causing me to feel every pinprick of sweat and the heat leaving my body. My mouth feels as dry as a baking desert. My hairs bristle with vitality, my fingertips tingle with electric currents. My heart rate and blood pressure continue to creep up. I follow the flow of blood through the chambers of my pumping heart. I feel my brain ticking over. This heightened self-awareness is accompanied by an unprecedented bliss, a swaddling euphoria.

I am so happy . . . *So happy . . .*

My eyes swell with tears of joy, and, in that instant, it is like looking through an exquisite, sparkling, multi-faceted diamond before they roll down my cheeks, leaving glistening snail-tracks.

Psybient experiences. I can hear Kasabian in my head—or is it in external space? Not the Doors or Jefferson Airplane. Got any Quo? Perhaps their *Pictures of Matchstick Men*? Forever in search of their fourth chord? Nope? What about the condition the First Editions were in or Fifth Dimension's New Age astrological nonsense or the Hurdy Gurdy Man bringing songs of love? No, it's Kasabian, *Cutt Off*, instead. Why? Go figure!

My senses merge, overlap. I see the notes and chords of the tune exit my ears and flow across the air, just as in similar synaesthetic terms I can taste the vanilla-essence of the light surrounding me, illuminating my physical frame.

Depersonalization. The boundaries between me and the world begin to break down, dissolve, accompanied by the multiple splitting of my ego. I am entering some kind of trance state, but I know I'm still talking, and my voice sounds strange, weird, otherwordly. I am approaching something akin to ecstasy.

Suddenly the drug ignites my entire body like a hit of adrenochrome. The shock wave radiates along my polished network of bones, races up the curve of my crystal-quartz spine, makes the gleaming enamel of my teeth resonate with the acoustic beauty of tuning forks, the statically-charged coruscation frying my brain and exploding out of my nostrils and ears and the orbits of my eyes and the seams of the skull in a blinding flash . . .

My body feels as floppy and lax as a bonfire effigy, but my expanding, profoundly-altered consciousness has developed an aura.

And condensed within that exuding luminescence of my shiny brain is the Knowledge of My Life.

Deep-store memory has suddenly become accessible, mental images and experiences rising to the fore.

I realize that I know everything.

I know EVERYTHING.

The Entire History of Me lies at my fingertips. And like any computer I can access any memory of the past I have ever had the luck to hear, see, touch or taste, even the most incidental of incidental memories. No matter if it's a memory buried in the depths of my subconscious, repressed, abandoned, forgotten. Even material—every *minutia*—you'd normally painstakingly retrieve under hypnosis.

The colour of the tank top—*pink*—my First Love, Verity, wore when I first laid eyes on her in Mr. Rennie's A-Level Biology Class... the rewind-play-stop-rewind-play experience of our first kiss together under the bleachers, the taste of her balm-moistened lips, the grapefruit scent of her honey-blond hair . . . mournfully sitting by her bedside in a hospital room as her body, twenty years older and withered by cancer, breathes its last breath. The exact pattern of freckles on my best friend's face in Sixth Form . . . Best Man at my wedding a month after I graduated from medical school . . . His face would grow corpulent in later life and become further mottled by liver spots. I think I can speak Czech proficiently after watching that foreign film last Tuesday: *Vsadím se, že nevěděla, že jsem mohl mluvit česky*. I see my father driving us on a camping holiday to the South of France in the summer of 1989, the sense of safety and calm reassurance the King Edward cigar protruding confidently from the corner of his mouth imbued, his lips curled into a soft, self-assured smile, imparted upon his two nerdy and needy teenage sons constantly seeking his validation...I remember the sudden peculiar agonized look on his face as it droops horribly on the left side, his whole body sagging abysmally, eyes growing glassy and fixed, as he drops dead of a massive stroke while celebrating my Sixteenth Birthday in an Indian restaurant. I remember sitting at precisely two-twenty-one in the morning, unable to sleep, and seeing a spider conscientiously spinning its web the day after I attained Tenureship. Recalling every spoken narrative of every episode of *Horizon* I have ever watched. I can recite every word of every line of every page of every book I have read with perfect photographic memory. I can sing every note of every song I have ever heard, better than any wannabe pop idol. Every painting by the Old Masters is fresh in my mind, ready for reproduction, more convincingly than any forgery, hopefully as perfectly-rendered as the original. Every recorded memory stored in the deepest parts of my subconscious, everything I have heard, read or seen is available to me. It's all there—every gesture, every conversation, every sound, every emotion, every *thought* I have ever experienced—available to me as clear as day, stretching back from the right-here-right-now to the memory of me stroking our cat when I was still in my crib to the sweet taste of my mother's milk as I latched onto her breast . . . to the day I was born.

The sensation of reliving my own birth.

Or maybe even before I am squeezed out from between my mother's blood-and-slime-streaked thighs. Could it be I can hear the steady thumps of my mother's heart or her attempts to talk to me through her distended belly, hoping to familiarize me to her voice, as I float unborn in the dark of her womb? Exploding cell divisions of my zygotic nuclei just after I'm conceived. Transcendental experiences that go even further back. Ancestral memories . . .

The minutest details. Every scrap of personal, historical,

experiential knowledge. Memories I never thought I had. I am finding significance in things that shouldn't have meaning. I realize my name Artemis means 'wise'.

My brain power is such that, without sounding grandiose, I could take on all the champions of *Mastermind* together and win. I feel smart. Superior. *Invincible*.

Side-effects, half-life and metabolites do not even enter the equation.

William James began the 'Ten percent of the brain' myth in the 1890s, suggesting we only used a fraction of our mental capacity, believing that we all had a potential for genius, if we could harness all 100% of our brain's computing power. However, this has been proven false. Brain scans have shown that no matter what one is doing, including sleeping, all areas of the brain are active, some areas more so than others. Despite taking up only 2% of the human body's weight, the brain requires 20% of the body's energy. If 90% of the brain were dormant or silent, the process of natural selection would have eliminated the large brain size in favour of smaller, more efficient brains. Synaptic pruning, a spring-cleaning for the brain, partly driven by the hormones of adolescence, removes redundant brain cells, those with a tendency to degenerate. If 90% of the brain were inactive, autopsies of the normal brain would reveal large-scale degeneration.

So am I experiencing a chemically-enhanced intelligence or is the drug just tapping into the potential already there? I wonder if I am capable of precognition or psychokinesis . . .

Any drug that supposedly enhances intelligence interests me as a cognitive scientist. One of the stories I dig up is *Flowers for Algernon* by Daniel Keyes, a tale of a mentally-challenged menial worker whose intelligence skyrockets following an experimental surgical procedure, and as his intelligence continues to accelerate and he gains a greater understanding of the world around him, it precludes relationships and emotions since he becomes unable to relate to others, doesn't see the object of it, resorting to that old ego-defense mechanism, intellectualization. His prodigious intelligence is only temporary for he soon regresses back to his original IQ and, in many respects, his humanity.

But what is the relevance of that story? Why should that story come to the fore? Do I fear that I will crash and burn, that my intelligence will dwindle, or that I shall revert back to an earlier, primitive state of consciousness?

I glance at the clock above the entrance to the lecture hall: 7:36PM.

The clock has stopped. I cannot explain the profound time dilation. Am I faster than time? Or is it only an illusion of my perception?

Yet there is more. Oh, significantly more . . .

The geometric boundaries of reality continue to disintegrate. The lecture hall is no longer a wibbly-wobbly, play-doughy kind of place. The walls are rapidly draining of colour, turning translucent, transparent, appearing increasingly crystalline like the walls of a glass house. And in between the walls I see rat spoors and the culprits themselves: bristly, beady-eyed creatures scurrying about their business. I can see—and *smell*—the silverfish, and the spiders in their webs, together with other tiny, scuttling bugs and curly, slimy wriggly things. Damp mould presents as a dark, bubbling fungus, as ripe as a cluster of giant puffballs, the swollen heads popping and dispersing spores amidst the dust and fust and must.

The walls, ceiling and floor continue to utterly deplete of pigment, perfect transparent windows in all directions.

I see human beings—students, the few eager ones who remain behind after class, as well as a couple of lecturers and the domestics—on the different floors of the building.

People upstairs, downstairs, sidelong, all around . . . walking in predictable straight lines at an optimal speed of 1.3 metres per second. I hear people talking on their mobile phones, the conversations they're having, and I can somehow hear the person on the other end of the line. I spot a young female student, Clare Keating, whom I've taught, and I can see into her handbag, the scrunched-up tissues, her make-up kit, the £3.60 in her purse, her NUS card, the sequence of numbers on her

National Insurance card, the Date of Birth and Address on her Driving Licence.

My eyes adjust, grow in sensitivity, carry on inputting impossible visual data. How can Miss Keating not be wearing any clothes? Or, for that matter, the rest of stragglers around here? They seem to be in different states of undress, most wearing only bras and underwear. Now they're abruptly naked—this is hilarious and rather sensual—the individuals unaware, oblivious to my new-found X-Ray vision. Their integumental system gradually starts to disappear, as I see deeper still, and they look like living, breathing skinned specimens from dissection class: bulks of pure red muscle attached to bone by ligaments and tendons, slotted compactly together their vital organs and nerve bundles and pulsing blood vessels. There's Dr. Linus whose lateral anterior descending coronary artery is vastly narrowed, risking a heart attack if he doesn't get that seen to. A male Biochemistry student walks above my head, separated from me by the physical see-through barrier of the ceiling, and I'm already witnessing the onset of fibrotic liver disease in someone so young, probably on account of downing ten pints every night with his rugger mates at the Student Union. The flesh, too, of all these once-nameable individuals evaporates and I am looking at walking skeletons as they forge on ahead towards invisibility and slowly fade away . . .

And it doesn't stop there. My consciousness—my range of perception—continues to expand. *Exponentially.*

And yet, *somehow*, I maintain my lucid reasoning.

Floor upon floor of the medical school skips by, and I finally see up and through the roof. Although it's past sunset and night has fallen, the sun is blinding, spilling out a rainbowed spectrum of light. Normally we see only one-tenth of the wavelength of light. Presently, my vision can accommodate the rest of it, beyond the confines of our rather limited, conventional reality. I can see the interactions of radio-waves, I can see infra-red. I glimpse reams of digital data, deflected off communication satellites in orbit.

I see way, way beyond.

I feel the vibrations of the air, the pull of gravity. I penetrate the foundations of the city: brick and concrete and metal; the huge, gnarled roots of the trees feeding themselves, the phloem carrying nutrients up the tree, xylem transporting water; the homes of burrowing animals; a priceless, yet-undiscovered Roman coin collection still buried in the earth; the maze of old, Victorian sewers; downward still, a secret river running through a vast underground cave system; the ribcage of a mammoth and other fossilized remains. I am cognizant of everything.

I understand Nature in its absolute entirety . . . how the energies of the Earth are connected, epitomized by the mysterious network of ley lines, a source of unlimited power, which Man has sought to harness for centuries, unsuccessfully. A mathematical code pervades all of Nature. I see the Fibonacci sequence in action, its relationship with the Golden Ratio and the Euclidean elements, the applications of Fermat's spiral and fractal patterns. Most of the body parts follow the numbers one, two, three and five: one nose, two eyes, three segments to each limb and five fingers on each hand. The Grand Design of All Life. DNA molecules follow this sequence, measuring 34 angstroms long and 21 angstroms wide for each full cycle of the double helix. They say Beauty is in the Eye of the Beholder, something subjective, but it can actually be objectively measured: there is a mathematical basis to beauty. The secret to physical beauty is based on how closely the features of one's face reflect the golden ratio, Phi = 1.618, in the shape, symmetry and proportions of the face, the relationship between the eyes, ears, lips, nose, mouth, etc. The closer the faces are to the Phi ratio of 1.618, the more beautiful they are perceived to be. Our faces conform to Phi proportions when we smile as opposed to the ugliness of a sneer or a look of contempt. Such numerical laws govern the natural world. Pi = 3.14 for circularity. These fundamental units are woven into the leaf arrangements in a plant or the pattern of florets of a flower as they maximize sunlight and seed arrangement, applicable to the growth of every living thing, including every cell, grain of wheat, ancestry of bees and even all of mankind. Consider the similarity of growth in spirals between a sunflower, the horns of a ram, a conch shell on a beach, the curvature of a wave and stars moving to the centre of the galaxy. Fractals depict the same degree of complexity at different levels—near or far, they look the same. The basic footprint of Nature on which it has built the world: the clouds, the mountains, the trees. From the geometry of a crystal or the shape of a virus to the perfect symmetry of a snowflake, as unique as any spider's web, Nature works in the most economical, efficient, least-energy-expending way. And Nothing is Random; there is always a Pattern, a predictable Cause-and-Effect, unless you put too much emphasis on Chaos Theory, how sometimes the most insignificant moments can escalate to change our lives forever—the Butterfly Effect—which, again, only highlights the Interconnectedness of All Things.

Nothing dies, so to speak. The First Law of Thermodynamics dictates that energy cannot be created or destroyed. The energy in ourselves is the same energy that has driven the Universe since the very beginning, the aggregate measure of matter and energy remaining consistent throughout Time and Space. We are composed of those fourteen billion years of atoms, and the nuclear fusion in the stars surges, reticulate, through my veins. Consciousness survives even after its human vessel has returned to the dust from whence it sprang.

We are all, in a sense, a completely different person every seven years—it takes seven years to replace every single atom in our body, for the human body to regenerate—and we do not die since the molecules in the chemical decomposition of your cells and tissues are recycled and redistributed throughout Nature, creating new life. So do not grieve—your loved one is still in this world, even if he has passed away.

I want to share this glorious knowledge about the mysteries of Creation with you, pass on my enlightenment, explain how everything works, but my brain wrestles with sensory overload to neither fully pause nor reflect.

I can see beyond the sky, surpassing the stratosphere, higher than even the exosphere, directly into the cold, stygian loneliness of infinite space.

And with it, I catch a sound, a dull vibration, a faint but steady thrum. I am hearing the background hum of the Universe.

I recognize the constituents integral to the very core of Reality. As I crack open Reality, I am able to reconcile the dynamic chaos at the quantum level with the physical laws governing the greater Universe. Quarks, mesons, even the Higgs-Boson particle that has eluded the CERN scientists thus far, I know how to isolate. Even the dark matter binding the Universe. I know how to design the perfect perpetual-motion machine. I know the square root of minus one.

Mathematical impossibilities aside, I see the rotation of the planets, hear the music of the spheres. The dark, undiscovered fields of space are alight with spiralling constellations of stars, their cooling gases forming rock and the foundations of life over billions of years.

The Ultimate Equation to describe the Theory of Everything? The Answer to Life, the Universe and Everything? Pure coincidence that I should have just turned forty-two only a week ago?

There really is only a single, definite, precise law for this Universe, with no approximations, which in a sense deterministically specifies how everything in the Universe happens. Certain things can look incomprehensible or probabilistic only because of the high degree of complexity involved. That is why the monkeys in the thought experiment are destined to type out the complete works of Shakespeare. We have been told that the hard and fast Laws of Physics are fundamental to the structure of the material Universe and the connectivity of Time and Space, and Chemistry fundamental to the study of Life. But truth be known, the Universe only exists because of an individual's consciousness of it, just as Cartesian doubt deconstructs Reality. Essentially, Life is central to Reality and it is Life that creates the physical Universe; the Universe itself does not create Life. The same applies to the concepts of Space and Time, which are simply tools of the mind. It explains Heisenberg's Uncertainty Principle and the so-called double-slit experiment, where the behaviour of a particle can be altered by a person's perception of it. In this experiment, when scientists watch a particle through a multi-holed barrier, the particle acts like a bullet travelling through a single slit. When the particle is not observed, however, the particle moves through the hole like a wave. It proves that particles act as two separate entities at any given time, challenging long-established ideas of Time and Perception. The behaviour of particles is inextricably linked to the presence of the observer; otherwise matter dwells in an undetermined state of probability, far from fixed or absolute. If Life came first, and Consciousness cannot exist without biological life to embody its perceptive powers of creation, there must have been an original consciousness to set it all into motion in the first place. Multiple universes, alien civilizations or cosmic intelligent designers aside, it goes some way in explaining our incredible, good fortune why we find ourselves in a universe fine-tuned for life.

Has my consciousness escaped the physical constructs of my body or am I still sitting there in the auditorium? I imagine spiking the water supply of Oxford with XY-99 and can envisage a universe of roaming consciousnesses, just as my consciousness is pouring out of its carbon-based constraints.

As I explore the finer workings of the Universe and the very nature of Existence, I gain deeper insights into my immersive metaphysical experience and glimpse realms parallel to our own, doorways to other universes and other possibilities, perhaps higher planes of existence penetrating into our own limited dimension. I stand at the interface between the spiritual and tangible realms while something—some unfathomable, sentient force—pulls me deeper and deeper towards it.

And what is this? What are these incredible floating, flying entities? Alien beings? Winged angels?

My consciousness-expansion has taken me here. I gaze in wonder and awe at the majestic white brilliance before me. A brilliance almost indefinable, indescribable. A transcendent peace descends over me.

It is like the beatific vision saints speak of or the light at the end of the tunnel just before I am born. From the birth canal to this very moment, it was meant to happen.

From the Dawn of Creation to the entire course of Eternal Recurrence, I am in the Infinite.

I can sense—*feel*—a presence occupying the fundamental interstices of the Universe. A numinous presence older than Time itself. I think I know what this immaculate presence is. Perhaps schizophrenics are genuinely blessed or damned. Maybe they exist in a different state of consciousness and like the holy prophets and the mystics and shamans really do have a direct link to this archetypal deity, Abrahamic or otherwise. But if science has revealed a Universe grander and of a more elegant design than previously thought, why should conventional religion still revel in its own narrowmindedness and prefer its god to be an old god, a small god? Incredible, that the senses of a godless figure such as I can acknowledge and give himself completely to this original, widely-worshipped Universal Consciousness.

My observations cannot be proved or disproved.

What a trip! What a Tryp!

The Tryp with a y—or a why?

As far as my perceptions can stretch, not in any sane, normal human capacity, I must embrace the Ultimate Truth—this Theophany, this Eternal Radiance, this Dazzling, Swirling, Pulsating, Trailing Transcosmic Numenescence—like Michelangelo's Genesis.

In that fabulous moment of clarity, I see.

I can see, oh my God, I can see!

I SEE...

And as I attain divinity, absolute nirvana, cosmic unity—call it what you will—my mind is poised on the cusp of reaching its full potential.

For I am only just peaking . . .

August 2013—September 2013

Strange Meridians

"Two possibilities exist: either we are alone in the Universe or we are not. Both are equally terrifying."

Arthur C. Clarke

```
IPv4<55.89.144.233.>
USERNAME<Xander07>
PASSWORD<* * * * *>
LOGGED ON <05/06/2007@18:43>
RUN PROGRAM<DONTYOUHAVEANYTHINGBETTERTODO?>
```

Some would argue that the Internet Revolution was a terrible curse, but in Xander Hubley's opinion, and thousands of millions like him, it was an information superhighway that could transform the way we think, feel and live our lives.

True, it could be used and abused like any other great invention, a world where the modern criminal could break into your home without ever stepping foot and steal your identity, where our children risked daily exposure from real creeps and online predators looking for someone to seduce and groom, and where computer hackers with little else to do sought to access our nuclear defence codes and set off World War Three—just to prove they were smarter than the average expert system programmer.

Stranger danger, identity fraud, and other acts of cyberterrorism aside, the government keeping tabs on even the books someone borrowed from the library just in case the individual posed a risk to national security, Xander and the rest of the GoogTube generation accepted the Internet as the single-most, greatest technological event since the birth of the microchip. It was up there with the discovery of fire, the creation of the wheel, the alphabet, the internal combustion engine, and maybe even more remarkable than the Moon landings. Satellite communications at your fingertips, connecting you to anywhere in the world in ways generations of visionaries could once only dream of. The very concept of video-link, Skyping, gave the humble telephone an extra dimension and took you into the realms of science fiction. The ability to download any movie to your laptop would soon render the TV, a contraption people had relied on for more than half a century, a thing of the past. The Internet had developed into an innovative, expedient medium for work and relaxation, education and commerce, sharing and socializing, connecting you to anywhere in the world . . . all from the comfort of your living room. For some, it had become an absolute substitute for life and even replaced masturbation as the leading cause of Repetitive Strain Injury.

Did man—as the technophobes led you to believe—face a dark, dystopian future plugged into this all-embracing nexus of perverts, piracy and paranoia or—as its many advocates described it—could the Internet possibly hold the key to ultimate enlightenment, be hailed as 'the new town square for the global village of tomorrow'? Or did it *really* matter on which side the fence the jury sat? To Xander, it simply provided a convenient means by which to escape his mundane existence.

He wasn't one for the chatrooms, those electronic asylums full of babbling lunatics. Like any self-respecting geek, he preferred to spend his evenings surfing the 'Net, hunting down strange and rare websites, pretending he was doing something useful. He hated his job, being a lowly cubicle slave at a software firm, working under management wolves and corporate sharks, who seemed far more intent on downsizing the company than checking on the wellbeing of the staff. The suicide of a former employee, recently laid-off after three decades of faithful service, had done precious little to melt the cold hearts of the consultants or curb their soulless enthusiasm for cost-cutting. Not that Xander expected to keep his job, either. Fortunately for him, he had given up caring a long time ago.

Never was he troubled by family or friends, since he possessed none. Both his foster parents were long gone, and growing up, he had always kept very much to himself. He fancied the neologistic term "Aloner" to "unsociable" for he felt there was a magical ring to it, something cool and darkly romantic. Fantastical even. Blade, Constantine, Ghost Rider, the Caped Crusader. Shyness didn't figure into it. The comic-book years soon progressed to science-fiction's finest (Asimov, Bradbury, Clarke). *Precious few sci-fi films made these days as the population gets thicker.* Conspiracy theories, *Lone Gunmen*-style, were the next stage in the evolutionary process . . . until he demanded greater kicks, something more bizarre to sustain his attention and interest. Something different, something offbeat, something utterly unconventional. Alone each evening in a rundown apartment block in the urban jungle, eating plasticky-tasting microwavable dinners and drinking guanabana juice, he searched the network for these peculiar, seldom-visited websites.

Tonight was no exception.

Free of commitments, without the hint of any 'hotchick@ home.envyofmyfriends.com' to beguile and exploit this particular 'domain user', Xander sat in curtained darkness, save for the steady glow from the monitor. Xander selected a track on the MP3 player, setting the scene. *Weirdo* by the Charlatans, a song he could identify with, came rolling out. He adjusted his glasses as he explored the mad space between the plain weird and the downright twisted.

The enquiry 'WEIRD WEBSITES' had produced over 1,800,000 hits. Mons Olympus for the novice climber, but for the more experienced web-user, this was not the mean feat it appeared to be. If you wanted to research the eccentric and the unnatural and the completely freaky, these two keywords essentially covered the entire repository of information on the subject. Then it was just a case of navigating through the results and focusing in on the nuttiest. Many, if not most, of the sites he recognized from previous excursions. However, new ones were cropping up all the time. You could never browse through all 1,800,000 sites in a lifetime, but you could come damn close.

Xander always carried on from where he left off, guided on by reminders as simple as undeleted cookies placed strategically at selected pages to the more complex task of time management to sift through the enormous stream of data. One thing you couldn't fault Xander on was his efficiency. So far, he had inspected over one-and-a-half-million weird-themed websites, which had taken him almost twelve months to accomplish. He could plod on at the pace he was going or he could go all-out and try and achieve resolution. He didn't want to admit it, but he was beginning to feel he was covering old ground, the information becoming repetitive to the point that he could anticipate it and rattle it off word for word.

Could he get to the end? Could he know all there was to know about the unknowable? Could he gain an Honorary Fellowship with the University of Life-But-Not-As-We-Know-It?

Xander enjoyed crawling the fine line that separated reality from fiction, scenarios or situations that were way too weird or strange or surreal or bizarre to be true.

The majority of links he had visited before. Others, previously untapped, he glanced over very quickly. *Is your computer on?* was a site solely devoted to checking if you were plugged in. *Testing, testing . . .* The *Weak Password Tester* poked fun at weak passwords. There was a site dedicated to people with a third nipple. *Why? Who knows? Send Me Your Wounds* offered you an opportunity to see photos of some really sick, infected wounds. *Gross, but strangely compelling. When Good Toilets . . . Go BAD!* explained what happens when the relationship breaks down between people and the john. *The remedy: couple's therapy. HoldTheButton.com* invited you to undertake the most pointless exercise in history. *How long can you push it? Revolting Recipes* showed you how to boil a whole hog's head. *Mmmm . . . Nice!* He passed a link about people who molested statues. Another listed the *Top Ten Things To Do When You're Manic*. And another, *Tattoos In Strange Places*. *Pretending To Cure Boredom*. *Bill Gates Is Dead*. *Lip Balm Anonymous*. *Son of Spam*. *Male Pregnancy*. *Street Lamp Interference*. *Snow Peeing*. *Bill Gates Is Alive*. *Gun-crazed Grannies of the NRA*. *Plunging Buses*. *iLLiTeRruT muNThLee*. *Buddhist Wrestling*. *My Name Is Jesus Christ*. *Bill Gates Is Satan*. *Buy My In-Laws*. *Streetmattress*. *Fun with Asbestos*. *Bubblewrap For Beginners*. *Bill Gates Is Cryogenically Frozen*. *NOBODY HERE*. *Zzzz zzz zzzzz*.

Xander yawned. Checking his watch, he noticed it was approaching midnight. He had been going at it without a break for almost six hours straight. Yet, oddly enough, he wasn't feeling tired. Not at all. His faculties seemed sharper than ever, as though he could go on forever. *Screw sleep!* he decided, taking a sip of guanabana. *I've come this far. Why not go all the way? I've expended so many months, years, so much time and energy, why not see how it ends?*

He would ring up sick tomorrow, citing the oft-used excuse of irritable bowel. And, meanwhile, he could prowl the Wilderness of the Far-out to his heart's content. *Just a few more hundred thousand sites to explore . . .*

So, in the small hours of the morning, Xander indulged himself in an old pastime. A pastime which was fast becoming an obsession. An obsession which would soon take him over the edge to a place he never thought existed.

And a fate he dared not imagine . . .

Now there's something you don't see every day! considered Xander, studying the text on the screen. It was two days later, and he had barely slept or eaten, washed or shaved. He was completely absorbed in what he was doing, or as he might refer to it as 'In The Zone'.

Find A Grave: Collect dirt from the graves of famous people. Search our extended database of historic cemeteries and find out where your favourite actor, politician or Nobel Prize-winning scientist is buried. And, if it's a person you hate, we'll locate so you can DESECRATE!

People do the weirdest things. Weirder than those weirdos who do gravestone rubbings. But, still, nowhere near as crazy as Corpses For Sale.

Xander clicked on to the Related Links. *The Celebrity Dead Pool* caught his attention: *Make money from the death of a celebrity. Pick ten people you reckon might die in 2007, and if by the end of the year, your list comprises the most dead celebs, you win $2007 tax-free. Go ahead, make THEIR day!*

Macabre, Xander thought, grinning. *Positively macabre*. So far, the year had seen off the likes of Kurt Vonnegut, Sidney Sheldon and Boris Yeltsin. What else did it hold in store? Although Keith Richards from the Rolling Stones always made everybody's wish-list, that guy had somehow defied the cream of medical science for the past forty years. No, the pollsters were hedging their bets on diminutive British supermodel, Kate Moss's heroin-addled idiot-of-a-boyfriend, Pete Doherty . . . which would probably disappoint Old Keith. They had good reason to since Doherty was exactly the kind of jackass who might feed hash to penguins at the local zoo and such a prodigious talentless shit he might manage to daub together a painting using his own [allegedly] infected blood and auction it off to the biggest sucker. *A Writer's Guide to Death* discussed some of the strangest coincidences involving famous authors. A case in point is Mark Twain, whose fate was inextricably linked to the appearance of Halley's Comet. Twain was born on the same day as the appearance of Halley's Comet in 1835, and he died, as he had already prophesized, on the very day of its next appearance in 1910.

Eerier still, Morgan Robertson's *Futility*, published in 1898, details the fateful voyage of a fictional transatlantic luxury liner christened Titan. Although touted as unsinkable, it strikes an iceberg in April-month and sinks with the loss of over 3000 passengers. In April 1912, the RMS Titanic, a transatlantic luxury liner set off on its maiden voyage. Heralded as unsinkable, it struck an iceberg and sank, resulting in the loss of nearly 2200 lives.

Reaching new heights of creepiness, Edgar Allan Poe's only

complete novel, *The Narrative of Arthur Gordon Pym of Nantucket* tells the story of four survivors of a shipwreck, who floating adrift on an open boat, decide to murder the cabin boy, Richard Parker, for food. In 1884, almost half a century later, a yawl named the Mignonette, floundered, its only four survivors drifting helplessly in a lifeboat. Severely hungered, the three senior crew members eventually killed and ate the cabin boy. The victim's name was Richard Parker.

Impressive, pondered Xander. *Three tales to chill the blood. Amazing what these researchers can dig up if they know where to look. As creepy at the mysteries of the Mary Celeste, the Flannan Isles Lighthouse and Dyatlov Pass.*

He discovered an equally-weird website called *Questions That Cannot Be Answered.* Xander looked at some of these searching, insoluble questions. *Why doesn't the fattest man in the world become a hockey goalie? How does the guy who clears the roads with the snowplow get to work in the morning? Why doesn't McD's sell hotdogs? Do Jewish vampires still avoid crosses? Why doesn't Tarzan have a beard? Why do superheroes wear their underwear on the outside of their clothes? If Wile E. Coyote had enough money to buy all that ACME equipment, why didn't he just buy himself a nice dinner? Where on the Ark did Noah keep his pair of woodpeckers? Are children who act in 'R'-rated flicks allowed to see the movie? If nobody buys a ticket to a movie, does the cinema still show it? Do Siamese twins pay for one ticket or two tickets when they go to the cinema? If a queen gives birth to a pair of Siamese twins, who gets to be king after her? Can hermaphroditic humans fertilize themselves? Can atheists get insurance for an act of God? When atheists go to Court, do they have to swear on the Bible? Why aren't the Judge or the lawyers sworn in during trials? Why do they sterilize lethal injections? Can cannibals be arrested for being under the influence of alcohol, such as drunk-driving, if they happen to have eaten someone who was drunk? If a patient is addicted to counseling, how do you treat them? What is another word for 'thesaurus'? If fortune favours the brave, why do fools rush in where angels fear to tread? What happens to an irresistible force when it hits an immovable object? Can you imagine a world without hypothetical situations?*

He continued to browse . . . and stopped dead in his tracks.

Hey, what have we here? Xander had spotted something worth investigating. The site was simply called *Death Clock*. When he opened up the file and read the instructions, he learned that just by filling in a few personal details (Date of Birth, present place of residence, whether or not you smoked or drank and any current health problems), this program could, by scientific means (or otherwise), calculate the date of your death to an accuracy of five years.

A tall order if you ask me, he thought. *Let's give it a whirl.*

Come on, Hubley, do you really want to know when you're going to croak? an inner voice protested.

"Why ever not?" he murmured, intrigued. "Who doesn't want to know their destiny?"

The inner voice went silent. As he entered in the relevant information, butterflies fluttered in his stomach and his mouth tasted like pennies. His fingers paused over the final key. *Maybe I shouldn't . . .*

He considered aborting for a moment, then brushed his doubts aside. *To hell with it! What's there to lose?*

He hit RETURN.

The program went about its calculations and seconds later spat out an answer:

26/05/2007

Xander stared at the screen, puzzled and a little perturbed.

That can't be right, he debated. *Must be some mistake.* He followed the instructions again, careful to input the correct information, and the same apparent glitch stared coldly back.

Unease turned to mistrust as he tried to make sense of the numbers presented before him. It suggested that three weeks from now he would be dead. How could it possibly be true when he was still in the prime of life?

It was a program designed for the purposes of

scaremongering, he concluded. Aside from perhaps being a program error, the reading itself was false and deliberately misleading, never meant to be taken at face-value, except by those who believed in the ambiguous predictions of the Zodiac or those who accepted unquestioningly divination by crystal gazing. Even then, the joke was on them. In other words, a simple means of putting the fun back in death.

He laughed it off and moved conscientiously to the next set of files. Nevertheless, despite his best efforts, somewhere a nerve had been touched and a dark, disquieting uncertainty lingered.

Xander sped through a series of files devoted to UFO-lore. Most contained documents borrowed from websites he had browsed earlier: photographic evidence of mysterious lights in the sky, eyewitness reports of close encounters with unearthly entities, episodes of missing time and unexplained cases of radiation sickness, conspiracy theories concerning government cover-ups, crop circles and cattle mutilations. Adamski, Foo fighters, Men-In-Black, the Visitor from Taured, the Voynich Manuscript, the Valentich Disappearence, the Solway Firth Spaceman, the orgiastic teachings of the Raëlian Movement . . .

Sensing he would gain no new insight into this popular phenomenon, he skimmed through the pages, stopping to view the occasional interesting article.

Coping with Alien Abduction spoke of a higher incidence of autism amongst children of alien abductees.

The Black Knight Satellite was a dark, tumbling object that had apparently been orbiting the Earth for thirteen thousand years, transmitting mysterious radio signals, first intercepted by Nikola Tesla in 1899.

Ancient Astronaut Almanac suggested that previous visitors to our world had left a secret message in our DNA, a kind of cosmic greeting which the Human Genome Project was close to unravelling and decoding.

The Gnostic claimed that both organized religion, particularly Christianity, and capitalism were created and perpetuated by

Manipulative Extraterrestrials in order to enslave mankind through greed, exploitation and violent oppression and divert him from his true calling of uniting with the Highest Consciousness of the Universe: God.

Three weeks had passed. During this time, Xander had neither showered nor changed his black clothes. His stubble had burgeoned into a straggly beard and he looked gaunt and pale. He had been living off Pot Noodle and water. He hadn't been to work or called in sick—he just hadn't bothered. Mrs. Scarsdale, the ill-tempered landlady, had called round twice, demanding this month's rent, but Xander had already bolted the door so she could not enter using her skeleton key. Realizing he was in and refusing to open the door, she had uttered some unrepeatable falsehoods about his mother, then threatened him with eviction. So far, she hadn't come back.

Xander no longer attached any great importance to these 'chores'. All that mattered now was completing his monumental quest. Rooted at his computer, totally immersed in the slipstream of data, he cruised on Auto-pilot around the Twilight World of the Weird and the Wonderful. He had become a willing captive of The Zone.

Congratulations, Hubley! To use the words of Licklider, you've achieved Advanced Man-Computer Symbiosis!

Xander left the UFO archives behind, shifting to an athenaeum of sites conceived in different languages. Xander did not pretend to be multilingual, so instead of trying to translate these curious foreign articles (which would have proved futile), he settled for the visual content. He made out a French bulletin about an old lady arrested for riding along the Expressway on her electric wheelchair. He seized upon the tale of a cunning hypnotist who, during the Spanish Civil War, managed to brainwash an entire battalion of Franco's troops into switching sides and fighting for the anti-Fascists. German bloggers argued as to whether or not conjoined twins, participating in a soccer match, counted as two players. An undisclosed source from the Vatican was offering to sell a Jesus petroglyph, reputed to be as authentic as the Turin Shroud, for a reasonable price. On a separate note, a young

Czech atheist wondered if he should file a lawsuit against his school because a Bible course he was forced to attend violated his religious liberty. A Russian medical journal discussed the rising epidemic of so-called 'Yellow People', an outbreak of jaundice in men below the breadline brought on by drinking bootleg vodka, generously infused with floor polish.

Xander delved deeper into the foreign languages' section of this, the heir apparent to the traditional library. From Eastern Europe, he journeyed forth to an article in Hebrew about an Israeli mathematician who had supposedly discovered a universal equation which could finally unlock the secrets of the Torah in relation to its place in the wider scheme of things. An Arabic scholar warned that the Time of Judgement was at hand and two monsters, Gog and Magog, were poised to escape their eternal prison and be unleashed upon the Infidel. Red rain, according to a Hindi correspondent, descended over Kerala, southern India, raising the possibility that the winds had carried fallout from a meteor shower or, from the cellular nature of the particles, extraterrestrial spores; perhaps the first-ever reported case of *panspermia*, as Xander had read elsewhere.

He journeyed on . . . and soon found himself in the Far East. Looked like Korean—or maybe Vietnamese. Something about restaurants adding narcotics to their dog stew to entice customers . . . Next up, grainy photos of the actual manifestation of a haunting on the set of *A Chinese Ghost Story* . . . A Japanese still-shot of a lightning-quick robotic arm slicing through fired bullets using a simple *Sashimi* knife . . .

He scrolled down a page. Xander's self-made project suddenly saw him tramping through uncharted territory.

Here, he encountered languages he genuinely didn't recognize. HTML documents speaking in dead and forgotten tongues, possibly set up by some passionate professor or avid linguistic revivalist. Whether these webpages were printed in Sanskrit or Aramaic, Hunnic or Ancient Sumerian, Xander couldn't tell. He did, however, feel like an archaeologist stumbling across the ruins of an extinct civilization. Perhaps, somewhere in this section he would find a sacred Mayan codex.

There must, of course, be sites written wholly in Or'zet . . . or canonical Klingon. Not that Xander would ever know the difference. *All very Martian*, he mused. *I've surely located the basement and what lies buried within . . .*

He followed these digital footprints further into the past.

Tablets of archaic symbols—unidentifiable, indecipherable, completely obscure—accompanied sinister rock-carvings of gigantic, tentacled, cyclopean creatures, and hooded, misty beings with a fiery-green stare, and shapeless, mutating forms covered all over in eyes and mouths. *Demented*, thought Xander, fascinated, *the work of a twisted imagination, definitely basement-dwelling material*. The images of these frightening bas-reliefs recalled the pantheon of Elder Gods of Lovecraftian mythos. Knowledge of their very existence was likely to drive you mad and the mere glimpse of them could kill you. It was also rumoured they were once rulers of our world when man was but a primitive worshipper, only to succumb to a perpetual sleep, and although the ordinary mind of man forgot about them and moved on, their memory did not entirely fade from history. For, through the ages, underground cults sprang up, and these seekers of the arcane and the forbidden and the unspeakable extremes of human experience, *remembered*.

Now the gods sleep, their long hibernation full of dreams of waking . . . They dream and bide their time . . . Waiting to rise up again and be masters once more . . .

We are like dragonflies to them, Xander reflected, pitiful of what humans essentially stood for. *Ephemerals with our short, lowly, meaningless lives*. Appraising these perfectly-hewn stone monstrosities, he could feel a melancholy setting in. He quickly cautioned himself. *Hey, you're taking this way too seriously. They're just stories. Acquire, appreciate and turn the page.*

He did.

Xander skipped to the next entry . . . and let out a gasp.

He had scarcely considered the eventuality . . . but here it was, staring him straight in the face.

He had done it! He had actually made it!

He had accomplished the unthinkable, reached the

unreachable. Endless corridors he had travelled down to arrive at this place.

The final entry in all the two million results listed on the Google Search Engine.

This was it! This was definitely *it*!

The occasion was distinctly overwhelming, complete with a strong, unquantifiable dose of Nerd Rapture. Xander took a gulp of water to steady himself.

Twelve months, he thought, *an intensive twelve months of solid sacrifice.* The last three weeks—working day and night, pretty much non-stop—had been particularly taxing. And, yet, surprisingly fun at the same time, like the paradoxical agony and joy of childbirth. Because this was what it had all been about. This was supposed to mark the climax of his year-long mission. The culmination of his hard work, reward for his toils.

The payoff.

He looked at the outlandish text. Somehow, he knew this amounted to the special, singularly strange thing he had been searching for. He shouldn't have been able to interpret any of it, but he could without even trying. It was as though the symbols before him were being transmitted directly into his higher centres while undergoing some form of decryption process. Further still, Xander deduced that the carrier wave comprised a built-in universal translator and was broadcasting in every conceivable language and in all known frequencies. The transmission could adapt to the unique, intricate pattern of the synaptic pathways in the language centres of each human brain. In other words, you saw what you were mentally equipped to see. The message read:

EXAMINED VOYAGER CRAFT

INITIATING CONTACT

GREETINGS

ENTER

Xander puzzled over it for a few moments, before his eyes widened in stark realization. "It can't be," he murmured. And saw it for what it was.

It was a signal from another world.

A signal from another planet, marvelled Xander. *I must confess, not the terrible let-down I dreaded. Credit to Dr Frank Drake, despite the limitations of his equation. Got to be coolest gem I've ever unearthed. I've hit the Jackpot!*

True, he had neglected himself to the point that his clothes didn't fit any more. And, yes, he had trawled through volumes of crackpot ideas and downright weird stuff to get here, but this final hit provided irrefutable evidence of the existence of intelligent life elsewhere in the vast infinity of space. Ultimate proof of otherworldly sentience, justifying his long and exhaustive twelve-month search.

Better than the alogarithm design, reverse engineering and logic gates I'm forced to endure day after day. Doesn't anybody know the cure for cyberslacking is the application of proxy settings, you idiot? ALWAYS—so don't bother me again!

But, of course, it begged the question: why had S.E.T.I. not spotted this extraterrestrial communication—if this was in fact an extraterrestrial communication?

Maybe because it's so obscure, tucked away in the deepest recesses of the World Wide Web. Those boffins at S.E.T.I. are probably searching for it in the wrong place—somewhere unmapped and inconsequential and far, far away—when it's been hiding here all along, right under our very noses. God bless the Age of Information.

The cursor pointed calmly to the legend, ENTER, awaiting further instructions. Yonder lay the way to eternal wisdom. *But do not haste. Sit back and savour the moment. The moment before your head swells with metaphysical conundra, when you discover the secrets of hitherto unknown realms. Places unheard-of and unseen, places mankind would probably never physically visit even if he managed to make it as a space-faring species.*

Dare you enter, he composed himself. *You've come this far! This, ladies and gentlemen, is the moment of truth!*

Something awesome lay behind Contestant's Door Number One-million-eight-hundred-and-fifty-three-thousand-four-hundred-and-twenty-six. Xander just knew.

Setting his sights on the target, eyes on the prize, he pressed ENTER.

At first, nothing happened. The screen went blank and, for a short while, Xander almost feared the system had crashed.

Then, he sensed a vibration. The accompanying hum went unnoticed until Xander removed the buds from his ears. The humming grew steadily louder, resembling the sound of an old electric generator. The table and chair began to tremble, shake, reverberate as though a train had passed overhead. The computer screen suddenly came to life, emitting a bright pink glow.

[. . . *T minus 9 . . . 8 . . . 7 . . . 6 . . . Initializing boosters . . .*]

The hum increased to a deep throbbing, keeping in rhythm with the stuttery pink beams streaming from the computer and the shuddering of the walls and furniture.

[. . . *5 . . . 4 . . . 3 . . . 2 . . . 1 . . . Zero Hour . . . Ignition confirmed... Mission Control, we have LIFT-OFF!*]

The rise and fall of each deep-throated, mechanical throb intensified further. The walls shook violently, as if an earthquake had struck. Xander was forced to squeeze his eyes shut by the psychedelic light show, its unearthly brilliance consuming the entire room. It was as though his whole apartment was wired up to the entire power supply of the National Grid.

A new sound entered the fore, a high-pitched ripping noise. Xander squinted amidst the plethora of dazzling pink as a conduit opened up. All around him, the pounding commotion reached a deafening crescendo, as thunderous as a jet engine howling down a wind tunnel.

[*We're now leaving Earth's orbit . . .*]

The rip widened, the room dissolving around him like a reel of film combusting outwards, the pink ethereal light dimming, harmonizing, gaining some measure of stability.

Soon, the ever-expanding opening had dilated to an absolute swirling, spatial rift which swallowed up the room and every inch of reality he knew. The sinister background pulse subsided, echoing away into nothingness.

Xander straightened up, blinked.

He had completed an incredible transition.

Before him stretched a vista unlike any place on Earth. He beheld a harsh, rugged landscape, where most of the rocky formations took on strange and fantastic shapes. Helices of rock jutted up from the ground, spiralling up like corkscrews while elsewhere tall monolithic spears, grouped like missiles, pierced the heavens. Twilight bathed the world, a pink twilight, methane-rich, shimmering and fabulous. An enormous, blue-hued, crescent moon hung low on the horizon, its extensive cratered surface accessible to the naked eye. Occasionally, a meteor would come trailing down, burning up in the atmosphere in a golden, flaming spectacle. Somewhere in the west, an electrical storm raged.

One small step for man, reflected Xander, overcome by the unutterable beauty of the place, *one giant leap for mankind . . .*

He might have been forgiven for thinking he had inadvertently stepped into a Virtual Reality simulation, with everything around him nothing more than the sum of its pixels and terabytes. Except he knew this wasn't just some finely-detailed computer projection. This was the real deal. He had experienced a sequence of events nobody would possibly believe. He had picked up a signal from across the stars, merged with the user interface, been sucked through a portal and transported billions of light years away to eventually touchdown on a distant alien world.

An alien world which, from its rust-coloured sands and auroral skies and random meteor bombardment, appeared remote and desolate and inhospitable. What scientists might call a 'dead world'. Yet, there was life here. The seemingly barren terrain was broken by brief oases of vegetation. Sparse, yes, but life nonetheless. Clusters of black puffballs, their heads pregnant with spores, waited eagerly for the winds to do their duty. Exotic plants, with fleshy, blood-red leaves and spines full of poison, ingested juices from beneath the ferrous sand with greedy, sucking motions. A small army of purple-backed scuttling things marched past him in a single, precisely-organized file. And, overhead, the silhouette of a giant bird that looked like a scraggy cross between a bat and a vulture swooped down to collect its evening snack, promptly soaring away with a piercing shriek into the distance.

And there was something else. Xander could feel it.

An intelligence far greater than man.

Xander saw the tower and its blinking light. What at first glance might have easily been mistaken for a natural geological formation, on closer observation, awakened the real possibility that, like the Pyramids, it had actually been constructed to serve a particular purpose. To the north-east it stood, rising up from between two outcrops of rock, a dark, imposing, sky-flung edifice, once a graceful piece of architecture, now an abandoned, crumbling ruin. An antenna winked on and off at the top of the spire—the same distress beacon which had summoned him.

Xander could see it now. A civilization that had once been indigenous to this planet, a powerful and advanced race, until tragedy struck when the planet itself rebelled against its masters. Soon, the world they had taken for granted could no longer sustain them, and they began to die out. But, although their bodies withered away and their bones turned to dust, their souls lived on, immortal and as insubstantial as ghosts, trapped on a world which had become a prison to them. So, with a technology significantly superior to our own, the last, able-bodied members of their race had built this tower and set up the signal in a last-ditch attempt to contact other worlds.

They must have heard the benevolent hails of the Voyager probe by chance and sensed a glimmer of hope.

On a fundamental level, it made total sense. The tower was an unassailable monument to their survival.

Deserving his complete attention, Xander was about to head off in the direction of the tower when something he had not been anticipating occurred to him. He realized he possessed no corporeal form. He, like the disembodied spirits of this world, was composed of pure consciousness, floating invisibly and seamlessly above the ground. Soul, consciousness, sentience—same difference. He was now a being of pure energy. *This is what death must be like, the moments after death, that thing they call an out-of-the-body experience.* The revelation came as both a shock and a sweet, welcome release.

It was at that stage that the final pieces of the puzzle fitted into place. They had devised an ingenious way out. The tower was not just a transmission station, but housed equipment of an unimaginable scale designed to serve as some sort of soul-transfer device, designed to displace the target soul, ultimately leading to a case of bodysnatching, in the absolute sense of the word, and a means of migration to another world. Somewhere back home sat his actual body, presently commandeered by one of the former inhabitants of this planet. There would be no way of reversing the process; Xander could not get back. He could only but marvel at the ancient alien hardware at work.

He vaguely recalled reading something about the portentous relationship between Mark Twain and Halley's Comet, and remembered the prediction of the Death Clock. If he remembered correctly, today *was* the twenty-sixth. Not that it mattered. He had found his niche in the wider Universe.

Mustn't be late for my own funeral . . .

Travelling interstellar distances to this world was worth the price of the ticket alone. He had touched alien shores and would spend the rest of eternity roaming his new home as pure energy as omniscient as a free spirit. This was his greatest adventure, the summation of his dreams. At that moment, Xander felt a belonging with this planet . . . and felt like a god.

What of those who were disillusioned with the practicalities of mundane life and thought the human race was doomed anyway, those who chose escape in the Internet, those thousands of millions like him?

Learn they soon would of how an alien invasion by stealth had begun . . .

But maybe the final word should belong to Carl Sagan and his shrewd—and sanguine—interpretation of the human race: *You're an interesting species. An interesting mix. You're capable of such beautiful dreams, and such horrible nightmares. You feel so lost, so cut off, so alone, only you're not. See, in all our searching, the only thing we've found that makes the emptiness bearable, is each other.*

THIS IS XANDER07... LOGGING OFF.

April 2007—June 2007

Perfection on Demand

"Acceptance of the impermanence of being. And acceptance of the imperfect nature of being, or possibly the perfect nature of being, depending on how one looks at it."

William Gibson

As with any Saturday night, the CONSTANTINOPLE was packed. Turkish music filled the air, its spiky exotic beats almost drowned by the constant buzz of human conversation. Well-to-do customers tucked into their meals, talked and laughed boisterously amongst themselves and puffed away merrily on the hookahs supplied by the proprietors. Fine membranes of blue smoke drifted up to the rafters. The evening's entertainment was provided by a voluptuous belly-dancer, who was provocatively going through the motions in the spotlight, aware that her main audience was a group of Middle Eastern businessmen, who seemed utterly entranced by her every move and whom she thought were wondering whether she might offer a different kind of service at a negotiable price.

Two old friends sat in a candlelit corner booth, finishing off their dessert of pistachio-and-sultana baklava whilst openly contemplating what the future held for both of them. Their main course of spiced kobedahs with pomegranate tagine had been a delicious revelation.

"I'm fit to burst," declared Hector Delgado. "I couldn't eat another morsel."

"So stuffed you might explode and shower the place with the undigested contents of your stomach?" Marisa van der Rijk asked with mischief in her eye.

"Monsieur Creosote," Hector replied without the flicker of a smile, "from that Monty Python sketch in *The Meaning of Life*."

"Nothing gets past you," chuckled Marisa. "You're a regular walking encyclopedia."

Hector looked thoughtful for a moment. "I'm curious. Why this place?"

"Ever remember coming here before?"

A look of puzzlement crossed his forehead. "No, I don't think so. Should I?"

"I thought you might appreciate it. Cheer you up a bit. You've been kind of down lately."

"Down, what do you mean down?"

"No offence, but you never go out. You spend your evenings drinking and shunning decent company. I want you to get a life."

"I *have* a life!" Hector protested weakly.

"Drinking half a bottle of vodka a night inside an empty apartment does not a life make."

"I'm dead inside," Hector said dolefully.

"No, you're not," Marisa observed. "You're just stuck in your ways."

"What if I like the way things are?"

"The problem is, you don't," she said with complete understanding. "You only think you do." More brightly she added. "I now solemnly take it upon myself to break your daily routine. I order you to have some fun. Think of me as your morale officer."

Hector sighed resignedly. "And as my morale officer what is your first act of duty?"

"You don't wear black."

"And why not?"

"I mean, all black, every day, that's not normal."

"So?" Hector replied gloomily. "*I'm in mourning for my life*, as Masha tells Medvedenko in Chekhov's *The Seagull*." Marisa tutted in mock-despair. "Besides, black will never go out of fashion," Hector argued. "It's the colour for all occasions and saves time thinking about what else one should wear. It's simple, it's functional and, most of all, it's downright cool!"

"Lucky it suits you or I'd drag you down to Savile Row myself." The espressos had arrived.

"Mind me asking why you decided to take me out?"

"Like I said—to cheer you up!"

"Forgive me for being a paranoid fool," Hector apologized, "but I sense an ulterior motive."

Marisa sounded a little annoyed. "Why do you have to ruin a perfectly good evening by analyzing everything? Why can't you just enjoy the moment?"

Hector looked away, a little embarrassed.

Suspecting she might have upset him, she gently added: "I didn't mean to be hard on you, but you can be really exasperating at times. You have a tendency to overanalyze things when you should be having a good time." She studied him closely. "Aren't you having a good time?"

"I suppose," replied Hector, still rather shamefaced.

Marisa downed the rest of her Arabian flower and started on her espresso.

They sat awhile in silence, listening to the Eastern-themed music and snatches of conversation around them. The belly-dancer had stopped dancing and one of the interested businessmen was making her a proposition she could not possibly refuse.

The architecture of the place fascinated Hector. The Moorish crescents and arches and pothooks took him back to a time when the Crusaders were besieging the evil Saladin's last surviving stronghold. *Strangers in a strange land,* he thought. *Power to the Cruciform sword.*

The espressos drunk, Marisa paid the bill. Hector expressed his displeasure at her refusal to split the bill. They slowly made their way to the door of the restaurant.

"My treat, remember?" Marisa said cheerily.

"Your treat," said Hector, sounding disgruntled. "A gentleman never allows a lady to pay for dinner. Next time it's on me."

"Who says there's going to be a next time . . .?" Hector stopped in his tracks. "I'm only teasing," Marisa said, playfully punching his arm. "Don't be so serious. You really do need to lighten up."

Hector appeared slightly bemused. "That's just the way I am."

"Not true," Marisa corrected him. "It's just the way you *think* you are. You were once a very sociable, outgoing person."

"Then why can't I remember?" There was genuine anguish in his voice.

"In time you will," reassured Marisa. "You must give the therapy time to work and it'll soon come flooding back to you." She touched on a lighter note. "You know what they say about us Cancerians, don't you? Hard outside, soft on the inside."

"Oh?"

"We're supposed to be summer people. That's why we get on with everybody. We live in the eternal sunshine."

Outside the restaurant, the autumnal night fell cold and dark. A half-moon rode high in the heavens, peering down on a land flourishing with romantic dreams. The wind gusted softly, air-kissing any face it could find.

Marisa hailed a cab. "Want to come back to my place for a nightcap?" she asked Hector, her breath condensing into mist.

"I don't want to impose . . .." Hector began.

"You won't be, I promise."

Hector mulled it over, eventually accepted the invitation. "Okay, if you insist."

The lack of enthusiasm in his reply did not deter Marisa. "Oh, I insist!"

The cabbie was a jolly fellow named Dave.

"7, Ocean Drive," Marisa instructed him before she and Hector clambered in.

"Ocean Drive, hey?" Dave said, letting out a whistle, "Must be a nice place you have. Right by the sea. You must do well for yourself."

"I get by," Marisa said modestly.

They left behind the Arab Quarter and sped out of the city. "Good night out?" Dave inquired pleasantly.

"Exquisite, thanks," replied Marisa. "I couldn't have asked for anything better."

"I'm not one to pry, but can I detect some romance in the air?"

Hector intervened. "We're just good friends."

"I suspect your ladyfriend begs to differ."

"You're quite the intuitive genius," Marisa remarked.

"When you've been in my business as long as I have," Dave explained, "you tend to pick up on things. Little hints, small gestures, subtle signals. I consider myself something of an expert in non-verbal communication."

"We could use someone like you at our organization," Marisa said, smiling. "I ought to put you on our payroll."

"And what kind of work do you do?"

"I'm a genetic designer. Government research, Top Secret, confidential, hush-hush and all that."

"Mum's the word," Dave laughed, tapping his nose. "You can count on me to be discreet. If anybody asks, I never met you."

"Much appreciated."

Hector had remained preoccupied during their exchange, looking out the window at the passing headlights and dwindling number of upmarket dwellings.

Dave addressed Hector. "Why the long face?"

"Nothing personal," Hector responded, "just got a few things on my mind."

"Want to share?"

"Not particularly."

His reply killed the mood of the cab-ride, and although Marisa tried to make conversation with him, Hector kept his replies to an absolute minimum.

They arrived at the seafront, just after ten. Marisa paid the fare and handed Dave a generous tip.

As Hector wandered off up the beach, Dave spoke to Marisa quietly, conspiratorially. "He's a strange one, your date. Fair enough, he's good-looking, but other than that I really can't understand what you see in him."

"Believe me, he's been through a lot lately. He just needs time to recover."

"I hope it works out between you guys."

"Thanks," said Marisa. "I hope so, too."

She watched the cab drive away, and once its rear-lights had faded into the distance, she slipped off her toe-hooped sandals and ran barefoot towards Hector.

Marisa opened the door to her beach house. "Come. Let me show you inside."

Luxurious, spacious, three-bedroomed, the beach house was the epitome of modern living. A gigantic TV screen covered the entirety of one wall whilst a patio window constituted the opposite wall. The remaining walls and ceiling of the lounge, lit by chandelier, appeared as dazzling-white as the Pearly Gates. There was a small collection of abstract paintings down the hallway. A corner showcase boasted an authentic Dali sculpture called *Homage to Terpsichore*.

"Make yourself comfortable," Marisa asked of Hector.

"Your wish is my command," he said, trying to sound casual. He slumped heavily into the white leather couch, staring out to a darkened sea, hearing the surf crash against the rocks, smelling the salt tang in the air.

Marisa returned from the kitchen with two brandy glasses, each partially filled with her favourite Cognac.

They clinked glasses.

"To the future," Marisa toasted. "May nobody ever fall out of love."

"To Peace on Earth."

Marisa swirled the glass before taking a sip. "The secret is to unlock the flavours—just like any good Cabernet."

Hector sipped his Cognac meditatively. "What are you thinking?" she asked.

"Nothing,"

She glanced at him knowingly. "Is it about the incident at the bank?"

"I'd rather not say," he muttered.

"Therein lies your problem. Instead of brooding over it, you ought to talk about your ordeal and come to terms with what happened."

"What if I don't want to?" Hector replied, distressed. "What if all I deserve is to re-live that nightmare over and over again?"

"Stop punishing yourself. Try to understand it wasn't your fault. The pregnant mother got in the way and those bastards shot her. These things happen all the time. The world is an unjust place and Fate itself a petulant prankster. For chrissakes, Hector, you thwarted a bank robbery! You're a national hero! You should be proud of yourself!"

"But the mother and her unborn child . . ." The actual robbery was still a blur to him. All Hector could recall was the pregnant woman screaming hysterically before one of the masked gunmen approached her angrily and shot her at waist-height, her swollen belly deflating suddenly as thick, red amniotic fluid splattered on the floor, the bullet exiting her lower spine and decorating the back wall with a fine spray of blood. She died instantly. "I failed her," he mourned. A tear trickled down his left cheek.

"Hector, please," implored Marisa. "I know it's tragic, but it's been over a year. You have to let it go and concentrate on the positives."

"What positives? Her death is all I can remember from that day!"

"You mustn't blame yourself," reiterated Marisa. "I assure you, your amnesia will gradually lift."

"Maybe . . . maybe not . . . but my conscience won't let me rest."

Marisa moved closer to him on the couch. "Then let me make it easier for you."

She reached for his hand, but he snatched it away. "Don't...!"

"Why? I want to help you get over it."

"I have intimacy issues."

"I kind of figured, but I'm not going to lie to you, Hector. I've been attracted to you since I first laid

[made] eyes on you. And we're talking eighteen months. That's a long time for a girl to wait."

Hector went silent.

"Don't you find me even vaguely attractive?"

Her question produced a pained expression on his face. He looked at her longingly, wistfully. Her features like fine bone china, her multi-toned red bobtail, those emerald eyes into which one could drown, that perfectly rounded nose with its slight upward dimple and her soft, delicate, extremely kissable lips—her face pure and natural and seraphic and unenhanced by cosmetics. Even her style of dress deserved some mention—quintessentially bohemian yet so utterly chic. Only someone like Marisa could pull it off. "I think you're cute, sexy, intelligent and stylish with a great sense of humour, an air of girlishness and the graceful figure of a ballerina. Your body is a temple and I would worship at that temple every night if I could."

"Why don't you?" whispered Marisa, setting aside both brandy glasses.

"I can't . . ." said Hector in the midst of a guilt

[chip] trip. "You have a boyfriend. Sixteen years you've been seeing him."

"Our relationship was based on nothing more than a business arrangement. I don't love him anymore and the feeling is mutual."

"I thought he was supposed to be your soulmate."

"I thought so, too," Marisa said distractedly. "But he lost interest in me a long time ago, started taking me for granted. I'm going to tell him it's over. He won't mind as long as we part on good terms."

"You're not just saying that because you're on the rebound?"

"I could never use you or take advantage of you—I'm not that kind of girl. I find you mysterious and fascinating and a little bit sad."

"What if you're just trying to recapture your youth and all I'm looking for is a pleasurable distraction?"

"Hector, I mean every word I say," Marisa persisted earnestly. "Sometimes you just have to let go and seize the moment."

Still, Hector resisted. "I could not do this to you or your boyfriend. This is not me!"

"How do you know it's not you if you haven't tried it? So please stop stalling! I really, really like you . . ."

"Likewise, but . . ."

"No buts," Marisa mock-warned, putting a finger to his lips.

But Hector was suffering the agonies of the damned. "I can't go through with this."

Marisa's eyes welled up with tears, appealing to his humanity. "Oh, Hector . . ."

Sensing her desperation, her sweet, uncontrollable yearning, her deep unrequited feelings for him, Hector leaned over and placed his lips on hers. Marisa responded by pressing harder. Their tongues connected, warm and moist and arousing. Mouths locked in a crushing embrace, their hands busied themselves, excitedly removing the other's clothing. Soon they were naked, touching and caressing and exploring one another's sensitive, sweating, vulnerable bodies.

"I want you inside me," breathed Marisa at the height of passion. Hector obliged without hesitation, carefully manoeuvring his gorged manhood into her willing sacred pit. They moved together as one, in perfect rhythm, her soft, silky legs wrapped around his rugged waist. Like a smouldering fire splashed with oil, their flesh blazed and the gods rejoiced.

They made love all night and both reached the peak of ecstasy many times over. Eventually spent and exhausted, Hector held Marisa in his arms, her head resting on his chest. As dawn broke and the seagulls cried, Marisa pulled away to her side of the bed and gazed into his sleeping face, full of affection and wild desire. The intensity of their lovemaking had surprised her, even frightened her, for she had never experienced anything like it before. For the first time in her life, Marisa felt she was home.

Sex on demand . . . the perfect love on demand . . .

She kissed him on the cheek. Hector stirred, opening his eyes briefly. "I love you," she whispered sincerely.

"Likewise . . ." he moaned and closed his eyes again.

Likewise? Marisa thought, smiling blissfully instead of feeling like a discarded object. It wasn't Hector's fault he didn't feel for her the way she felt for him. But in time he might learn to love her. Hector hadn't been kidding when he'd told her he felt dead inside. He was an empty, soulless thing, constructed by the finest engineers and powered by renewable fuel cells. Although programmed in multiple techniques of lovemaking, he was still vastly inexperienced in the emotional aspects of love.

Lying there, Marisa hummed that old tune in her head, *Black Coffee*, by a long-forgotten girl band called All Saints from the turn of the century.

Oh, how she loved this beautiful creature, this perfect replacement for the real Hector Delgado, who had abandoned her for another woman. The spark had faded from their relationship long before he and his mistress were killed in a horrific car crash. Their bodies had been burnt beyond recognition; nothing could have been salvaged from their charred remains.

Her Hector replicant, on the other hand, had indeed foiled a bank robbery, the incident not the product of some false implanted memory as some might speculate. He had been shot so many times in the process, that if the professional clean-up crew from ANDROIDS INC. hadn't arrived on time, the doctors at the local general hospital would have been shocked to discover a real-life walking, talking biomechanoid.

Marisa had downloaded Hector's personality herself and she found his melancholic tendencies adorable, so Shakespearean. In true Stepford fashion, he looked like an upgraded version of her erstwhile boyfriend, free of all the deceits, reckless behaviours and irritating quirks of the real thing. Except she did not wish to mould him to her own high personal standards, but let his program evolve of its own accord, develop the way he saw fit. He was capable of independent thought and of incalculable logic, self-repairing and an extensive repository of knowledge. He also possessed a heart—she had made sure of that—a heart that was synthetic and durable, a heart that could possibly beat for all eternity.

Now Marisa could live out the rest of her days with Hector until she was old and grey and wrinkly. The Hector she had designed would be her bestest of friends, her companion and confidante, her silver angel and guardian to watch over her, her new soulmate and all-time hero, not forgetting the greatest, most versatile lover in the world. And when she would one day breathe her last dying breath, the Advanced Neuro-Cybernetics Division at ANDROIDS INC. would upload her brain into her new artificial body, so she and Hector could live as machines together forever.

A perfect chance for them to meet and fall in love again.

February 2008

Love of a Machine

"The marriage of reason and nightmare which dominated the twentieth century has given birth to an ever more ambiguous world. Across the communications' landscape move the spectres of sinister technologies and the dreams that money can buy."

J.G. Ballard

Something spurred me awake—a noise, a faint whisper of song, an unidentified voice calling out a name "Zane, can you hear us?"

And with this gentle mental nudge, my muscles twitched and my eyes fluttered open. Darkness surrounded me, heavy and obsidian. Vestiges of memory drifted out from the time-fog, hazy, indistinct, unshaped. I groaned, stirred, found I was lying on my stomach.

Oh, my head! What the hell was I drinking last night?

"Lights, please!" the same voice decreed.

Suddenly, I was slammed in the face by a fierce blaze of light, harsh, blinding, unbearable. For a moment I could not see. Blinking against the glare, arm protecting my stunned eyes, I tried to make sense of the white confusion engulfing me. Then, as my vision gradually adjusted, I realized I lay on a king-size bed with silk-white sheets, face-down, the brilliant illumination overhead hitting me from all sides in an arrangement photographers termed 'four-point lighting'.

Am I in trouble? Am I in some sort of interrogation chamber about to suffer the tortures of the damned?

"Zane, glad to see you back with us," said the voice from the darkness beyond. "Are you ready for the final scene?"

Final scene? What final scene? "I don't understand," I croaked, the words coming out dry and awkward. I noticed I was wearing only black Armani jeans. I examined my rugged physique, touched my six-pack in a curious manner.

"What's wrong with him?" someone else—another male voice, vaguely foreign—asked, concerned.

"I think he's disorientated," the first, earlier voice replied. Speaking directly to me, [*Zane, yes, I remember, my name is Zane*] it gave me a quick rundown. "Your name is Zane Harglow. You're on a film set. We're shooting the final scene of a movie. Ring any bells?"

"Not particularly," I replied, more bewildered than ever.

"Don't worry, it should all come back to you."

"And who exactly might you be?"

The voice introduced itself. "I'm Elliot Webber, the director of this visual feast. Beside me is Maurice Roquefort, our cameraman and lighting engineer."

"Zane . . ." There was just the hint of a French accent in that elementary greeting.

"We've also got a technical consultant from your organization here with us: Dr. Ernst Durant."

"How're you doing, Zane?" Dr. Durant said, his reassuring voice coming at me from beyond the lighted stage. "You've done a bang-up job so far, and we're all very proud of you."

"And the rest of the film crew," Webber went on. "They're right behind you, dying to see you do your thing."

A cheer surged up from the darkness yonder, a rousing faceless chorus offering the warmest encouragement, support and gratitude.

"Why can't I see you?" I asked, propelling myself into a sitting position, straining to see into the darkness.

"Because we don't want any unnecessary distractions when you're doing your scene," answered Webber.

But my mind drew a blank. "I don't get any of this. What scene?"

"Come on, Zane, get it together," floated the voice from the dark. Webber seemed to be losing patience. "You're the ubiquitous Zane Harglow, the greatest Hollywood actor since Chase Carver. We're on the brink of finishing a masterpiece in celluloid. There's only one more scene to go before we close for the season."

"So you keep reminding me . . ."

"Why can't you remember?"

"I don't know. I can't recall ever being an actor."

"Not recall being an actor?" Webber exclaimed, astonished, quick to consult his technical advisor. "How can he not remember, doc? Could the action sequence at the oil refinery have damaged him in some way?"

Webber's use of the word "damaged" instead of "injured" struck me as slightly odd, but I didn't dwell on it. At least, not at that particular juncture.

"Something's not quite right," Dr. Durant replied, getting suspicious. Then, addressing me directly, he asked: "Zane, what's the last thing you remember?"

"I'm not sure." I searched my mind, unearthed nothing concrete. Except . . . "Wait, I remember a stack of paper, a desk-lamp and a typewriter . . . wasn't I some kind of writer?"

"You *were* a writer," Dr. Durant informed me. "You wrote a number of screenplays, all highbrow works, one of which turned out to be a Hugo Award-winning effort. *Love of a Machine* caught the public's imagination and made you a star overnight. But because you as a person were always more interesting than your stories, we moulded you into an actor."

His explanation dislodged something. The memory rose up like an old shipwreck from the dark abyss of my mind. A jagged, rusted hull, a ghost of its former glory, but visible enough, like looking through a dirty lens. The World Science Fiction Convention in San Francisco, paparazzi and spotlights, myself going up on stage to collect my award to a round of wild applause and delivering an emotional yet uplifting speech. Through the circus of fragmented images, I remembered Zane Harglow the Scriptwriter, but where did Zane Harglow the Actor come from? "I must insist I have never acted before in my life."

"This is getting us nowhere," stated Webber.

"I may need to run a diagnostic," suggested Dr. Durant.

There, again: another curious turn-of-phrase. "What's with the technical jargon? I don't want to sound ignorant, but for what reason should you want to conduct a 'diagnostic' on me?"

Maurice Roquefort, the French cameraman, joined in the conversation. "He doesn't know."

"Know what?" I demanded, gripped by frustration. "Could someone please tell me what the hell is going on?"

"The real Zane Harglow was a notorious womanizer and a hardened drug addict," Dr. Durant said frankly. "He eventually died from a heroin overdose."

"What are you talking about?" I burst out, rocked by the revelation, trying desperately to grasp the enormity of what he'd uttered. I felt a dark shiver ascend my spinal column as though someone had stepped over my grave. But my startlement was only momentary since his outrageous claim raised the obvious, logical question. "If I'm supposed to be dead, how can I still be breathing?"

"I don't know how to put this without being blunt—*you're not human.*"

"That's crazy! If I'm not human, then what am I?"

"A machine. Very lifelike, granted, but a machine, nonetheless."

I thought of *The Six Million Dollar Man* from my childhood. "A machine? As in bionic?"

"Not quite," recounted Dr. Durant. "You're a machine through-and-through. An android. Top-of-the-range. The most versatile and sophisticated model we ever produced. We extracted your brain, pruned away all your negative traits and memories, downloaded the remainder of your personality into an artificial neural net, which explains why you can think and feel like any human. When you died in real life you weighed 120kg—you'd really let yourself go. Our genetic engineers rebuilt your body to the specifications of what it once was in its heyday, using the latest cutting-edge technology and the finest, most durable synthetic materials. We fine-tuned you, perfected you, granted you a new indefinite lease of life. You will neither age nor die, except perhaps require an occasional overhaul. In many respects, you are immortal and almost indestructible."

"Can't you see, Zane?" Webber followed on. "You're the ideal candidate for the big screen. Your come-hither looks, your heroic personality and formidable intelligence, your unbelievable feats of endurance command the attention of the whole world over and Mars too. Worshipped by the public, who can't get enough of you, and hated by your fellow human actors, since you've practically made them obsolete. ANDROIDS INC. even manufactures a line in Zane Harglow pleasure models, programmed in over two hundred sexual positions, very popular with the ladies, satisfying the desires of the bored housewife, and a few men too I can tell you! Your name alone is a huge, money-spinning industry. You almost singlehandedly reshaped the landscape of modern cinema. You are an inspiration to millions. You are the legend that is Zane Harglow!"

I took a while to digest the information. It was both incredible and sad. I suppose I should have been flattered, that I had physically evolved into the ultimate mechanical being and was Hollywood's number one leading man, but there was something tragic about the loss of my individuality. I could no longer call myself human. "There still persists the matter of why I can't remember acting in any movie."

"He's malfunctioning," concluded Webber, "Why don't you just deactivate him, doc, and set the reboot sequence?"

"No-one's deactivating no-one," I warned, suddenly feeling threatened with extinction.

"That's what I like about him," remarked the film director. "Irresistible when vulnerable. Harrison Ford all over again."

Dr. Durant spoke up, thoughtful, out-of-sight. "I seriously doubt he needs reprogramming because I don't believe this is a case of misfiring circuits. I think his amnesia is based on something empirical." He went out on a limb. "Zane, what year is this?"

"2007, of course," I said, puzzled by the question.

Dr. Durant summed up what he had already suspected. "This,

gentlemen, is not the Zane Harglow we've been working with. What you have before you is the prototype, the *original* Zane Harglow, the one from which we designed all our future models."

"My God!" exclaimed Elliot Webber. "How did this happen?"

"They must have brought the wrong Zane Harglow out of storage."

"But that means . . ."

"Yes, we've just made history," responded Dr. Durant, his fascination evident. "We've revived the first-ever Zane Harglow." He seemed as excited as a person who had just rediscovered an old toy, forgotten from childhood, during an attic clear-out. "Zane, how do you feel?"

"Confused."

"That's understandable."

I had an awful feeling. "You asked me about what year it was. Why?"

"Because it's the year 2046."

Was there no end to these seismic revelations? Decades had lapsed, my parents were dead, the life I once knew was a skeletal relic buried in the distant sands of times and, worst of all, I had been turned into a robot only to be exploited. Grief welled up inside me. I fought back the tears.

"What about my picture?" demanded Webber tersely. "Unless you're going to ask Buck Rogers over there to finish it off for me."

Dr. Durant sounded distracted, annoyed. "For once, Elliot, think outside the box!"

"I keep telling you I *can't* act!" I reiterated.

"Hold your horses!" Webber declared prematurely. "That amounts to a breach of contract. The movie studio execs won't like it."

"Why so glum?" Dr. Durant asked me, supportive, sympathetic in tone. "You're the original. You have an actual living brain inside your head, something which the later models don't. Modified, agreed, missing chunks of your memory, but with your humanity still intact."

"So?"

"You're still *you*, only physically more advanced."

~ 79 ~

It made sense, absolute and perfect sense. I was still me, only better. Why should I despair, mourn my old life, when the future stretched out ahead of me like the mysteries of the night sky to an amateur astronomer? I was supposed to be a science-fiction writer, dammit, and wasn't it every science-fiction writer's dream to see what the future held? "I wrote for a living because I sucked badly at every audition. However, the circumstances seemed to have changed. For the sake of my reputation, I'll give it a shot."

"That's more like it!" Webber said, wasting no time in getting down to business. "One last scene—I really don't care which Zane Harglow we use as long as it doesn't end up on the cutting-room floor. Ought to be straightforward."

"What is this final scene you speak of?"

"Get a load of this: you've uncovered an international conspiracy to cripple the global economy, travelled to some dreamy, exotic locations during the course of your assignment, defeated the cyberterrorists in truly spectacular fashion and rescued the girl."

I struggled to access my residual memory. "Sounds like something I know . . ."

"Now it's time for you to seal your relationship with the heroine."

"You mean I have to do a love scene?"

"What else? It's what the people expect."

I was alarmed, aghast, afraid. "You mean I have to perform naked in front of all these cameras?"

"Is that going to be a problem?"

"I've never done this kind of thing before, least of all for the entire planet to witness."

"Sure you have," Webber attested. "Maybe not you exactly. But together Zane Harglow is one big institution, incarnations of the same, most sought-after actor in movie history. What could possibly go wrong?"

My plumbing might not work, having been in deep freeze for nearly half a century. But I chose not to express my fears out aloud.

"Wait until you see whom you'll be making love to . . . Zane, meet Selena Tremaine, voted the most beautiful woman in the world!"

She emerged from the shadows, wearing a white, dragon-gilded kimono . . . and not much else. I glimpsed her fabulous body through the silk. Her skin was olive-toned and flawless, her light blue eyes sparkled like Bombay sapphires, her full lips appeared as succulent as strawberries and her hair was dyed mauve, cut short *anime*-style. Although I'd been out of operation for such a long time, I doubted I'd be disappointing my fans, even if I tried. The prospect of making love to this gorgeous thing no longer instilled me with fear. I would have gladly foregone my multi-million-dollar fee to ravish her. A song from the early-'Noughties, *Fantasy* from the old Appleton sisters, ran through my head. "Hello, Zane," she greeted me with a honeyed tongue.

"Come hither," I requested, patting the bedspread invitingly.

Selena padded barefoot to the bed and sat down beside me. She undid her sash and her perfectly-formed breasts fell out. "Shall we get acquainted?"

I spoke to my invisible audience, unable to keep my eyes off my desirable new friend. "When I've done this I'm free to go?"

"You're free to go," Dr. Durant assured me.

"Thanks, I've got forty lost years to catch up on."

"Selena is an artificial lifeform just like yourself," explained Dr. Durant. "Get it right and you'll be imprinted on her. She'll be yours to keep forever."

"You're kidding . . ."

"No, we owe it to you."

"The biggest, iconic mega-stars in the motion-picture business together at last," Webber said, drooling with anticipation. He approached the quiet Frenchman. "Maurice, get the cameras rolling."

"By the way, what's the movie called?"

"We're shooting a big-budget adaptation of a story I think you just might be familiar with: *Love of a Machine* . . ."

. . . AND ACTION!

July 2009—August 2009

A Question of Empathy

". . . Seeing with the eyes of another, listening with the ears of another, and feeling with the heart of another."

Alfred Adler

When Humphrey brought Jayne round for dinner that Friday evening, Connie didn't quite know what to say. The woman standing on the doorstep, claiming to be Jayne, was a different person altogether to the one that she was accustomed to. Connie tried to discuss it with her husband, Noah, but he appeared not to perceive anything amiss with Jayne's altered general physique since their last dinner party exactly one week ago. Noah just informed her she was imagining things. Why didn't the silly man notice?

The Abingdons had known Dr. Humphrey Carlyle and his wife, Jayne, for the best part of ten years. Dr. Carlyle was a reputable psychiatrist and Jayne worked as his receptionist at his Harley Street practice, whereas Connie and Noah ran their own interior design firm in Notting Hill, an untaxing Tube journey from their posh semi in Wimbledon.

As usual, Humphrey and Jayne were fashionably late by fifteen minutes. Humphrey previously pointed out that, with any given appointment, people living locally always seemed to arrive late than those from much farther afield. He never apologized for his tardiness, as though believing he was only conforming to some unwritten social norm. But, on this particular evening, he arrived with a completely different woman, Connie was one-hundred-percent certain of it. Why could nobody else see? And why did everyone keep referring to her as Jayne?

Although preoccupied with this fact, Connie maintained polite conversation, without openly voicing her doubts and this most glaringly obvious of observations. She spoke with the woman posing as Jayne, discussed old times, probed more deeply into topics of nostalgia, but somehow Jayne described everything correctly, just like the real Jayne would have, and Connie could not understand how this particular Jayne could possess an accurate knowledge of all the good times they had shared. However, the more she spoke with Jayne, the more Connie got the sense that, although Jayne could rattle off each one of their moments together in perfect, sequential order, there was no emotion or feeling attached to any of those good times, as if she had not really lived them but instead been spoon-fed the real Jayne's life and was recalling everything from rote memory. Humphrey caught Connie's gaze a couple of occasions, and she quickly averted her eyes, but not before she spotted an odd, almost smug knowingness in his expression. Did he know something she didn't?

Sipping limoncello cocktails on the patio while catching up with long-term friends and admiring the lovely sunset of an Indian summer evening proceeded to events in the dining room, tucking into the meal prepared by Connie. Theme for the evening was Italian, and on offer was an antipasti selection of cured meats, cheeses and olives, a main course of chicken liver and wild rabbit linguine accompanied by sliced garlic-and-rosemary focaccia, cappuccino-flavoured tiramisu for dessert, washed down with a nice, full-bodied Chianti. All by candlelight.

"Can't you see how different Jayne looks?" Connie confidentially pestered Noah while bringing the food in from the kitchen.

"Yes, I know, it's a different look for her with her hair up like that," Noah said pleasantly. "I like it, though."

"No, that's not what I mean," Connie said, getting exasperated. "Jayne is *not* Jayne. She is not the same person. She talks the talk, but she looks nothing like Jayne. I mean the real Jayne was brunette, not blond, and easily three inches shorter."

"Are we back to that again?" Noah replied, a tad irritated himself. "I have no idea where you've acquired this fantasy or delusion, or whatever it is, but that woman out there is the same Jayne we've known for almost a decade. Don't start mouthing off this nonsense, because there's a shrink in our house and he just might commit you. You need to seriously get with the schedule."

Connie sealed her lips and spoke no more on the subject. Dinner passed cordially by. Despite being consumed by suspicion and frustration, Connie kept her dialogue with this incarnation of Jayne casual and relatively low-key, taking care to observe social etiquette and not to offend her guest. She began to question her own thinking. Was she going crazy? How could only *she* see what was really going on?

So what exactly is going on? Connie demanded to know of herself.

"One thing I can't complain about is your culinary skills, Connie," Humphrey complimented. "But I cannot help but notice that you seem strangely distracted. Is there something on your mind?"

"No, it's nothing . . ." Connie murmured, wearing a slightly embarrassed smile on her face.

"Come on, Connie," Humphrey encouraged. "We're amongst friends here." He recited that old cliché: "You can trust me—I'm a doctor."

An uncomfortable silence descended, seemed to stretch out for an eternity. The flickering candleglow etched dark, grotesque lines on all the faces around the dining table. Despite the unseasonably warm evening, the dining room suddenly felt cold and cramped. The background music drifting in from the adjoining living room, *Freak Like Me* by the Sugababes, presently took on louder, more sinister overtones.

Noah broke the deadlock, using a deliberate light tone to downplay his wife's frankly absurd perception of their friend. "It's actually really funny. Connie's got this crazy notion that Jayne is actually someone else pretending to be Jayne . . ."

"I see . . ." said Humphrey, suddenly staring hard at Connie, brow furrowed. "Is that true?"

Connie was at bursting point, and she could not hold it back any longer. Besides, Noah had already spilled the beans. "I've been so desperate to let it all out since you arrived, Humphrey. What Noah is saying on my behalf is the woman you've brought this evening is not the same woman I remember. As I mentioned to Noah—whom you'll be glad to know doesn't believe a word I'm saying, and at risk of sounding like one of your patients—I don't think that woman sitting there is Jayne."

The woman Connie thought was masquerading as Jayne appeared mildly surprised, far from shocked or offended as ought to have been the case, in Connie's opinion, to such an outrageous accusation.

"Very interesting," Humphrey said, nodding slowly, taking on the role of the therapist. "What makes you say that?"

"She looks similar to Jayne, granted, but the comparison I'm making is between an actress and the real-life person she's impersonating. Either that or this really is Jayne and she's not only had a makeover but also plastic surgery to modify and make subtle but noticeable changes to aspects of her physical appearance." Jayne looked blankly back at her, made no attempts to protest or defend herself. "And that's the other thing. This Jayne has no emotional depth to speak of. Without sounding disrespectful, her conversation is very superficial, dull and fact-based, lacking any colour . . . *without feeling*."

"That is extremely observant of you, Connie," responded Humphrey, impressed. "With powers of observation like that, you'd make an excellent psychiatrist."

"I'm half-hoping you three will tell me that this is all one, big joke, and I'm on *Candid Camera* or something, and now the charade's over and we can get on with things as they really are." Connie hesitated for a moment, reasoning with herself, weighing up the situation, eventually opting to give a balanced argument. "Or, alternatively, I've gone bonkers and I don't know it, or I've possibly had one of those strokes where you misidentify people."

Humphrey turned to Jayne, directed her gaze to the wall and

the framed reproduction of a famous painting of a man carrying a boulder over his shoulder up a slope. "What's that?"

"*Sisyphus* by Titian, finished in 1549," Jayne recited, almost encyclopaedically. "Based on the Greek myth of King Sisyphus of Corinth whose punishment for his deceitfulness, greed and lust was to perpetually roll a giant boulder up a hill, watching it tumble back down, having to roll it back up again, forced to repeat this punitive task forever."

"What do you think of the painting?"

"What do you mean?"

"What do you think about when you first look at the painting? How does it make you feel?"

Jayne looked perplexed, unsure. "I am indifferent to it. It is merely a painting from the Renaissance."

"What does the painting represent?" explored Humphrey. "Can it be important in a modern contextual sense?"

"I cannot see any other relevance."

"The painting might symbolize the loneliness, emptiness and meaninglessness of life because of constant, daily repetition, or it might refer to the universal truth that it may take a lifetime to build a great career but only an instant to experience its downfall." Humphrey turned his focus back on the Abingdons. "As you noted earlier, Connie, there's no genuine warmth to Jayne. She's concrete in her thinking and very shallow and matter-of-fact in her conversation."

"Hey...!" Jayne uttered, hurt, albeit without any genuine conviction.

Humphrey winked at his hosts conspiratorially, flashed them a cunning smile, and went back to testing Jayne out some more. "Okay, Jayne . . . whilst you were having a comfort break, Connie told me she has endometrial cancer."

Jayne took the news well—a little too well. She exhibited no distress or made any effort to find out a bit more or even endeavour to reassure her dear friend. Instead, she told Connie unemotionally. "You should get it operated on. I suggest a hysterectomy."

Humphrey continued, took the bogus news one step further.

"The doctors discovered the cancer's spread to the other organs. Unfortunately, Connie's developed brain mets."

Again, the bad news should have been met with sadness and anguish and sympathy. Condolences might have been in order. "There's no hope for you, Connie. Survival rates are very low. I think you should put your affairs in order . . ."

"Noah was telling me that their house was broken into last night and burgled," Humphrey informed Jayne, changing the subject. None of the 'Are you okay?', 'Was anybody hurt?', or 'I hope nothing important was stolen', but simply: "You should report it to the police."

"How do you think they felt when their house was broken into?" Humphrey searched of Jayne. "What are your thoughts?"

Jayne shrugged her shoulders. "It's against the law to ransack another person's house."

"How would you feel if I told you I read a newspaper article about a single mother with paranoid schizophrenia who drowned her eight-month-old baby?"

"She shouldn't have got herself pregnant!" said Jayne, unblinkingly, insensitively. "Doesn't she know the baby would have carried a genetic loading for paranoid schizophrenia?"

Humphrey decided to bring the cross-examination of his wife to an end, offering a scientific explanation to the peculiar nature of Jayne's answers. "As you can see, the thing Jayne lacks is *empathy*. She has no concept of the victim's perspective. She cannot relate to you at your frequency or on any worthwhile emotional level."

"Empathy?" said Noah, still confounded by the exchange he had witnessed moments ago. He was evidently finding it difficult to reconcile the bewildering responses Jayne gave with the same kind, caring, generous woman he and Connie had known for nearly a decade. Maybe Connie's suspiciousness was justified after all.

"Empathy is probably the most human of qualities," Humphrey lectured. "Empathy is the ability to recognize and experience the beliefs and emotions of another person, providing a corresponding socially-appropriate response, thereby blurring the distinction between self and other. The psychologist, Edward Tichener, coined the term in 1909, derived from the German word 'einfuhlung' meaning 'feeling into'. According to Aristotle, *To perceive is to suffer*. George Eliot advised us not only to rejoice in the joy of another but share in their troubles. Without empathy, you don't have sympathy or pity or compassion, or even guilt or anger or a sense of injustice at another's suffering. Theory of mind and perspective-taking, putting yourself in the shoes of another, become practically non-existent, no different from the psychopathic or narcissistic personalities or those on the autistic spectrum, rendering them cold, detached and aloof. Cruelty and Torture are born from that void vacated by Empathy.

"There's been a lot of psychological research done on the subject of empathy by the likes of Carl Rogers and Fritz William, how '*the leap of empathy transports us into the soul and heart of another person*'. Daniel Goleman brought the terms 'social intelligence' and 'emotional intelligence' to the public consciousness. No point being highly intelligent, cognitively-speaking, an academic highflier, when you can't interact in the simplest prosocial ways. Dr. Simon Baron-Cohen, a leading expert on autism, spoke about the need to learn double-mindedness rather than remain consistently single-minded. The human capacity for empathy even allows the person to immerse themselves in sophisticated imaginative processes such as fantasy, helping them to identify with fictional characters. Method actors have powerful, trained empathic responses—part imitation, part authentic—as they live and breathe the role they inhabit, feeding off one another's emotional states on stage."

It seemed 'empathy' had become the buzzword for the day. "Am I to suppose that Jayne is an actress," said Connie, "and a bad one at that?"

"Hey...!" Jayne repeated, as though insulted, unconvincingly, mind.

Humphrey decided to let them in on a secret. "No, Jayne is a *machine*."

Noah didn't quite get what Humphrey was driving at. Neither

he supposed did his wife, judging by her puzzled frown. "I don't understand . . . *machine*?"

Humphrey elaborated. "Jayne is a robot—an *android*—designed by the robotic engineers at ANDROIDS INC. Very lifelike in appearance, composed of durable, unaging, genetically-enhanced flesh, but a machine, nonetheless, mentally lacking any significant emotional language, in some respects still in her infancy, operating only by a series of logic circuits. I am retained as the Chief Psychiatrist at ANDROIDS INC., assigned to program emotions into their creations."

Connie stared at Jayne in wide-eyed astonishment, reeling from the staggering revelation. Noah appeared dumbstruck. Jayne just looked on incuriously, continued to absently fiddle with her napkin. "That's incredible!" Connie cried.

"We've been experimenting with emotions for a while," Humphrey continued. "Our purpose is to build autonomous machines that can serve as domestic servants, provide round-the-clock care to the terminally ill or, perhaps, simple companionship for the elderly. Our final objective is for them to be able to respond in socially meaningful ways, whether through voice contact or touch, facial expressions or body language. The problem we encountered was either our androids were smothering, unable to dispense the appropriate level of comfort and emotional investment, or prone to engaging on an intellectual rather than emotional level, when it came to reciprocity. We've come a long way in developing empathic androids . . . *You, Noah, for example, are also an android, and you don't even know it.*"

Noah favoured Humphrey with a confused, does-not-compute kind of expression.

"That's crazy!" exclaimed Connie, indignantly, leaping to her spouse's defence. "He's my husband! I should know if he's a machine or not!"

"Believe me, he's an android," Humphrey reiterated. "But with a wider range of emotions than Jayne. Not as socially-inept." He paused, wondering how to proceed. He decided to name it, ultimately. "I'm sorry to dump this on you so unexpectedly,

Connie, but you're a mechanical person, too, the most advanced and emotionally mature of our social robots. It further saddens me to inform you that your whole life is a dream. You don't live in Wimbledon or go to work in Notting Hill. They're all implanted memories. Only this residence and the dinner party we have all partaken in is real, except it's on the secure grounds of ANDROIDS INC. This dinner party happens daily, an objective assessment tool designed solely to observe and improve your emotional development, progress human-robot social interactions. Once this evening is complete and the data collated, we switch you off until the next day, when the experiment starts all over again."

Connie took a while to digest the mind-shattering announcement, the staggering knowledge that she was nothing more than a machine, grown in a laboratory, composed of synthetic flesh and fitted with an artificial brain. She handled it well, she realized, unlike most humans would have. She reached acceptance . . . too soon for any human. "None of this is real? And your wife?"

"I don't even have a wife," admitted Humphrey. He caught the sorrow in her eyes. Was her look of disappointment for him, or herself, or both? "Don't despair, my dear. You are a sentient being and a remarkable individual—so innocent—with your own unique personality constructs. You are indeed a thing of beauty. One day you might even pass the Turing Test. Rest assured, we will perfect you, and you will be able to live your life as you please."

That lifted her mood, brought a fresh, edifying sparkle of hope to her face.

"In today's day and age, empathy is something of a moot point. The last great American president, Barack Obama, alleged that we lived in a culture that discourages empathy, a culture that too often insisted our principle goal in life was to be thin, young, rich, famous, and entertained . . . Perhaps, androids will eventually become *more* human than their actual human counterparts."

"I always look forward to our dinner parties, you know," said Connie, positively brightening up.

Humphrey appreciated her warmth, visibly gladdened by her reaction, her quick recovery from the edge of despondency. "As do I, my dear, so do I . . . I will always consider it the highlight of my day . . ."

August 2013

The Janus Factor

"Have we ever met before?"

Somewhere in Time (1980)
Richard Matheson

The car was everything Charlie Hammond imagined.

It posed irresistibly in the old woman's driveway, like some Rock Star strutting his stuff on stage, wilfully daring every pretty young thing not to fall under his thrall and give way to temptation. Legend, consummate performer and pure sex on legs, caught in the camera eye and frozen in time, destined to seduce generations to come.

"What do you think?" Mrs. Phelps asked. "Like it?"

"Love it!" Charlie whistled. He still couldn't believe his luck. There were so few of these actual classics left in the world and to actually spot one for sale on eBay, well . . . he felt utterly blessed.

Many a motorist magazine had voted the Audi UR Quattro Coupé the Car of the Decade on account of its smooth handling, aerodynamic design and cutting-edge features, such as Anti-Lock Brakes, Power-Assisted Steering, unique Turbo-Charged Quattro engine and a lightweight, stainless-steel chrome body, concepts unheard-of and foreign to the carmakers of the time. The rear spoiler and alloyed wheels only added to its smouldering charms. This particular model had originally rolled out of the showroom in 1985 and there was not a chip or a dent in its shiny, metallic-black coat. Its single previous owner had looked after it extremely well.

As though she had read his thoughts, Mrs. Phelps remarked: "My husband, God rest his soul, had the same look in his eyes as you when he first saw it. He laboured on it every weekend, come rain, snow or shine. He believed it a crime against Art to let something so beautiful fall into disrepair. It became his pet project. Sometimes, I thought he cared more about the car than he did me. But that's just silly . . ."

"He certainly did an amazing job," Charlie stated, nodding. "I would never have guessed it's clocked over two hundred thousand miles." He produced his cheque-book from his jacket pocket. "Name your price."

"Same as was bid."

He scribbled down the amount as promised. He would have happily paid double for it because this was the car he had always dreamed of owning. None of the Mercedes or BMWs ever built could hold a candle to its genius, and in a world of bubble cars conforming to convention and convenience, this machine was a Revolution in Automotive Design and Engineering. Never were truer words spoken than *Vorsprung durch Technik.*

Charlie handed Mrs. Phelps the cheque and received the keys for his efforts. Brushing his hand down the polished, rust-free, black wing, he opened the driver's door and sat in. Eyes closed, he inhaled deeply, savouring the moment, and immediately picked up the smell—exactly the same smell as when he had bought his brand-new Audi TT a few months back. It shouldn't have been possible since this car was nearly a quarter-of-a-century old, but there was no mistaking that new-car smell. It must have taken a lot of dedication to keep this vehicle in such pristine condition. Charlie opened his eyes and looked around contentedly. Black leather seats, manual transmission, electric windows and sunroof. The modern accessories included a CD-changer and a Sat-Nav.

The coolest thing on wheels, thought Charlie, *mine by right!*

He turned the key in ignition and powered down the window. "Does it have a name?"

"My husband christened it Janus, after the Roman god."

Janus? considered Charlie. *Intriguing!* The old man had given the Audi Coupé a masculine name when most men generally referred to their own motors, no matter how macho in design, as a 'she'. There was a certain manly feel to the Audi, which Charlie couldn't deny. "He must have thought highly of it."

"He did."

Charlie decided not to outstay his welcome. "I think I'd better be off. Thanks, Mrs. Phelps, you've definitely made my day."

Mrs. Phelps smiled back. "Think nothing of it. I'm only glad to help someone find their dream. All I ask is that you keep the car in the spirit that it was born, for the memory of all the hard work my husband put into it. If you take care of Janus, Janus will take good care of you and show you places you never dreamed of."

Her unexpected comment took Charlie by surprise. He had been so wrapped up in the car that he hadn't given the old woman a passing thought. He studied her curiously. He wondered how old she was. With her flowing white hair, gentle wizened face and large rotund frame, he would have estimated her age to be around eighty. Except for the eyes, of course. Her eyes were those of a young lady, strangely sensuous and full of vitality, meadow-green with flecks of red. He imagined that, once upon a time, she must have been a real stunner. "What do you mean?"

There was nothing sinister in her tone, only warmth and kindness. Again, that knowing smile. "Oh, just that it can do things no other car can."

Without appearing disrespectful, it occurred to Charlie that Mrs. Phelps might be a little senile. Her extreme age, the loneliness of widowhood, selling her husband's favourite plaything, her slightly doddery manner all pointed towards this possibility. He looked up at the sky, its lower reaches painted with the orange hues of sunset. It was getting late. "Mrs. Phelps, I really ought to get going." He started up his newly-purchased Audi and listened to the cool, steady hum of the V5 engine.

"Call me Eleanor . . ."

"Okay, Eleanor, pleasure meeting you. Best wishes for the future."

"Perhaps we'll meet again . . . in our dreams," she suggested mysteriously.

"Perhaps . . ." Charlie replied, not sure what she meant or how he should respond.

With a cursory wave, he shifted the raunchy, rock-starry car into gear and crept down the short driveway of the elegant bungalow, turning right on the road. In the rear-view mirror, he could see Eleanor Phelps waving back at him. He managed to catch her last words as he sped away, "Remember, all sales are final!"

The following evening, Charlie was preparing to go out on a date.

The journey back from the old woman's retirement roost in Chistlewick to his place in Upper Nasebury, the night before, had been an uneventful affair. The Audi Coupé hadn't disappointed. It had driven like a demon in the wind, perfectly tuned but possessing of a glass-darkly edge. He had spent much of today marvelling at its aesthetic shape, washing and waxing it so that its black paint produced a mirror-shine in the mid-afternoon sun. He could imagine his jet-black Audi TT, which was locked up in the double garage, growing green with envy and feeling neglected and second-best, sensing a genuine rival for the affections of its owner. Extraordinary how the old woman had considered the Audi Coupé as nothing other than male. Even the name, Janus, seemed strangely apt.

The tax disc was still valid which meant either the old man had passed away within the past twelve months or his wife had renewed it for the sake of selling the car.

Charlie lived the quiet life of a bachelor in his five-bedroomed detached house in the leafy suburbs of Upper Nasebury. He worked as a scriptwriter for television and radio. He had done some work on The Archers, but his claim to fame was an award-winning documentary about the founding fathers of modern science fiction called The ABC of SF.

He never married because he felt a little awkward around girls, but now on the wrong side of thirty-five the urge to find a suitable partner seemed almost paramount. Blind dates were not his thing, but his sister, Matilda, had a close friend called Ellie and had set up this particular date. Ellie, a Sixth-Form History teacher, apparently didn't live far—in Lower Nasebury, in fact—and had requested that Charlie ring her up before he visited her. There was something unorthodox about meeting a girl he hadn't met before in a less-than-neutral place like her house, but if she wanted the home advantage, who was he to complain? Presently, he was in the process of dialling her number. Someone picked up the phone on the other end. "Hello . . ." came the female voice.

"Hi, this is Charlie. I hope I'm not disturbing you."

"No, not at all," she replied cheerily. "I'm Ellie."

"Well, Ellie, my sister was very insistent I call you. She does talk a lot and she can be very persuasive sometimes."

"You shouldn't blame Matilda," Ellie said openly. "I hope I'm not being too forward, but *I* insisted you call me. I'd heard a lot about you and I was very interested in meeting you."

"I'm impressed," Charlie remarked, trying to sound lighthearted. "I like a girl who uses her own initiative."

"Then, I suppose, we should get on like a house on fire," Ellie speculated, laughing. Suddenly, there was a short pause before she announced, "Hang on a minute, there's someone at the door . . . Back in two ticks." Down the line, Charlie heard retreating footfalls, the creak of a door, followed by the sound of muffled voices. Then, Ellie was back on the phone. "Charlie, you still there?"

"Yes."

"I've got to go now," Ellie said, hurriedly. "Say, why don't we meet up at my place at eight?"

"I really don't want to intrude if you've got company."

"No, you won't be," Ellie assured him. "It'll just be you and me, and a juicy rump cut from an animal that once grazed on the South American pampas. We can get to know each other better."

Charlie relaxed, quickly checking that it was a quarter to seven. Time enough. "Okay . . . see you later?"

"Wouldn't miss it for the world . . ." Ellie promised breathlessly and hung up.

Charlie held the receiver thoughtfully for a short while before eventually replacing it. He felt they'd made a good first impression together. Ellie seemed nice. Mature yet surprisingly playful. If things worked out between them, he might actually have to thank Matilda for being discerning for once.

In the bathroom, he applied a whiff of Eternity to his freshly-shaven face. Downstairs, he buttoned up his silk shirt and threw on his dark jacket. He picked up the bouquet of red roses and bottle of Chianti he'd bought earlier before heading for the door. Outside, the Audi Coupé reminded Charlie of a fine breed of cat, stretched out on the rug and waiting patiently for its master. Golden rays from the setting sun glinted wickedly on its sleek black coat.

Opening the car door, Charlie climbed into the driver's seat. He dumped the wine and roses in the back seat. He sat in silence for a while, stroking the steering column and taking in the atmosphere. He smiled smugly. This was a fairytale come true. He considered himself neither materialistic nor a collector of classic cars, but here he was with the car of his dreams in his possession— what more could a man ask for?

Better start making tracks, he eventually decided. He could sit here all night if he so wished, overawed and free of boredom, but that wouldn't go down well with his date. Besides, this was a great opportunity to show off his new car. Clipping on the seatbelt and adjusting the rear-view mirror, he started the engine. Its soft, inviting purr comforted him.

He checked his jacket pocket and found a crumpled piece of paper. It contained the address of his impending date, an almost illegible scrawl from his sister. Lower Nasebury wasn't far, a half-an-hour journey depending on the traffic, forty-five minutes at the most. Reason enough for testing out the Sat-Nav. Charlie switched it on.

The monitor sprang to life. The myriad of colours evened out into a simple WELCOME message. A male voice spoke up, corresponding to the network. *"Thank you for using New Space Synaptics . . . I am Janus . . . Where would you like to go?"*

Charlie jerked when he heard the announcer's name. It was as though the car itself were speaking to him through the Satellite

Navigation System . . . which was absurd, of course. Unfortunately, he always found these new-fangled gizmos with their own inbuilt personalities somewhat creepy. Artificial, superficial and still a good many years away from the buddy-buddy relationship between the fictional Michael Knight and his supercar, K.I.T.T. *With my enthusiasm for all things science-fiction, I should be embracing new technologies, not acting like a technophobe.*

"*Please key in your destination,*" continued the automated voice. Charlie typed the relevant information into the miniature display and set off. He left behind the leafy suburbs of his home town and was soon on the road to Lower Nasebury to rendezvous with his destiny.

Upper and Lower Nasebury were connected by a winding, twelve-mile stretch of road—precisely the route Charlie was taking. The B436 was a country road, allowing Charlie to revel in the delights of the countryside as well as ride his dream-machine at speeds he dared not exceed in the city.

Late summer in the Home Counties was always a pleasant affair. Today was no tall exception. As he cruised down the road with veritable ease, Charlie soaked up the sights, sounds and smells of Mother Nature. The wind rushing through his hair, the fragrance of grass, tracts of squirrel-dwelling woodland broken by floral-rich meadows: plantains and buttercups, cowslips and clover, dandelions and Ox-eye daisies, royal ferns and wild mushrooms. A red fox darted across the road ahead and disappeared into the undergrowth. A murmuration of starlings took to the sky as a single sweeping body, pirouetting again and again in an amazing spectacle of unrehearsed shapes and formations. In the distance, the horizon shimmered with deepening shades of red, completing the kind of idyllic scene one might find in a Constable oil painting.

Despite the compelling beauty of the world around him, Charlie remained conscious of the Audi's manoeuvrability. Its slick performance continued to astound him. It responded with unerring precision to the rhythm of his thoughts, man and machine moving in perfect harmony. The car wanted to be driven and, so far, it hadn't let him down. It had heaps of character and experience, phlegmatic and sublime if not with a slightly roguish quality he found deeply satisfying. His mind wandered back to the Knight-K.I.T.T. comparison.

"*Hard right in one hundred metres*," instructed the disembodied voice from the smart Sat-Nav. "*Please reduce your speed.*"

"You bet," acknowledged Charlie. He'd already spotted the sharp bend on the screen.

He slowed down and took the corner smoothly, hitting the gas again when he was clear. *Not far to go*, he thought. *Ought to be on the outskirts of Lower Nasebury soonish.*

Except what struck him as odd was that he couldn't remember passing another car in either direction. The road was strangely deserted for a Saturday evening.

Perhaps people were staying in to watch the England-Germany game at the New Wembley Stadium. *But still—*

Onwards, he drove. He passed a remote farmhouse surrounded by fields of barley. Then, the landscape opened up into untamed wilderness.

Why's it taking so long? Charlie asked, getting impatient. *I should at least be seeing some sign that I'm almost there.*

Dusk was falling, the sun having long since set.

And, with the descending night, Charlie stared dead ahead at a queer whiteness that was coming towards him. At first, he thought it was a fogbank but dismissed the idea when he realized it was incredibly white, well-coordinated and a little too clean-edged. Then it was on top of him as he sped through it.

A sudden downfall of snow. The temperature dropped a staggering thirty degrees and a biting wind sprang up from nowhere.

Shivering, Charlie dropped his speed and pulled up the car windows. He closed the sunroof, as big, fat snowflakes drifted in, and quickly switched on the wipers.

What the hell's going on? he thought, trying to make sense of the white limbo. *It never snows in summer.*

Yet there was no escaping the fact that he was suddenly driving through a blizzard, as cold as the Siberian wastes. Thinking this might be some sort of transient freak of nature and cursing the Met Office for failing to mention it, he was greeted by the now-familiar voice of his trusty Sat-Nav. "*Strange weather we're having.*"

Startled, Charlie skidded to a halt. Was the Sat-Nav attempting to strike up a dialogue with him. "What did you say?"

"*It's a bit chilly out there, wouldn't you say?*"

Charlie realized he wasn't dreaming, that maybe he hadn't actually fallen asleep at the wheel. "Who are you?"

"*I told you: Janus.*"

"And what exactly are you?"

"*I am the Before and the After. I am What Once Was and What Is Yet To Come. I am as Ancient as the Earth and yet Unborn.*"

"This is madness," Charlie uttered, both terrified and fascinated. He couldn't believe what he was about to say next. "You're a ghost in the machine?"

"*If you prefer to think of me in those terms, then, yes, I am the ghost in the machine.*"

"What do you want with me?"

"*May I interest you in a tour of the Borderlands? I have so many sights to show you.*"

"I'm not interested. I have a date and I don't want to be late."

"*Your date can wait, Charlie. I own you, now, and you own me.*"

When exactly did this Sat-Nav or Janus—or whatever the hell the Audi was—get to know him on a first-name basis?

As though having read his mind, Janus explained: "*I've known everything about you the moment you stepped into the car—your life, your loves, your every intimate secret.*"

Charlie felt exposed, violated, at the mercy of a haunted car. "You can't intimidate me."

"*I have no desire to,*" the car replied. "*Remember, it was you who sought me out. Now you have the privilege of witnessing what I am capable of.*"

"And if I refuse?"

"You won't because you must satisfy your curiosity. All your life has been spent searching for something beyond this world. I can show you what lies there."

The car caused Charlie to summon up a quote from Jack Finney: *The strongest instinct of the human race, stronger than sex or hunger, is curiosity: the absolute need to know. It can and often does motivate a lifetime, it kills more than cats, and the prospect of satisfying it can be the most exciting of emotions.*

Who knew where this car had been and where it would be taking him. Charlie, being the consummate sci-fi buff, accepted the offer to quench his own curiosity. The Audi did not appear to harbour any sinister motives, but that didn't mean it might not turn out to be crazier than the Plymouth Fury in that Stephen King novel. The engine rumbled and the wipers swished back and forth. The way ahead was as white as a Norwegian winter. "Show me!"

Something even more disturbing and unexpected happened next. Dark, silky tendrils sprouted from the steering column and strapped Charlie's hands, moving up his arms with almost fluid motion towards his shoulders. More silk cables emerged from the edges of his seat, wrapping themselves around his legs, flowing upwards like liquid metal to encase his stomach and chest with both points of attack eventually converging at his chin. Nearly completely cocooned in an alien suit, Charlie moaned and shook violently, utterly panicked.

"*Do not resist,*" came Janus calmly. "*Let it take you.*"

Charlie stopped shaking.

"*Now we can be as One.*"

A micro-tendril slithered over his chin, around his mouth and crawled up his nose, attaching itself to his brain, his mind now locked in the neural bridge, the interface between man and machine.

"*How do you feel?*"

"I don't know," Charlie replied in awe. "I can't describe it."

"*Like you have a second sight?*" suggested Janus.

"Exactly!" He could see a lot more now. It was like looking through a blue filter. The blizzard was subsiding, dissipating into a few light flurries of snow. "The snowstorm isn't real, is it?"

"*Not in your world. You prodromed back there—I was testing your potential as a hypnotist might test the hypnotic potential of a subject. But now you are beginning to experience the full effect of our union.*"

There were monsters in the snow. Charlie had seen nothing like them before. They were shaggy, six-legged things, and on a very fundamental level resembled scavenger wolves. Six-legged because, although they possessed powerful haunches and sinewy arms, an additional pair of limbs evolved directly from their torsos. Their faces were vaguely Cerberian, their mouths, which opened vertically from forehead to chin, were crammed with shark teeth, and their eyes glowed yellow like Chinese lanterns in the dark. Despite their grotesque physiognomy, they moved with reasonable grace—sometimes walking on two legs, other times slinking on four legs and then there would be moments when they would use all six legs, crawling insect-like. They circled the Audi, howling and snarling and drooling.

Charlie knew they had only one intention, thinking of Diana, Roman goddess of the moon, who would normally be pictured hunting in the company of wolves. That's if these otherworldly animals were indeed wolves. "What do I do?" he demanded, afraid.

"*Nothing,*" replied Janus. "*As long as you are in the car, you are safe.*"

The wolf-thing nearest the driver's side suddenly stood up on its hind-legs, and Charlie estimated its height to be well over seven feet tall. Its eyes shone cruel and vicious, filled with an insatiable hunger. Its right middlemost claw curled into a fist, and like some one-armed pugilist, struck the driver's window with devastating force, causing the car to shake and Charlie to duck reflexively. But, somehow, the window held.

Not on your chinny-chin-chin, Charlie thought, slightly alarmed. "I think we'd better get out of here."

"*Then get driving.*"

Charlie didn't need to be told twice. He put the car into gear and applied the accelerator. The Audi shot off, Charlie swerving to avoid another wolf-like creature waiting to pounce from the front.

The wheels gripped the road comfortably, as Charlie took a quick gander of life in the Borderlands. There were all kinds of weird, unnatural creatures to behold.

He passed a large troop of albino-skinned toads, each the size of a beach ball, their bodies covered all over with boils which at intervals would pop and release their milky, gestating young. In the world he knew, all amphibians were cold-blooded, unequipped to survive the gruelling winter months.

But not in this reality.

For a moment, the pale sky was filled with gargantuan, screeching, unrecognizable flying creatures, each possessed of a triangular head and a huge, hooked beak and a pair of flapping, leathery wings. They looked less like prehistoric pterodactyls than hellacious phantasms from a Boschian nightmare, particularly when taking into account the stalks attached to their heads which ended in hideously bulbous eyes, the colour and shape of pomegranates. Charlie saw one such Brobdingnagian flying thing swoop down with flexed claws and seize an abject six-legged, wolf-thing cub. It came to rest some distance away on a nearby boulder, hunching forward, wings enclosing griffin-like around its wriggling prey, securing a firmer, unbreakable hold from which to feed. Charlie imagined its mighty beak piercing the skull of its young victim and scooping up small chunks of brain. Something thudded against the windscreen of the car, causing Charlie to start. Some sort of noisome bug, the blush of mulberry wine and on the scale of a large fruit-bat, clung to the glass with sucker pads on the underside of its obscenely plump, multi-segmented, slime-coated body, obscuring the view from the driver's seat. It carried feelers instead of eyes, yet Charlie was sure it could see, and for some reason he thought of the hookah-smoking Caterpillar from Wonderland. Charlie sprayed the windscreen with screenwash, and the otherworldly, purple bug flew off with an electric buzz of its membranous, mosquitoey wings in a furious, scrittering protest.

In this bleak, frozen wilderness, the colossal trees formed strange, gnarled, twisted shapes, pupae of an indeterminate nature suspended from their skeletal branches. Dangling from one tree by a hi-tensile silken cable, an enormous adamantine-black spider with a curled scorpion's stinger of a tail, unlike any of the cellar spiders that brooded over the dead flies festooned in their webs in the dusty shadows of the garden shed, watched Charlie pass by with its multitude of intelligent, rapt *human* eyes: *Come into my parlour, said the spider to the fly.*

"Quite the tour," said Charlie, astounded by these territories. "Is this world populated . . . with people?

"Yes, by the Spindlers," indicated Janus. *"But I won't let them find you . . ."* Rather than elaborate, Janus intimated: *"Shall we dance?"*

"Why ever not?" Charlie declared, getting the hint, and stepped on the accelerator. "Show me what you can do."

The world outside began to whizz by as the Audi picked up speed. Sixty . . . seventy . . . eighty. Soon Charlie was going at one hundred miles an hour. No bends, no crossroads, just straight up. One-twenty . . . one-thirty . . . one-forty . . .

This must be what it's like racing at Silverstone! If only Jeremy Clarkston could see me now!

One-eighty . . . one-ninety . . .

They crossed the two-hundred-mile-per-hour barrier with the Audi still going strong. Charlie couldn't believe such speeds were attainable in this car. The speedometer was already off the dial.

The rush, the intoxication, oh, the adrenaline surge!

As the world outside streaked by when even the parallax view could not be sustained, the Audi continued to accelerate. Past the two-fifty mark, Charlie began to feel hot and queasy. The G-forces were kicking in. Faster and faster they sped, man and machine moving as one. Running on maximum overdrive, plugged into the car in some kind of neural, symbiotic link, sensing the friction on the wheels and the aerodynamic body, united with its every electrical circuit and ticking mechanism, Charlie felt invincible, like a superhero.

This is what I call driving!

The G-forces were strong now, crushing Charlie in his seat. The lightheadedness grew worse as blood pooled in his legs from the sheer weight of gravity. Every muscle in his body seemed to be tied down by lead balloons. He thought of stars collapsing upon themselves and space-cruisers swallowed up by black holes.

Are we there yet? his mind mustered, confused, in the grip of a painless euphoria.

It was as though the world had ceased to exist. Outside was a white, blurry, formless nothingness, crackling with a lightning field that transcended every available colour of the known spectrum.

Still faster . . .

[*Than light?*]

Sealed tight in his seat, yet exponentially expanding in consciousness, Charlie tasted Omnipresence, a gift endowed to the deities of old and the newer Christian god. The Universe was revealed to him in a nanosecond. For an infinitesimal moment in time, his multi-sected essence resided in every corner of this world, in every living organism, every last cell, every atom. He occupied the infinite points of this universe—and every other universe—seeing realities unfathomable from every miniscule angle, in sublime detail, with crystal clarity—all at once. He was everywhere . . . and *nowhere*.

He saw his old Oxford chum, Professor Artemis Higham test out the effects of a hitherto-unknown hallucinogenic drug, and for a tiny, transitory split-second, their distinctly-separate, unbounded consciousnesses met.

He entered the mind of the black-robed Spindle King as it surveyed its sovereign kingdom from the High Tower at the heart of the Borderlands . . . and sensed an *intruder*.

He glimpsed a grotesquely-tall and spindly figure, with yet-unspoken, sinister motives and mischief on its mind, step otherwise-unseen into our reality . . .

Then, they were slowing down.

Charlie gradually recovered his senses. As he awoke from his indescribable godlike experience and his normal vision returned, he found he was doing a steady forty. The question on his lips begged an answer. "How fast?"

"*187,000 miles per hour.*"

"*You're shitting me!*" exclaimed Charlie, amazed the Audi was still completely intact, that the shear forces had not ripped it apart or gravity simply crushed it like a tin-can. Forget breaking the sound barrier or smashing the land-speed record for a jet propulsion engine, Charlie had attained *Lightspeed*. "That's one hell of a ride!"

"*Worth repeating?*" Janus inquired.

"*Heck, yeah!*" Charlie affirmed, ecstatic, exhilarated, energized. "As often as is humanly possible!"

"*Then, we shall merge again when the time comes,*" Janus advised.

"Can we go again?" Charlie asked, as excited as a schoolboy at the end of a rollercoaster run.

"*Not today. Your body would not survive another trip.*"

A look of disappointment crossed his forehead, as he stared out at the road ahead. Falling snow, dark, ambiguous shapes in the forest and not much else—perpetual winter in the Borderlands, like Narnia under the spell of the White Witch.

Something appeared out of nowhere in the middle of the road. Charlie braked hard. The Audi ground to a halt.

It looked like something out of that computer game, *Silent Hill*. The figure was essentially human but spectral and faceless, with rudimentary arms and legs. It moved towards the car in an almost floating, rolling manner. Its insides were completely visible, its organs swirling and rotating within its membranous body. There was a sense of sadness and regret about this pathetic creature.

"What is that thing?" Charlie wondered in morbid fascination.

"*That, Charlie, is you eighty years from now.*"

Somehow, Charlie found himself on the doorstep of his date in Lower Nasebury, having parked his audacious Audi on the kerb, silencing the radio which moments earlier had been chugging out Rihanna's commandment to *Shut Up and Drive*. The house was a Queen Anne. He rang the bell.

There came the sound of approaching footsteps and the door swung suddenly open.

"You must be Charlie!" the young lady of the house announced. She was a decent-looking brunette in her early thirties who had modestly primped herself for her blind date.

"Indeed, I am," replied Charlie amicably. "And you must be Ellie!"

"Guilty as charged," Ellie remarked pleasantly.

Charlie handed her the bottle of wine and bouquet of roses. "I thought you might like these."

"Thanks," she said, sniffing the roses. "You're an absolute gentleman." She invited him in. The reception room was as immaculate as the hallway, bright white with a touch of beige. "Make yourself at home. I'm just on the phone. I'll be as quick as I can." Ellie disappeared into the hallway.

Charlie seated himself on one of the leather sofas, looking around the room. There were a couple of paintings on the wall, nothing fancy, merely nondescript landscape art. A stereo-system rested in the corner and the shelves were lined with books and CDs. His eyes moved to the mantelpiece above the fire-grate. Either side of the expensive carriage-clock were a set of framed photographs. They were mainly pictures of family and friends, but one particular photo caught his attention. Charlie got up from the sofa and walked over to it, astonished. He picked it up. It was a wedding photo, the happy couple standing outside the church doors, laughing as they're sprinkled with confetti. The bride he recognized as Ellie . . . and the groom . . . the *groom*—?

"That was *you* on the phone," came a voice from behind him, making him jump. Ellie had returned and was carrying a vase accommodating the roses he had brought. She placed the vaseful of roses on the windowsill. "And that's *you* in the photograph."

Charlie checked his Rolex. Nearly a quarter to seven. He had got here ten minutes *before* setting off.

"We'll get married one day in June."

Charlie stared back at the prophetic photograph of his wedding. In the photo, he had never looked happier or more alive.

"How is this possible?" he murmured, bemused.

"Your car," Ellie explained, a familiar knowingness in her smile, "the one you buy from me many years from now? It can do special things no other car can."

Charlie looked at her closely. Although she had shed decades of her life, there was no mistaking those eyes. Eyes that were expressive and full of life, pasture-green with red flecks. "Eleanor Phelps?"

"They call me 'Ellie'."

"But how—?" Charlie tried to comprehend, work it out, but failed miserably.

"The same way you lost two stones during a single car ride—drains you like a battery."

Okay, yes, Charlie needed to tighten his belt or his trousers would fall down and, yes, he looked miraculously younger and fitter—

"Hasn't it already shown you what it is capable of?"

Charlie vividly remembered the frozen, foreboding otherworldliness of the Borderlands, how its stygian forests teemed with dark myth and scowling, shuddersome things. "Yes, but . . ."

"Then accept things as they are," she said with a serenity that was as soothing as it was seductive. "We were meant to be together. Janus made it possible."

"Janus?" *The uncommonly-chatty Sat-Nav? The sentient being that commandeered the Audi?*

"Two-faced Roman deity, who since the birth of the gods of man, has earned a special place in the pantheon of gods. Once the god of all gods, he became known as the god of change and transitions, presiding over the passage of time, the progression of the cosmos, even gatekeeping the points of access from one universe to another. His dual nature means his two faces can simultaneously watch entrances as well as exits, delve deeply into the inner, dream state yet look out beyond the external, waking world. He is both male and female, the alpha and the omega, all beginnings and endings, the before and after, with one face retracing the Past (which is no longer) and the other pointing towards the Future (which is yet to come)."

"And what of the Present?" Charlie demanded, still struggling to fathom what she was getting at. "The In-between Time. The Here and Now."

"The Present has no meaning in the land of the gods." Ellie

moved towards Charlie and kissed him softly on the cheek. "You are awake in the dead space of the Present, unaffected by your Past or Future, contained in your—or should I say, *our*—reality. Trust in Janus and the Present can be anything you want it to be."

For the first time since arriving at Eleanor Phelps' house, Charlie Hammond seemed to understand what she was driving at, gained some appreciation into her metaphysical insights. Nothing was ever pre-destined and everything goes full circle.

And, of course, all sales were final.

June 2008—September 2008

Mindforce

"Because mind has no mass it takes no time to travel."

Chocky (1968)

John Wyndham

I: THE DREAMS

Ever since he could remember, Edgar Byers had always been told he was a special boy. From the moment he was born, indeed four weeks premature, until Social Services snatched him away from his violent, alcoholic parents when he was only six months old, he was considered to possess a 'certain quality'. He rarely cried as a baby, which spooked out his caregivers, and reached his developmental milestones much later than his peers, which greatly troubled his caseworkers. Despite his solitary nature, he went through a string of foster carers, most of whom seemed far more concerned with negotiating their fee for looking after him than actually looking after him; neglect was often cited as the primary reason for moving him on to the next placement. Whereas most children his age were inventing imaginary friends to keep them company, Edgar would spend hours rigidly building straight towers of like-coloured Lego bricks. He stumbled through school, his short stature and detached, awkward manner making him an easy target for the bullies. Because of his poor academic skills and innate inability to mix with his classmates, he gained a Certificate of Special Educational Needs early on together with a diagnosis of Low-functioning Autism. He received speech therapy to help him learn to speak, mentalization-based techniques to address his mind-blindness and allow him to read people, unfortunately to no avail. Although socially-inept and intellectually-challenged, he maintained a firm preoccupation with order, symmetry and fastidiousness.

He was eventually thrust into the big, sabre-toothed world, albeit with the necessary supports in place.

Now fast-approaching adulthood, Edgar Byers took a low-paid job at SPALDING'S LO-COST SUPERMARKET. His inflexibility of thought and difficulty shifting sets meant that stacking shelves and directing customers to the appropriate aisles suited him just fine. He excelled in knowing the number of cans of chicken soup on the shelf and always volunteered to mop the floor every evening, bringing it to a brilliant shine time and again. Quiet, passive and unassuming, he got on well with his colleagues, who seemed impressed by his level of conscientiousness and his rigid, uncomplaining adherence to routine. If they were ever to ask him, he would have told them in his own odd, inanimate way that he was doing something that made him happy . . . if this was what real happiness was. Edgar knew that the store manager, Mr. Spalding, believed, like the succession of authority figures before him, that Edgar was special.

And, when the day was done, Edgar would return to his flat, eat his microwavable meal and work on his Lego sets.

Imagination never figured into the equation, for Edgar was not your archetypal dreamer.

Until, one day, he began to dream.

Dream of places, remote and unimaginable and of impossible time and distance.

His life was about to change.

The light rap on the door plucked Edgar Byers away from his favourite activity.

He knew who was at the door even before he answered it. Colin Hendry stood in the hallway, a friendly smile on his face. "Hi,

Edgar, just thought I'd pop my head round and make sure there wasn't anything you needed."

Edgar wandered back into the lounge without returning the greeting, sat back down in front of the Lego world he was busy constructing, the repetitive, restricted aspect of his autistic play. Colin didn't take Edgar's coldness personally. Edgar was funny like that. He didn't mean it—he just had difficulty expressing his feelings. Being autistic couldn't be an easy thing for anyone to bear in this modern time of mass communication, corporate greed and degenerating moral values. Edgar had suffered so many injustices in his life—from abusive parents who sent him into hospital with a fractured skull when he was only a baby to those cruel schoolchildren who would beat him up in order to get an emotional response—that it amazed Colin how Edgar could have survived the lack of nurturance and the hurt and the horror without exhibiting the psychological damage that frequently went with the experience. Even his careworkers, teachers included, had treated him inconsistently, either shunning him or infantilizing him. But, knowing Edgar, he had taken it all in his stride, despite his resistance to change and lack of interpersonal skills. A special kid, it seemed, as tough as he might be vulnerable. A credit to his resilience. At least now, aged seventeen, Edgar had achieved a period of stability, close to a normal existence, and with the job at the supermarket, found his niche in society. And, as warden of ST. ANTHONY'S LODGE, the supported housing complex inhabited by Edgar and his peers, Colin wished only to protect the lad, keep him safe. He took it upon himself, if he was on duty, to check in on Edgar, however briefly. Colin was sure Edgar appreciated his visits, even if Edgar didn't verbalize it. There was a kind of unspoken respect between them. "So how are you today, Edgar?"

"Alright," Edgar replied without looking up.

The lounge was spick-and-span as always, kept stringently neat and tidy to the point of obsession. Colin joined Edgar at the island in the middle of the room, the five-foot-by-four table atop of which rested his Lego base. *Lego: the best toy any growing boy could own . . . a greater resource than any Hornby railway set or Sony PlayStation.* "What are you making?"

Edgar's natural monotone resembled that of an automaton. "A town. I'm making a town."

Colin studied Edgar's little showpiece. Edgar had created something different from his usual sterile, Council-style tower blocks. It appeared to be a Legoscape of black, peculiar-shaped pyramids, nothing that Colin had seen before. The overall design, vaguely Mayan but with a bold futuristic slant, was astonishing and completely unexpected. The larger central pyramid reached out from all four corners like arms to smaller, symmetrically-situated satellite structures, each a downscaled version of its mother. The mat on which these buildings were attached was red and dotted with curious objects, preexisting plastic casts of flora that Edgar had obviously modified. "Where'd you get the idea from?"

"I sometimes see things in my sleep."

"You mean dreams?"

"Dreams . . ." Edgar contemplated. There was no pitch or range in his voice despite his undoubted interest. "Yes, I see dreams."

"Inspired . . ." commented Colin, patting Edgar on the shoulder. He took one last look at Edgar's unique, X-shaped model city. "Carry on like this and you could end up an architect of some distinction."

Edgar did not respond to the compliment, avoiding all eye-contact, absorbed in his lifelong hobby. He rooted through the *Star Wars* box of the Rogue Shadow Colin had bought him as a birthday gift and added a few more black bricks to the foremost pyramid. Just like Edgar to be emotionlessly and purposefully going about his business with no sense of reciprocity.

Yes, he was funny like that, thought Colin, heading for the door of the studio flat. Simple, patently honest, straight as a ruler. A true survivor.

Special.

Once more, Edgar stands in the plane of astral dreams. The normally parched ferrous-red sands stretch out to the distant horizon. The sky darkens overhead: alternating cycles of short, scorching days with prolonged, cooler grey nights.

Edgar surveys the configuration of pyramids which dominates the landscape. They never cease to fascinate him. They bear little resemblance to the pyramids he has seen in the photographs where he comes from. First, they are many times as big as the pyramids his world is accustomed to. Secondly, they are flat on top, lacking any visible peak, affixed with an all-seeing eye, a symbol of divine providence. Finally, the pyramids are black, neither painted nor built from stone—Edgar, during a previous trip, has already touched their smooth, shiny surface, making him think of beetle-armour.

One can immediately tell from the damage the pyramids have sustained each was a victim of war, a war that supposedly ravaged the land aeons ago. Thereafter, Time did the rest.

"Would you like to go inside?" an unseen presence asks him. "I can show you the Psychetron."

"Not tonight," replies Edgar. "Next time, maybe."

All he wants to do is take it easy, lie awhile amongst the ancient ruins and look up at the crazy helter-skelter of stars, no-one to disturb him or his new friend.

Revel in the dark beauty of this place before he unfortunately wakes up in the ordinary world.

Everyone noticed a big difference in Edgar in the days that followed. He seemed brighter in mood, more approachable and receptive to conversation. For someone blessed with the mind of an eight-year-old, Edgar also appeared a lot sharper, on the ball. Mr. Spalding entrusted him with recording the stock, which Edgar successfully completed without raising any concerns. His colleagues at LO-COST puzzled over his sudden boost in confidence and wondered whether he'd taken to using that experimental oxytocin spray, which was supposed to improve sociability, or if in fact he'd got himself a girl. More upbeat and prosocial, not so closed-off, Edgar's change in personality and attitude would become impossible to ignore when the Brothers Grime paid the supermarket a visit.

The Brothers Grime, as they came to be known, were a trio of teenage thugs. If not standing on the street corners, wearing their customary shell-suits, drinking Buckfast and smoking cannabis, they would run around like a pack of wolves, terrorizing the neighbourhood. Every deprived area in Britain has its own Brothers Grime. They are often well-known to the local Youth Correction Officers. Expelled from school for violent conduct when not truanting, slapped with multiple, ineffective ASBOs, they develop a pattern of recurrent offending behaviour which typically includes Breach of the Peace, Property Damage, Common Assault, Possession of a Dangerous Weapon and Attempted Robbery. Shame, because they're only kids at the end of the day who took the wrong path in adolescence, destined to spend their adult lives in and out of the Criminal Justice System.

They burst into the supermarket, that day, like lawless gunslingers entering a saloon. Whooping with doped-up glee, they jostled past the startled customers and made straight for the the liquor aisle. They soon began stuffing bottles of alcohol into their holdalls.

Mr. Spalding was the first to the scene. "What on earth is going on?" he demanded.

"What does it look like, Fatty?" Scott Grimes, the eldest of the trio, jeered.

When Mr. Spalding saw who the troublemaker was—that evil, high-strung expression and those bulging, bloodshot eyes—the anger immediately drained from his face. He gulped, took a step back, continued weakly. "I can't allow you to leave with goods that you have no intention of paying for. Even if you could, you've got to be over-18 to buy alcohol."

"We take what we want, got that, Fatty?" Scott told him, full of menace. "Who's going to stop us? You?"

The store manager gestured nervously to the security guard at the doors. Wilson Banks, well-beyond retirement age and frail-looking, merely shrugged his shoulders, throwing in the towel.

"Him?" Scott derided cruelly. "He's older than Nelson's Column."

"Put those bottles back and leave quietly," Mr. Spalding managed to muster, sounding and feeling totally powerless, "or we're calling the police."

"The police?" cackled Scott. "They're shit-scared of us! Aren't they, gang?"

His kin, Reece and Leo, agreed, joining in the crazed laughter.

"Please do as Mr. Spalding tells you," arose a voice from behind them, interrupting the flow of their inexplicable amusement.

The young hooligans spun round and found Edgar Byers standing there like some government marshal.

"Edgar," Mr. Spalding said, alarmed, "you mustn't get involved."

"But they're not being very nice," Edgar observed, innocently enough.

Scott Grimes advanced towards him, rounding on the diminutive shop assistant. "What are you—his bum-chum?"

"That's not a very nice thing to say," Edgar replied simply.

"Aren't you that retard who works here?"

"Leave him alone!" Mr. Spalding intervened, trying to defend the poor boy.

"Or else what, Fatty?" Scott half-challenged, half-mocked. He went back to tormenting Edgar. "So, Retard, how about it? You and me outside, right now! I'll make you eat shit before I'm through with you!"

"I don't want to fight you."

"Why not?" Scott said, striding over, grabbing Edgar by the apron, yanking him off the ground, faces inches apart. "Too chicken-shit or too soft in the head?"

"Please don't say those things. It's not nice."

"Show him who's boss, Scott," egged Reece Grimes.

It was the profound lack of fear in Edgar's expression that finally got to Scott Grimes. Here Scott was, being an absolute bad ass, and the message didn't seem to be getting through to this half-wit. Frustrated, Scott spat into Edgar's face and hurled him into the opposite aisle. Edgar landed on his back in a tangle of arms and legs, boxes of washing powder tumbling over him.

"I just stacked them this morning," Edgar said in dismay.

"Well, I guess, you're going to have to stack them again, won't you?"

"I don't think I like you!" Edgar protested. "You're *bad* people!"

Scott spoke with a murderous edge, eyes bulging insanely. "I don't think I like what you're saying! You want some more, Retard?"

Edgar got up slowly and, composing himself, said something nobody expected. "You wander in here, high on 'Crack', like you think you own the place. I'm not surprised you've turned out the way you are. Never disciplined by parents who are, for all intents and purposes, absent, sitting on their arses all day long and sponging off the State, breeding like plague rats just because they have nothing better to do, unwilling to carry out their duty of raising their offspring in the proper fashion. Then they moan like the morons they are when their kids turn into drug addicts and lay blame elsewhere when their twelve-year-old gets shot at two in the morning in a bad part of town. Since you've already failed in life, with not a glimmer of a decent future in sight, you deserve no place in our great country. You're the motherless, fatherless cancer on society, needing to be surgically excised."

It wasn't so much what Edgar said as how he said it—in sinister, threatening overtones and with a cold primeval stare that could have cut through diamonds—that caused Scott's voice to falter. Except, Scott's wired, misplaced pride got in the way. *"What did you say, Retard?"*

"You heard me."

"No-one dares disrespect a Grime and gets away with it! Oh, you're about to suffer a world of pain, *Retard*!" Scott warned, grabbing an unopened wine bottle by its neck.

A frightened gasp rang through the watching shoppers.

Waving the bottle in Edgar's face, Scott suddenly lunged at him.

Edgar ducked, swung his right leg out in a semi-circular motion, catching Scott squarely in the shins. Scott collapsed to the floor, bottle falling from his grasp, instantly shattering. His face landed in the broken glass.

"Oh, my face! My beautiful face! What have you done to my face?" Scott shrieked over and over, crying like a big girl, his street-cred suddenly in tatters.

Edgar knelt down beside him and lifted his head. Shards of glass pierced his countenance like the quills of a porcupine. "Like white powder, do you, Fuckhead?" Edgar asked calmly. Tearing open a box of Persil, he poured its contents into Scott's yapping mouth, causing him to choke. "This'll help wash your mouth!"

Scott's younger brothers had seen enough. "Let's get out of here!" Reece suggested loudly. But Leo was already bolting out the supermarket doors.

As a parting shot, Edgar stuck his leg out, tripping Reece. Reece went sliding along the floor, grazing half his face. He quickly got up and followed in the footsteps of his brother, leaving the prodigal son with multiple cuts on his face and a mouthful of washing powder, at the absolute mercy of the enraged adults.

The rest of the customers clapped and cheered.

"The police are on their way," the check-out girl informed Mr. Spalding.

While Scott coughed and spluttered and nursed his bleeding, splinter-ridden face, Mr. Spalding took Edgar aside. "I don't know what to say. How you pulled this off I'll never know, but we're all indebted to you." His stark astonishment gave way to a glowing smile of gratitude. "I guess you've earned yourself a Duvet Day."

"You did well today," Colin Hendry congratulated Edgar. "Above and beyond the call of duty." He showed him the local paper, the *Utterston Herald*. "Look, you made the front page: *Have-a-go-hero foils robbery at supermarket.*"

"I only did what I thought was right," Edgar replied, glancing up from his Lego set. "Miracles happen when you speak with the angels."

"I wish I was there," Colin said wistfully. "Don't let me ever get on your wrong side."

"I would never hurt you."

"I suppose you need to rest now the excitement's all over." Colin was alone with Edgar in the lad's flat. Edgar had been allowed to leave the supermarket after the police had taken down his statement. The newspaper reporter, who'd also interviewed Edgar, had quickly rushed the story into print.

"I can see your Lego city is coming along rather nicely," Colin said, examining the pyramid-themed showpiece. The same restricted fixation, true, but it was the noticeable degree of geometrical sophistication that intrigued Colin. It was, he thought, as courageous a piece of work as Edgar's heroic behaviour at the supermarket. And, yet, the piece of construction was so utterly foreign-looking like something from an old, half-remembered *Stargate* episode.

The shape of his dreams . . .

"Should I make us some tea?" Edgar asked pleasantly. "I've got some Earl Grey if you like."

The invitation surprised Colin. Edgar was certainly not one for social gestures. Come to think of it now, where was the stereotypical, colourless language everyone was so familiar with, the intense robotic manner in which it was spoken? Gone, too, was the gaze avoidance. Autism involved an imbalance, a systemizing-empathizing deficit, a clear absence of the 'cold' theory of mind. However, at the present, one could almost say that Edgar was acting like any normal adolescent. Could autism burn itself out with age? Colin doubted it very much. It was a neurodevelopmental disorder, you were born with it, your brain hardwired in a completely different way from most people. The condition was lifelong but those on the autistic spectrum learned to compensate for their social inexpressiveness/communication difficulties over the years. Maybe, in this case, the events at the supermarket had simply improved Edgar's self-esteem, done wonders for his confidence, but Colin remained unconvinced by this superficial explanation. "No thanks, Edgar, it's getting late. I'm due to have supper."

"When will I see you again?"

Another prosocial question, never before asked in living memory. *So completely un-Edgar-ish*, thought Colin. *What's the deal here?* His mind went back to a comment Edgar had made earlier, which he had nearly overlooked. *Miracles happen when you speak with the angels*, Edgar had philosophized. Colin felt an ominous twinge of disquiet, sensing he was seeing only a tiny fraction of a much larger picture. He responded warmly: "Soon, Edgar, soon."

"Come with me," Edgar hears the voice softly calling.

Edgar is not surprised to discover that he has returned to this place, just as he's done every night for the past two weeks. He doesn't mind. There is something peaceful about this place, this so-called Psi-world, a strange tranquility he welcomes and enjoys escaping to. Yet, he can't help but feel he is walking in someone else's dream.

Night has fallen, a cool, ashen night. The stonewashed sky twinkles with weird constellations of stars which Edgar doubts can ever be witnessed by the cosmologists of his world. The red desert is a dusty shade of purple and crawling with sparse spindles of vegetation. There is no animal life here, no people, as he remembers his spirit guide once telling him. The indigenous population, a powerful war-like race, perished in the Last Neutron War, several thousand millennia ago.

Edgar reaches the plateau, from where rises the Giant Pyramid, tall and godlike and adorned with its inert Eye of Providence. Its scorpion-black walls shimmer in the half-night. Chunks of it are missing, blown apart by missile fire. It smacks of abandonment, ruins of a lost civilization. Emerging from each corner of its base, limbs extend to what should be other smaller pyramids, a number of them nearly completely demolished, razed to the ground, reduced to rubble. This entire site was a military base, according to Edgar's guide, and the stronghold of the High Imperial Monarch. Despite the devastation on display, the place still manages to retain its stark magnificence.

Hypnox, Edgar's invisible friend, speaks again. "Care to look inside?"

How can Edgar possibly refuse? He's come this far, hasn't he? It would be a terrible waste of a dream if he doesn't at least take a peek inside, considering how obsessed he has recently been with reproducing this place in Lego. Standing there, under the mad, glittering stars, gazing across the purple-hued landscape at the ancient, black edifices of the night, on this occasion Edgar resolves to take Hypnox up on his offer. "I would like that."

"Then all I ask is that you think. Think of being inside and your wish will come true." Edgar closes his eyes and simply imagines... and, in a flash of thought, is instantly transported. The fabled genie-of-the-lamp couldn't have done better.

He suddenly finds himself roaming the great halls, which are immense and filled with silence, cold and desolate. The walls are embossed by curious writing and strange hieroglyphics, different aspects of a language long-since dead and forgotten.

The corridor Edgar is wandering through opens up into a vast, pillared court. Edgar realizes from the bejewelled splendour of this chamber that this was once the seat of power of the High Imperial Monarch. Improbable gemstones stud the walls, gleaming with iridescent light. Shadows streak and flit by like discarnate ghosts. Edgar's eyes are drawn to the webbed, pulsating column of alien flesh that commands the centre of the hall, looming up like a leviathan, multi-lobed and sulcified, as though consisting of a thousand individual brains melded together, each extending out its own separate network of nerves.

"This is the heart of the Giant Pyramid," explains Hypnox. "The nexus of thought we call the Psychetron. The collective memories of my fellow Psi-beings are trapped in its core, searching for a passage out. Their knowledge along with their pain is magnified within. You must help release us, revive our dying civilization. We are the last of our species, and extinction beckons. You, Edgar Byers, are our only hope. Your task will, in time, become clear to you. You shall be our special ambassador on Earth."

An astral traveller on a distant, alien world, Edgar understands and accepts his new role.

It began with the dreams.
Then came the powers . . .

II: THE POWERS

Life ticked along at a leisurely pace over the next few days. Edgar Byers went to work as per usual, his colleagues at LO-COST treated him like a minor celebrity, and Colin the Warden checked on him during the evenings.

One such evening, while Colin was visiting the flat, Edgar asked a question which had obviously been bothering him for some time. "Why are people so mean to each other?"

Colin deliberated for a moment but could not come up with a satisfactory answer. "I suppose it could be because of their tough upbringing. Life has dealt them so many blows that the only way they can survive is by hurting the person nearest to them. Or maybe sometimes they're just born bad . . . Not everyone is mean, you know."

"You're not mean," admitted Edgar. "You're a good friend." Colin felt flattered by the vote of confidence, Edgar's touching acknowledgement. "Are you thinking about what happened at the supermarket the other day?"

"Yes . . . I really wish people could be nicer."

"I think most people dream of world peace and living in a utopian society."

"I want to put the world to rights," Edgar said thoughtfully.

"How do you propose to do that?"

"I could work for a charity."

"That's an excellent idea. But your duties at the supermarket keep you extremely busy. You don't want too much on your plate right now."

"I just think I could do more to benefit Mankind. Give back to the world a little of what the world has given to me."

The warden found Edgar's choice of words surprising and his enthusiasm heartening. *Is it me or is he getting smarter? I want whatever brain-enhancing serum he's taking.* "Very selfless of you. Perhaps we could figure out a way in which you could carry on in your job at the supermarket and still commit to doing voluntary work on a part-time basis."

"I would like that."

"So it's decided then," Colin concluded. "I'll start making some enquiries."

"Could you try the NSPCC?"

Colin smiled, getting up to leave. "Of course . . ."

Soon after, Edgar experienced his second run-in with the Brothers Grime and his faith in the goodness of humanity sank forever.

Edgar had just finished his shift at LO-COST and was heading home. His usual route incorporated a shortcut through an alleyway behind THE JASMINE GARDEN. The night was dark and drizzly, broken only by the yellow light spilling out from the kitchen window of the Chinese restaurant. As he passed by, he heard the clinking of dishes and the chatter of Oriental conversation.

"Hey, Retard!" yelled someone from behind him.

Turning round, Edgar saw Scott Grimes and his gang striding towards him with less-than-friendly intentions. Reece and Leo were wielding weapons, a crowbar and a length of metal piping respectively. Scott shoved Edgar hard in the chest and a startled Edgar went crashing into the dumpster. Scott reached into his pocket and clicked open a flick-knife. Its blade glinted wickedly in the dimness of the alley. "So you think you're some sort of hero, do you, Retard?" Scott hissed contemptuously. "You caused me a lot of grief, made me look stupid. The police kept me for hours. They were going to put me back in Juvy."

Edgar rose from the damp ground, wiping the dirt from his clothes.

"Time you paid for our last encounter," Scott added.

The backdoor to the restaurant opened, providing a wide oblong of light, and a man, possibly the dishwasher, stepped out with a lighted cigarette. "What's going on here?"

"What does it look like?" Scott sneered. "Murder!"

The dishwasher assessed the situation—three kids with some nasty-looking weapons harassing another small, defenceless young man—and quickly decided he shouldn't get involved. "I'm calling the police . . ."

"Be my guest," advocated Scott, "and I'll firebomb your restaurant first thing in the morning!"

The dishwasher hurried back inside, closing the door behind him. The alley grew dark again.

"Now, where were we, you little squirt?" Scott enunciated, seething with vengeful hatred. "Yes, I'm going to cut you up so bad you're going to beg me to kill you." He began making vicious, jabbing gestures with his flick-knife, dangerously close to Edgar, with the sole purpose to intimidate and frighten. Reece banged the lid of the dumpster with his crowbar, the rattling cacophony of sound echoing down the alley. Leo slapped the palm of his other hand callously with his metal pipe.

But the initial fear in Edgar's eyes was gone. His expression had taken on a cold, steely quality.

The humiliation in front of all those shoppers had been bad enough, but now, despite being outnumbered and outgunned, the fact that Edgar still appeared undaunted was just too much for Scott Grimes to bear. "Why aren't you scared, Retard? Do you want to die?"

Edgar was imperturbable, an immovable object. "I'm only going to ask you once," he warned in a calm, judicial tone. "You either leave of your own accord or I fuck you over . . . for good."

The threat sounded so real that Scott almost thought twice about carrying on. Except he was too determined to inflict pain on this miserable rat, just too jacked-up on drugs to abide by his natural instincts. "Bring it on, you fucking Retard! Let's see what you've got!"

Edgar did nothing, merely stood there stiff, maintaining his impenetrable stare.

Scott looked into those eyes and saw the distillation of his own worst fears, the darkness within his own soul reflected back from a cracked mirror. He could not resist raising his flick-knife and stabbing his own right eye. He watched himself doing this, unable to will his arm to stop. When his eye popped open in an oozing red jelly, he fell to his knees, releasing a long, horrible scream. He glanced up at Edgar briefly with his one good eye, the blade of the flick-knife wedged in the other socket, as Reece and Leo raised their weapons and brought them down on his head. Again and again, their metal implements delivered lethal blows, smashing into their brother's skull as easily as if it were a rotting pumpkin. Blood sprayed out in a mist with each strike. Reece and Leo did their gruesome work uncompromisingly, unflinchingly, glazed-eyed, held in an inescapable trance. They continued to pummel Scott until he collapsed on the ground, face-down, flick-knife sliding smoothly into his brain, his head a shapeless, raggedy pulp of gore-soaked hair and splintered bone. More blood seeped out, forming a dark, glistening pool by the light of the kitchen window.

When the restaurant owner and his staff came to investigate the commotion outside, Edgar had already fled.

"Did you hear the news?" Colin Hendry asked Edgar Byers the following evening. "Scott Grimes was savagely beaten to death by his own younger brothers. So much for your old nemesis."

"Did the police give a reason?" Edgar inquired nervously.

"Not really. The attack was totally unprovoked. His brothers are now in police custody, mute and catatonic. It's predicted they may never speak again and could possibly spend the rest of their lives in a mental institution."

"How have the public taken it?"

"I won't lie to you. The local community is obviously in shock, but it's also breathing a deep sigh of relief."

"Did the police mention anything else?"

"Come to think of it, there was something else—glad you reminded me. It's claimed there was an eyewitness to the crime, someone who apparently fled the scene before it was reported to the authorities." Colin caught Edgar's brief, uneasy glance, immediately growing suspicious. "But you know all this, don't you?" He looked at Edgar long and hard. "Did you have anything to do with what happened?"

Edgar's eyes dropped, implying certain involvement. "Why do you ask?"

"You must go to the police if you know something," pushed Colin.

"*Do not dare to dictate what I should or should not do!*" snapped Edgar, irritable, fractious, confrontational. "I've got bigger fish to fry!"

Colin was startled by the sudden outburst, the sheer anger on display. "Bigger fish?"

"Have you seen today's newspaper?" Edgar reached down beneath the settee and pulled out a folded copy of *The Times*. "Drug-mule babies. Child soldiers in Africa. A high-school massacre near Stuttgart. The unending Israeli-Palestinian conflict. The subjugation and rape of women by the Taliban. The unchecked development of nuclear-missile technology by North Korea. A hostage situation in Kiev orchestrated by Chechen rebels. The indiscriminate bombing of a Peruvian peasant village by the Shining Path in retaliation for the murder of one of their commanders. Spillage from an oil tanker kills off the local seal population. Racism in the Metropolitan Police Force. An idiot of an American President. CEOs of crisis-hit financial organizations hiking up their obscene salaries with substantial bonuses using government bail-outs." Edgar hurled the newspaper at the wall in disgust, the pages spilling open. "I won't stand for it!"

Colin was thunderstruck. Never before had he seen Edgar so emotional, so gripped by rage, let alone so acquainted with world events. *Whether or not this amounts to simple angst is another matter, but when did he start reading the newspaper?* "The evil that men do along with the grace of others are what make us human."

"I will put the world to rights!"

He spoke with such assertiveness that Colin almost believed him. "How do you propose to do that, if you don't mind me asking?"

"Hypnox will guide me," explained Edgar. "I shall even provide you with a demonstration of my powers. Keep your eyes peeled for the fate of the International Space Station. At ten o'clock tonight, it will cease to be and all aboard shall perish."

Dear God, he's cracking up! Colin thought, greatly concerned.

He's talking grandiose nonsense. How could an armchair teenager affect the running of something that was ordinarily in low, geosynchronous orbit some two hundred nautical miles above the Earth? *I think I should consult his doctor and ask for a mental health assessment.* "Why target the International Space Station?"

"I was thinking the Hubble Telescope, but where would be the loss of life? The International Space Station is an absurd, self-congratulatory extravagance, costing billions of dollars when half of Africa starves and floods destroy the meagre homes of the impoverished Bangladeshi people."

"But the International Space Station is a joint venture between the various space agencies," Colin argued, "a symbol of world unification, questing to explore and catalogue the wildest frontiers of the Universe."

"I understand more about the frontiers of space than any NASA scientist. Before long, this mechanical monstrosity will usher in a new age of space tourism, another pointless diversion for the undeserving elite."

Colin decided to bring this heated conversation to a close. He was utterly nonplussed. Edgar seemed focused on the crimes of the few and the suffering of the many, and Colin didn't know why. "What's wrong, Edgar?" he importuned. "Mr. Spalding told me you didn't go into work today."

Edgar laughed a dark, unpleasant laugh. "Nothing's wrong with me, only with the world we live in," he continued, sounding like a crazed emperor. "I can tell you I've never felt more liberated. Tonight, the peoples of Earth will know me . . . and *tremble.*"

Colin went back to his own office on the grounds of ST. ANTHONY'S LODGE, distinctly unsettled. The warden did not know what to make of Edgar's sudden grievances over the bad elements of the world, let alone his outrageous claim that he could endanger an orbiting space station. Anger notwithstanding, Edgar had seemed so earnest, so sincere, so utterly canny in his final analysis that his subsequent inflated warning nearly convinced Colin. However, it would take significantly more to make a believer out of Colin than the moral condemnations of a distressed teenager. Indeed, there was a lot Edgar was saying that made total sense, righteous without being self-righteous . . . except Edgar had appeared overwhelmed by the knowledge in his possession . . . or could his over-aroused state and big talk possibly indicate the onset of a mental breakdown? Hardly surprising, considering the stress he'd been under lately, what with the press and police attention he had received. Lord knows autism made you four times more susceptible to becoming psychotic. Why not take medical advice, nip this in the bud?

As to the threat posed to the International Space Station... *well, there's only one thing for it* . . .

Colin put on the TV, switching channels to BBC News 24. He watched and waited, glued to the set, the tension welling up inside him as the seconds ticked by.

Ethnic riots in Paris, wildfires spreading towards Melbourne, the systematic abuse of prisoners at Guantanamo, the violent crushing of a student demonstration in Tibet . . .

Then, as seconds became minutes and the designated hour approached, along came the Breaking News. A sombre-looking newscaster addressed the camera, solemnly informing the world of the absolute destruction of the International Space Station. It had simply exploded in space. At this stage, the cause of the disaster was unknown, but it was suspected that an electrical fire, sabotage or otherwise, had arisen in the fuel tanks, sweeping throughout the rest of the superstructure with such frightening speed that the crew had no chance to evacuate. This constituted the biggest unforeseen space tragedy since the Challenger disaster in 1986, shaking the very foundations of the world's scientific community and placing the future of space exploration in grave jeopardy. Tributes poured in to the families of the brave men and women who had lost their lives on board.

Colin turned off the television, feeling giddy, his mind whirling with dark thoughts and unanswerable questions.

It had happened. It had actually happened. It seemed Edgar wasn't self-aggrandizing, blowing his own trumpet. Either he had developed into an oracle of doom or he had managed the unthinkable: destroyed a space station by the power of thought alone.

I will put the world to rights . . . Miracles happen when you speak with the angels . . . I understand more about the frontiers of space than any NASA scientist . . .

Edgar's words now took on a darker, portentous significance, a whole new sinister meaning, following the shocking events in space.

I think we need to talk about Edgar. He has created a shockingly curious incident. I don't know how he did it, but he did it. I need to find out how.

Overcome, Colin felt he could proceed no further tonight. He needed to lie down and recover. He decided he ought to examine the evidence with a fresh mind, in the merciful glow of the morning light.

Still in a relative daze, he changed for bed . . . but could not sleep.

"Tell me about Hypnox . . ."

Edgar pondered Colin's question, the next evening, with a look of mild surprise. "Hypnox is a Menos, a Psi-being, and his pneuma lives within me. His voice, like those of his fellow Menos Grex which threaten to invade my mind, consoles, instructs, *empowers*. Their chatter is like listening to various radio frequencies, switching different channels."

Hypnox, Colin ruminated. *Sounds like a variation on the name Hypnos, supposedly the Personification of Sleep in Greek Mythology. Either that or it's the brand name for an over-the-counter natural sleep remedy.* "Where does Hypnox hail from?"

Edgar pointed towards the night sky visible through the open curtains.

"Outer space?"

"From a binary star system in the constellation Orion."

Orion, also more commonly known as the Hunter. "How did Hypnox get here?"

"He journeyed across the stars."

"But, according to a physicist called Einstein, it's become an accepted fact that nothing travels faster than light."

"What you mean is that an object approaches infinite mass the closer it accelerates to light speed. Einstein didn't take into account the fundaments of mind-travel, the speed of thought. Since you cannot weigh consciousness, the trip is practically instantaneous."

As far as Colin gathered, Edgar talked about being possessed by an alien consciousness, how one could not measure the speed of thought. The leap in his intelligence was staggering, potentially proof positive of otherworldly involvement. He thought of the Mysterons, the villains from one of his own favourite TV serials as a child, and their relentless war of nerves. Colin gestured towards the Lego pyramid site, something he had earlier assumed was Edgar merely dreaming out aloud. "Is this a representation of Hypnox's home planet?"

"Astutely-put," said Edgar, matter-of-factly. "The Menos Grex were a race of powerful warriors, of both mind and matter, who at one point had conquered half the galaxy. Unfortunately, a power struggle ensued, where they turned on themselves, almost wiping out their entire civilization. The few who survived cheated death by storing their souls in an operational Psychetron Generator. Although the Psychetron is capable of projecting their thoughts, it also amplifies their pain and suffering."

Colin picked up on an important detail, ran with it. "If what you're saying is true about this Psychetron-machine amplifying their pain, ever thought it must also amplify their rage?"

Edgar ignored the inference. "Hypnox has helped awaken genes lying dormant in the human brain, once harnessed by mystics, magicians and alchemists across the ages. Minds capable of applying a measurable force over solid matter and physically changing the precepts of reality."

"You mean telekinesis," acknowledged Colin.

"Indeed. Most religious texts were never meant to be

interpreted literally as the commands of an omnipotent deity but provided cryptic instructions on how humans could harness their own natural Godlike, psychokinetic powers. Centuries of scientific skepticism and organized religion continue to fuel the fundamental misinterpretation of this esoteric knowledge."

"What does Hypnox want with you?"

"To escape his captivity and start a new life on Earth. He is the avatar and I am his vessel. Soon others will join him."

It was so much clearer now in Colin's mind. He had agonized over it all night and much of today. The coming of the dreams, the heightened imagination, the remarkable upswing in intelligence, thinking in the abstract, these infernal powers Edgar had acquired, the displaced, expressive rage. Poor Edgar couldn't see he was being used. Hypnox, it seemed, was grooming him to be an instrument of destruction, turning his mind into a weapon of infinite power. "You didn't have to kill those astronauts."

"Humanity is a plague on this planet," Edgar said harshly. "History is littered with zealots, despots and madmen, who have instigated war and genocide—every witch hunt, purge, invasion, occupation and exterminations—in the name of religion and greed. Your primitive, solar-based economy, with its over-reliance on fossil fuels, is killing the environment and driving innumerable species to extinction."

"What about Man's achievements: the Sistine Chapel, the Shakespearean sonnet, Mother Teresa, the Moon landings, stem cell therapy?"

But Edgar wasn't listening. "It is my ultimate duty to cleanse this diseased world. There is no-one greater than me in the history of thought."

Colin could not escape the absolute wrongness of leaving such apocalyptic powers in the hands of an autistic teenager. "Most people would construe your hostility as misanthropy."

"The misanthrope fears nothing and nobody. He believes in self-preservation at all costs."

"Maslow would disagree. Our purpose in life is to fulfil our higher needs, rise above our shortcomings, reach the level of the aesthete. In short, it's about self-actualizing."

"Schopenhauer didn't think so. He viewed Mankind as a futile, aggressive, self-destructive animal, on his last legs, destined to die out."

"The same can be said of the Menos. Except they're the ones who died out. *We're still here!*"

Edgar didn't take kindly to the remark. Colin suddenly became aware of the stare, the cold silent stare, regarded by many anthropologists as the most hostile gesture in non-verbal communication. Then Edgar spoke in a deliberately condescending manner that made Colin shudder. "You do realize, dear Neurotypical, that my intellect is now superior to yours."

"With power comes great responsibility," said Colin, trying to avoid the Medusa-like stare. "But what do us empaths know?"

It would seem Edgar had already selected his next target. Upper lip twisted in a contemptuous sneer, he said: "I shall purge this sick, shameful society, starting with your own crooked, unworthy government with the recent investigation into MPs' expense accounts, the peerages-for-sale controversy and the neverending stream of smear campaigns. If I remember correctly, today *is* Prime Minister's Question Time." He recalled an old rhyme from childhood. "*Remember, remember the Fifth of November.*" Suddenly, his tone turned icy-cold. "I'm going to do what Guy Fawkes should have done four hundred years ago."

"You can't!" Colin protested, appalled. "I forbid it!"

"Duly noted," said Edgar coldly. "I think you should go now. I have important work to do . . ."

But Colin held his ground. "Whatever you have in mind, I can't let you go through with it."

"I don't want you to visit me anymore because I can't be held responsible for what happens to you."

The threat, pre-emptive and lacking any subtle sugar-coating, completely broke Colin's defiant resolve, chilling him to the core. As Parliament stood on the very eve of destruction, he fled Edgar's flat without uttering another word, fearing for his own life and the safety of his fellow citizens.

Ten minutes later, a jumbo jet crashed into the House of Commons, killing most of the Cabinet, silencing the chimes of Big Ben and sending the country into chaos . . .

III: THE METAMORPHOSIS

The United Kingdom descended into chaos and anarchy the very hour the Houses of Parliament went up in flames. The media considered it a catastrophe of 9/11 proportions. The initial shock was followed by swift—if not misinformed—retribution. Islamic terrorists were suspected and whole communities took to the streets, beating up anyone who looked even remotely Muslim. Riots soon broke out in every major city, on the scale of Brixton, Handsworth and Toxteth, angry mobs of people leading pitched, running battles with the overstretched police force. Shops were looted and burned. Thousands were killed or seriously injured. Thousands more were arrested. The unfortunate passengers of the doomed plane seemed to be all but forgotten, overshadowed by the panic gripping the nation. The Anglican Church believed the horrible demise of the government and the subsequent, unprecedented urban chaos heralded the Beginning of the End. Geoffrey Burnham, the Defence Secretary, who somehow survived the destruction of Parliament, took up the mantle of acting Prime Minister and declared a national state of emergency. The British Army was called in to restore law and order. The only thing missing were the zombies.

"The inspector will see you now," Sergeant O'Hara of Utterston police station announced.

Colin Hendry was escorted by the police sergeant down a short corridor and ushered into an interview room, sparsely-furnished apart from a table and two chairs and what looked like a one-way mirror along the wall. Colin took a seat at the table opposite the plain-clothes detective after shaking his hand. Sergeant O'Hara closed the door behind him, leaving the two men alone.

"I read your statement," Inspector Ragg told Colin with a furrowed brow. "I really don't know what to make of the information you submitted."

"Do you think I would waste your time if I didn't see it happen?"

"I'm yet to figure that one out," remarked Inspector Ragg.

"I have nowhere else to turn."

"We've got Ground Zero in Westminster, the country's gone down the crapper and you're saying this is all the work of an angry autistic child with psychokinetic powers?"

"He purposefully sent the plane crashing into the Parliament buildings. The civil unrest comes as a direct consequence of the people's fears and need for justice."

"Powers allegedly acquired through an alien spirit inhabiting his body?"

Colin nodded.

Inspector Ragg went on skeptically. "And he destroyed the International Space Station at a stroke with the power of his mind?"

"Look, I know how far-fetched it must sound," Colin maintained, "and I'm at risk of being detained on a Section 136 and ferreted away to a mental hospital, but the facts are exactly as I stated."

"How do you expect me to respond to your testimony?"

"Can't you at least entertain the possibility?" Colin impressed. "There's been so much research done into psychokinesis over the years, largely by the Soviets during the Cold War. They possess silent black-and-white footage of Nina Kulagina stopping the beating of a frog's heart by the sheer force of her will. Another Russian psychic, Sergei Mendoyev willed a pane of glass to shatter and remote-influenced the spinning of a compass needle under clinical conditions. Wolf Messing walked out of a bank with 100,000 rubles after handing the cashier a 'cheque', which in fact turned out to be just a blank piece of paper. Then, there's the

Indian yogi master, Chandaraman, who was caught on camera levitating three inches above a bed of nails for approximately half-an-hour. The Global Consciousness Project is an ongoing scientific experiment, originally set up by Princeton University, to measure the randomness of major events in relation to large crowds of people. Even the Ministry of Defence has its own Psionics Division."

"Maybe so," Inspector Ragg said querulously, "but you're describing paranormal events on a miniature scale, not the highly improbable notion of some kid whom you claim has the ability to direct planes into buildings."

"Why is it so hard to accept?" Colin insisted, beginning to lose patience. "Edgar caused the death of Scott Grimes, blew up the International Space Station and murdered most of Her Majesty's government. If you don't do anything about this, there will be more disasters. His ambitions extend to wiping out all of Humanity from the face of the Earth."

The sheer desperation and urgency from a normally level-headed and rational man, working as a warden at ST. ANTHONY'S LODGE and looking after those with mental health needs, caused Inspector Ragg to revise his opinion. "You really believe this stuff, don't you?"

Colin said nothing.

Inspector Ragg flashed a consolatory smile. "We just can't spare the resources at present, but when we get a moment's respite I'll see what I can do."

"Oh, thank you," Colin sighed, his body relaxing a little.

"I'll contact you in due course . . ."

Sergeant O'Hara returned and escorted Colin to his grey Rover Metro, which was parked in a side-road. The windscreen was cracked—someone had thrown a rock at it while Colin had been in the police station. Colin got into his car and slumped back in the driver's seat, suddenly feeling a great weight lifted. He had done his bit, offloaded his fears; it was now in the hands of the authorities.

He looked out at the scene before him.

It was hell out there; Utterston High Street was down on its knees. Thugs, most of whose faces were concealed by scarves, were overturning cars, smashing shopfront windows and hurling Molotov cocktails at the advancing line of riot police.

With caution called-for, Colin drove off slowly, keeping only to the side-streets, avoiding even the slightest hint of a crowd. He felt it imperative he should evacuate the residents of ST. ANTHONY'S LODGE, for their own safety and protection, and because the authorities would soon be coming for Edgar.

How would they fare against the unique, mind-controlling genius of Edgar Byers?

No contest.

The black, armoured truck roared up the forecourt of ST. ANTHONY'S LODGE and came to a juddering halt outside the main doors. Six big men jumped out from the back of the truck, clad in black military gear and carrying SA80 assault rifles. They were joined by their driver. The day was overcast and dreary, the faint, acrid smell of smoke lingering in the air from the running street battles of the night before.

Grim-faced, Colin Hendry watched the men organize themselves from his car parked some distance away on the grounds. They didn't seem to be regular army lads or a tactical police unit. They encapsulated a ruthless, mercenary quality. What were the chances that these spooks hailed from the Psionics Division of the MoD? It appeared Inspector Ragg had taken Colin's disclosure seriously and telephoned through to the big guns. Colin hated snitching on Edgar, but what choice did Edgar leave him? An intergalactic war raged, unbeknownst to Mankind, with Edgar unwittingly serving as proxy agent to the Menos, a crucial catalyst in unleashing their devastating telekinetic powers. The very future of Mankind hung delicately in the balance.

"Right, men, you know what to do," said Captain Prosser, adjusting his beret. "This is a strictly seek-and-capture operation. Remember, we want him alive."

"What if he won't come quietly, sir?" Private Dooley inquired.

"Then we simply incapacitate him . . . with minimal force,"

Captain Prosser reminded him. He gestured to the main doors. "Let's go, men."

Captain Prosser led his crack team of soldiers across the threshold and into the lobby.

As expected, the lobby was deserted.

The soldiers crept up the stairs in smooth formation, wary of any sign of movement, Captain Prosser ahead, Private Talbot bringing up the rear.

All of a sudden, one of the lead soldiers froze up.

"What's wrong, Jenkins?" Captain Prosser demanded.

"I c-c-can't go on any f-further . . ." Private Jenkins responded tremulously. "I think I'm . . . *afraid*."

"Me too," admitted Private Wismer.

"Can't you feel it?" said Corporal Burke, glancing around nervously. "The atmosphere's thick with it. I sense a powerful mind reaching out. He *knows* we're here, sir."

"All the more reason to bring him in," Captain Prosser said determinedly. "He'd make an excellent research subject."

"The feeling'll only get worse," Corporal Burke warned.

"Don't give in to the fear," Captain Prosser advised his troops.

Private Gilmore was holding a small electronic device in front of him. Its red light was blinking madly. "Look, Captain, the PKE-meter reading's off the scale."

"I don't want any more dillydallying, men!" barked Captain Prosser. "Look alive! Focus on the task at hand! Now, get moving!"

They began climbing again, their pace steadily slowing down the closer they got to their destination.

Arriving on the third-floor landing, Private Jenkins let loose a hideous shriek.

His startled colleagues reacted instantly by training their weapons on him.

"No more . . . no more . . ." Jenkins gibbered. The others noticed the faraway look in his eyes, as though he were re-living some kind of waking nightmare. The mixture of dread and despair on his face spoke volumes. "No more . . . no more . . . no more..."

His captain showed not the slightest trace of sympathy. "What the hell's the matter with you?"

"No more, please, no more . . ."

"Snap out of it!" ordered Captain Prosser, shaking him roughly by the shoulders.

They watched in pure horror as Jenkins raised his gun and shoved the barrel into his own mouth.

Captain Prosser released him and backed away. "Don't do it, man—!"

Private Jenkins pulled the trigger.

The back of his head blew outward like a volcano, spewing forth a conical jet of blood, brain and bits of bone across the wall behind, forming a scarlet splatter as ill-defined as an abstract expressionist painting. His knees buckled beneath him and he went down gracelessly, his rifle clattering to the floor beside him.

Nobody spoke for nearly a minute.

Then, Private Dooley broke in, his voice tight with emotion. "Poor Jenkins . . . He completely lost it . . . Never figured him to be the type to commit suicide . . ."

"He didn't do it of his own volition," said Captain Prosser, marvelling at the pitiful, bloody corpse on the floor.

Corporal Burke failed to see the fascination. "This is getting incredibly dangerous. Jenkins bought it. I think we should abort."

"We will do no such thing!" Captain Prosser growled back. He knew it wasn't a confident start to their dawn offensive, but they had to soldier on. "We're going to see this mission through, no matter what the cost! We have a duty by our emergency government!"

"But captain—"

"No buts, Corporal! I won't tolerate insubordination in the ranks! Anyone who disobeys my orders will be Court-martialled! Is that clear?"

Private Dooley swallowed hard while the others looked at their superior sheepishly.

The PKE-meter Private Gilmore was carrying suddenly fizzed and sparked, its screen growing dead an instant later in a wisp of smoke. "It's overloaded, sir."

"Not to worry, Gilmore," Captain Prosser replied, "we're almost home . . ." Gesturing severely to his men, he added: "Let's maintain our shape and discipline. We're supposed to be highly-trained specialist agents."

Conversation lagged.

Prosser moved stealth-footed down the corridor, passing a series of closed, numbered doors. He could not ignore the sense of nameless dread weighing down his guts and how every step seemed a conscious effort. His men followed as professionally as they could. Approaching the door marked 14, Captain Prosser silently instructed his men with finger codes.

Privates Dooley and Gilmore immediately took up positions on either side of the door-frame, Private Wismer stood directly in front, poised to strike, gun at the ready. On the signal from Captain Prosser, he lashed out with his right foot and kicked open the door. "MoD!" he cried, storming into the flat.

His colleagues burst in after him, quickly spreading out around the room.

The lounge was otherwise empty. "Where is he?" asked Dooley.

Private Gilmore's attention was drawn to the showpiece on the centre table. "More to the point, what's he building?"

It was shaped like a flying saucer, only half-built, constructed largely from black Lego blocks. A network of mysterious wires connected the surrounding mechanized components to the tiny cockpit. There was an inherent, unearthly beauty to the polished, aerodynamic design.

"What is it?" Private Gilmore said, examining the display more closely.

"A spaceship of some sort," replied Captain Prosser, sharing Gilmore's curiosity. Doubtlessly a prototype, wondrous and innovative. "I can bet it would be fully-operational when he finishes. Large enough, I suspect, to house an alien consciousness."

"What was he planning to do with it?"

"Fly out of here, of course . . . maybe wish himself away."

Someone—or something—coughed.

Vigilant, the soldiers turned their guns in the direction of the noise. The sound had emanated from the adjoining bedroom. The door stood wide open, nothing but darkness visible from the chamber.

"Didn't anyone bother to secure the other rooms?" Captain Prosser said reproachfully.

His men didn't reply, probably embarrassed by this apparent lapse in procedure.

Captain Prosser spoke into the blackness beyond. "I know you're in there! Come out at once! I don't want any funny business because we're armed!"

"*Do not tell me what to do!*" sprang a voice from the darkened bedroom, a rasping, bubbling voice, foul and inhuman. "Haven't you seen what I'm capable of?"

"No, come out and we'll talk."

"Then let me show you once more . . ."

The vision of Private Jenkins' untimely death was nothing to what followed. Private Wismer yelped like a jackal, dropping his rifle. He began to tug and claw frenziedly at his uniform as though it were infested with soldier ants. "I'm so hot! *I'm burning up!*" His skin began to redden, blister, crack, blacken, smoke . . . and, in one agonized scream, he erupted into bright, orange flames, arms flailing, his body performing a dreadful, jittery death-dance. The fire consumed him in a matter of seconds, leaving behind only a pile of ash together with the scorched remains of his legs.

His colleagues watched his swift, horrible demise, stunned. The stench of charred flesh was thick and gagging. "Pyrokinesis," Captain Prosser eventually commented, not without a measure of awe, "spontaneous combustion—very impressive!" From the corner of his eye, he caught Dooley and Talbot edging nearer the door of the flat. "Nobody's going anywhere until we've taken home our grand prize!"

A despairing Corporal Burke tried to reason with him. "We don't stand a chance, sir!"

"That's for me to decide!" Captain Prosser responded, wild-eyed. "Can't you see what this means? It means we've got ourselves possibly the greatest weapon of mass destruction known to Man! I'll be damned if I'm going to let it fall into enemy hands!" He took a step towards the bedroom, but Private Gilmore abruptly barred his way.

"I can't let you in there."

"Get out of my way, soldier! That's an *order*!" But Gilmore stood his ground.

Captain Prosser saw the vacant look in his eyes, the expressionless face, and concluded Gilmore was slave to a vast, unbreakable hypnotic trance. His current dissociated state reminded Prosser of the assassin, played by Laurence Harvey, in *The Manchurian Candidate*. "If you don't get out of my—"

Private Gilmore raised his rifle, but Captain Prosser was quicker off the mark. He fired his Browning semi-automatic straight into Gilmore's chest, the gunshot echoing like a thunderclap in the small confines of the flat, with Gilmore dead before he hit the floor. Captain Prosser couldn't have asked for a cleaner kill. Or so he thought.

"Captain, are you okay?" Corporal Burke said, concerned. "You've been shot."

Captain Prosser felt the pain in his side and collapsed to the floor.

"I'm going to call an ambulance . . ."

Except it wasn't Corporal Burke any more. It was one of Saddam's Republican Guards, looking down menacingly at Captain Prosser, who seemed to be lying on the baking desert, sweating profusely, a ragged bullet-wound in his stomach. Two more dark-skinned Iraqi soldiers were approaching. Prosser glimpsed a township in the far, shimmering distance.

How he'd got back to the Iraq war he couldn't tell, but he knew what he needed to do. The British convoy had been ambushed, the foremost tank demolished by a landmine. The handful of Allied troops had perished in the ensuing gun-battle, heavily outnumbered, with only him—Captain Prosser—the sole survivor. Now it was his firm duty for the sake of democracy to punish those who had annihilated his brave battalion.

The Republican Guard stood over him, chattering triumphantly in a foreign language. He kicked Prosser in his wounded side, causing Prosser to groan in flaring agony.

He checked his immediate vicinity and spotted his Browning half-concealed in the sand less than three feet away. Luckily, the Republican Guard hadn't noticed it.

The plan was simple. These heathen bastards didn't take Prisoners-of-War and he was in no mood to, either.

The sun glared down. The vultures circled the burnished sky. The wreckage of the army tank blazed fiercely by the roadside. The domes and minarets of the next town shimmered like a distant mirage.

The Republican Guard stopped chattering when he saw two of his comrades approaching, his attention drawn momentarily away.

And Prosser took his chance. Before his captor knew what was happening, he rolled across the sands, and in one fluid movement, picked up the gun and took aim. He pumped several bullets into the near-most soldier's head, shredding it apart in a claret-coloured nimbus. Instantly switching direction, he fired again, twice. The two incoming men went down with relative ease.

Only two miles to Basra, he thought. The Mercedes didn't seem to have sustained too much damage. He could drive there and inform command—

—Captain Prosser found himself back in the present at ST. ANTHONY'S LODGE. He looked around the flat and discovered that his entire Special Ops unit was dead: Dooley, Talbot, Gilmore. Burke's face was particularly unrecognizable.

Prosser realized he had killed his own men.

Obviously, he had been under the influence, his own mind entangled with the will of another—psychic terrorism, in a manner of speaking. "That was a lousy thing to do!" he told the presence in the bedroom.

"You pulled the trigger, not us," gurgled the gleeful, congested voice from the dark.

"I need to see what you look like..." Captain Prosser murmured, eyes glittering with madness. He propelled himself up on his arms and began to crawl towards the bedroom, dragging his wounded body behind him. He gasped at the excruciating pain in his abdomen, losing frank freshets of blood with each ghastly effort. ". . . Even if it's the last thing I do."

"Then behold your new god!"

It emerged out of the darkness, and the sight of the thing sent an already-deranged Captain Prosser to a place from where he knew he would never return. He wanted to scream but could only produce a low, lurching moan. His eyes filled up with blood, the skin, musculature and skull-plates of his face gradually stretching, ballooning outwards, straining all known anatomical limits, as though he had been jettisoned on a moon with no atmosphere. The corresponding pain was enormous, like a scythe ploughing through his brain. He got up on his knees awkwardly and clutched his temples as he tried to drown out the uncontrollable pain and the dreadful memory of the unspeakable horror he had just glimpsed.

Then, an instant later, as if his mouth had been stuffed with a live grenade, his head exploded.

When the armed contingent of government agents didn't re-emerge from the building after a whole hour, Colin Hendry decided to go in. He stepped out of the Rover Metro, turning off the radio and, with it, songstress Alanis Morissette's cover of *Crazy*.

He checked his watch again and carefully lifted the briefcase from the back seat.

Almost time . . .

Carrying the briefcase, he walked across the courtyard, past the silent, unmarked truck and into the waiting doors of the entrance. Through the lobby, he plodded up several flights of stairs.

This is a bad idea, but it's the only way I can be certain. Arriving at the third-and-final-floor landing, he encountered the first gruesome casualty of the raid, lying motionless on the blood-stained carpet. The mess on the wall, the consistency of which reminded him of bolognaise sauce, had already begun to congeal. The nametag read JENKINS and, judging from the cavernous hole in the back of his skull, it looked as if he had deliberately blown his own brains out . . . or maybe not so deliberately.

Hovering over the corpse a moment longer, Colin wondered why he felt no fear, why the dead body did not alarm him, when most people under such circumstances would have run a mile or risked experiencing nightmares for the rest of their lives.

I suppose dealing with the mentally-challenged day in, day out would desensitize anyone.

He carried on down the third-floor corridor, not very hopeful. The door to Flat 14 had been forced open. Without the slightest hesitation, Colin entered.

He surveyed the scene before him—the aftermath of a massacre—stoically, objectively. He counted six more dead, making up the remainder of the platoon. If he wasn't too much mistaken the captain seemed to be missing his head, one of the soldiers had literally been reduced to ash and the rest had shot each other. A right, royal bloodbath.

They failed in their mission, thought Colin with a grim sense of inevitability. *Kind of expected—no amount of gung-ho military muscle can take down an autistic kid with extraterrestrial powers, a rage magnified a millionfold. Their fate was sealed the moment they stepped into the building in their bid to apprehend him, but none of them deserved to die in the manner in which they did.*

On the lounge-room table, where the Lego temples had once been was what appeared to be a half-completed alien spacecraft, undamaged in the shoot-out.

"I expected you sooner," issued a voice from the shadowy depths of the bedroom, noisome-sounding like words spoken through sludge.

"I came when I thought prudent . . . How are you keeping, Edgar?"

"Edgar is well. He exists among us."

"Among you? How many of you are there?"

"Thousands. Edgar now carries the entire surviving population of Menos Prime, our collective consciousnesses that were stored in the Psychetron. We projected our pneumae into his body last night. He is a most hospitable host."

"Why are you lurking in the shadows?"

"Edgar suffered a slight complication during the transfer process."

"What kind of complication?"

"His genetic constitution was irreversibly altered by the influx of our pneumae. We, the Menos Aggregate, have reconfigured his body to the physical dimensions of our race when we were in mortal form. We have made him in our image."

"Can you show me?"

And the dark shape shuffled slowly out of the shadows. The creature was roughly four feet tall and pyramidal in shape, the flesh densely corrugated, the colour and slickness of tar. Just below the apex was situated a lone, green saucer of an eye, and directly below that, the horizontal sliver of a mouth, a wrinkled, lipless, gumless, toothless thing. Four serpentine tentacles on either side of the small squat body pulsed and writhed, each ending in a single razor-sharp talon. Short, multitudinous polyps beneath its bottom-heavy base produced a rhythmic, anemone-like motion which allowed it to crawl in any direction it desired.

Colin tried not to show his disgust. He choked down the contents of his stomach, staring dispassionately at the creature Edgar had become. It was hard for him to accept that this repulsive, genetically-reprogrammed abomination had once been a normal, regular human kid. These psychical beings had not only turned him into a receptacle of ancient knowledge, gifting him with the keys to unlock some of the Universe's deepest mysteries, they had rewritten his DNA in their own alien image. *Hell-awful things happen when you commune with demons.* "You disposed of the troops in a hurry."

"Rather a fitting end to the special taskforce, wouldn't you agree?" rasped the resurrected Menos. "Our survival is paramount."

"Evidently."

The Cyclopean eye watched Colin with avid intensity. "You betrayed us."

Colin kept a cool head. "With much regret . . . believe me, you didn't give me an alternative. The survival of my people is equally paramount."

"There can only be one victor. Your combined military might is no match for our collective mental abilities. We will claim this planet as our own when all life has been extinguished from it."

"And how do you plan to go about it?"

"H3M-4Pi. Nearly seven billion people on this planet and not a clue."

"H3M-4Pi? And that is code for what?"

"You will find out soon enough. Child's play, as Edgar might say. Rest assured, the suffering of your people will be but fleeting."

"You know I can't let you go through with whatever you have in mind."

"You are in no position to threaten us."

"Threaten, no. Stop you, yes." Colin placed the briefcase on the floor and glanced at his watch.

"Why are you so anxious? What's in the briefcase?"

"Oh, something I made . . ."

The burbling, wheezing voice was suddenly brimming with suspicion. "What is it you're hiding from us? Tell us!"

"I don't think so . . ."

"Don't you know we can tell what you're thinking? We can scan and detect the pattern of firing synaptic connections in the brain, allowing us to read your thoughts. And our combined will is more powerful than anything on your planet."

Invisible hands seized Colin's neck and lifted him off the ground. "Edgar, if you're in there, I'm sorry for what I'm about to do . . ." he managed to whisper.

The eye bulged balefully and the amplified telekinetic forces generated from the collective hive mind continued to strangle him, crush his windpipe. He felt his mind being invaded, probed, plundered and he did his best to think of a secure, steel-reinforced vault in the basement of a bank.

Colin recognized the voice which rose to the surface, previously lost among the legion of alien spirits. "No, it is *I* who should be sorry, Colin. You showed me nothing but kindness. I shall always be your friend." Dangling several inches above the ground, his mind forcibly and irreparably raped, while unseen fingers continued to throttle him, deprive him of air, Colin felt a last, conciliatory pang of sadness. *And you were always special, a prince among kids . . .*

And as the Menos reached deeper into his mind, burning through the complex lock with a thermal lance and twisting open the vault door to the strong-room, they glimpsed the secret he had been hiding all along, the makeshift bomb in the briefcase... counting down to zero hour.

I do this, son, as your surrogate father and friend . . . in lieu of your real parents.

They released him, retreating like a panicking shoal into the farthest recesses of Edgar's mind, and Colin dropped to the floor like a sack of flour, gasping for air. For a moment, he saw only Edgar looking back at him in that single, gleaming eye, serenity, affection and understanding in that gentle expression, bound by friendship. It seemed Edgar had finally overcome his pervasive social deficits, found a cure for his mind-blindness through his union with an alien species.

The last thing Colin remembered was the ringing of the alarm-clock in the briefcase, followed by a bright, blinding, all-consuming flash.

In the dark gulf of space, the asteroid H3M-4Pi hurtled at five-hundred kilometres per second on a direct collision course with Earth . . .

February 2009—April 2009

Encounters of the Liminal Kind

"There is nothing in the dark that isn't there when the lights are on."

Rod Serling

1

Seraphim Park proved to be Corporal John Harding's regular haunt. Not that he ever actually walked on the grass or fed the pigeons or traipsed gaily through the woods.

Never there in person, he served as an unseen presence, but he was far from a ghost, if using the word in its literal sense.

Physically-disabled, Harding preferred instead to watch the comings and goings of Seraphim Park from his apartment window, a constant reminder of what might have been and what he had lost.

This cold, grey November day was no great exception.

Summer might have come and gone—lasted an entire weekend this year, according to the cynics—but there was still plenty happening at Seraphim Park. The number of park-goers may have dwindled over the autumn months, but there was still a consistent hardcore of people who frequented the grounds almost every day.

Harding watched them (sometimes through his binoculars if he needed a close-up view, other times without), giving them nicknames, making up stories about their lives. It was an idle occupation at the best of times, but Harding had gradually grown accustomed to it. Besides, how else could a major cripple avail his time when it really was too much pain and effort to go outside? He had made a conscious decision to remain solely within the confines of his apartment like some tired old recluse, with precious little company apart from the physiotherapist who visited once a week. At least, out there, through his third-floor window, he took comfort in seeing a semblance of normality and knowing the world still turned on its axis.

He was safe in the knowledge that nothing could upset his life so dramatically again or shake the foundations of his daily routine. He valued his privacy, a relatively peaceful existence free of undue complications or any unexpected surprises.

That was before he first noticed the MacMen.

2

Johnny Harding termed them 'MacMen' because of the peculiar manner in which they dressed, in long brown Macintoshes and matching Trilbies, as though they had travelled up from the depths of the Cold War.

On the day he would see them, Harding had suffered horrendously all morning. The pain had been worse than usual, practically unbearable, bringing tears to his eyes. The result of the severe injuries he had sustained during the Persian Gulf War. A Corporal in the British 1st Armoured Division, he had lost both legs when he had inadvertently stepped on a landmine—a novice's mistake—the same day Iraq surrendered and the Kuwaitis rejoiced in the streets of their capital. A large whizzing piece of shrapnel had lodged in his forehead during the explosion. Miraculously still alive, his mangled legs needed immediate amputating above the knees and the embedded jag of shrapnel was surgically removed and a small metal plate fitted in its place to protect his exposed brain. Two years he convalesced in a military hospital, traumatized, receiving grief counselling, mourning the loss of his former life. The bitterness slowly turned into acceptance, and the government compensation in the form of a modest army pension helped him adjust to his new life, and the intensive physical therapy programme allowed him to function again, albeit as half a man. Regaining some of his confidence and pride, he opted for independent living instead of going into a residential home. The surgical plate sometimes produced blinding headaches and, on those very rare instances, had been known to pick up long-wave radio, a phenomenon he found utterly bizarre and somewhat amusing. The phantom limb pain he experienced was the worst part, however, causing him to sit in sweaty, teeth-gritting agony for hours on end, dulled only by mood stabilizers and opiate painkillers. Even though as a soldier he had been trained to withstand all manner of hardships, he found the chronic, inexhaustible nature of his pain ultimately soul-sapping if left untreated.

Today was a particularly bad day. The stumps of his thighs hurt like a sonofabitch, and it wasn't the first time he thought about doing himself in. Except, over the years, he had got used to the persistent awfulness of his suffering to some degree and, as always, he ought to give medication a try. He dry-swallowed several tablets of morphine sulphate, more than the prescribed dose, and waited it out.

Forty minutes later, he could feel the pain letting up. The accompanying euphoric effect of the morphine was a bonus; he could not deny he had developed a taste for it. Able to think a little more clearly now, filled by a pleasurable sense of wellbeing, he rolled his wheelchair up to the lounge-room window and looked out.

From his perfect vantage point, he peered down at the familiar world outside, the expanse of parkland opposite.

The morning rain had stopped. The afternoon sky was grey and overcast, threatening a further downpour later. To Harding, late autumn held its own unique attraction. The oaks and maples were moulting and half-skeletal, shedding their leaves on the ground in richly-coloured abundance, heaps of browns, reds and golds.

Grey squirrels scurried up and down the trunks, making ready to throw off the shackles of the old year and negotiate the journey towards hibernation and renewal. Flocks of birds visited the park, setting off again in search of warmer climes.

All the regulars were out in spite of the inclement weather. There went Jogging Girl, following the course of the footpath, listening to her MP3 Player, her blond ponytail bouncing gaily behind her. Sitting on a park bench, wrapped up warm in a scarf and reefer jacket, was Handsome Guy, watching the progress of the swans, white and graceful, as they floated silently on the lake. A few benches up from him sat Rex the Codger, reading a newspaper, preferring the open air instead of the stuffiness of the library or the stale smells of the social club. Lady with Pushchair trundled past, doting over her infant charges, possibly twins. Man with Dog, a sprightly Yorkshire terrier, was also doing his usual rounds.

Prerequisites are: must be retired, in the service of housewifery or work directly from home, thought Harding, feeling a strange kinship with these people. It was as if he had known them all his life so familiar was he with their daily routine. *Because, my fellow citizens, I've got the best seat in the house.* Moreover, he imagined them walking *for* him, allowing an amputee like him to reconcile with the envy he felt for their intact, fully-functioning legs. *After all, a man is the sum of his memories—a legless wonder like me more so.*

Daylight was fading fast, and it wasn't even four o'clock yet. Lady with Pushchair had already gone, probably to feed the little ones and make dinner for her hard-day-at-the-office husband. Rex the Codger finished his reading and headed on under the arch of the park entrance, maybe to catch a couple of swift ones down the local spit-and-sawdust. Jogging Girl did a few more laps round the lake before calling it a day—wouldn't she and Handsome Guy make an excellent couple? But Harding was almost certain that a stunner like her would already have a man about the house, and if not, then home she might go to curl up on the sofa and watch a cosy chick-flick with her girlie-friends. Handsome Guy remained on the bench, studying the swans, even as twilight fell. Definitely no girl in the wings, suspected Harding, otherwise why spend an entire cold afternoon at the park without the slightest tinkle on his mobile? No, he must be a writer, in between books, searching for inspiration to kickstart his latest novel.

Then, just like clockwork, entered a rabble of young teenagers, dressed in school uniforms, taking their usual shortcut through the park. They spilled onto the grounds, laughing and joking and talking animatedly, hoping for any way in which to delay the homework pending or, better yet, cunningly sneak onto their PlayStation when their parents weren't around. Harding watched their numbers diminish . . . and his eyes suddenly caught on the curious figure sitting on the park bench nearest the entrance, by the bins. Harding was surprised he hadn't noticed him before, as if he had appeared out of nowhere.

Must have missed his arrival, rationalized Harding, not wholly convinced by the explanation. *Too fixed on the kids.*

It was getting quite dark now and colder still, and groundmist snaked up from the shrubs and grass. There was hardly anybody else in the park now, apart from Handsome Guy.

Harding picked up his binoculars and trained them on the figure sitting by the park entrance. He was oddly-dressed in a brown Mac and Trilby hat, and for a disturbing if not amusing moment, Harding thought he was some kind of pervert—or *flasher*—waiting for his chance to rise up and spring open his coat in order to terrorize the schoolchildren, if any had been loitering.

But when he turned his head a fraction, Harding noticed the waxy pallor of his skin and that he was wearing heavy sunglasses, a mystery considering it was dusk at the height of autumn.

Who was he and why hadn't Harding ever seen him before? Intrigued, Harding continued watching him through his binoculars when, all of a sudden, a second figure came into view from just outside Harding's line of sight.

The second figure, too, was dressed incognito, in identical Mac, Trilby and Sunglasses.

Where did he come from? thought Harding, fairly perturbed.

The first of the figures got up from the bench, and Harding saw, even from where he watched, that both men were similarly slim but extraordinarily tall. *Nearly seven feet tall.*

And both gangling giants were carrying something, which Harding quickly realized were corrugated metal briefcases. He saw them swap briefcases in a single smooth exchange.

Their impassive manner made Harding think of Communist spies with secret documents plotting the downfall of the West and blueprints in microfilm to create weapons of mass destruction, together masterminding the advent of World War Three.

And as Handsome Guy went ambling past, finally done for the day, Figure #1 pulled out an extendable, ornate-looking spear from his silver briefcase and, with the pointy tip, callously jabbed Handsome Guy in the right ankle. Handsome Guy loosed an inaudible cry of agony as his ankle twisted beneath him, stumbling for a moment. Bending down momentarily to check his ankle, glancing around in utter bewilderment, Handsome Guy limped off down the footpath and out of the park.

Handsome Guy doesn't see them, Harding thought, suddenly certain of this one, terrible fact. *Why doesn't he see them?*

Harding stared as each man extracted a small, futuristic-looking device from their respective coat-pockets and, turning some sort of dial . . . *vanished in front of his eyes.*

One minute they were there, the next they were gone. Harding blinked, not sure what he was seeing.

Where did they go? he thought in a giddying mixture of surprise and consternation.

He carefully scanned the park against the descent of darkness. Tendrils of mist drifted up from the lake, the swans seeking shelter for the night along the reedy banks . . . but there was no-one to be seen; the park was otherwise deserted.

People don't just vanish into thin air . . .

Still a little startled, Harding tried to make sense of the strange events of the afternoon. He understood very little of what had transpired. He even questioned his own sanity, wondered if he had witnessed what he had actually witnessed. No answer, however, was forthcoming.

Who are those mysterious figures and what do they want? He remembered their pale complexions, their incredibly tall, lanky frames, their identical dress code as though it were some kind of inconspicuous (or not so inconspicuous) disguise, their briefcases crammed with puzzling gadgets. He remembered them gently prodding Handsome Guy in the foot with something that looked like a retractable lance, somehow causing the ankle to sprain, and the unfortunate victim limping away, bewildered, without noticing their sinister presence (even though they, quite frankly, stuck out like a pair of sore thumbs). Then those mysterious strangers had come up with the most spectacular *pièce de résistance:* disappearing in the wink of an eye, as if they'd never been there in the first place.

Harding thought he would call them MacMen . . . and he knew he would be seeing them again.

3

Johnny Harding spent the next day in his usual spot once the pain in his thighs eased off. He found it remarkable how Seraphim Park had, since the upheaval in his soldiering career, become the lynchpin of his existence, with his constant prying into the lives of others reminding him of some nosy old lady who also doubled as Dame of the Grapevine.

After last night it didn't bother him. He didn't care. Everything he had glimpsed in those few singular moments the afternoon before was too crazy to be believed. Was it possible he had uncovered some kind of shadowy conspiracy? Strange foreign men in the park stealing State secrets and plotting a nuclear (or biological) strike on British soil? Crazy, yes, but not completely outside the realms of extreme possibility. And just when the politicians were trying to convince us the Jihadists were the world's latest aggressors. It was simply naive not to look in your own backyard for the instigators, having set foot in this country some years ago with dark, cataclysmic motives in the forefronts of their minds, quietly spreading their manifesto of hate. They were more commonly known as Sleeper Cells.

Why can't it be ex-KGB agents, pissed at the fall of Communism, forever dreaming of the day when their embittered ranks would rise up from their vodka glasses and take over the world? I mean 007's still fighting Russian terrorists, even today— albeit Russian terrorists who've grown fat off the profits of the Free World.

Harding was hooked the moment he looked out of the window. He felt like a private detective, about to uncover something big, something earth-shattering. Nothing could shake his enthusiasm. He hadn't felt this good since he had been kicking ass in the Gulf. He might even earn himself a much-coveted Victoria Cross if he singlehandedly—and, moreover, as a disadvantaged, legless cripple in a wheelchair—foiled a potential terrorist plot.

So far, however, it had been a slow day, but Harding was nonetheless hopeful.

Jogging Girl maintained her fitness regime. Lady with Pushchair gave her twins a taste of fresh air. Rex the Codger kept himself abreast of current affairs. Fats Solomon, so-called because he was the exact spitting image of corpulent soul-singer Solomon Burke, was out for a stroll. But of the MacMen—whoever or *whatever* they were—there was no sign.

With considerable patience, Harding watched and waited. He didn't intend to miss a thing.

The clock ticked by. The afternoon grew late and windy. Fats Solomon stood by the banks of the lake, feeding the swans. Jogging Girl did another lap round the lake. Rex the Codger got up and left. Billy the Friendly Neighbourhood Tramp took his place. Man with Dog came passing by. Even Handsome Guy, whom Harding thought would be housebound for the next few days, made a guest appearance, limping along at his own manageable pace, eventually sitting himself down on one of the benches. Schoolchildren swarmed the park at the close of play, lingered in loud, unruly numbers and quickly dispersed. But still no MacMen.

Just when Harding was beginning to have serious doubts, that he might have imagined the events of before (Handsome Guy's injury notwithstanding), his eyes picked them out.

Freaky though it might sound, it was as though they had simply shimmered into existence . . . and at that precise moment, as if it was their time to appear.

Harding checked the wall-clock. It was getting on half-four. Outside, Seraphim Park was bathed in an eerie, prescient twilight. Harding surveyed the gale-swept grounds against the darkening gloom.

There weren't two like yesterday. This time, Harding could make out at least five or six MacMen, each stationed in different quadrants of the park. All prodigiously tall and worryingly gaunt and attired in the same ridiculously retro get-up, each carrying a metal briefcase. Like '50s-style government spooks, caricatured brilliantly in that Dom Joly sketch.

But it wasn't just their presence that disturbed Harding. It was what they were up to. Sat in the darkness of his flat, he stared in horrible fascination as each individual MacMan trailed alongside the various park regulars, doing some seriously spooky shit to them.

Fats Solomon had a hose fitted to his big belly like an umbilical cord, the MacMan in his vicinity pumping him full of a nameless silver liquid [perhaps to tamper with his genes and force him to retain vast quantities of fat]. Billy the Friendly Neighbourhood Tramp had some kind of medieval torture device pinned round his head as the MacMan assigned to him adjusted the insertion depth of the needles in his skull. Every so often Billy the Tramp would rub his temples, literally through the bars of the illusory steel head-brace [possibly to ward off the onset of a migraine brought on by an emerging brain tumour]. Jogging Girl had stopped running and was taking a short breather. Her MacMan was busy examining her stomach with sophisticated scanning equipment, lighting up the growing foetus she seemed unaware she was carrying in rufescent pulsing radioactive waves. [Several months down the line she would, Harding was sure, give birth to a congenitally-deformed baby, the damage inflicted on her unborn child occurring on this *very night*]. Another MacMan was expertly using a syringe to extract some spinal fluid from the back of Handsome Guy's neck [*which could probably explain why the fellow was going through the worst depressive episode of his life, soon to be contemplating suicide*]. Man with Dog did not escape the onslaught. A MacMan walked along either side of them, each occupied with testing their subject. The dog-owner strolled on, coughing and sneezing, not noticing the phosphorescent powder being sprinkled over his nose [*containing a particularly aggressive strain of virus that would in the coming days take root, multiple at a frightening rate, and what he thought was a simple cold would progress into a life-or-death case of pneumonia*]. His Yorkshire terrier, who already appeared strangely on edge and seemed to be barking at something behind him, as though sensing the MacMen, suffered an even more gruesome fate. Its accompanying MacMan, realizing animals might possess a sixth sense, removed a flamethrower from his briefcase, activated the nozzle and set the dog alight. Its fur instantly catching fire, the dog went berserk and shot off down the footpath, a blazing, howling thing. Still sneezing, his owner chased after it, wondering what the hell had got into it. Of course, in the real world, he would not be able to see the actual flames cremating the dog's flesh, only recording a nasty fever.

Harding turned away from the scene of carnage and closed the window, appalled. He sat in the dark, trying to compose himself. His suspicions had been correct. He understood the MacMen a lot better now, their purpose all too clear.

The fat generator, the contraption of needles designed to aggravate an existing brain tumour, the glow of a nuked uterus, the induction of suicidal thinking in an already-depressed individual, the nasty, life-threatening chest infection, the burning dog.

The MacMen were conducting experiments on those unsuspecting humans. Harding knew this more than anything else. Their behaviour suggested a scientific unit, and they weren't Russian. In fact, Harding was certain that they weren't even human. It didn't require a trained eye or a science-fiction writer to tell him they hailed from another world or even another reality.

Here, to bring misery to the human race in their pursuit of scientific knowledge.

Why couldn't those people see what was happening to them? And why was it only he who could see the MacMen?

Maybe it was a case of the metaphorical white elephant in the room. Maybe those people *could* see the MacMen, but *refused* to acknowledge their presence, choosing to ignore the unignorable.

However, Harding dismissed this idea after objectively re-evaluating the evidence.

A word floated to the surface of his mind, a rarely-spoken word from the English lexicon. The word was *liminality*. It was a fascinating word, very erudite, significant and rather apt in this particular situation. Its meaning? The transitional middle ground between two otherwise dominant states. Liminality of Time, for instance, referred to the ambiguous half-lit worlds of dusk and dawn.

Harding was suddenly sure the MacMen had been around all day, but only became visible at dusk. *There must be something about the twilight. The MacMen must exist in a liminal state that is a second or two out of sync with our reality.*

The other question still stood: why could *he* only see them?

Surely, they ought to be invisible to me, too.

It occurred to him, then. He tapped the right side of his forehead where the skull plate resided. *Liminality of Consciousness*, he reasoned. Whether it was the metal plate (capable of picking up band-width radio under the right meteorological conditions) or the pills he popped, or maybe a combination of both, only he possessed the ability to tune in on their particular frequency. *I must be blessed . . . or, rather,* cursed.

I'm living in my own Twilight Zone . . .

How long had these hideous experiments been going on? Ordinary people going about their everyday lives, oblivious to the knowledge they served as mere lab rats for a more advanced species. Yet, Harding conceptualized, could it be humans were created perfect, and all the physical ailments they endured during the course of their lives sprang from these alien beings tampering with their vital systems and DNA? Could it not be equally possible that this entire planet was in fact one giant Petri dish?

No, thought Harding, *I'm reaching too far.*

Night had fallen. Harding switched from his binoculars to his Army-issue, night-vision goggles and looked out.

The park had emptied of its visitors, both human and alien. Not a soul to be seen. Just gale-force winds and the invisible secrets of the dark . . .

White elephant or not, theory of liminality or otherwise, Harding decided he should tell someone about what he had witnessed tonight. Blow the whistle on their inhumane activities. After all, this might be the prelude to a full-scale invasion, a war between two worlds. He had been trained to protect civilians, and he wanted, again, to do his bit for Queen and Country. For all Earthlings.

He realized the glaring drawback in his plan. Who would believe him?

4

Harding didn't know to whom he should disclose his alarming discovery. He still kept in touch with some the lads from his old regiment, occasionally attending the reunions, but he doubted 'Froggy' Marsh and Freddie 'Four Fingers' Tucker would take his story at face value if he rang them up. Those dolts would probably think he was yanking their chains and laugh their asses off till the cows came home. Even his own normally open-minded Commanding Officer, Brigadier Letwin-Smith, would struggle to accept his outlandish story. No, Harding had to convince someone who trusted him (and whom he trusted), and he knew just the person.

Jenny Bingham, his blond-haired, white-smocked-and-sneakered physiotherapist, arrived at the apartment at her normal designated time of two on the Thursday afternoon. If Harding still had his legs he would have had no hesitation in making a play for her. But, then again, if his legs were still intact he would probably never have met her. So he supposed there was a minor upside to losing his legs.

"Hello, Johnny," she greeted him, as he let her into his apartment. "How are you faring today?"

"Can't complain," he replied, pleased to see her. "And what about you? How goes your love-life?"

"Same-old same-old, thank you. Non-existent, as I keep telling you every time."

"Can't get enough of me, hey?"

"Keeps me coming round, doesn't it?" She assisted him up from the wheelchair and onto the foldable exercise plinth. "Any problem with your legs?"

Lying on his back, Harding looked up at her with mischief written all over his face. "Aside from the fact I don't have any?"

Jenny glanced down at him with a small wry smile. His greying crewcut and designer stubble, his penchant to dress in black, those friendly blue eyes, full of courage and acceptance of the nightmare he once suffered, and his constant desire to flirt with her as though he harboured a secret crush. Shame, because he wasn't all that bad-looking and she might have gone for him in a different life. But best to keep everything amicable and professional. Harding had come a long way in the years she'd known him. Not easy overcoming the bitter heartbreak of losing both your legs in combat. There was a massive gulf of difference between a victim and a survivor. And Jenny considered Harding a true survivor, having successfully discarded the perpetually-suffering victim role many years ago. Still, it would be nice if she could convince him that prosthetic limbs weren't the mark of a robot so he could go out a bit more. A former soldier like him might even shine in the Paralympic Games, if he were interested. "Prevention is always better than cure. We don't want you developing any nasty contractures."

For the next hour-and-a-half she helped him exercise what was left of his legs in an attempt to maintain healthy circulation and muscle mass. Harding appreciated her systematic approach and put up with the accompanying pain exceedingly well. There was such a massive difference between pathological pain and therapeutic pain. She pushed him harder than ever and Harding did not yield. The heavy toil-and-sweat left Harding feeling drained if not a lot fitter. "Can't do any more . . ." he gasped, trying to catch his breath. "I'm pooped."

"I'm impressed by how much you managed today," commended Jenny. "Well done!"

"Care for a bevvy?" Harding said, bringing out a carton of OJ from the fridge.

"No, I'd best be going," Jenny said, packing her bag. "Same time, next week?"

"Jenny, stay awhile," he requested, all of a sudden. "I really need to talk to you about something."

Jenny stopped by the door. For an absurd moment, she thought he was finally going to ask her out on a date, but the urgency in his voice made her reconsider. She looked at him, puzzled. "What is it, Johnny?"

"You trust me, don't you?"

"Yes, we share a good rapport."

"Then, what I'm about to tell you is in the strictest confidence." Harding brought his wheelchair to the window and looked down over the park. Within this temporary twilit window of opportunity, Harding could see the cabal of MacMen at work again, attired in their identical dress code, conducting their own brand of Nazi-style experiments on the regular park visitors, who had no clue what was happening to them.

Jogging Girl ran on with a glowing uterus, the foetus inside slowly gestating and mutating into something grotesque and obscene. As it began to drizzle down, Rex the Codger finished with his newspaper and made the journey to the park entrance, hunched forward with excruciating back pain inflicted by a triangulated laser beam trained on the length of his spine by the MacMan walking behind him. Handsome Guy, too, decided to take a raincheck and hobbled away from the park bench, looking old, tired and miserable, uncharacteristically agitated like a junkie withdrawing from drugs. Despite the drizzle, Fats Solomon stood by the lake, feeding the swans, the artificial umbilicus attached to his navel area streaming in liquid metal; with an ever-increasing girth, he looked easily two stones heavier since yesterday. Home-time, the park was suddenly invaded by schoolchildren, and Harding noticed several MacMen quickly and quietly latching onto them, putting electrostatic mesh hoods over their heads like suffocating plastic bags.

Shit, thought Harding, aghast, *they've started on the children! Fewer kids, I bet, in class tomorrow, forced to stay at home with headaches and colds and tummy problems.*

Curious, Jenny joined him by the window, peered out into the deepening twilight. "What are you looking at?"

"You don't see them?"

"See what? What am I supposed to be looking for?"

Why would she see them? thought Harding, despairingly. *She isn't the one with a metal plate in her skull.* "Take a seat and brace yourself. I'll explain."

Jenny did as he requested. She wondered what this could be about. "Okay, fire away."

And Harding told her. He told her of what he had witnessed at dusk in the past couple of days. He told her of the liminal beings he called the MacMen, how only he could see them. He told her about the weird experiments they seemed to be conducting on the park regulars and the dangerous effects their research might be having on their subjects. He didn't exactly know the origins of the MacMen, but he was more than certain they had arrived here from elsewhere, probably from beyond our world altogether. He was thorough. He tried not to miss anything out.

Jenny listened to his account silently and fully, without passing judgement.

When Harding finished his tale, he gave Jenny a few moments to digest and dissect the material. He valued her opinion. "What do you think?"

Jenny did not speak for a while. She was caught in two minds. On the one hand, she wanted to believe him—*really* believe him—so detailed and earnest were his observations. Poor guy, seeing what he claimed he was seeing would freak anyone out. Yet, she could not ignore her clinical expertise. The emotional trauma of getting both legs blown off in the combat zone and resorting to living the rest of his life as a virtual recluse, watching over the park like a sentinel, must have snapped something inside him and caused him to create this elaborate fantasy. Poor sweet paranoid, deluded Johnny. It would be unfair on him if she agreed with his delusion and didn't report her findings to his doctor. She decided she would maintain the mutual trust she had established long ago with Harding to get him the help he needed. She owed it to him. "I think what you've seen is disturbing and completely unacceptable. Have you mentioned it to anyone else?"

Harding shook his head.

"Good." Tactfully, she said: "Let's see if we can put a stop to it. I think it's important I consult somebody about the matter, somebody who may know what to do."

"But how? It's impossible to interfere with them in their present liminal condition. The MacMen exist in an indeterminate plane of reality in tandem with our own which is why they're invisible to practically everyone. We need to find some way to bring them and their research out into the open, allow the rest of the world to see what they're doing."

And there was her thinking he only read Andy McNab novels. Jenny never thought he took an interest in science fiction, let alone would ever express a belief that aliens had infiltrated our society. "Leave it with me . . ." She glanced down at her watch. "It's getting late. I really have to go." She hurried to the door with her sports bag. "I'll see you soon, Johnny, I promise."

Then she departed.

Harding watched her leave with a sinking heart. He had scared her off. He knew exactly what was going through her mind. He was positive she believed he'd gone off his rocker from sheer loneliness and had concocted a mad conspiracy about invisible aliens experimenting on humankind with the objective of colonizing the planet. He'd made a terrible mistake confiding in her. He had thought he could pull off Hitchcock's *Rear Window*, with himself taking on James Stewart's role and Jenny stepping into the shoes of Grace Kelly. Fat lot of good it did! Jenny was probably en route to speak with Dr. Kirchner about everything she'd heard. And Dr. Kirchner, a real hardcase, would definitely be calling round at some point with legal papers sanctioning Harding's detention to the loony bin.

Harding realized he had very little time left to prove his story before Dr. Kirchner and the men with the butterfly nets came a-knocking. He required hard evidence. Indisputable evidence. Anything substantial that might support his wild claims.

He looked out again. That metaphorical, transitory window had closed. The park was dark, empty and silent, on the edge of night. The squally winds continued to sweep the land, more rain and gales expected later.

He was now reduced to stopping the MacMen all by his lonesome, whether by hook or crook. He now made it his mission for he had an axe to grind. And it took several hours of intense, painstaking brainstorming for Johnny Harding to come up with the ghost of a plan.

5

The plan Johnny Harding devised was at least partway workable. The gist of it was to draw media attention to Seraphim Park and make the MacMen think they were being watched and that the authorities were on to their game. In essence, call their bluff.

Not the most ingenious of plans, granted, but one that at the very least deserved a try.

The next day, as mid-afternoon approached, Harding got his plan into action. BBC News 24 provided the background noise, bringing a welcome wealth of calmness to the growing apprehension he felt. He sat by the window in grim anticipation, waiting for the right moment, the coming of twilight when the MacMen would reveal themselves to him in that short-lived reality breach. The low whine of the November wind outside caused him to shiver despite the closed windows and the full, prevailing warmth of the radiator. Harding didn't have to wait for long because, as half-three came round, he spotted the MacMen materializing all over the park.

There they are . . . the MacMen, doing their thing. Torturing the few lingering park visitors in the name of science.

Back to feeding the swans, Fats Solomon appeared to have ballooned considerably, almost into a human blob. The MacMan standing over his shoulder continued to pump shiny liquid through the umbilicus attached to his belly. The strain showed in Fats Solomon's expression as he piled on the stones and acquired new folds of flab. Soon, he would not be able to walk and the risk of organ failure would turn into a foregone conclusion. Handsome Guy looked worse than ever: unkempt, unshaven with dark arcs under his eyes that betrayed many sleepless nights. As he limped his way down the footpath, a neural syringe sticking out from the back of his neck, Harding saw the wild look on his face. It bespoke madness, the deranged, wearied look of someone who has come to the end of the road. Tonight, Harding suspected, Handsome Guy would fashion a noose and hang himself. Instead of seeking medical attention or sustenance at the soup kitchen, Billy the Tramp was curled up on a park bench, the MacMan beside him fiddling around with his array of skull-burrowing needles. Every so often, Billy's body would physically shake and seize, more out of tumour-focused epileptic activity rather than from the cold weather. Jogging Girl stopped running and doubled over, clutching her stomach. Her womb glowed as red as a stop-light. She touched the crotch of her jogging bottoms and discovered it was stained with blood. She realized for the first time not only was she pregnant, but she was also in the process of miscarrying.

About time he executed his plan, Harding decided. *Should be enough to ruffle their feathers. Maybe even bring them out into the light. Must do it before school closes and the MacMen start targeting the kids.*

Harding picked up his mobile and dialled the number for the Emergency Services. He demanded Police, Fire and Ambulance. He informed the operator there was a bomb in the park, set to go off in the next hour. When asked how he knew, he hung up.

Within five minutes came the sound of wailing sirens, growing louder and nearer. Seconds later, a series of police cars, a couple of ambulances and a single fire engine came to a screaming halt on the street outside the park entrance. A police van soon joined them—Bomb Squad, guessed Harding. Policemen flooded the park, escorting out the visitors and cordoning off the entrance. Harding was pleased to see Jogging Girl, Handsome Guy, Fats Solomon and Billy the Tramp tended to by the paramedics. *Look after them well. They've been through hell. I just hope they can recover from the physical abuse their bodies have suffered at the hands of the MacMen.*

The outside world was a sensory overload of flashing blue lights and blaring sirens and multiple human voices. A crowd of curious onlookers, including many excited schoolchildren, had gathered on the fringes of the suspected crime scene, held back by several police officers. The sight of all those people reminded Harding of that grungy Foo Fighters' cover of Numan's *Down in the Park*. Strong gusts of wind battered the trees and spectators alike, the breath of winter in its throat. Dusk steadily crawled towards night.

But what of the unearthly MacMen? How were they responding to this interruption in their scientific project?

Harding could see them with his hawk's-eye view of the park. Invisible to the humans and impervious to touch, the MacMen were dotted around Seraphim Park and looked far from impassive; in fact, they seemed positively bemused, watching the organized scurry of police activity around them. Then, one by one, as if feeling threatened, they began to vanish. Harding saw them each dial a small box they were carrying and simply vanish. Their ability to appear and disappear at will never ceased to amaze him.

Except for one particular MacMan who stood motionless by the red telephone box to one side of the park entrance, avoiding the heavy police presence.

Yes, YOU...! challenged Harding. *Have a good long look! We're on to you! Not joining your mates, hey? Why don't you just piss off back to whatever place you came from?*

Down in Seraphim Park, the single remaining MacMan glanced

up. Removed his sunglasses and glanced straight up at Harding's apartment, even though the ex-Army man was sitting in near-darkness. Met Harding's gaze directly, fixed him with a cold accusing stare . . .

For an endless moment Harding could not move, could not breathe, dread of the utmost racing through his body. He could hear a loud hammering sound, realizing seconds later it was his beating heart. Then, using all his inner strength, he ripped his eyes away from the hypnotic stare of the MacMan and wheeled himself back into the sanctuary of his gloomy, unlit apartment.

He saw me, panicked Harding. *How the* hell *can he see me?*

Keep it together, Corporal! the other, more rational part of him contested. *You're mistaken. You only* think *he saw you, but it's merely your imagination getting the better of you.*

Taking a minute to compose him, Harding peeked out from behind the curtain, slowly, cautiously, fearfully.

The MacMan was still staring up at him.

Then, the MacMan dialled up his teleportation device and blinked out of reality.

Knowing precisely where the MacMan was heading, Johnny Harding swivelled his wheelchair round and turned on the desk-lamp.

6

The MacMan did not disappoint.

Harding heard an ominous noise—a high, kinetic *zip!*—and a dark human shape appeared in the middle of the lounge. The image was initially unclear, obscure, like looking through frosted glass. The figure fiddled with the hand-held teleporter, and the shadowy manifestation rippled, gained definition and clarity, gradually came into sharp focus, became more substantial, more real, more *there*.

There stood the MacMan, trenchcoated, enormous and lanky, his trilby-bearing head nearly touching the ceiling. For the first time, Harding was able to study the MacMan close up. The face possessed a deathly pallor, an almost albino, vampiric quality. His sharp features for some reason were vaguely reminiscent of Richard O'Brien of *Rocky Horror* fame. But it was the eyes that sent a stab of fear through Harding. With no sunglasses to conceal them, the eyes could have belonged to a blind man, except for the unnatural pink irises that surrounded black pinpoint pupils.

The MacMan tried to speak, but no sound emerged. Realizing he still occupied a different frequency, he turned the dial of the device he held. Shimmering briefly, he now stepped out of his own reality into the reality Harding knew. Acquiring a physical presence, he brought with him a blast of cold, Arctic air.

Pain suddenly flared out from the metal plate in Harding's forehead, presumably due to the claustrophobic nearness of the MacMan. Wincing, Harding uttered the first thing that came to mind. "What's up?"

Huge and gangling, the MacMan loomed over him like a demigod. "You have been spying on us."

He had a good command of the English language, though his voice was odd, tonal, full of clicks and grunts, as alien as those pink eyes. Harding struggled to maintain his composure. "What if I have?"

"We know you have been watching us for some time."

The revelation caused a momentary chill. Harding quickly steadied himself. "So can I assume you're from outer space?"

"From a galaxy your astronomers call the Andromedus cluster."

"What brings you to Earth?"

The MacMan went on to explain, "We have been visiting your world for many centuries now, watching its inhabitants evolve and advance. You are still a primitive race based around an industrialized society, but sturdy, resilient creatures . . . perfect material for experimentation." He soon disclosed a statement of fact Harding had already considered but dismissed as over-the-top. "The bubonic plague, the Ebola virus, the AIDS epidemic, SARS—that was *us*. We hope to apply the principles of our extensive research into disease processes and find a nostrum for our own ailing civilization. We already have the ability to cure every disease on Earth . . ."

"But you *won't* . . ." Harding finished the sentence for him.

"No, our research on the human subjects is more important us."

"I don't understand you. Why roam around the park in the cold and the wet? Why not abduct those people and take them up to your Mother Ship to carry out whatever experiments you fancy?"

"We do not wish to bias our experiment. We prefer to observe the effects of disease on your species in its natural habitat to the absolute limit your physiological systems can withstand."

Natural habitat? thought Harding. *As if we're just expendable animals for biological testing.* "What you're doing to my people is unacceptable," he said, pledging not to feel intimidated. "I can't allow you to continue."

"Interfering with our plans will only bring about your destruction."

"Are you threatening me?" Harding demanded, defiant. "I don't take kindly to threats."

"If we are forced to prematurely terminate our experiment," the MacMan intoned in a series of vocal clicks, "the protocol of our scientific council dictates we must release a plague of engineered nanoparticles and eradicate all life on this planet."

Harding deliberated over the apocalyptic ultimatum. His head throbbed. It seemed the MacMan was well past negotiation. He realized the fate of all Mankind rested in his hands. He reached into the back of his pants. "You arrogant bastard!" he snarled angrily. "I'm asking you one last time to leave our world!" He pulled out his gun, a keepsake from his days of soldiering, training it on the towering MacMan.

Another icy blast of air radiated outwards from the MacMan. "Your attempts to frighten me will not work."

"L9A1 Browning Hi-Power, .9mm semi-automatic. Robust and reliable, particularly when its owner is a superior shot. Like me . . ."

The MacMan glared fiercely at him. "You have no idea how far up our work extends." He pointed a long, crooked finger at the television set. "Behold and tremble."

His attention drawn to the TV screen, Harding froze, his jaw dropping open. In a live broadcast, the British Prime Minister was addressing the nation. He stood outside 10, Downing Street, warning of the growing epidemic of Swine 'Flu. Except there was a MacMan (only Harding could see) standing to the left of the PM, attaching a sophisticated pacemaker-shaped device to the pocket of his shirt, designed (Harding assumed) to test the limits of cardiac function by bringing about palpitations and other cardiac-related stresses, conveniently leading, one day, to a fatal heart attack. It explained why the PM had been feeling under the weather lately. The MacMen were part of a reality the rest of the world was oblivious to. *The MacMen aren't exclusive to the park,* Harding thought in nauseous dismay. *They're everywh—*

The distraction proved untimely and costly. The giant MacMan swooped down and batted the gun away from Harding's startled grasp. It went clattering across the floor, coming to rest beneath the radiator.

But Harding was a man of action, a seasoned veteran of the Gulf War. He had faced so many dangers on his tours of duty, fought on the side of democracy and freedom, even if his politicians sought only to get their grubby hands on the oil. He would not forget that black day when the landmine blew off his legs, leaving those two charred, smoking stumps, his nostrils assailed by the acrid, disgusting stench of explosive and his own burning flesh. Most people would have folded under the shock, never recovered, but not Harding. In spite of his obvious physical impairment, Harding had worked through the memory of his spirit-crushing ordeal with a determination praised by his superiors, emerging out the other end a stronger person. He never forgot those long, gruelling months of rigorous training as a young cadet, a combination of sharp-shooting, endurance and survival training he would build on and perfect throughout his military career and implement on the battlefield. Once a soldier, always a soldier, as the saying went. And, of course, Jenny the Physiotherapist had, following his honourable discharge from service, helped him maintain his physical fitness with whatever was left of him.

Using the power of his buttocks, Harding propelled himself out of his wheelchair. He cushioned the fall with his hands and crawled like a seal across the floor with a courage and determination reserved for military heroes. He was on to the fallen gun like a shot. As his fingers clasped round the butt of the Browning, the MacMan, who had momentarily been taken off-guard by Harding's lightning speed, stepped forward and crushed his heel on Harding's wrist. Harding yelped in pain as he heard the bones crunch. Harding reacted spectacularly. He swung the entire weight of his body in a perfect arc, forcefully catching the back of the MacMan's legs. Unbalanced, offering a look of surprise, the MacMan fell backwards, hitting the floor with a hard thud. His trilby slipped off his head, and Harding recoiled in repulsed horror not at the bald, shiny cranium but the third pink eye staring out from the forehead. The shock evaporated quickly, and Harding picked up his gun with his other hand, aiming it at the MacMan. "You can't keep a good dog down," he gasped, sweating like a pig. "You might be assessing human endurance with your sick experiments, but you will never be able to crush the human spirit."

"You are making a terrible mistake," the MacMan warned, propping himself up on his elbows. "Do not risk your life and the lives of your people."

"I think I'll take my chances," replied Harding, still reeling at the MacMan's physiognomy. If there was ever proof that the MacMen were alien in nature, here it was in the shape of those three blinking eyes . . .

"If you let me go, we will not use you as a test subject," the MacMan bargained, his click-laden, droning voice hiding a sinister edge. He probably wasn't thrilled he'd been bested by a member of the 'primitive race' he'd been sent here to study.

"You're not using anyone as a test subject!" repeated Harding firmly. "You're getting back in your spaceship and travelling back to wherever you came from!"

But the MacMan was biding his time, and Harding knew it. "One man alone cannot order around an entire fleet of super-scientists."

"You're not hearing me—"

And that was when all hell broke loose as the MacMan, still supine, revealed the ace up his sleeve. He jerked out what appeared to be a raygun from the pocket of his trenchcoat and fired. If he had been a more accurate marksman, Harding would have been playing harps with the angels. Instead, the bright, spinning laser-bolt whizzed past Harding's head, singeing hair, and struck the desk lamp, vaporizing it on contact. The room was plunged into darkness, save for the steady glow of the fourteen-inch television screen. As the MacMan tried a second time with the matter disintegrator, Harding fired his own more down-to-earth weapon. In a loud, echoing blast, the bullet from his gun ripped through the third eye of the MacMan, spraying the surrounding area with a starburst of pink, incandescent jelly. The MacMan keeled backwards, his head slamming the floor, motionless, hopefully dead.

The moment Harding ditched his gun, the door to his apartment came crashing down, and several figures, some wearing police uniforms, others dressed in military gear, rushed in. They gave the dead MacMan a wide berth, going straight for Harding. A lab-coated technician injected Harding in the arm before he could resist.

Harding instantly experienced a sense of dislocation. "What are you do—?"

"So you're the fellow who called in the bomb threat?" said one of the more senior police officers. The badge on his hat and the stripes and decorations on his uniform suggested he was the Superintendent.

"Don't you see?" Harding mumbled, the effects of the drug taking over his system. He pointed shakily to the giant, still shape on the floor, fully-exposed to reality, runnels of neon-pink fluid flowing from the gaping wound in the forehead.

"We see, all right," the police superintendent replied. "*You just killed Dr. Kirchner.*"

The news produced a small, troubled frown. "It can't be . . ." As the tranquilizer continued to overpower his senses, Harding saw the dead figure on the floor wasn't a MacMan at all but none-other-than Dr. Kirchner, grey hair in disarray, horn-rimmed spectacles askew, blood pooling around his head from the bullet-wound in his shattered skull. Bleeding ordinary, fresh, claret-coloured blood.

A man with a bristly white moustache and smart military uniform stepped forward. "Remember me, son?"

Harding recognized him at once. "Brigadier . . .?" He tried to salute, failed, began to giggle.

"Listen carefully, son," Brigadier Letwin-Smith explained, "we think you've suffered a psychotic break. We're taking you to a safe place where we can look after you."

But Harding heard his former superior's voice from somewhere faraway. He wasn't even sure if he was still in the real world any more. This stuff they'd injected him with was so much more relaxing than any of the morphine tablets he consumed. "Do with me as you will . . ." he murmured, giggling, his vision growing dim, his eyelids heavy. No longer able to stay awake, Harding slumped across the foot-rests of his wheelchair, unconscious but evidently breathing.

7

The following few days were a bit of a blur. Heavily sedated, Johnny Harding drifted in and out of consciousness as though in the grip of a delirium. He vaguely remembered getting injected, the periodic stinging sensation of a needle in his arm. He didn't mind; he was swaddled in bright, wonderful layers of narcotic dreams. He dreamed of surgeons operating on his missing legs. He dreamed about Seraphim Park, of a bright saucer-shaped light emerging from the lake, hovering up to the night sky and flying off beyond the clouds. He dreamed of Jenny the Physiotherapist bending down and kissing him passionately on the lips as he lay on the exercise table.

When he finally awoke, Brigadier Letwin-Smith was looking down at him in fatherly fashion. "How do you feel, son?" he asked. "Not too great," Harding replied, groggily. His mouth felt dry, his tongue as rough as sandpaper. The words came out clumsy and awkward. "Wh-where am I?"

"Military hospital," said the Brigadier. "You've been here five days. We had to bring you here until the furore died down."

Harding realized he was lying in a hospital bed, the room around him white-walled, clinical, air-conditioned. He spotted the pretty-looking nurse standing behind the Brigadier, making a note on the patient's flipchart. "Furore?"

"Yes," the Brigadier reminded him, "you killed a very important and distinguished member of the medical establishment. The Press are baying for your blood. Quite the pickle you've found yourself in."

Harding recalled the crumpled, pitiful form of Dr. Kirchner lying on the floor of the flat, a bullet through his head. *Did I do that?* "What about the MacMen?"

"Yes, of course, the fabled MacMen," mused the Brigadier. "*That* will be our defence. Our lawyers will handle the case and should get you off on diminished responsibilities by virtue that you were severely mentally impaired at the time of the incident."

"I know what I saw," insisted Harding.

"Perhaps . . . But we'll talk about it later . . . You need your rest...We want you sufficiently recovered to provide a statement." The Brigadier headed for the door, pausing to tell Harding, "By the way, there're some people here to see you . . ." Informing Harding she would be bringing him lunch, the nurse followed the Brigadier out the door.

Harding was suddenly alone with his thoughts. Five days, the Brigadier had said. Harding had been in hospital five days. Time enough, he supposed, to reflect on the staggering events that brought him into hospital. Could it actually be that, as the Brigadier claimed, Harding had lost his grip on reality and done the unthinkable? What if years of loneliness had finally driven him insane?

I know what I saw, his mind reiterated.

Really? his rational self argued. *Sitting in your usual place, day after day, staring out the window, dreaming up crazy stories of alien conspiracies and even crazier experiments. You sure you didn't imagine the whole thing?*

"Maybe, I did," Harding muttered to himself, resignedly, laying his head back down on the pillow. "But the Court will rule if I am, indeed, criminally insane. Having done so much time in hospital when I lost my legs, it won't matter if I do some more . . ."

Imagination . . . its limits are only those of the mind itself, as Rod Serling, creator of The Twilight Zone, *once declared.*

The door opened and the visitors the Brigadier had spoken of entered the room. Harding watched the two of them silently cross the room and take up positions on either side of his bed. They stooped a fraction to avoid the ceiling. The chill of winter accompanied them.

Harding suddenly didn't feel very well. His heart instantly leapt up into his throat and his skin broke out in a cold sweat. Pain exploded in his head. The glue holding his mind together began to slowly separate.

"Hello, Corporal Harding," said the MacMan on the right.

"What do you want with me?" Harding murmured, inexpressibly afraid.

"You caused an interplanetary incident," spoke the second MacMan, a perfect clone of the first, his words interspersed with glottal clicks.

"Very unfortunate," opined the first MacMan gravely.

"You're all ours now to do as we wish," said the other. "We mean to take good care of you."

"Nurse! *Nurse!*" Harding began to yell, at the same time frantically thumbing the red button for nursing assistance.

But no-one responded.

"We even gave you new legs," intimated the first MacMan, not without a noticeable, stomach-turning degree of glee and pride. "Various accounts, apocryphal or otherwise, speak of the third-century Saints Cosmas and Damian who miraculously replaced the gangrenous leg of a Roman deacon with the leg of a dead, black Moor. Your medical archives mentioned a Russian scientist called Dr. Vladimir Demikhov, who transplanted the head of a one-month-old puppy onto the shoulders of a German Shepherd in 1959. The puppy's head remained fully viable for eight hours. Dr. Robert White, an American neurosurgeon from Case Western University, conducted similar head transplant procedures with monkeys in the early 1970s, the attached monkey's head surviving two whole days before suffering the effects of tissue rejection. So we operated on your legs." He whipped off the bedsheets. Harding was met with the sight of an anatomical nightmare. Sure enough, he possessed lower limbs again, but they belonged to another creature altogether. Sewn to his stumps were the pale, writhing, sucker-cupped tentacles of a giant octopus. "We hope you like them."

Staring down at those sickening Frankenstein legs, Harding's mind finally ruptured. He started to scream hysterically. He screamed and screamed like a madwoman possessed, but none of the hospital staff heard him or came to his rescue . . . or, like the white elephant, they chose not to.

October 2009—January 2010

The Litter Patrol

"Adapt or perish, now as ever, is nature's inexorable imperative."
Mind at the End of its Tether (1945)
H.G.Wells

Litter, or garbage, or some call it trash. Same difference. Land pollution at its most elementary level, waste-material adulteration of a world that gave us life and sustenance.

When we consider that the average family produces up to one-and-a-half tonnes of rubbish every year, imagine what would happen if there were no-one to collect our garbage. Society would effectively become a stinking, decaying hell. Fortunately, in the industrialized world, we have the small but indispensable luxury of refuse collectors and dump custodians who, although professionally frowned upon, do our communities a great service with their sewage works, landfills and junkyards. Then we have the ecologists and conservationalists who, despite being viewed as tree-hugging fanatics or rich, crazy liberal outcasts, keep us aware of our environmental blues.

Since the smog-choked Industrial Revolution of the eighteenth and nineteenth centuries, we have despoiled our land, sky and sea shamelessly and we leave a grim legacy for our future generations. From the horrors of DDT to the radioactive disaster at Chernobyl, from the depletion of the Ozone Layer to the deforestation of the Amazon basin, and as we stand on the cusp of a runaway Greenhouse Effect venting its rage through El Niño and the freak weather events around the globe, our ecosystems are dying and we must all be held accountable. Something must be done . . . and *fast*.

But, in Woods End, something had already been done about the issue of mass litter. The people of this sleepy community had discovered an ingenious and terrifying way of dealing with this problem. It was called the Litter Patrol, unleashed whenever Mankind sinned against Mother Nature.

Because whoever met the Litter Patrol never went home . . .

Stepping off the train at Woods End, Percy Heaton took in the sweet breath of the countryside.

It had been a pleasant, uneventful journey from Oaks Fold— Percy hadn't seen so much greenery since visiting Dublin two years ago.

It might be a little out of the way, he contemplated cheerily, *but it's certainly worth the price of a ticket.*

He had passed so many fields and meadows and tracts of woodland that he thought he had been transported back to the Days of Yore.

Percy walked up the near-deserted platform, through the archway marked EXIT and found himself on the road outside the train station.

Now, how do I get to Leanne's? Percy delved into his pockets but could not find the piece of paper on which he had scribbled down the route. He searched his person for the best part of a minute and eventually gave up. *I should have bought an A-to-Z. I guess I'd better ask someone for directions.*

The morning was bright and sunny and perfect for a walk. The Indian summer was over, according to the weathercasters, but Percy wasn't so sure. Autumn may have officially begun, but summer was intent on making one last comeback.

He ambled down the stone-bordered country road, listening to the agreeable chirruping of blue tits and katydids in the enchanting oaks and elms and silver birches. Individual driveways led up to half-glimpsed cottages. He passed a road sign:

WELCOME TO WOODS END
VOTED THE CLEANEST VILLAGE IN THE COUNTRY

"Good for you," said Percy to no-one in particular. "I could live here—"

He came across another sign:

PLEASE KEEP WOODS END TIDY
LITTERERS WILL BE PUT DOWN

—*Or maybe not* . . . he puzzled, finishing the thought. He found it an odd turn-of-phrase. It didn't read *Litterers Will Be Prosecuted* or *Punished* or *Put Away* as it should have said, but *Litterers Will Be Put Down* . . . *Put* Down?

He thought of an old, incontinent dog taken out to the shed and shot and felt a cold tingling up his spine. *Must be a misprint? As radical as chopping off the hands of thieves like they sometimes do in the oil-rich regions of the Middle East.*

And as he walked on, he encountered yet another sign:

NO LITTER!

"No kidding!" he murmured at the menacing impact of this inarguable imperative. "They seem obsessive about town cleanliness."

He had been walking for, perhaps, twenty minutes when the houses on either side, mostly traditional semis, became dominant, and five minutes further on, he reached the village high street with its post office and library and shops and banks. And thought no more of the series of litter-admonishing signs he had witnessed.

The shop-door bell tinkled as Percy Heaton entered WILFRED'S NEWS & MART.

Business was slow, the aisles well-stocked. A white-haired, old man with rimless glasses stood behind the counter, chatting away contentedly to a blond, good-looking gentleman. The Beta Band performed *Dry the Rain* on the radio.

Percy approached the two men, cutting into their conversation. "I wonder if you could help me. I'm looking for Percheron Avenue." The shopkeeper did a quick, discreet appraisal of the newcomer. "Percheron Avenue? New here, are you?"

"How did you guess?" said Percy affably.

"Woods End's a small place. Everyone knows everyone around these parts. Here on business or pleasure?"

"Actually, I'm visiting my sister. I thought I'd grace her with my presence. I suppose that's what Sundays are for."

"Do I know her?"

"I wouldn't think so. Leanne moved down here recently with her husband, Macaulay."

A ray of recognition filled the shopkeeper's eyes, as deepest green as those of his very blond friend. "Macaulay Crawford?"

"Yes, that's right!" Percy acknowledged, a little excitedly.

"Macaulay comes in here often," the shopkeeper told him. "Nice fellow."

"I guess so."

The shopkeeper introduced himself, "The name's Wilfred Soames," and, gesturing to his hunky friend, added, "and this here troublemaker is Rick Henderson."

"Percy Heaton. Pleased to meet you." Percy shook hands with them and, for the first time, noticed the slogans on their T-shirts. Wilfred's read: MAN IS NATURE'S SOLE MISTAKE, a direct quote from a play by W.S. Gilbert. Rick's was more interesting and almost impossible to get one's head around: SAVE WATER. DILUTE IT.

Percy decided against pointing out the absurdity of Rick's motto. One step crazier than the tongue-twister he read somewhere: *It's only an illusion that the solution to pollution is dilution.* Percy thought Rick looked like someone who might be affiliated with Friends of the Earth, the kind of guy who seemed equally at home swimming with dolphins or orchestrating violent protests at the G8 summit. And, on that note, Wilfred's ponytail and goatee suggested he might also have served as an eco-warrior in his salad days. Yes, Percy speculated, amused, he was surely confronting a pair of tree-huggers.

[*And those eyes, those bewitching green eyes . . . Are the two of them possibly related?*]

"Turn right out the shop," explained Wilfred, "right again at the lights, straight on for two hundred yards, turn left by the off-licence, up Hedge End Road, third exit down and you're on Percheron Avenue."

"I'm extreme grateful," Percy said sincerely. Then, something occurred to him. "Oh, and before I forget . . . a packet of ten Silk Cut, please?"

An awkward silence followed. Wilfred's forehead wrinkled with a mixture of surprise and alarm, as though Percy had propositioned him for a bag of heroin. He and his blond-haired friend exchanged furtive glances. When he spoke again, the good humour was gone from his voice. "Ten Silk Cut, is it?"

Sensing their disappointment and implicit disapproval, Percy felt he should justify his request. "My last and only vice, Scout's honour!"

"That so?" The shopkeeper picked out the specified brand of cigarettes from the rack behind and handed them to Percy. "You do realize cigarettes are hazardous to the environment. Unlike what you might have heard, the filter is non-biodegradable. Cigarette filters have been found inside trout, pigeons and foxes, who have unfortunately mistaken them for food."

Percy tried to smile, suddenly filled with guilt, not caring for the lecture.

Wilfred brought the conversation to an abrupt end. "Your custom is much appreciated, sir. Please call again."

But Percy knew, from the hardness in his tone, Wilfred didn't mean one word. The old man probably didn't give a damn if he ever clapped eyes on Percy again—probably hoped he never would.

Bewildered, feeling like a pariah, Percy paid for his goods and from the newsagents beat a hasty retreat.

*****

What was all that about? puzzled Percy. *It's not as if I'm going to pass the cigarettes on to some schoolkids.*

Outside, traffic was sparse and there were very few people on the street.

Percy walked up the High Street, glancing occasionally into the shop windows. He retrieved his newly-purchased pack of cigarettes from his jacket pocket and removed the cellophane wrapping. This he scrunched up in his hand and, through force of habit, dropped it on the pavement.

[*Awaken, spirit of the earth!*]

He proceeded to pull out a cigarette, attaching it to the corner of his mouth in a deliberately rakish manner. Lighting up the end with a match, which again he deposited on the ground without thinking, Percy inhaled deeply. The headrush was almost instantaneous. He walked on, enjoying the aromatic taste of the tobacco and the sweet lightheadedness the nicotine produced.

Filthy habit, he thought gaily, *but, boy, does it feel good! The secret with these little carbon footprints is not to smoke your lungs out and chase an addiction but to take a puff once in a while, as God intended. Leanne might give me an earful later, but she knows I only very* seldomly *dabble in the evil weed.*

Percy came to a set of traffic lights, a clothing store on the corner. He took a right, as instructed.

I should have got me a Sunday paper, he thought, tempted to go back to the newsagents and catch the latest on the ever-declining fortunes of the government. New Labour were on the verge of coming to power, the upshot of the public's overwhelming condemnation of the countless scandals and inexcusable mismanagement of the country under the Tories. However, after a moment's deliberation, Percy decided against buying a newspaper. *Leanne'll keep me occupied, I'm sure.*

He was suddenly jolted from his reverie by the worryingly-near barking of a dog. Behind him, a trim, athletic-type woman [*with eyes of emerald-green*] was trying to keep her Great Dane, normally a majestic, docile breed, in check. It was tugging fiercely at the leash, teeth bared into a snarl, a look of vicious hatred in its eyes. Percy was almost certain it would break free and attack him.

"Sorry about this," the woman said to Percy above the racket.

"No need for apologies," Percy reassured her, trying not to betray his discomfiture.

"Don't bother the poor man, Duke," she told her canine friend. "The mark is upon him."

The dog stopped barking, and with a cursory farewell, the woman and her Great Dane walked away.

Percy watched them disappear around the corner, mystified.

What a peculiar thing to say! The mark is upon him? Words, he considered, that would not entirely be out of place in the Middle Ages. And the dog had responded as if it understood what she meant. *Does she think I've got the plague or something? Or I'm—*

[cursed . . .]

He didn't want to think it, but it just popped into his head like a polished gem. He laughed at the ridiculousness of the idea, but it was a nervous, humourless laugh.

Percy took another drag from his cigarette and went on his merry way, past a row of shops. Outside the entrance to the park, on the opposite side of the street, hung a small group of teenage boys, carrying skateboards. They couldn't have been more than twelve years of age. They were pointing at him and sniggering, derision in their

[GREEN!?!] eyes.

Appalled by their rudeness, he had a good mind to cross the street and ask them what they found so funny.

Meaning for Percy to see him, one of them ran a finger across his throat in a quick, switchblade motion. Another boy bent his neck to one side and tugged at an invisible noose in an unmistakable hangman's gesture. The third boy recited, "The folly of the outlander shall bring/The dreaded wrath of the Copro-King!" Thereupon, the trio burst into maniacal laughter.

Their sinister performances caused Percy to shudder. Not one for confrontations, he decided not to get involved. The thought of seeing his sister kept him moving. All of a sudden, he didn't feel so great.

The dog spooked me out, and now these scallywags. A good hiding is what they deserve, and a good hiding is what their parents should administer. Maybe they just don't like strangers around here.

Except Percy could not escape the disquieting feeling in the pit of his stomach. The very name, the Copro-King, brought up hideous connotations of demon-raising sacrifices made at pagan altars, of hoary, baby-snatching druidesses dancing naked inside a stone circle during the summer solstice, of an unclean god sitting on a throne of skulls, planning the end of civilization.

Percy completed the last drag and dropped the cigarette-butt on the ground, crushing it underfoot. He carried on ahead, blissfully unaware that somewhere in Woods End the Litter Patrol stirred.

Percy Heaton hadn't gone far when he realized he was being watched. He was perturbed to discover vague, dark shapes behind the veiled curtains along almost every house, not-so-secretly watching his progress.

I bet they don't get many outsiders here. And what were the chances that all these people possessed green eyes?

[everybody knows everybody around these parts]

The sky clouded over. Thunder rumbled.

My God, I've stepped into The Twilight Zone . . .

But the sense of being observed by the inhabitants of this street did not compare to the mounting feeling that something else, something significantly more sinister was keeping tabs on him, maybe even following him. He heard a cruel chuckling, not from the jeering skateboarders he had passed, but from somewhere beneath the ground.

A sharp chill accessed his bones, and his heartbeat cranked up a notch.

The sound had come from the gutter—Percy was sure of it—and he suddenly considered it essential to his very survival that he should take the situation more seriously. His world changed in a single mental newsflash. He began to jog, to run, but the wicked, ugly tittering gave chase, growing louder, closer.

Percy picked up his pace, starting to panic.

The hellish titterings, now swelling into a harsh minatorial growling, matched his pace.

Soon, he was running full-pelt, trying to get away from the thing that dwelled in the sewers.

He shouted for help a dozen times, but the street appeared eerily deserted. Or, in all likelihood, nobody was prepared to help him.

From the houses, half-seen shadows watched his plight. Thunder expressed its choler in the overcast sky. A high, fulsome odour of putrescence assailed his nostrils.

What the hell is down there? And why does it want me?

The sky already looked in danger of falling. Literally terrified the earth would swallow him up, Percy pushed his legs harder.

He came to another landmark the newsagent had promised, an off-licence curiously called WILFRED'S FOOD & WINE.

Percy dashed into the store, hoping for a moment's respite. "Please, you've got to help me!" he cried shrilly, quaking with fear. "There's something after me! *Call the police!*"

He stopped in his tracks when he saw who sat behind the counter. "The police won't help you now," replied Wilfred Soames, clean out of sympathy. "You wronged Nature and you must be made accountable for your actions."

"*How did you get here so fast?*" Percy asked, blinking, utterly confused.

"You broke the laws of our village," said a certain blond-haired male customer. "Now the Litter Patrol will not stop until it has hunted you down."

"Why me?" Percy demanded distractedly. "What could I have possibly done?"

Rick Henderson spelled it out. "*Litter.* You dropped litter on the ground. More than once."

"Litter? What litter?" Comprehension suddenly dawned: the cellophane when he had first opened his pack of cigarettes, the match to light his cigarette, then the cigarette-butt which he extinguished on the pavement. *Strike three!* "But how can it be a crime?"

"Contaminating the environment is a capital offence here," Rick answered calmly.

"What if I go back and pick up my rubbish?" Percy bargained.

"You missed the bus on that one, pal," Wilfred remarked indifferently.

Percy's heart sank into a quagmire of despair. *"There must be something I can do!"* he implored. "It was an *accident!*"

"Ignorance is not an excuse," said Rick flatly, "Go out there and face the music. The life you once knew is over."

Desperation turned to anger. "This is *insane! It's only LITTER!*"

"Still the outlander doesn't see the severity of his blasphemy against Nature," Wilfred told Rick with a note of sadness. "Isn't that tragic?"

Percy could take their brand of patronizing religion no more. *"Go, stuff your laws!"* he yelled, incensed, and, shooting past the shelves of liquor, fled the off-licence. Outside, he checked his bearings.

Left at the off-licence—wasn't that what Wilfred, the earlier Wilfred, advised?

Sure enough, he saw Hedge End Road.

He had to get to Leanne's house. Leanne was a rock. She would know what to do.

The Litter Patrol was definitely near because the air reeked of putrid, rotting waste.

Percy got moving again, carried by a sense of urgency, determined to outrun the underground horror that had set its sights on his destruction.

He ran like the wind, ran like he hadn't run since he was in school, almost two decades ago.

He had expected the Litter Patrol to consist of a single, dim, officious Environmental Inspector, punishing the litterer with a small, on-the-spot fine . . . and not whatever lurked and flowed and seethed beneath the village, snatching up passersby unfamiliar with the code of the countryside.

This can't be happening . . .

Overhead, thunder pealed in a darkened sky, full of menace, demanding rain. But it would not rain, as though the stormclouds were saving their burden of water for later.

Behind him, the ground shook with the passage of the Litter Patrol.

This can't be happening . . . this can't be happening . . . this can't be happening . . . Percy repeated over and over in his mind like a mantra.

Hot on his tail, the Litter Patrol muttered and growled and shrieked like the voices of a thousand lost souls.

Percy took the third exit, as advised earlier . . . and found himself on Percheron Avenue.

Not far now . . .

He crossed the street, siding with the odd numbers. He staggered past the residences, searching for his destination.

The Litter Patrol pursued him with single-minded purpose, unmerciful and relentless and unstoppable. And, in the background, the dry storm raged. Then, before he knew it, Percy finally arrived at 73, Percheron Avenue, an elegant white bungalow. He stumbled on the short driveway, spilling to the ground. Exhausted, his legs felt like lead balloons, his heart pounded like a wrecker's ball in his chest and he thought he tasted blood in his mouth.

The stench grew thicker and unbearable as the Litter Patrol bore down on him.

From the storm-drains emerged a cluster of dark, glistening, squirming tentacles, rows of yawping-and-puckering, flamingo-pink suckers on the underside, a rolling green octopus-eye embedded into each tip. Smoky at first, almost spectral, but presently beginning to take on substance, a physicality. Percy daren't imagine the enormity of the size of the entire creature lurking within the dank sewers of the town.

The pulsing, blinking tentacles, now fully-realized and substantial, slithered towards him, questing for his legs.

One particular tentacle managed to wrap itself around his ankle with the convulsive death-grip of an anaconda. Its chain of pinkish sucker-mouths began to clench, chew, *eat* away through his trousers, their corrosive saliva burning into the flesh beneath. Disgusted and panicking, Percy kicked at it hard with his other foot. The heel of his shoe struck its wide, startled eye, which immediately popped, oozing a thick, noisome, yellowish fluid. The execrable, subterranean titan shrieked in infinite pain, an ear-splitting squealing of stressed, twisting metal. The tentacle relinquished its hold and retreated, slipping and sliding and sloshing away aimlessly, hurt, reverting back to its vaporous, incorporeal form, gifting Percy the opportunity to get to his feet.

He limped up the driveway, ignoring his stinging ankle, and started hammering at the door with his fists. *"Let me in! Please, Leanne, let me in!"*

The slither of tentacles surged again with a vengeance, growing tangible in the process, seeking out the exposed, vulnerable, terrified man yelling at the door. They were mere inches away from coiling round and seizing his ankles and wrists and yanking him backwards when the door opened, and Percy barged in. He pulled the figure answering his screams into the bungalow and slammed the door behind him.

Leanne stared at her brother, startled by his half-crazed, dishevelled appearance. "Percy?"

"Whatever you do, don't open the door!" he warned, relieved to see her.

"Why, what's out there?"

"You *really* don't want to know . . ."

"What's going on?" she asked, as concerned and afraid for him as any big sister would be. "What did you do?"

He gave her his best I-screwed-up-so-bad look and memories of them sneaking into a derelict factory as children came flooding back. "Believe me, a minor violation. Now there's something chasing after me. We've got to call the authorities."

"You dropped a cigarette," she reminded him.

A frown furrowed his forehead. "How did you know?" he asked, alarmed, suspicious. He studied her face and recognized what he had found peculiar. "Your eyes . . . What happened to your eyes?"

"You like them?" she said, beaming. "I think their greenness is rather fetching."

"You're *not* my sister," Percy whispered, taking a step back.

"Of course I am, silly," replied Leanne. "Just not the sister you know." She smiled at him again. "Cigarettes aren't exactly ecologically friendly. No-one can go around poisoning the land—certainly not here, at least. We have laws, firm-and-fast laws punishing anyone who transgresses them. There is a great power at work, protecting the planet from those daring to contaminate it. We must all—including you—bow down before this incorruptible force and accept its soul-cleansing benevolence. Only then can we be at one with Nature."

Percy could not hide his incredulity. When had Leanne—shrewd, level-headed Leanne—turned into a world-class loon? Her preaching came off sounding as though she had signed up with some deranged, Nature-worshipping cult. "I'm not bowing down before *anything*!"

She suddenly gave him a dark look, causing him to shiver. "The choice is not yours to make any more. Be reborn and behold the beauty of the world with the Eyes of Nature."

He felt a spectral gust of wind float in through the window as if something invisible had just entered the house. The toilet, visible through the partially-ajar bathroom door, began to rattle, shake. As the lid flew open with an abrupt smack, a brown sludge gushed upwards from the bowl like a geyser, pouring over the brim, splashing on the floor. Percy stared, flabbergasted, as the pool of slime crawled, coalesced, took shape, formed a small dwarfish mound.

The accompanying unholy stench made him think of neglected septic tanks and clogged sewers. He coughed and gagged at the unholy stink, bringing his handkerchief to his face while wishing for his nose to be amputated.

The mound enlarged, soaked up all the muck on the floor, rose to a formidable height, touched the ceiling.

Percy watched, avid with a kind of moronic terror, as before him stood a man-shaped giant composed entirely of the foulest, vilest-smelling goo, a cloud of fat horseflies buzzing indolently around its head. Leanne gazed up at the repulsive, looming monstrosity with a look of high adoration.

Eyes flicked open, shone green, fixed on Percy. "We are the Copro-King," the unspeakable creature declared agelessly and pointed a dripping, gunky finger at Percy. "You are charged with profaning the sanctity of Nature! As Nature's Watcher it falls upon us to sentence *you* to Purification! Any last words?"

Percy hadn't a clue how he should respond to the pronouncement. He had been charged, tried and sentenced in the space of a few seconds. He was struck by an almighty epiphany. "Ironic," he observed starkly, "how *you*, the Copro-King, the metaphysical embodiment of Mankind's crimes against Nature, are, in fact, nothing more than a man of animated shit!"

The dung monster chuckled, a low bubbling sound. Yet Percy detected no malice in that voice. "Excrement is the natural component of composts and fertilizers, the nutriment of Nature."

And that was when things got really messy.

The pendulous head of the Copro-King yawned open into a gaping maw and, arching down, clamped itself like a helmet to Percy's scalp. Percy did not scream—not that he possessed the strength to—for the enormous mouth gobbled him up headfirst, as a snake swallows its prey, enveloping his neck and upper torso in a series of rapacious gulps until the rest of him, too, was consumed. Leanne watched the disgusting spectacle with an expression of weird serenity, contemplating the mechanics of the purification process. She could vaguely see Percy in the brown, bloated, translucent belly of her god, curled up in the foetal position. When the baptism was completed and Percy fully purged, the Copro-King regurgitated him up from its engorged belly in a single, heaving motion. Percy tumbled to the floor with a wet splash. He looked and smelled squeaky-clean as though he had just come out of the shower. Calmly, the Copro-King deflated, shrank, became amorphous, and the living sludge oozed its way back to the bathroom. The trail of sentient goo disappeared down the toilet bowl, leaving the lounge and bathroom clean and Spartan once more and the air as fragrant as a summer meadow. The toilet flushed of its own accord, then a peaceful silence descended.

Leanne crouched down next to Percy and helped him up. She was gratified to see the dazed tranquility in his fresh green eyes. "Now, don't you feel much better?"

Percy Heaton got up from the floor a different person. He ate Sunday lunch with his sister and brother-in-law as though nothing had happened. Thereafter, he returned to Oaks Fold and went about dismantling his former life. In the months that followed he quit his job as a highly-paid actuary and moved to the country, carrying with him a new-found respect for the laws of Nature. He bought a sustainable property and grew his own vegetables. Birdwatching turned into an agreeable pastime. He experimented with solar-panelling and took to driving an electric car. He attended street rallies promoting environmental awareness while condemning industrialized capitalism and made regular contributions to the Global Green Network, spreading the Gaian philosophy—a religion as good as any other—of how our planet was one, vast ecosystem that relied on the interdependence between its diverse species . . . or maybe we were even tighter than that and the Earth actually operated as a single, sophisticated, self-regulating superorganism.

His was a lesson learned and a warning to those who decide to enter Woods End. For whoever encounters the Litter Patrol never goes home . . . unless they behold the beauty of the world with the Eyes of Nature.

June 1997—August 1997

Shades of the Underground

"The whole point of meditating on the ultimate nature of reality is to ensure that you are not fooled by appearances that can often be deluding."

Dalai Lama

"Know what 'snagging' is?" Luke Hembrey asked the lady of the house.

Mrs. Ursula Delacourt responded, "Can't say I do."

"In the building trade," Luke explained concisely, "snagging is when the new builder throws up a fuss over the 'shoddy workmanship' of the previous builder and marks up his quote by twenty-five percent to that of his predecessor's . . ."

"I see . . ."

Luke Hembrey and his potential client stood on the steps of TULPA VILLA in the process of early negotiations. Dusk encroached on the damp November day. "We won't hike up our daily rate," Luke promised. "We'll keep the same quote as the last handymen. I couldn't put it fairer than that."

"I'm ever so grateful," Mrs. Delacourt said sincerely. She invited him in. "Come inside. I'll show you the bathroom." She led him into the rambling, four-bedroom bungalow, out of the wet, and took him to the main bathroom down the hallway. It was a lovely space for whatever work had already been done, ample-sized albeit unfinished. A globe light, made of translucent glass, hung from the industrial-grey ceiling. The floor-tiles imitated a distressed, wood-grain effect. The shower had already been fully-fitted and the modern toilet employed an automatic flush. The Duravit sink rested on a floating vanity unit and, above it, was an oval mirror attached to a string which could turn on the inbuilt, pastel-blue shaving light. Although only partially-complete and nowhere near touching the ceiling yet, as Mrs. Delacourt had previously indicated, the tiles on the walls were the most interesting feature, small, white and oblong, metro-style. "I wanted a London Underground theme for the bathroom."

"I noticed . . ." Luke observed. "Why?"

"It's the latest trend, but there is a lot of history surrounding the London Underground. You should read up on it some time. It might surprise you."

"Will do," promised Luke, adding: "Speaking of trends, this brickwork-type of tiling's been around since the 1900s and gives a very contemporary finish. I also see the grouting is a dark shade of grey."

"Anthracite," Mrs. Delacourt informed him, identifying the exact colour.

Luke hoped she would elaborate on whatever information she had already given him over the phone. "Sounds like the whole thing's been quite a palaver."

Mrs Delacourt nodded, slightly aggrieved. "Indeed. A real snafu. Unnecessary stress, if you ask me." She gave him the backstory, a more comprehensive breakdown of the work already completed. "I think the first lot of handymen, the Tattersalls, husband-and-wife team, did a sterling job to begin with. They stripped the entire bathroom. When they removed the old bathroom fittings, the condition of the walls was shocking. They discovered black mould, along with slugs and snails, across a rotted substructure. You can imagine the horrendous, health-damaging effects of such mould. Removing the old shower unit revealed another horror story: a mud gulley. Thick, black sludge, along with mud, served as the floor beneath the shower tray. The external drains that serviced the bathroom and kitchen had been blocked for a considerable length of time by a root, as evidenced by the swamped garden along with the stench from the drain, which, needless to say, necessitated unblocking before work could commence on the bathroom. The Tattersalls kindly cleaned up the mess and re-plastered the walls, straightening them up so as to accommodate the little tiles. They did the flooring, adjusted the drainage, attached the overhead light fixture, fitted the new shower unit and the toilet, transferred the stopcock from outside, ran the water pipes up to the loft for the convenience of a combi boiler which I plan to put up there. The Tattersalls started off working nine-to-five, all good to begin with, but they gradually shifted their work hours. Soon they were drifting in later and later in the day until they were coming in the afternoon and finishing in the evening."

"That's taking the mick," Luke sympathized, shaking his head.

Mrs. Delacourt continued: "I didn't complain because I didn't want to upset them since I wanted them to take their time over it and do a good job, which I suppose they did in some respects. Bizarrely, though, even if you include the time-consuming care spent on the tiling, it took them eight weeks to do one lousy bathroom."

"Wow!" exclaimed Luke, genuinely astonished. "It would have taken me one week, tops!"

"But do you know what the really odd thing is?" Mrs. Delacourt explained, mystified, "The Tattersalls just disappeared. I never heard from them again. I've tried to reach them, but they remain completely uncontactable. So I stopped chasing them. They still haven't sent me the invoice . . ."

"Yes, I can see how that would be puzzling," Luke admitted, scratching his head. "I call that unprofessionalism."

"The Tattersalls had done most of the work to a reasonably decent standard, mind, but their finishing touches left much to be desired. You didn't need to be an aesthete like me to see the overemployment of mastic and the misalignment of the window trims. I guess they can get away with their lack of refinement with the Nepalese community, their usual clientele, who really don't know better or are not in the position to complain."

"I think you've hit the nail on the head."

"The second handyman I hired to finish up the tiling and tidy up the existing work, a South African fellow whose name escapes me, turned out to be not quite up to scratch. Very clumsy and utterly hopeless. He tiled the window sill in a godawful manner, left the window trims sticking out even worse than before and ran more mastic up the corners of the bathroom. He fitted the sink wonky and scratched the shower frame, so I had to order an entirely new shower unit. He bled the radiators for some reason only God knows, leaving air in the system and no heating in the house."

"Incompetence," categorized Luke, shaking his head again.

"But the gall of it was," Mrs. Delacourt went on, "he compared himself to a GP. He claimed handymen, like a family doctor, know a bit of everything and have certain special skills."

"I suppose there is some truth to what he's saying. We handymen are all-rounders. I certainly consider myself a jack-of-all-trades. But you're right. His work was way off the mark."

"Milking it, too," Mrs. Delacourt recalled out aloud. "He stretched out his day with lots of lengthy break periods just to justify his fee."

"Yes, not acceptable," agreed Luke. "I certainly won't be cheating you out of house and home."

"He vanished, too," Mrs. Delacourt suddenly announced. "Same as the Tattersalls. He never responded to any of my communications. He never got back to me. Doesn't make a jot of sense."

Already Luke could tell there was a pattern developing here. Both sets of handymen had disappeared inexplicably. He didn't think much of it at the time, despite the cold stirrings up his spine, just thought they'd done a runner, probably ashamed of their finished product. Luke could only advise. "It's very simple. I'd let sleeping dogs lie. You've tried to contact them. They should contact you if they want to get paid."

"You know, I think I'll do just that," decided Mrs. Delacourt. "You're the third lot, about to undertake the repairs of the repairs. We're in the process of renovating the entire house, giving each room a different theme. After the bathroom, I plan to extend the kitchen, French country-style."

"I'll be bringing my nephew along to get the work completed on time," said Luke, summarizing: "Seems like a simple enough job. We'll straighten your sink, install the replacement shower unit, attach the radiator to the wall, seal the base of the toilet with silicone, line up the window trims and get them flush, take the subway tiles to the ceiling and replace the mastic with grout. Did you know there are tradesmen whose sole area of expertise is grouting—that's how specialist a job it is?"

"Thank you for taking on this job at such short notice. It's a headache I don't need . . ."

"No problem. Leave it with us. You won't get any trouble from us. That's why we come highly-recommended. And if you like our work, my brother is a brickie, and he can extend the kitchen for you cheaply and in timely fashion, regardless of what the weather throws at him."

"I'll let you know," Mrs. Delacourt said, slightly more reassured. "When can you start?"

"How does tomorrow sound?"

"Sounds like a plan," she said, impressed. "I hope the work goes smoothly and swiftly . . ."

Mrs. Delacourt had left the housekey under the doormat for Luke Hembrey to let himself in with. He arrived at Tulpa Villa bang on nine the following morning, accompanied by his sister's son, Brooklyn Spalding. Whereas Luke was in his mid-forties and possessed the stereotypical frame of a builder, ruddy face and beer belly and visible butt crack when he crouched down, Brooklyn was twenty-one and as thin as a stick. Brooklyn was extremely hard-working and eager to learn, and Luke was proud to have his nephew under his tutelage. Neither person was the sort of builder accustomed to wolf-whistling at women in the street, even if Luke concurred with Brooklyn's impression that Mrs. Delacourt was a good-looking woman of mature age and a typical sexually-frustrated housewife—or was it only the wishful thinking of intractable youth?—and, in her loneliness, probably experiencing the pangs of 'empty nest' syndrome, since her only son had upped and gone off to University. Her husband, too, was away a lot. Mrs. Delacourt had made it clear she wanted only salt-of-the-earth, home-grown builders from now on to complete the work on the house rather than the Polish kind, even if the latter were generally reliable and hard-working and cost-effective. She was proud of her country and a true-blue Brexiteer.

"Let's boogaloo . . ." Luke kicked off the team.

As they set to work, reproducing the walls of the London Underground, Luke remembered Mrs. Delacourt's words: *There's a lot of history surrounding the Underground. You should read up on it some time. It might surprise you.* Last night, Luke had done just that. Even if he was an absolute salt-of-the-earth fella, he liked to think of himself as 'educated', through his own learning. He enjoyed reading. Gaining knowledge. Last night, he'd read up about the London Underground on Mrs Delacourt's suggestion. And, as a matter of fact, it had been something of an eye-opener, very enlightening. *Did you know there's a hidden world beneath London?* Ancient Roman amphitheatres, where gladiators once fought each other, praying for the protection of the goddess, Minerva. Unearthed plague pits with the preserved skeletons of Black Death victims. Haunted limestone caves. Rat-infested Victorian sewers. Allied secret bunkers and the Churchill War Rooms. A hydroponics' farm, below ground. The London Silver Vaults, showcasing the largest collection of shiny, glittery silverware on earth. The British Library, a book depository that numbered a hundred million items, including the Magna Carta. But the most famous thing about subterranean London was its underground railway system, a network stretching two-hundred-and-fifty miles. Its statistics were staggering. The Tube transported one-point-four billion passengers around the capital annually. The London Underground also boasted the oldest section of underground railway track in the world; the line between Paddington and Farringdon Street first opened circa 1863 and which now belonged to the Metropolitan Line. Two-hundred-thousand people—students, drunks, the homeless—crashed overnight at the station each year. The place was popular with jumpers, done with life, wishing to throw themselves in front of an oncoming train, with a peak suicide time of eleven in the morning. Then there were the Mole People . . .

All very interesting . . .

Two days was all Luke and Brooklyn had allocated themselves. As he'd informed Mrs. Delacourt, the job seemed straightforward enough. Most of the work had already been done, and it just needed fine-tuning, finishing off with a bit more class, some finesse. What could possibly go wrong? Ursula Delacourt would, in the meantime, make herself scarce, go off to work as medical secretary to a community mental health team and had instructed the handymen to help themselves to tea and coffee and cookies in the kitchen. Her husband was a member of the Royal Geographical Society and always away on business. If Luke remembered correctly, Mrs. Delacourt had mentioned her husband was in Kuala Lumpur, presently.

Luke located the kitchen down the hallway for his midmorning cuppa. The existing kitchen had a pleasant wild, rustic look, like the kitchen of a French farmhouse, painted a shabby baby blue, but he understood why Mrs. Delacourt wanted it redesigned and extended. It wasn't particularly roomy, and he imagined she wanted it capacious enough to accommodate an island in the middle and an Aga. French country-style, she had stipulated, maybe at the time of the French Revolution? Luke wondered what work it would entail in her specific desire to capture aspects of the period in question, as opposed to something more generic. Guillotines came to mind, but Luke didn't dwell too much on the thought. As he made a strong brew for himself and his nephew, he glanced through the kitchen window and the grey drizzle outside and saw a couple of pigeons tucking into scraps of old bread scattered on the secluded front lawn. He watched a squirrel gather an acorn and scamper along the fence and out of sight, preparing for the coming of winter. A noise broke him out of his quiet contemplations.

It was a low growl, like that of a wild animal.

He swung round, nearly dropping the mugs of tea.

There was nothing there. He put the mugs down and cautiously stepped into the hallway. Nothing unusual.

Maybe he'd imagined it, he thought.

Grrrrrrrr!

The fierce snarl caused Luke to jump. He realized the growling was coming from a closed door on the opposite side of the hallway. Could be a dog in there, he considered, although he couldn't remember Mrs. Delacourt warning him of any pets in the house. He subsequently wondered why Mrs. Delacourt didn't tell him if there was a dog in the house. He didn't mind dogs—he had a mastiff of his own—no matter how huge and mean the thing might be. Curious, he tested the doorknob. It was locked.

He decided to give it a rest and went back to the bathroom with the steaming mugs of freshly-brewed tea. Luke and his nephew took a comfort break and he shared his eerie experience from the kitchen with him.

Brooklyn was on the same page. "Yes, probably a dog, a big, savage thing . . . that's probably why the door is locked. Not to keep us out but to keep it in. I reckon that's what scared off the last few handymen. Either that or it gobbled them up."

It was meant to be a joke, but it didn't come off sounding like one. His remark caused Luke to experience a strange dread deep in his stomach. Yes, if his memory served him well, Mrs. Delacourt had used words like disappeared and vanished, instead of describing the former handymen as having abandoned their work and run off.

"Maybe the owner's an evil murderess and she chopped up the last guys and fed them to the dog . . ." Brooklyn followed up, laughing. Except it was a forced laughter, because the first inklings of disquiet had already tainted the atmosphere.

It didn't go down well with Luke. "Quit it! That isn't funny."

"Sorry, boss," Brooklyn said sheepishly. "What do you think it is?"

Luke decided to put the whole, unsettling business aside for now and not entertain any further creepy thoughts. "Let's say it's a dog, a big, savage thing, and it's locked up for that exact reason. Let's speak no more of it."

"I won't if you won't!" Brooklyn replied, thankful they were moving away from the subject.

They went back to work and completed the first day's graft by half-three, but even as he managed to focus on the task at hand, Luke's mind kept drifting back to that locked door from behind which he had heard the distinct, fearsome growls of a vicious animal.

"There's something not right about this house," Brooklyn remarked.

It was the second and final day, and the two handymen were busy on the bathroom. "What do you mean?" asked his uncle.

"It's an odd house," repeated Brooklyn. "Something ain't right...*can't you feel it*?"

"You feel it too?" corroborated Luke. "Ever heard of the Winchester Mystery House?"

Brooklyn shook his head.

Luke went on to explain: "It's supposed to be a haunted Victorian mansion in California that once belonged to Sarah Winchester, the widow of the gun magnate and founder of the Winchester rifle. After his death, legend has it she went crazy and ordered ceaseless, round-the-clock building works for nearly forty years to turn the house into an absurdly-sprawling, one-hundred-sixty-room warren of staircases and corridors and doors leading off into nowhere."

"Weird . . ." whistled Brooklyn. "What happened to it?"

"It's now just a historical landmark, an architectural curiosity," explained Luke, divulging, "but the point I'm making is Tulpa Villa reminds me of the Winchester Mystery House. There's a lot of locked doors, and I'm wondering what dark secrets they hide. That's not all. Unless I've got my bearings all mixed up and it's all down to perception, there's way too many doors inside the house than there should be, making the house look bigger on the inside than outside."

"That *is* weird . . ." said Brooklyn. "Maybe her husband's a Time Lord!"

It was meant to be a stab at humour, but neither of them laughed. For there seemed some truth to the canny observations Luke had shared. Moreover, a muffled growling from somewhere down the hallway jolted the men out of their conversation, adding fuel to their supernatural musings.

The two men stared at each other, spooked.

"I think we should leave . . ." Brooklyn suggested, with a fearful expression.

Even if impulse demanded they skedaddle out of here, Luke held off. "Let's just see the job through, shall we? Only a few more hours and we're done."

"What about that noise? It sounds *hungry*."

Luke decided he would man-up. "I'll investigate."

But Brooklyn grabbed his arm. "No, please, don't leave me. What if you don't come back?"

"Stop trying to freak me out!" Luke snapped at him. Except he didn't feel brave at all. He was shaking inwardly. unlike his nephew who was visibly shaken. "I'm going to look."

"Then, I'm coming with you . . ."

"Fine!" said Luke, trying not to betray the anxiety welling up inside. He picked up his cordless power drill. "Anything comes near us and I'll rip it to shreds."

Luke looked down the hallway ready to spring the drill into action. The hallway was deserted. He began moving stealthily down the hall, followed closely by Brooklyn. Trepidation dragging them down, each step grew heavier as though their boots were slowly filling up with cement. Soon they arrived at the door opposite the kitchen, the same door that had attracted Luke's attention yesterday. They could hear it now, more clearly, a low-pitched growl, the sound of an incarcerated fierce animal. As Brooklyn had mentioned, a *hungry* animal.

They paused by the door, afraid. Luke put his ear against the door, listened in. The growling persisted, a formidable, deep-throated sound. He reached for the doorknob—an excruciating moment.

"Don't do it . . ." Brooklyn implored his uncle, backing away.

"Must . . ." Luke replied. He had to know. Fear or no fear, his curiosity needed to be sated.

Heart trip-hammering in his chest, skin prickling with cold sweat, he called on all his reserves of courage to turn the doorknob. This time, the door was unlocked. Power drill in hand, prepared for some monstrous beast to lunge out, Luke pushed open the door, ready to close it in a flash, if necessary.

The growling abruptly ceased.

They encountered nothing frightening. Nothing challenged them. Nothing came rushing at them. No sign of a wild beast.

The two men stood in the doorway, surveying the large, elegantly-tailored room. It was a sitting/drawing room, done up tastefully in Old Colonial-style. The décor captured the time of the British Raj, and the room was filled with decorative pieces of Indian furnishings, mango-wood cabinets, silk-red curtains, a globe of the world, a sofa and a couple of armchairs, made of leather, pointed towards the silent fireplace; there was even a fainting couch. A fan whirred quietly on the ceiling, attempting to dispel an unseasonable sweltering heat that was singularly located in this room. As a matter of fact, the two men began to sweat profusely as though struck by a wall of heat. But the most eye-catching aspect of the room was the mural painted across one entire wall. It exploded with colour and depicted a tableau of scenes all compressed into one picture with no attention to perspective. Recognizable within the mural was the Taj Mahal, elephants bathing in the Ganges, monkeys swinging from coconut trees, a Bengal tiger emerging from the jungle . . .

Luke's focus was immediately drawn to the tiger, life-size, graceful, all sinews and black-striped, golden fur, jaws open in mid-roar, its sharp, flesh-ripping canines set like an unsprung bear trap. The tiger looked poised to pounce and there something slightly disconcerting staring at its lifelike appearance. He thought of Rudyard Kipling's Shere Khan and William Blake's iconic, short poem *The Tyger*, a spiritual meditation over the duality between the exquisite beauty and wild ferocity within one divine creation. "Here there be Tygers . . ." he murmured, thinking of the uncharted edges of navigational maps mariners used in the seafaring days of old. The thought did occur to him that the mysterious growls may have originated from the painted tiger, but he dismissed it as preposterous. *My imagination's running away with me, and, whatever it is, it's catching . . .*

Yes, it was a strange house. Each room, according to Mrs. Delacourt, was custom-made, would have its own theme. The drawing room captured the era of the Viceroy. The study was supposed to be devoted to the English Civil War. The wallpaper of her son's former bedroom purportedly depicted the Wild West, full of cacti and tumbleweeds and stampeding horses and wagon trains and guns and arrows. And the main bathroom, nearing completion, replicated the Underground.

Takes all sorts, thought Luke, and closed the door. "Let's get back to work," he told Brooklyn. "*Tempus fugit*. Especially when you're enjoying yourself."

Luke and his young apprentice kept to their schedule and, with one final push, were on course to complete the work by half-five. And, indeed, the tiles made the bathroom looked spanking-new, immaculate. The design emulated the beauty of the London Underground with ease.

Whereas Brooklyn worked as a DJ of hard-house music out of hours, and he was due to deliver a gig tonight, Luke was a reader. His passion did not exclude poetry, and the London Underground was synonymous with poetry. *Orpheus on the Underground*. Another contemporary poem imagined Tube drivers as cats since they operated in absolute darkness, an eternal midnight, and the need for a practical sanitary arrangement in the cab. There was even a clever meta-poem, about 'London Underground' possessing five syllables and deserving a haiku, in the form of a haiku.

Outside the bathroom window, the sky was darkening, as the two handymen headed down the final strait. Tired from their labours, Luke fixed the last tile to the wall and stood back to admire their handiwork. "All done," he declared, satisfied. He shook hands with his protégé. "I think we worked well together."

Brooklyn was chuffed. "I think so, too."

"I've got a few more jobs lined up in the coming days," Luke informed him, with a straight offer: "Let me know if you're interested."

"Will do," Brooklyn said, appreciatively. "Thanks." He was already thinking about what selection of music to put together for tonight.

"Time to wrap up," Luke said, starting to pick up the tools. "I've already emailed Mrs. Delacourt the invoice and my bank details."

It was Brooklyn, who first noticed the sound. "Do you hear that?"

Luke stopped what he was doing and listened. His ears picked it up. Faint, at first, echoey, but the sound began to swell, to gather momentum. And Luke noticed how different the bathroom air had become. The air seemed thicker, heavier, began to vibrate. His nostrils picked up a curious smell, a sootiness combined with the odour of underground rivers, carrying a subtle hint of decay . . . and *something else*. The atmosphere thrummed with electrical potential, what one might expect if one stood within close proximity to a power station.

Brooklyn was a smart boy, sharp as a tack. He identified the sound before Luke. "I think there's a train coming . . ."

It was a crazy observation to say the least, uttered in a moment of confusion, but neither man could deny it was the most accurate observation.

The vibrations increased. The sound of the subway train grew louder. The world inside the bathroom stuttered, as something absorbed the light from the overhead globe, and the walls grew dim, misty, insubstantial. Suddenly, up ahead, in the distance, appeared an ominous glimmer of light, that started to expand and fill the disappearing bathroom, pinning the two men, like deer caught in the headlights of a car.

Eyes widening, Luke managed to produce a few sluggish, startled words. "I think we should get out of here . . ." But he could not move, transfixed by the sight of the approaching train.

As the bathroom walls continued to dissolve, fade, to gradually lose their physical reality, Luke realized they were standing on the sleepers of an underground railway line. Waist-height, the image of a platform was forming either side of them, gathering substance, striving for three-dimensionality. The emerging logo painted across the subway wall told him the name of the station.

He remembered reading somewhere the place had once served as the biggest air raid shelter during the Second World War, but it had later been abandoned in 1994. The black roundel on the wall confirmed his suspicions. For the horizontal bar that crossed the circle read: ALDWYCH. Across the wall, next to the sign, some subway poet had scrawled a sinister ditty:

> *Hail, oh Shades of the Past,*
> *Faith-summoned Haunters of Today.*
> *Thy Power shall Everlast*
> *If We wish upon Yesterday.*

The lights from the train intensified, filling the low-ceilinged, underground tunnel in a blinding radiance. The walls reverberated violently with its approach, the ground shook. As the train closed in on the two men, the faceless driver in the cab must have seen them on the tracks for he blasted the horn, producing a huge, deafening wail. In the same instant, he hit the brakes and the ghost train slowed down with a screeching crescendo of sparks, the clash of steel on steel. Luke nearly choked on the overpowering acrid mix of soot and diesel fumes.

"ALL CHANGE . . ." boomed a deep, inhuman voice from the overhead speakers, unseen and somewhere too close for comfort, as though the two men had already stepped on to the train. "*THE TRAIN TERMINATES HERE . . . MIND THE GAP . . .*"

[... *between this life and the next...*]

"Let's get the hell out of here!" Luke yelled above the thunderous, mind-rattling din, doom-stricken, and, grabbing his quaking nephew, he bolted out of the bathroom door and beat a hasty, hysterical retreat into the evening outside, leaving his tools behind, before both men could get swallowed up by a disused underground station resurrected from another space and another time. As the Yardbirds once raved: *Train Kept A-Rollin'*.

Luke did not see any shame in fleeing, particularly since he valued his own life, and, in the coming days, he would downright refuse to do any more work on the damned house. He now realized what had frightened off his predecessors. The clue, he would discover in the comfort and safety of his own house as he read up on the terrifying phenomenon he and his nephew had experienced, this collision of two disparate worlds, was in the name of the cottage: TULPA VILLA. Tibetan mystics spoke of thoughtform—or *tulpa*—when faith was absolute and enough belief in something could will a thing into existence. Luke guessed that the husband had learned the secret of tulpamancy during his many travels in the East. In other words, each room reflected supernatural events consistent within its own thematic décor, conjuring up otherworldly ghosts, or *shades*, faith-summoned emanations of the mindstream, and if Mrs. Delacourt thought he was going to renovate the rest of the house, then she had another thing coming.

January 2018—February 2018

Tales from Space

"Whatever the truth may be at the end of the road... all I can provide you with are brief, imperfect, vexing glances of 'something'—a something that may be a kind of truth or just the lie within the lie . . ."

Jerome Clark
UFOlogist and debunker

1

Casey Jones had always considered herself a serious journalist. Unfortunately, as apprenticeships were so extraordinarily tight to come by at the leading broadsheets, she ended up settling as a reporter for *Weird World*. Despite her disappointment at not being erudite enough to work for *The New York Times*, she was the best journalist at the magazine, the top-dog, one might say, or 'blond bitch' as some of her colleagues liked to affectionately think of her. And who could blame her for being bitchy. Although they paid her well, she hated the ludicrous stories she was asked to report on.

Weird World was no *Ripley's Believe It or Not!* The former lacked the respectability of the latter and dealt with fringe news stories, the world of the paranormal, chiefly UFOs, swamp monsters and haunted houses. Mercifully, at least, it was viewed as one step up from that all-time kooky supermarket tabloid, *The National Enquirer*.

Not that Casey had seen anything bizarre herself, if you didn't count the loons she had to interview to obtain her story.

The witnesses were always screwier than their accounts. It was difficult to keep a straight face when you were interviewing a porn addict who just happened to be raped by a sexy, six-feet-tall Venusian blonde, or when eliciting accurate details of an erotic vampire attack on a desperately lonely Suicide Girl. And, lately, these were precisely the types of stories coming her way.

Except one. Except one that seemed like a genuine case, not a fourth-rate reject from Bullshit Boulevard or the delirious rantings of someone on Freaky Fungus.

This hopefully-not-so-crummy assignment had been assigned to her by her boss, the Editor-in-Chief, Charlton Frobisher, whom she considered a cut above the rest. Unlike most of the strange people who worked alongside her, Frobisher—a balding Englishman with a garish smile—knew everything *about* everything. If you were to ask him anything he would provide you with the answer in a matter of seconds, let it be the life-cycle of the hookworm, the number of islands in the South Pacific or more classified information such as Dubya's real IQ and the size of his wiener when fully aroused. Casey had often wondered why such a blistering genius as Frobisher worked on a downmarket rag such as *Weird World*. The answer when it came surprised her. He liked it.

"If you think you know all there is to know about Life, you have surely gained a Scholarship to study the Great Unknown," was his personal motto. He always reminded her of the magazine's mission statement: *It is not we but the world that is weird*.

That was why when he selected Casey with overwhelming enthusiasm for an article on the curious events in the small coastal township of Pinewood Bay, New England, her interest was immediately piqued.

She drove from her home in Boston to Pinewood Bay in under four hours and booked into a homely Bed-and-Breakfast at two on a sunny late-September afternoon. The journey across had been uneventful, Casey getting into the spirit of the thing by listening to *Is That You Mo-Dean?* by The B52s on a perpetual loop.

Pinewood Bay wasn't a bad place to live, a typical North US retirement resort with plenty of sun, sea and swimming. What separated Pinewood Bay from most other places was the sinister, conspicuous presence of Magna-co, a government atomic research station, located merely fifteen miles north-west of the town's suburbs. Although the site of Magna-co was listed as secret, the dark, domed edifice could be seen in the distance like a foreboding sentinel from some grim, alternate future.

Casey had a half-three appointment with a certain Tim Hallaran at the local hospital to discuss the weird business he had experienced. She arrived promptly and was ushered into the Psychiatrist's plush, book-strewn office by his spinsterish secretary. The fact that Dr. Hallaran was a sane, skeptical, responsible, respected MD was the key feature that provided an incredible twist to the unusual tale she had been asked to report on.

Dr. Hallaran greeted her jovially and invited her to take a seat. Casey's initial impression of the shrink was that he was quite handsome and well-spoken, certainly dapper, far removed, reputation-wise, from the normally obsessed, suppressed, repressed, stressed and depressed members of his medical specialty. He could have dropped out of an episode of *St. Elsewhere*, the kind of doctor who could make nurses swoon and patients blush.

It was only when Casey crossed her legs to reveal her curvaceous sun-brown legs below her short, lime-green-and-chilli-red dress that she came to the opinion that maybe Dr. Hallaran wasn't so much different from his peers. His appraisal of her form was more than just perfunctory and less than professional—Casey thought he was drooling with his eyes.

Obsessed, suppressed, repressed, stressed and depressed, she thought. *And now he wants to see me undressed.* She smirked silently at her own witticism. *Not a long haul for a shrink.* Her eyes happened to glance at a plaque on the wall: A PSYCHIATRIST IS SOMEONE WHO HAS MORE COMPLEXES THAN HIS PATIENTS.

Tell me about it. She laughed again inside. *He's like some sweaty pubescent discovering a skin magazine in his father's drawer.*

"Do you mind?" she said aloud, sounding indignant at his continued leery inspection of her. "I believe in hot stories, not hot skirts."

Dr. Hallaran stopped ogling her legs, his eyes flicking to attention. "I beg your pardon," he apologized, smiling weakly. "God, it's been such a long time since I—" He suddenly realized he was mumbling to himself and thinking a little too loudly for comfort. "Forget I said that."

"That's okay," she answered, slightly reassured.

"Shall we start over?" Dr. Hallaran declared, more businesslike. "I'll tell you all you need to know about what went on here. Would you care for some coffee?"

"No thanks," Casey said politely. She extracted her notepad and biro.

"How about something stronger, more medicinal?"

She declined again. Dr. Hallaran pulled out a bottle of Remy Martin VSOP from a cabinet marked FIRST AID and poured himself a large shot in a coffee-mug. "Use only in case of emergencies." He grinned. "Like now." He downed the liquor in one gulp. "You'll need a stiff one by the time I've finished."

"Excuse me?" Casey looked at him mistrustfully. His sexual innuendo was appalling. Or was it because he was a shrink?

Dr. Hallaran coughed. "What I meant was: by the time I've finished telling you the story. Aboveboard, I swear."

"Oh," she murmured, decidedly relieved. Maybe she had misunderstood him, although she noticed his gaze kept wandering to her legs.

Dr. Hallaran opened his account, nevertheless. "It all began with…"

2

Natalie Cole.

She was a smart, together fifteen-year-old, not the kind of girl who rebelled against authority or hung around with the hoky wild boys of the township or smoked grass with her friends. Merely an average, happy, obedient, Rock-'N'-Roll-loving, with-it teenager.

The twenty-seventh of August was a hot, sultry evening, not a patch of cloud in the russet-indigo sky, not a spot of rain expected for a week. Natalie was strolling barefoot on the beach, lost in her own universe. The sun had already set, the clear, rippling waters reaching for the glorious horizon and the warm, rolling waves idly kissing the shore.

It was getting late, and there were hardly any tourists or visitors on the beach. Yet Natalie appeared oblivious to all this. Occasionally she'd bend over and absently pick up a seashell or examine a stray starfish brought in by the tide and buried in tangled fronds of seaweed, but her thoughts were focused elsewhere.

Her boyfriend had split up with her and she was devastated. The news that Steve Bell, the school jock, was secretly dating Sammie Willis, of all the airhead chicks in the place, had come as a shock to her and she had spent much of the afternoon in tears. His unfaithfulness, his awful betrayal of her trust and his subsequent lack of emotion when admitting his terrible indiscretion had made her feel like shit, used and abused like some French tart. She had come to the conclusion that she hated men and wished they would all die from syphilis.

Something cold and smooth touched her foot, making her start.

She looked down. It was a lump of metal, silver and vaguely cuboid in shape. Curious, Natalie picked it up and studied it. *This shouldn't be here*, she thought. *The beach patrol is going to be furious*. The edges of the cube were as sharp and jagged as those broken bottles she sometimes discovered discarded dangerously by a significant number of thoughtless tourists.

She noticed something odd about the piece of metal she was holding. There was a dull shine to it, a kind of cold inner radiance. She stood quietly gazing into it, unaware that a steady humming sound was coming from somewhere out to sea. It was only when the distracting vibration increased in pitch and intensity and a blast of air ruffled her brown hair that she glanced skyward and froze instantly.

The twilit sky was lit up by a hypnotic array of fabulous colours, emanating from a singular saucer-shaped object which, at first, she could not make out. Then, realization struck, followed by morbid fascination.

It can't be! Natalie's thoughts screamed disbelievingly. *It just can't be! A UFO . . . I'm seeing an* actual *UFO!*

She had heard stories of UFO sightings in the area, from her friends over a campfire barbecue, but Natalie had always considered them silly and nerdish, reserved for the overactive imagination of attention-seeking nuts. Yet, what she was witnessing now, in real time, was far from silly and nerdish. There was without a doubt a UFO in the sky and it looked nothing like a plane or weather balloon, or chain-lightning, one occasionally read about. The immense, glowing disc glided closer and closer to the shore, travelling at a speed and trajectory that appeared impossible for any man-made craft. Soon it hovered less than five hundred metres from Natalie's transfixed position, the swirling central ring spilling dazzling stroboscopic reds and blues and yellows and greens onto the beach, the whirring, grinding noise now loud and thunderous, shaking the ground and unsettling the tide.

Natalie stared helplessly at the incredible spectacle, her throat dry, her mind dazed. She had little opportunity to ascertain the circumference of the space vessel when there was a tremendous roar and a cone of brilliant white light exploded from the underbelly of the colossal flying machine. Half-blinded and close to being unbalanced by the maelstrom, Natalie watched as something emerged from the resplendent illumination,

[*Do you believe in monsters?*]

a figure that was seven feet tall, thin, humanoid, naked-grey...

Enormous black eyes watched her from beneath the bulbous, bald cranium, hollow stygian pits that glittered with crazy, unearthly intelligence and sinister intent.

Natalie didn't stay to see what would happen next. She turned around and fled, clutching the piece of metal tightly, her thoughts held by the terrifying notion that the grey alien visitor was in hot pursuit. Time slowed down and the general forbidding silence of the bay seemed to spell out another dark fear—that maybe the whole town had been overrun by extraterrestrials and Natalie was the only human left.

She sprinted without her flip-flops to her house, a short walk from the beach, not daring to look over her shoulder or stop to catch her breath. As she passed through the porch, she slammed the front door shut behind her, closing her eyes to block out the vision of the UFO and its alien scout party. What should she do? Dial the number for the police? Call her parents urgently at Gramma Dorothy's? She felt cold, tired and scared as she considered her limited options.

Dropping the lump of metal on the sofa of the lounge, she had just lifted the receiver when there was a heavy knock on the front door, stopping her in her tracks.

It's the alien and it's come to take me away and conduct all manner of horrible experiments on my body. She had heard news reports of people who had been supposedly abducted by visitors from outer space and whisked away to the Mother Ship where their suffering could provide valuable research material for the alien scientists. It all sounded implausible, of course.

Except in light of the events of the last quarter of an hour. Another thud on the door broke Natalie's mass of dread, jumbled thoughts. Should she answer it and face the music? No way, she told herself. What if her parents were back from Gramma's? No, they had keys. If there really were an alien at the door, would it knock so patiently? Maybe if she were quiet for a few moments, whoever—or whatever—it was would go away. The litany of internal reasoning ended abruptly when Natalie realized she had overlooked a crucial detail.

But the door is unlocked . . .

She stumbled into the hallway in a desperate attempt at latching the front door but halted immediately when she saw that someone had already gained admittance. A dark human shape stood in the open doorway, the face obscured by the discomfiting gloom, their presence silhouetted against the retreating daylight and casting a long, crooked shadow over Natalie, who promptly collapsed with dumb apprehension on the foot of the stairs. The figure took a step forward and Natalie gawped back in bewilderment as his features hoved into view.

Oh, my God!

The visitor was dressed all in black, from his two-piece suit, shirt and tie to his scarf, leather gloves and Armani shoes. Although Natalie had never met him, his neatly-parted brown hair was unmistakable, his boyish good looks equally memorable from old news footage. The Bay of Pigs, the Cuban Missile Crisis, the Civil Rights Movement, the advent of the Space Race came to mind, springing up from her American History classes.

His lips were curled into a relaxed, if not charismatic, smile. "Er, hi there, little miss," he greeted her in that familiar Boston accent, caricatured with gusto by Mayor Quimby from *The Simpsons*.

Profundity clouded Natalie's thoughts. Of all the people in the whole world, he was the last person she expected to see walk through the door. Her heartbeat cranked up a notch and her body melted away in a mixture of fear and joy. She didn't know whether to sing 'Happy Birthday' to him or be terrified to the brink of madness. He was one of her all-time heroes and one of the greatest liberal icons of the twentieth century. The man, his life and his politics had changed the world. His *Profiles of Courage*, a non-fiction piece about certain Senators, who had risked everything by standing by their personal beliefs, had won the Pulitzer Prize. Even the last half-decent Leader of the Free World, Bill Clinton, owed a lot to this great man. "Wh-what are you d-d-doing here?" was the best Natalie could muster.

"Do I need a reason to see one of my upstanding citizens?" John F. Kennedy replied amiably.

"But you can't be here," murmured Natalie, fighting a swell of conflicting emotions. "You were assassinated over forty years ago."

"Now why do you want to go and say a darn thing like that?" JFK said, sounding slightly aggrieved. "What?" Natalie continued to stare at him, moon-eyed, unsure what to think, let alone what to say next. "Stop hurting my feelings, will you?"

"You're supposed to be dead . . ." she reiterated, entranced.

"What if I am dead?" Suddenly, JFK's tone turned cynical, stony. "I guess you're wondering how I can be standing here, ain't that so, miss?"

She could only nod, faintly.

"Maybe I'm not really here," he blared menacingly. He sounded like a demigod about to pass judgement on a condemned, lowly apostate. "What if the world outside isn't real? Perhaps this room doesn't exist? You absolutely sure *you're alive*?" He scowled at her, pointing his index finger at her cowering form. "Could it be your life is just a dumb dream in my head? Maybe you're peering into the Looking-Glass, and I am the Red King, who is dreaming about you, and once I awake, out you go—*bang!*— just like a candle! If you don't believe me, try opening your eyes tomorrow morning, little miss. You'll find everything's as black as a blind bat's ass."

The power and complexity of the statement, partially borrowed from the exchange between Tweedledum and Tweedledee, struck Natalie with the force of a shotgun. Adrenaline deposited in her veins as perspiration broke over her skin. Her heart felt light and fluttery and the muscles in her diaphragm and stomach tightened, making her groan with nausea. Her mind reeled with giddiness, confusion and contradiction, swirling with overwhelming, convoluted terrors that sent it plummeting into a deep, dark, nonsensical abyss. *What if her life REALLY was one big dream? And once JFK awoke she would cease to exist?* He was employing some kind of reverse, twisted logic, trying to convince her that she was merely a pawn in his meandering mind, that a living person was a figment of a dead man's imagination. Well, considering the absurdity of the circumstances, she was convinced!

JFK turned his head in the direction of the lounge and Natalie gasped in horror.

Glaring at her straight in the face was a large ragged hole, encrusted with dark blood, in his right temple. No awards for guessing what had caused it. She suddenly realized why he was wrapped up in a scarf. She knew that if he were to remove it she would find a similar deadly wound, where the assassin's bullet had entered the back of his neck and exited his throat.

Proof enough that the man confronting her

[*monsters do you believe in monsters*] could not be anybody else other than the erstwhile President.

JFK left her pale, speechless and trembling on the stairs as he gandered into the lounge. "I came for this here rock," he spoke, annoyed. He retrieved the lump of metal from the sofa, almost lovingly, as though one might lift up a small child. "You had no business taking it! The secrets of the cube belong to me!"

He returned to the hallway, rounding on her again. "Nothing happened. You didn't see or hear anything, is that clear?"

Natalie nodded weakly.

"Er, just one more thing," he sneered. "As you're such an admirer of my work, I'll leave you my autograph, since when I do snip the string to my dear little puppet, it'll be the last thing you'll see."

His comment brought another avalanche of bone-chilling incomprehension through her.

"As I once said: *Ask not what your country can do for you, ask what you can do for your country.*"

The contempt in his voice as he delivered these now-famous words made Natalie want to scream, but all she could produce were a few painful sobs. Dead Presidents with bullet-holes in their skulls aside, why was JFK being so nasty to her when she thought so highly of him, and respect for him still flowed from every corner of the globe? Not to press too fine a point, the man standing before her sounded like some sort of sick Republican parody.

Once again, a black daunting figure in the doorway, his features shrouded in shadow, JFK turned and informed Natalie casually: "Must dash. Cocktails at seven with Lady Babushka." Then he inquired, a harder edge to his tone: "Any questions?"

If he had been expecting any, he would have been greatly disappointed. Natalie merely sat on the stairs, weeping quietly, her hands clasped around her knees, genuinely fearing for her life.

After one last lingering look of satisfaction, JFK was gone, leaving the local authorities to stew in a sea of mystery and Natalie Cole to question her own sanity and seek urgent Psychiatric help.

A slip of paper floated down from the letterbox, bearing President Kennedy's official signature and the message: THINK BLACK.

3

"A flying saucer, an alien and JFK all in one hour—that's not bad going!" Casey Jones remarked, grinning.

"Knew you'd like it, though makes you wonder how crazy this world is becoming," Dr. Hallaran replied thoughtfully.

"*Crazy*—is that a technical term?" Casey humoured. She had to admit it was an impressive tale, if not rather far-fetched. Her own take on UFOs was rational and down-to-earth. We were definitely not alone in this infinite cosmos, but no extraterrestrial had, in the history of mankind, ever ventured onto our small blue world. To be frank, we had not yet learned to communicate with the great variety of intelligent species on Earth, let alone believing we might be able to speak with lifeforms from outer space. Still, it was nice to imagine we had been contacted by beings from beyond the stars as it gave us hope that there was more to life than the shit we were stuck with.

"*Crazy* would be the operative word," Dr. Hallaran declared. "I mean why JFK? Why not Elvis?"

Casey considered this carefully. "You're saying she wasn't obsessed with JFK?"

"You'd expect a regular teenage girl to dream of Elvis dropping in on her—or Jim Morrison or John Lennon or Kurt Cobain—than a President who's been in his grave almost half a century."

"Sightings of JFK aren't uncommon."

"True . . . but getting off with a dead rock star would make more sense."

"JFK was—and still is—a legend in his own right."

"It's extremely easy to dismiss the whole thing as a nightmare or a waking dream, but why concoct such an elaborate fantasy at your own expense?"

"You actually believed the girl's story?"

"There's more . . ." Dr. Hallaran poured himself another snifter of brandy and continued: "Natalie's parents brought her in at ten that evening. According to them, they arrived home to discover their daughter rocking gently back and forth in her bedroom, clutching a piece of paper, babbling incoherently. She was suffering from shock and amnesia when I got round to assessing her in the morning, mute, withdrawn, confused. She was terrified of sleeping and her initial sleep deprivation didn't help matters. It was only through hypnotic regression that I finally obtained the details of her encounter with JFK."

"That puts a different slant on the case," Casey said, suddenly less skeptical. "To get the information through hypnosis means that her experience must have been so traumatic that her mind blocked it out entirely."

"Precisely! But that wasn't all. We found numerous blisters on her hands, which we later identified as radiation burns."

"How is that possible?"

"I can only assume that, at some point during that evening, she must have come into contact with something that must have been radioactive. What, though, we didn't have a clue at the time."

"What other conclusions did you come up with regarding her medical condition?"

"Drug screen came back negative. After speaking with the police—who had no record of any unusual reports that day, such as lights in the sky, say—I diagnosed Natalie with an acute psychotic episode, triggered by something she must have actually witnessed, not forgetting her mysterious case of low-grade radiation poisoning or how the signature on the piece of paper was later verified by an expert as authentic."

"Wow!" burst out Casey, astonished and intrigued. "You mean it actually belonged to John F. Kennedy? This is getting distinctly creepy!"

Dr. Hallaran paused to take a few more sips from his mug before continuing. "Natalie was discharged a fortnight later, her health fully restored, and she returned to her normal way of life."

Casey jotted a few notes before raising an important question. "What are your views on the paranormal?"

"Fringe medicine is not my forte," explained Dr. Hallaran. "We doctors believe in hard evidence. I've seen a couple of cases of alien abduction wander into the ER, but I always analyze them from a neutral, scientific standpoint. Objectivity means everything. I am fully versed on the phenomenon of UFOs, but I'm certain there will be an underlying, clear-cut, non-supernatural explanation for each visitation, and if you look long and hard enough, you're bound to find it." Dr. Hallaran hesitated, shifting anxiously in his chair. "Having said that, what I experienced the same day we discharged Natalie was just as crazy as my young patient's testimony. In fact, it's safe to say that it put the frighteners on me."

4

A cold, wet September the Sixteenth.

It was Dr. Hallaran's weekend off and he had spent the day making arrangements for his forthcoming vacation to Bora Bora. He'd booked the flight, contacted the hotel he would be staying in and shopped around town for some suitable holiday-wear.

He came back to his bachelor pad, a large, four-bedroom house overlooking the bay, well past seven.

Depositing his dripping umbrella in the rack and his shopping bags in the kitchen, he turned on the TV, where Columbo was in the process of harassing his latest murder suspect, and then proceeded to make himself dinner. He knew how Columbo operated: the detective was an overworked slob who deliberately dressed himself down to lull the suspect into a false sense of security, and it always worked. Dr. Hallaran was famished, and he decided to make something quick and simple.

It didn't take him long to conjure up a Spanish omelette, which he was transferring from pan to plate when the telephone rang. Glancing through the kitchen window at the abysmal weather outside, he strolled over to the wall-phone in the hallway and picked up the receiver. "Hello, Dr. Hallaran here," he announced into the receiver.

"Good evening, Dr. Hallaran," a voice answered at the other end, a deep throaty voice the doctor didn't recognize. "I wonder if I might be permitted to have a word with you about one Natalie Cole."

"Yes, I know of a Natalie Cole. Whom am I speaking with?"

"That is irrelevant," came the curt reply.

The rudeness of the caller produced a puzzled look. "I'm afraid I'm in a bit of a hurry. I've got a date in less than an hour and I can't afford to be late."

"It is of the utmost importance we discuss Natalie Cole with you."

Natalie Cole? Why this sudden interest in Natalie Cole when nothing of logic lay therein? "And why exactly?"

"As yet, that is none of your concern," the fellow replied. The pleasantries seemed to be over.

"I'm sure you're aware of doctor-patient confidentiality—that I'm not at liberty to discuss any of my patients with outsiders, particularly total strangers."

"I'm afraid to tell you, doctor, that you *must*," the fellow demanded, "and *right now*!"

"Listen, mister, I don't know who you are, but nobody threatens—" The line went dead, leaving him staring at the mouthpiece. The SOB had cut him off!

There followed a rap on the door, which interrupted Dr. Hallaran's sense of bafflement and indignation. Who could that be? He wasn't expecting Amy, his hot date from Paediatrics, for some time yet. So who was it then, about to invade the doctor's privacy?

The sky was already twilit, the wind howling and whistling through the trees and the rain beating down at the window in relentless, smacking torrents.

Before he could answer the door, the door answered for him. It burst open with a tremendous force, snapping the safety-chain effortlessly and shattering the frosted glass.

Dr. Hallaran stumbled backwards, startled. He gawked at the two men who stepped into the hallway and the mess of broken glass on the hallway floor. They were the strangest characters he had ever seen. Each was a contrast to the other; whereas the first man was tall and brawny, his accomplice was short and slim. What made them comparable were their outfits: both were dressed in identical black suits, with black Homburg-style hats perched atop each head. Having gained entry, the pair advanced ominously towards Dr. Hallaran like evil hit-men from some violent crime drama.

Dr. Hallaran retreated to the lounge, half-fascinated, half-scared. "Who-who are you?"

"That is none of your concern," the taller of the two men, obviously the leader, declared, and suddenly Dr. Hallaran recalled the voice and comment immediately.

This was the guy, whom he had spoken to on the phone, only seconds earlier. What was more disturbing was how the two men had arrived at his house so quickly when the nearest telephone kiosk was at least half-a-mile away. (At this stage, stunned that he was, it did not occur to him they might have used cell-phones.)

He stared up at his visitors from the sofa, afraid for his own safety. There was something unnatural about them. Apart from their black attire, their features were semi-obscured by the shadow from their hats, giving them a sinister, almost bewitching persona. The nearest of the two men towered over Dr. Hallaran, who slumped on the sofa. "What do you want?"

"We require the absolute incineration of the file of Natalie Cole," the leading Man-in-Black ordered. "Why?" squeaked Dr. Hallaran.

"That is none of your concern," he repeated, his expression predatory and unmerciful.

Dr. Hallaran couldn't understand why they seemed so intent he should commit such an unethical act, insist he breach data protection laws. "But I'm her doctor . . ."

"Your medical skills have no bearing on her current mental state. I will therefore demand you dispose of her case-notes as soon as possible, preferably *to-day*!"

Dr. Hallaran decided to stand his ground, despite the fear generated by these dark intruders. "I can't do that."

There was a moment's pause. Then the leader of the duo asked with unwavering coolness. "Have you ever witnessed an Unidentified Flying Object?"

"Can't say that I have," the psychiatrist replied, wondering where this was leading.

"Then how can you persist in defying our demands?" the first Man-in-Black growled, as hostile as an angry bear. "What your patient disclosed to you was an absurdity. All absurdities must be presented accurately, otherwise they wouldn't be classified as absurdities."

Dr. Hallaran tried to comprehend the message, but its meaning seemed lost on him. "What are you telling me?"

The first Man-in-Black took a step forward, irritated and irate, and the doctor realized much to his perturbation that the figure was well over six-foot-four, a powerhouse of Herculean vitality. With a pink fibrous scar crossing his right cheek, he definitely wasn't the kind of guy to bump into in a dark alley, late at night. "You attest to be a man of medicine, yet can you postulate how the diverse physical components of your carbon-based brain generate consciousness? How does consciousness, integral to all life, beget thought, a function higher than mere instinct or any reflex? Do you deny that perception, a collaboration of sense and conscious experience, can be radically altered or deliberately manipulated? Is hypnosis not open to suggestion, to confabulation? So, pray explain, Dr Hallaran, why you hold credence to the immature ramblings of a child?"

Dr. Hallaran continued to look up like a dunce, stung and stunned. He got the daunting impression that he was dealing with people who were accustomed to life somewhere in the farthest reaches of the galaxy. These men could easily be mistaken for aliens. A greater dread wormed its way into his thoughts. Heck, what if they *really* were aliens? *Having travelled millions of light* years through hitherto uncharted regions of deep space, they decide to land in my backyard to give me a science lesson.

When Dr. Hallaran didn't speak, the first Man-in-Black added: "Maybe we can be more persuasive." He gestured to his silent partner with a simple flick of his gloved hand.

The second, smaller, slimmer Man-in-Black instantly removed his hat, and the psychiatrist got a good look at his face. It brought on a fresh wave of inarticulate fear. Whereas his overbearing colleague appeared human, relatively-speaking, the second Man-in-Black looked anything but. His head was completely bald, his face sallow and hairless without any hint of eyebrows or eyelashes. Worse still, he lacked even the slightest semblance of a nose. Smooth, glazed skin stretched from his lipless mouth to his narrow, Oriental eyes. He looked as though he had been moulded directly from wax like some exhibit in the Chamber of Horrors.

What followed was both staggering and terrifying in equal measure. The second Man-in-Black raised his leg and began to scale the wall. Not like a mountaineer on a major ascent but walking as proficiently as any biped would do on the ground. Neither did the ceiling deter him. He traversed the ceiling of the lounge, ludicrously defying gravity, and causing Dr. Hallaran to ponder his own sanity. Madness was his profession, except what he was seeing was beyond mad: it was *impossible*. When the unearthly figure was suspended upside-down, directly above Dr. Hallaran, he ceased his dizzying display of inverted perambulation, his feet remaining firmly planted on the ceiling. "You will obey us," he droned like a well-maintained automaton.

Too absorbed in the madness surrounding him, Dr. Hallaran wondered what he was referring to. "Obey you about what?"

"The incineration of your patient's notes!" the first black-clad man reminded him, blaring with more venom.

"Why is it so important to you?"

"That is none of your concern."

"If you want me to do something illegal, then you must tell me why."

"Stop locobobulating with us!" the leader boomed. From inside his coat pocket, he pulled out what appeared to be some kind of black raygun, not unlike a kiddie's water pistol. "Here's a demonstration of what we're capable of . . ." He aimed the gun at Dr. Hallaran, who froze in sheer panic, then focused it on the TV, where Columbo was on the verge of arresting the murderer. The detective in the crumpled brown mac was about to explain how he'd cracked the case when there was a high-pitched sonar discharge and the television screen exploded with a mighty coughing roar, fragments of glass and plastic showering the room. Dr. Hallaran's mouth dropped as he stared, horrified, at the blackened, smoking frame of his brand-new TV set.

"High-intensity ultrasonic device," the first Man-in-Black explained triumphantly. His tone grew fierce. "Next time it'll be *you*! I will fry your brain inside your skull!"

"You will obey us!" repeated the second Man-in-Black in a dull, emotionless monotone. He was now standing next to Dr. Hallaran, although the good doctor hadn't seen him detach himself from the ceiling.

"So do we have a decision from you?" the principal Man-in-Black commanded, confronting the doc like an ill-tempered judge asking a jury to return a verdict.

Damn right he'd made a decision, especially when considering the viciousness of the threats. Besides, he'd seen enough weird shit to last him a lifetime! He nodded timidly.

"We didn't hear you," Man-in-Black #1 challenged, pointing his futuristic weapon at the shrink.

Dr. Hallaran remained speechless.

"Our auditory sensors have not detected your response," Man-in-Black #2 warned impassively.

The leader's finger was beginning to squeeze the trigger when Dr. Hallaran's voice returned in shocked consent. "*I'll do it! I swear I'll do it! Just don't shoot me with that thing!*"

"It is pleasant to know that you are now operating on the same frequency as us," Number Two uttered. His colleague replaced the sonic gun back in his jacket, allowing Dr. Hallaran to relax, albeit only slightly. "Any refusal and our jurisdiction mandate demands termination of the non-compliant individual. *Any refusal and our*

*juris-dic-tion mandate . . . de-mands . . . term-in-ation . . . of . . .
the…NON-COMMMPLIIIANNNT…INNNDIIIIIVIIIIIIIDUUUAAAALLLLLL…"*
All of a sudden, his robotic speech ground to a halt like a broken-down gramophone.

Dr. Hallaran watched him become semi-quiescent. "What's wrong with him?" he asked, bemused.

"His energy modules are depleted," the first Man-in-Black answered, showing little sympathy for his sluggish partner. "He'll be fitted with a recharge and his alogarithms recalibrated."

Jesus H. Christ! Dr. Hallaran thought wildly. *It's a machine! An android! A freaking computerized synthetic human!* Even though artificial intelligence was still a hundred years from mass production. However, it was loonier to imagine such a technological marvel running out of charge at such a crucial moment. *I mean we wouldn't want to see Robocop turn into a pre-senile cripple whilst issuing a death threat.*

"NEEEED . . . RENNNNEWAAAAAALLLL . . ." the second Man-in-Black groaned, his voice distorted and dying.

"We must leave," the first Man-in-Black declared. He headed down the hallway, followed by the erratic, jerky movements of his companion. "You will carry out our instructions?" he demanded, requiring closure.

"Implicitly," Dr. Hallaran muttered.

"Today?"

"Today . . ."

"Nobody had better find out, Dr. Timothy Hallaran, if you know what's good for you." With this final chilling warning, the two outlandish visitors were gone.

Dr. Hallaran watched their progress through the lounge-room window, the rain already diminishing. They disappeared into a shiny black Cadillac, its windows heavily tinted, its twin exhaust behemoth. As the Cadillac roared to life and drove off into the prevailing evening mist, Dr. Hallaran noticed that the car boasted next year's number-plates which, after everything he had witnessed, wasn't so surprising.

Returning to his sofa, he suddenly felt ten years older, weary and frightened. He glanced at the wrecked TV set—which dispelled any notion he might have imagined the whole thing—then looked at the uneaten Spanish omelette resting on the plate on the coffee table. At that moment, he did not feel particularly hungry.

5

"Then what happened?" Casey Jones asked eagerly.

"I did as they told me," Dr. Hallaran said, leaning back in his chair, hands clasped behind his head, shoes resting on the table. "I came into hospital and destroyed her files."

"You actually went through with it?" Casey exclaimed, astonished.

"Shredded them," said Dr. Hallaran. "I had no choice. I was too spooked to consider any other option. I don't think I've been so scared since I was five when my mother introduced me to the concept of the Bogeyman during a violent thunderstorm on Halloween night."

"You don't seem very panicked about it now, though," Casey observed, utterly absorbed by the psychiatrist's tale. Her initial skepticism was no longer an obstacle.

"It's just that what occurred afterwards gave the entire thing a whole new perspective."

"Men-in-Black again?" Casey inquired.

"Not quite." Dr. Hallaran deliberated, consumed another shot of brandy and asked: "You familiar with eyewitness accounts of Men-in-Black visitations?"

"I know all there is to know about the colour black."

"I don't mean poetic or melancholic or biblical or philosophical definitions of black." His eyes unexpectedly roved back to her smooth, shapely legs, and when he realized she had caught his swift appraisal, he coughed to hide his embarrassment and resumed: "No, I'm referring to the generic name given to these mysterious charmers who have the austere intention of driving their victims round the bend. Markedly more

~ 226 ~

than discombobulate their targets. *Locobobulate*, to coin a phrase."

Casey sniggered. "That would describe them perfectly. The history of MiB dates back to the late 'Forties when people claimed to receive visits from them and were so mesmerized by their presence, they could not remember their experience or gave accounts that were too mindboggling and absurd."

"I must say they are extremely adept at applying the anchoring techniques of Neuro-Linguistic Programming."

"An essential element of their performance, I guess."

"I did a great deal of reading into UFOlogy after my encounter," continued Dr. Hallaran, "and I learned that the method of suppression of facts employed by the Men-in-Black gains them only publicity. Regardless of being shrouded in dark secrets and unleashing hellish warnings, there is no evidence of them ever actually harming anyone."

"Research undertaken suggested that the Men-in-Black were in some way linked to Majestic-12."

"Majestic-12?"

"Majestic-12," Casey explained, "was a secret committee supposedly formed in 1947, investigating UFO activity in the aftermath of the Roswell Incident. It consisted of scientists, military leaders and top-ranking politicians. It has been speculated that the Men-in-Black are the henchmen of this fabled organization since they only appear after a major UFO sighting in order to threaten the witnesses into silence.

Dr. Hallaran sounded dismissive. "I think MiB—and Majestic-12, for that matter—can be reserved for that hazy grey zone between reality and folklore, staples for the conspiracy theorists."

"You're probably right," Casey admitted. She'd never been a great believer of the occult in spite of her day job. "So what did the authorities make of your visitation—that's, of course, assuming you went to the authorities?"

Dr. Hallaran shook his head. "I'm afraid I didn't. Anyway, what happened later brought the case to a farcical conclusion."

Sheriff George Farnsworth was in the middle of eating his very late dinner when he received an emergency phone-call. All-in-all, it had been a quiet September the Eighteenth until about six in the evening when the switchboard had been swamped with calls from anxious residents at Pinewood Bay, claiming to have seen discs in the sky.

The sheriff hadn't been too troubled by all this, thinking that a couple of townsfolk had mistaken something ordinary like a blimp for a UFO. *Happens all the time.* He'd dispatched his deputy to investigate the reports. Then, at precisely ten-twenty, Deputy Sandy Scrubshaw called. He sounded excited. "Sheriff, you've got to come down here as quickly as possible!"

"Why? What have you found out?"

"Better hurry on down to Talunga Woods! We've just discovered an alien!"

Sheriff Farnsworth looked at the massive pile of pastrami-on-rye sandwiches with a sigh of resignation. Food would have to wait. "I'm on my way . . ." he told Scrubshaw.

Within minutes he had parked his dusty white police cruiser in a reservation at the entrance to Talunga Woods. He emerged from the vehicle and headed on into the copse of trees. The night was cloudy, but not too dark to see where one was stepping. He decided to withhold his torch for the time being until he discovered what was going on. He hadn't gone far when he saw a group of his own men and some civilians crowded round the top of a covered embankment, staring silently down with a mixture of awe and bewilderment.

Sheriff Farnsworth hunkered down next to Deputy Scrubshaw, who gave him the low-down. "One of the passersby found that thing an hour ago. We've been watching it since. Nobody's dared approach it."

Holding his breath, Farnsworth looked through the undergrowth. Sure enough, down in the hollow, was a figure that looked only vaguely human. It was grey, slim, with big black eyes and a prominent head, and seemed to have no idea it was being watched. It sat on the ground, resting against a tree. It hardly moved, its head bowed, as if meditating.

"That's all it's been doing since we arrived," Scrubshaw whispered to his superior.

Suddenly, there was a rustling noise down below and someone came into view. It was a woman, in her mid-twenties, dressed in skimpy clothes and high heels. Farnsworth recognized her immediately since he had busted her many times over. Kelly Danvers was the town's lady-of-ill-repute. She spotted the extraterrestrial and, instead of freezing on the spot with shock or running away in fright, she knelt down beside it and took its hand. It responded. The congregation of concealed spectators watched in dense amazement as the alien visitor stood up and put its arm round the woman's shoulder to steady itself.

Farnsworth noticed that it was staggering as it tried to walk and realized a split-second later that it was clutching a half-empty bottle of bourbon.

"Sheriff, don't you reckon something don't fit right?" Scrubshaw asked, evidently perplexed.

"You couldn't fool me," Farnsworth replied in mock puzzlement. "Why would an alien, a super-intelligent being, more advanced than our human race, one capable of constructing a faster-than-light spacecraft travel across the Universe to our tiny, blue world to pick up, of all people, *her*, a dumb floozie, for amusement? Well, if that's not a head-scratcher, then I don't know what is!"

"And to pick up Kelly," Scrubshaw exclaimed, not without envy. "Great choice, the lucky bastard's got great taste! Kelly's one of the hottest things in town! How come she settled for a guy from outer space?"

Farnsworth looked back at Scrubshaw, surprised at the sincerity of the question. "Maybe aliens have greater staying power." His tone changed, the humour gone. "Is this what you called me out for?"

"What's wrong, sir?"

"If that's an alien, then I'm Mother Teresa."

Scrubshaw's befuddled countenance was slammed by a wall of full realization. "You mean it's human?"

"As human as you and I, although I'm not too sure about you."

"Right . . ." Scrubshaw replied, nodding. As usual, he failed to acknowledge Farnsworth's sarcastic put-down. The deputy wouldn't know a sarcastic put-down if it ripped off all its clothes, painted itself Dayglo-pink and danced a waltz on the Empire State Building, singing: *I'm a sarcastic put-down!*

"Show's over!" Sheriff Farnsworth said, breathing out a long, exasperated sigh.

"Well, that's something you don't see every day," Deputy Scrubshaw observed.

True, one didn't normally see an alien wander around, swaying to-and-fro, drunk out of its head, taking long swigs from a bottle of liquor, a dumb harlot by its side, but when this kind of display happened to fool a police deputy, one wondered why the crime rate wasn't measurably higher.

"Where you going, Sheriff?" Scrubshaw asked as Farnsworth got to his feet.

"To bust its alien ass for wasting my time, causing a public panic and picking up a call-girl."

7

"That's it?" Casey cried, unable to hide her disappointment.

"Absolutely," said Dr. Hallaran with a winsome grin. "It's as simple as that. I know it's not quite what you wanted, but as I mentioned earlier, there's always a rational explanation for every paranormal event, even if it is sometimes out of reach. Do you really expect me to believe for one instant in the presence of aliens on Earth? I mean, why do they always have to be humanoid? Don't they have any other shape or form? The whole purpose of being alien is to look and act alien instead of an alien that resembles a human dressed in an alien's costume. Give me *The Thing* to *E.T.* any day."

"I guess you make a good point," Casey conceded. "What about the Men-in-Black?"

"That 'alien' they found was hauled into the drink tank," explained Dr. Hallaran. "He was a certain Dwaine Kessler, who turned out to be very human indeed. Under duress he admitted he had frightened Natalie Cole by dropping out of that UFO, which incidentally was nothing more than a helicopter disguised as a flying saucer. Its shell was constructed from a close meshwork of steel struts and fitted with multi-coloured strobe lights for effect. Kessler also played the Man-in-Black with the scar on his right cheek. Why he and his undisclosed employers had perpetrated this elaborate hoax became apparent later.

"Kessler's credentials confirmed that he had been hired by the Magna-co atomic research facility. Sheriff Farnsworth dug deeper and discovered the whole case revolved around the illegal dumping of radioactive waste."

"That's terrible!" Casey exclaimed. "They devised this ridiculous charade to cover up their own incompetence?"

"Correct. It explains why Natalie Cole had radiation burns. Magna-co's latest batch for testing was Cobalt-60. Unfortunately for them, one of their waste containers leaked."

"What about the android and JFK?"

"The android was just another government agent equipped with specially-designed, super-adhesive soles. Of JFK, or his handwriting for that matter, I haven't a clue, neither does the Sheriff."

"Could be a JFK impersonator with a talent for forging signatures."

"Quite possibly." Dr. Hallaran said, growing philosophical. "Didn't JFK once state, *You can fool all the people some of the time, and some of the people all of the time, but you cannot fool all the people all the time*?"

"No, I think that revered pearl of wisdom belonged to Abe Lincoln."

"Of course. But you get the point I'm making."

Indeed she did. She thought she would add one of JFK's actual nuggets: "*There is exists in this country a plot to enslave every man, woman and child. Before I leave this high and noble office I intend to expose this plot!"* She paused for a moment.

"Sounds like he knew something that the rest of us haven't yet figured out," observed Dr. Hallaran.

"I wonder what he found out . . ." contemplated Casey.

"Always the military industrial complex behind these sophisticated hoaxes," Dr. Hallaran explained, "Roswell, Dulce, Montauk, Area 51, Hangar 18—you name it, same nonsense. There will always be a secret agenda. The aim is to always confuse the UFO community—and indeed the public—by making everyone believe in something that was never there in the first place. The military just feeds the public scraps of misinformation, in a campaign of disinformation and denial and half-truths, claims and counterclaims, deliberately debunking any material witnesses, who seem to see into the conspiracy, only because it adds to the confusion. And this counterintelligence and deception sustains UFO folklore and keeps the public conveniently distracted, diverts their attention away from all the covert illegal shit the government is neck-deep in. I think UFO technology is nothing more than Nazi technology upgraded by the Airforce. Maybe advanced stealth technology—those wonderful men in those ultra-sophisticated, experimental flying machines."

"Makes perfect sense," said Casey, adding mock-conspiratorially, "but don't tell my boss."

Dr. Hallaran reciprocated, tapped his nose. "Mum's the word."

Casey stopped scribbling in her notepad, checked the clock on the wall. It was eleven minutes past five. "I guess I've got everything that I need. It's one hell of a story!" Complicated on the surface, but with a deceptively simple solution. "Thank you for your time."

Dr. Hallaran smiled. He looked a little intoxicated. "Think nothing of it. Maybe I can be permitted to ask you out to dinner?"

Casey returned the smile. "I don't know . . ."

"Please, I'd like to dine with you before you go, you know, to make up for my horny college-kid attitude. That is, if you don't have any other pressing engagements."

Casey considered the offer for a moment. "It's a deal. It's the least I can do to show my gratitude for your kind hospitality."

"Would the *Hampshire Restaurant* suit you?"

"As long as it serves lobster."

"The finest in New England," Dr. Hallaran affirmed, gulping down the remainder of the contents of his mug. "Clam-tastic!"

"Sounds ideal." She saw his obsessive gaze slip to her tanned legs and this time she didn't mind at all.

After all, he was only locobobulating with her.

8

Casey Jones returned to Boston the following day.

The drive back had been pleasant enough, but nothing compared to the previous evening. It had been fabulously filling, the exquisite experience guaranteeing a sensational journey to the peak of divine satisfaction. The lobster cuisine hadn't been bad, either!

It was past one when she socked home the key in the lock of her apartment. She sauntered into the lobby, half her mind replaying last night's date, the other half intent on typing up her jotted shorthand. Dr. Hallaran's anecdotal tale had the far-reaching potential for an article exclusive, so it seemed imperative she begin work with haste. A pot of steaming coffee and she would be well on her way.

The sound of a door slamming shut distracted her from her thoughts. Casey froze rigid. *There was someone here.* The idea that it might be a prowler, armed to the teeth, frightened her. Or maybe it was only the wind.

The apartment appeared unusually dim, the resident gloom seeming to sequester an unknown presence. That unsettling feeling of not being alone was too strong, almost tangible, to ignore. As alarm bells began to ring in her head, she chose the safest course of action. Turning round to beat a hasty retreat, she was stopped in her tracks by a deep, baleful voice, brimming with overwhelming authority. "Miss Casey Jones, would you please step into the parlour, said the spider to the fly?"

Behind her, at the entrance to the study, was a tall, hulking figure, his features veiled by shapeless, twisted shadows. When he emerged into the paltry lighting, Casey's nerves went ragged.

His black attire was both distinctive and spellbinding. The ugly scar on his right cheek brought everything into context. There was a Man-in-Black in her apartment, Dwaine Kessler incognito.

"What are you doing here?" Casey asked with cautious defiance.

"That is none of your concern," he decreed, dispassionately. "To the parlour, Princess of Trash."

Casey obeyed. Although she was lurching with apprehension, a part of her was enthralled. This was a scoop to end all scoops. She entered the sitting room to discover another unwelcome guest. A second man, wearing the same black get-up, sat unmoving in a chair. He was the same pale, mechanized human as described by Dr. Hallaran, except on this occasion he looked frozen in time, as inanimate as a statue. In his gloves, he was clutching a magazine, the page opened to *The Case of the Sexy Venusian Blonde*.

"What's the matter with him?"

"Energy modules overloaded. He read one of your articles and he short-circuited. I believe he struggled with the backwards rotation of the planet Venus and the concept that its day lasts longer than its year."

No-one spoke for a moment. She could hear the radio faintly from the bedroom, playing of all the tracks in the world, *Is That You Mo-Dean?* by the B52s.

"We advise you do not proceed with the composition of your article," the burly intruder ordered.

"Why not?"

"That is none of your concern."

Casey's patience was beginning to wear thin. Anger bubbled over. "Look, I know who you are. So don't try to act smart."

Kessler loomed over her like a cane-wielding schoolmaster. "You don't know anything. We are not whom you think we are."

"Yeah? Well, you and Magna-co's actions were mighty scandalous. The world's going to want to know . . ."

She broke off as the bedroom door closed and her jaw lost all tension.

There was another Man-in-Black present, and Casey stared, almost dumbfounded, at his avuncular face and his unmistakable chin curtain. "Hold your horses, lady," Abraham Lincoln, President, Statesman and Slavery Abolitionist, said gruffly. "Need I remind you, dear lady, that Life is a chore and Destiny a spiralling bullet in the head. The pain is over, and you are consigned to a deep hole in the ground, at peace with the Universe, a state banquet for the bugs. I ought to know—I've been there." He paused, declared contemplatively. "*And in the end, it's not the years in your life that count, it's the life in your years . . .*"

"This is some sort of trick," Casey managed to murmur, wide-eyed. "You're not really here . . ."

"You're half-right, dear lady," President Lincoln said, and grinning an uncharacteristic jester's grin, tugged at his hair and pulled off the latex mask he'd been masquerading in, revealing the handsome, boyish face Casey recalled from video footage of that fatal day in November, 1963, a face unchanged by death or decades of time. President Kennedy took a step forward, lifted a Cuban cigar from his pocket, lit it with a match without requesting permission from his hostess. "You know me and Uncle Abe go back a long way, little miss," he reflected, puffing away on his stogie. "You might even argue we are *one* and the same person! Jung spoke of 'synchronicities'—in other words, meaningful coincidences that have nothing to do with 'cause and effect'— he claimed there was *no* such thing as an accident. How're these for synchronicities?" Kennedy hit his stride, proving why he was the fastest and one of the most knowledgeable speakers ever to enter politics. "Uncle Abe was elected to Congress in 1846, myself in 1946, both of us leading the bill on Civil Rights. Uncle Abe was elected President in 1860, myself in 1960. Both our wives lost a son at the White House and each was present when we got shot in the back of our heads. Uncle Abe was assassinated on a Friday in 1863, myself in 1963. Uncle Abe and me were succeeded by

Southerners called Johnson, born 1808 and 1908, respectively. Booth shot Uncle Abe in a theatre and hid in a warehouse, I was shot from a warehouse and Oswald hid in a theatre. Both Booth and Oswald were assassinated before their trials. And we all know why. And we all know who *really* killed us . . ." Kennedy continued lecturing, rattling off opinion: "*Cui bono,* Latin for 'to whose profit'. You see, successful, high-profile assassinations generally rely on a middle man—a scapegoat or *patsy*—who takes the fall to divert attention away from the actual motive. *Failed* assassination attempts, like those conducted on Gerald Ford and Ronald Reagan, are often staged to gain public sympathy and boost the ailing popularity of the politician. Make sense, missie?"

"I think you've gone tooting," Casey reckoned, trying not to sound overwhelmed by the man's presence or the weird patter of information he had imparted.

"Nah, you're tooting," JFK replied amicably.

"If you write your story," warned Kessler, "we will not be held responsible for the consequences."

"Your circus act doesn't fool me," Casey said as defiant as ever.

"No?" JFK responded. "Well, maybe this'll convince you . . ."

He reached for his hair and, in one swift swipe, ripped off a second latex mask. Underneath was a face the journalist recognized instantly, and her blood ran cold.

"I bet you weren't expecting to see me again . . ." remarked Dr. Hallaran, with an absurdly friendly grin on his face.

February 2004—March 2004

Archly Amused Pan

"Anxiety is the poison of human life; the parent of many sins and of more miseries. In a world where everything is doubtful, and where we may be disappointed, and be blessed in disappointment, why this restless stir and commotion of the mind? Can it alter the cause, or unravel the mystery of human events?"

Tyron Edwards (1809-1894)
American Theologian and Christian Minister

Dr. Sebastian Havers, a respectable GP in the Malvern Hills, loved his fiancée, Hazel Spiers. He wished dearly to marry Miss Spiers to celebrate their love for each other.

Hazel was adored and respected by both Sebastian and me and our parents and grandmother. As Sebastian's elder brother, Marcus, I am also a family doctor of supposed equal reputation. Hazel was a sweet-tempered woman, generous and honest and caring, who saw the best in everyone, no matter what their shortcomings. Slim-figured and naturally-tanned, Hazel was blessed with a pretty face, kind blue eyes and short, dark-blond hair; her appearance was what had attracted my brother in the first place until he got to love the rest of her. Hazel worked as a Religious Studies teacher at the local Sixth Form College and kept up dutifully with her busy daily schedule. Hazel painted in her spare time, heavenly scenes involving choirs of haloed angels. Although Hazel and Sebastian had got engaged two months ago and she had moved into the Havers family home in recent weeks, I'm certain she and Sebastian had not yet embarked on intimate relations, since Hazel possessed strong Christian values, without resorting to fanaticism, hypocrisy or self-righteousness (unlike my grandmother), refused to wear make-up, was a resolute teetotaller and attended Church every Sunday. Hazel was therefore seen as perfect for my peace-loving, morality-driven brother, apart from one aspect of her personality: she suffered from anxiety.

Hazel not only suffered from anxiety but carried the full spectrum of anxiety traits. She had a compulsion to clean and tidy up, since Cleanliness was purportedly next only to Godliness. She could present as a hypochondriac with a tendency to somatize, i.e. develop transient bodily complaints that defied medical explanation, and would worry frequently about the quality of her motions, misconstrue abdominal pain as food poisoning, headaches that suddenly took on a sinister meaning and the suchlike, even fretting over Sebastian's physical health, which might have seemed cute in the beginning but had grown increasingly tiresome and frustrating for all concerned. There was an element of post-traumatic stress disorder stemming back to when Hazel's father used to beat her up while drunk during her late childhood, so Hazel would sometimes experience unpleasant, intrusive memories of the abuse and occasionally suffer nightmares. Her father's drinking had caused further problems when Hazel, during her adolescence, had witnessed him vomiting up stomach-loads of red wine into the toilet bowl almost every night from which Hazel had developed a huge, longstanding fear of vomiting. Emetophobia, as it is so-called, is one of the ten commonest phobias in the world. In Hazel's case, her emetophobia affected her appetite. She would not eat, afraid she would vomit, losing weight in the process, then panic that if she didn't eat, she would faint.

The worst, most crippling aspect of it was waking up in the small hours of the morning every night, shaking, highly agitated and panicky, burping up the air from her empty, churning stomach, struggling against the pounding heart, the severe cold perspiration and sickly, gagging feeling. Her panic symptoms increased her preoccupation with losing control and vomiting, which in turn exacerbated her sense of panic, which made her feel more nauseous, which further heightened the panic. To break this vicious cycle, she would try distracting herself: start cleaning, read the Bible, paint in the conservatory or, sometimes, when her panic was really bad, drive off to nowhere in the middle of the night. As Hazel put it neatly: *When I think I'm going to be sick, I have an overpowering desire to get as far away from it as I possibly can even though it goes with me.* Such avoidance and escape behaviours only risked reinforcing the phobia, perpetuating the anxiety. Hazel hated being touched during her nocturnal panic states, preferring to suffer in silence. Eventually her anxiety attack would burn itself out and she would get some much-needed sleep. You can imagine Hazel dreaded bedtime, afraid of waking up and puking. Even a mention of the word 'vomit' triggered all sorts of negative, distorted cognitions in her mind and set off the intrinsic 'fight-or-flight' response in her body.

Remarkably, her nightly panic attacks did not compromise her attendance at work. She still held down a demanding job, but it meant she went to college, aching and exhausted. She had done incredibly well for herself, worked doubly hard, when many people with her traumatized background would have gone on to self-harm or abuse drugs. It saddened Sebastian that he could not help her, with her refusal to be comforted when she was freaking out, making him feel like a terrible doctor, powerless, useless. He would have gladly shared her burden if only she let him, allowed him in.

When her anxiety reached a stage that she began to think Sebastian was throwing up every time he used the loo and that he might die, he turned to me for advice, hoping that my rather unconventional approach to patient management could address the problem.

"I can't give up on her now," Sebastian was telling me, having conducted a flying visit to my Fairview home one weekend. We sat in my spacious garden in bright, summer sunshine, drinking elderflower tea. "I love her, and it upsets me to see her suffer like this."

"Everybody would hate you if you claimed you'd had enough and broke off the engagement and decided to abandon her," I said, firm but supportive. "Also, she's the kind of level-headed woman who would resent pity. I think she would make an excellent doctor's wife, irrespective of her disability." Talking from experience, anxiety symptoms formed the commonest psychiatric presentation in the community, statistically-speaking, approximately one-third of GP consultations. Nothing wrong with being a little anxious. It's anxiety alone that allows most of us to get up in the morning and go into work, otherwise we don't get paid and we won't be able to afford the rent or the mortgage. But it was pathological anxiety that we must be wary of. Both Sebastian and myself were reasonably familiar with the various lines and combinations of treatment available to anxiety sufferers. "What interventions have you tried so far?"

"Hazel completed a private twelve-session course of CBT, which I paid for, in an attempt to challenge and ultimately alter her Negative Automatic Thoughts, allow her to de-catastrophize, unfortunately to no avail. The psychotherapist diagnosed her with Type 2 Trauma, meaning she has repeated exposure to the perceived threat/undesirable stimulus."

"She may need a more exploratory psychodynamic approach to deal with the underlying traumas. Could cost a few bob, though."

"Expense is no obstacle."

I referred back to the basics of anxiety management. "Does she try challenging her phobic thoughts? Perhaps, repeating over and over in her head, like a mantra: *I feel sick but there is NO rational reason why I should be sick?* After a while, the nauseous feeling should pass as ought the panic, and she'll calm down and fall asleep."

"Something similar, yes, ineffectively, though."

"Has she ever tried relaxation techniques/meditation/yoga?"

"Rather unsuccessfully," replied Sebastian. "She finds it

extremely difficult to perform breathing exercises, let alone relax, when she's having one of her episodes." A touch of gloom entered his voice. "All the anxiety management strategies—ventilation of feelings, distraction techniques, identifying both external and *internal* 'safe spaces' and potential self-soothing mechanisms—have so far proved ineffective. Poor girl understands the irrationality of her fears and feels so utterly guilty afterwards."

I didn't like how this sounded. "Her symptoms sound more entrenched than I first thought. It doesn't bode well for her prognosis." I turned to pharmaceutical means, all of which Sebastian would be familiar with. They were worth mentioning anyway. "Have you used medication: propranolol to cut short the autonomic arousal or diazepam for immediate management of the psychological distress alongside a trial of SSRI antidepressant—the dose optimized, of course—for medium-to-longer-term management?"

Sebastian shook his head. "Hazel refused flat-out. She doesn't want to be doped-up. She's also read that one of the early side-effects of SSRIs *is* nausea before it reaches a therapeutic level in your bloodstream. Besides, Hazel's never taken medication in her whole life—her parents didn't believe in it—not even Calpol as a baby."

I grew contemplative, took a sip of my elderflower tea. "You know it really narrows down our options."

Sebastian sounded despondent. "I still want to marry her, have kids with her some day. But I can't imagine her becoming pregnant and being able to cope with the morning sickness. Also, repeated high maternal adrenaline levels would affect the unborn brain, produce a jittery baby, as well as risking the male pattern thinking of an autistic child."

I said nothing for a while. The speck of an idea was forming in my mind, gathering mass, eventually crystallizing into a more elaborate pearl of a plan, almost radical in its simplicity. I thought I just might know how to manage her unquiet mind. "Hazel must know she's bad at vomiting. She hasn't vomited for over a decade. I would suggest adjusting her internal settings. An extreme variation on the dependable principles of graded exposure, as applied to all phobics, might be the order of the day."

"That's why I came to you," Sebastian said, suddenly brightening up. "I could use your rather unorthodox way of thinking. What do you have in mind?"

I pitched my cunning scheme with a degree of confidence. "Desperate times call for desperate measures. I'm thinking let's skip the preliminary stages of exposure therapy altogether and go straight to the fun part. Achieve the final product in one flash."

"And that would be?"

"Flooding."

The roots of the word *panic* lie in ancient mythology. 'Panic' derives its name from the Greek demigod Pan whom legend has it possessed the horns, legs and hindquarters of a goat. Apart from being the god of shepherds and flocks and the lover of nymphs, worshipped in fertility rites, and a genius on the panpipes, crafted from the clump of reeds that was once the nymph Syrinx, he took arch amusement from terrorizing passing travellers in the mountain wilds of Arcadia. Pan would hide in the bushes, waiting for any passersby. When he heard someone approach, Pan would deliberately rustle the vegetation, producing a sense of apprehension in the unwitting victim, causing them to pick up the pace. Then, Pan would quietly scurry on ahead, intercepting the person at another dark turn in the path. Still concealed and with growing excitement and mischief, Pan would again rustle the bushes in intimidating fashion and the traveller would make even greater haste, breathing heavily, heart beginning to thump harder and the sounds of their own quickening footsteps magnified ominously in the silence of the forest. Alarmed now, afraid they were being pursued by some dangerous, feral animal, the unsuspecting traveller would summarily flee Pan's forest kingdom. Never would the same former fright-stricken person re-enter the forest without experiencing a sinister degree of dread. Thus did originate the words 'panic' and 'pandemonium'.

Moving on from an etymological angle to a more scientific approach, the neurochemical cascade behind panic can be neatly distilled into the relationship between the inhibitory neurotransmitter GABA, which normally keeps the 'fight-or-flight' response in check, and the amydala, an almond-shaped set of nuclei that forms part of the limbic system of the brain and is involved in the storage of emotional memories and, crucially, the processing and expression of emotions, especially anger and fear. Simplified, reduced levels of GABA-A in the amygdala result in impulses to the hypothalamus for the activation of the sympathetic nervous system, saturating the body with adrenaline and precipitating a panic attack. Benzodiazepines, such as diazepam and lorazepam, addictive though they can be in the long run, inhibit the activity of the amygdala, this part of the brain responsible for fear, thereby leading to a short-lived reduction in anxiety.

With Sebastian's full blessing, I put my plan into action the following weekend at my old family home in Chertsford. Our parents had gone blissfully to the opera, and our grandmother, a sprightly ninety-three-year-old matriarch and Empress of the Grapevine, was taking in an early night, probably spent from a phone-filled day of idle chatter, character assassination and general malicious scandalmongering, leaving myself in the company of my brother and his dearly betrothed. A terrific cook, Hazel made dinner for us: homemade broccoli-and-stilton soup, pan-roasted red-snapper-and-dill on a bed of baby spinach, black olives and tomberries, and lime sorbet for dessert, polished off with a nice bottle of chardonnay (which Hazel didn't partake of due to her steadfast abstinent nature). We, then, retreated to the drawing room, where we enjoyed our after-dinner coffees.

"I'm glad you visited," Hazel said, with twinkling eyes. "We rarely ever see you. I know Sebastian calls you every so often. What's the occasion?"

"Does there have to be an occasion?" I replied amiably. "Sebastian gets on splendidly without me anyway. Isn't it enough I just dropped by because I miss you both?"

"It's great you're here," Hazel said, getting rather sentimental. I could imagine a tear of joy trickling down her cheek from the manner in which she spoke. "We all miss you too." However, her tone became one of gentle suspicion. "But I sense an ulterior motive."

There she was, sweet Hazel, chaste Hazel, *shrewd* Hazel, perceptive as ever. "I see that nothing gets past you." I recounted the conversation with Sebastian the weekend earlier. I broached the actual reason for my visit but deliberately did not include what we intended to do. "We have serious concerns over your ability to cope with your affliction."

"And what affliction would that be?"

"Your fear of vomiting and the episodes of panic it brings. I'm here to release you from your torment!"

Hazel produced an amused smile, curiosity piqued. "And how do you propose to do that?"

"There's nothing wrong with being anxious," I explained comprehensively. "Anxiety is a derivation of fear, which itself is a mechanism that has existed in us since man lived in caves and hunted in forests, designed to prepare us for any imminent threat. In a split-second, the brain evaluates the circumstances of the environment through the senses with whatever prior knowledge is available and fires a protective neurological command, mainly through the neurotransmitter adrenaline and the stress hormone cortisol, for our body to freeze, fight or flee, bypassing the conscious. Fear is a normal response to a dangerous situation. It becomes pathological when it starts to affect your daily functioning—I wouldn't call suddenly upping and leaving in the middle of the night for a drive as logical, rational or normal."

I read resistance in her voice. "I'm fine. It's who I am, it's what defines me."

"No, it's what you've *become*," I said darkly. "You've turned into a bit of a panicky girl these days. Your past haunts you every night, brings you no peace of mind. If we don't intervene soon, it will completely drain you, suck you dry. You'll burn-out, suffer a nervous breakdown and get committed to a psychiatric ward." I let my words sink in before I continued. "We don't mean to check you into a hospital, mind, nor do we plan to ask you to regurgitate all you're supposed to have already learned in your psychotherapy sessions. But we're determined to bring you peace of mind."

The smile had faded from her face, replaced by a look of unease. "I also take comfort in the Good Book or paint when I'm suffering. It does the trick sometimes."

"But I bet not always," I replied, carefully selecting a few choice quotes. "*Casting all your anxiety on Him,/because He cares for you.* 1 Peter 5:7. Taking refuge in Scripture and relying on prayer is all well and true, but I'm sure that although it might take the edge off your panic, it's not entirely alleviating particularly in the dead of night. And, as for painting, Edvard Munch, creator of *The Scream*, sublimated his deep-seated feelings of anxiety into his art. TS Eliot, arguably the most important Western poet of the twentieth century, called anxiety the '*handmaiden of creativity*'. However, even though you have a flair for art, I foresee the same shortfalls arising: I doubt you've honed your artistic skills enough to completely sublimate your intense anxieties into your paintings. In many respects, reading and painting aren't so much distraction as overstimulation, prolonging the crisis. Mentioning the philosophy of Aesop: *A crust eaten in peace is better than a banquet partaken in anxiety.*" I paused for a moment, proceeded forthwith using my most persuasive, confidence-instilling bedside manner. "Instead of living, you are wasting your life on worrying. You even worry about not being worried when you have nothing to worry about. Some might call you a delicate, fragile creature for you to suffer such extreme anxiety every night, but I say it is a testament to your resilience that your lovely personality has survived intact for so long. Work with us, Hazel. We both care terribly for you and hate to see you suffer so. Believe me when I say we only have your best interests at heart. Show us a little faith—I mean this is what we do for a living—and give us a chance to heal you."

Whoever invented the concept of flooding must have been an evil genius. Throw a man with an intense phobia of wasps in a room full of wasps and witness him scream and panic in absolute terror. His panic will reach a spectacular crescendo, then start to trail off, ebb away, until he is completely desensitized. He may get stung multiple times and drop dead from anaphylactic shock, but at least he'd be cured of his wasp phobia.

I had something similar in mind for my future sister-in-law.

Under strictly controlled, clinical conditions, of course.

Still sat in the drawing room, we finished off our coffees as Hazel mulled over my proposal. At this stage, I did not give away any inkling as to what we had in mind. Best to be economical with the truth. I could see skepticism in her expression or it could have been apprehension.

I dipped into my jacket pocket and pulled out a small plastic bottle containing a thick, amber-brown liquid, label consciously removed. "All we ask of you is you drink this."

I passed it over to her. Hazel handled the bottle, studied the contents closely. "What is it?"

"That, my dear, is our miracle cure. Works like magic."

"What does it do?"

"It should cure you of your vomit phobia. Make you as resilient as Cool Hand Luke fearlessly facing down an indigestible fifty eggs."

"Just like that?"

"Just like that!" I said confidently.

"Then why isn't this stuff—whatever it is—mentioned on any of the online Emetophobia forums?"

I lied, trying to sell the product. "It's a relatively new drug, only recently released on the market. Most people probably haven't heard of it yet. And very expensive, too."

"What do I do with it?"

"Simply drink it and all your troubles will vanish."

"What if it doesn't work?"

"I can declare with ninety-nine-point-nine-nine percent certainty that it will work. There is still that tiny, remote possibility that it won't, but at least we'd be satisfied in the knowledge we gave it a try."

Hazel continued to waver, but I seemed to be winning.

Sebastian watched our exchange in silence. "What if I refuse?" she asked suddenly.

I continued my negotiations, to coax her. "We can't force you to take it—we need your willing consent—otherwise it would be unprofessional of us. But it would mean you turned down a golden opportunity to rid yourself of your suffering once and for all."

Hazel glanced at Sebastian for validation, who gave a small reassuring nod. "Alright, I'll do it," she said, finally convinced, albeit with nervous trepidation. "All I do is drink it?"

"Down it in one go," I instructed her, watching her twist the top open with tentative slowness. "Trust us, you won't regret this." With one cautious sniff of the contents, catching the sweet, cloying aroma, Hazel consumed the intriguing amber liquid in one courageous gulp. At that moment, I respected her more than anyone else in the world for listening to me. Hazel had suffered horrendously. She was a gentle, virtuous God-fearing creature, a Theology graduate, a homemaker and the perfect soulmate for my younger brother. Despite her beauty, intelligence and obvious resilience, she had lived for decades with a frustrating, crippling mental disorder. The wishy-washiness of psychotherapy had not stopped her from waking up every night before REM sleep could kick in, shaking and panicking, leaving her feeling drained in the mornings. Pan was mocking her, in a manner of speaking. He had bestowed his blessing on her to go crazy, just as his roguish, unseen presence had aroused feelings of high anxiety in those travellers passing through his lonely, rustic wilds. Hazel deserved to find peace from her longstanding fears, to get on with her life without being plagued by undue reminders of her dreadful upbringing. Nobody should have to recover from their childhood. I would have gladly dropped a neutron bomb on her father's head, if he were still alive, for the complex traumas he had thrust upon her. I would have gladly desecrated his grave, if my dark side had its way.

"Tastes like pancake syrup," Hazel said, licking her lips. "You haven't just given me a placebo? I know how you doctors think."

"No placebo, I promise," I replied, satisfied she had no clue as to what would soon surely follow. I watched Sebastian return from the kitchen with a plain glass of water. "Now, wash down the foul-tasting medicine with this—the whole glass, please."

Hazel took the glass from Sebastian and swallowed the water in prim, ladylike fashion. She noticed us staring at her fixedly. "What? Did I spill some?" she said, delicately dabbing the sides of her mouth with a paper napkin. Then, without warning, a look of disquiet, of vigilance crossed her brow, as though she were beginning to experience something unpleasant, something unwelcome. "My tummy feels a bit funny."

It didn't surprise me. Her stomach would feel funny, and the queasy sensation would only get worse from now-on-out. I had resorted to deception to get her to drink that amber liquid. Except, in all honesty, I hadn't entirely misled her. The brown liquid she had unwittingly swallowed wasn't exactly straight out of clinical trials or a new miracle drug or even vaguely expensive. It had existed in the pharmacist's formulary for centuries, used only for one express purpose, until being recently discontinued, outlawed. Syrup of ipecac is derived from the roots of the ipecacuanha plant and is a gastric irritant and powerful emetic. It was once used to induce vomiting in attempted/accidental overdose patients until it was eventually replaced by activated charcoal as the first-line treatment of acute poisoning. Ipecacuanha juice is itself a poison, but because it acts very quickly in bringing up all the stomach contents, it is rarely absorbed. It has since gained wide and worrying favour with anorexic and bulimic sufferers. Ipecac syrup contributed extensively to the death of the popular singer, Karen Carpenter, at age thirty-two.

Why should I, you may ask, trick Hazel, who already had an unspeakable fear of vomiting, into ingesting syrup of ipecac? Reason: the concept of flooding involves confronting the perceived threat full-on. The perceived threat in this case would be nausea and the subsequent, unimaginable prospect of vomiting.

"Come with us, Hazel," I said calmly. "You don't seem to be feeling well."

Hazel's face was a mask of alarm and horror as she doubled over, clutching her stomach. Fully focused on her sickly feeling, she was having trouble getting her words out. "Where're we going?"

"Hold on, my dear," I said, as me and Sebastian walked Hazel to the upstairs bathroom. We made painstakingly slow progress, almost dragging her there, afraid she might actually hurl up on the way.

After a couple of minutes, we reached the marble family bathroom and we positioned her over the toilet. Kneeling, poised over the pan, Hazel uttered with a groan. "What have you done to me?"

"Let it all out," I encouraged her gently. "We know you want to."

"I *mustn't*...!" she protested between acidic burps. Despite wrestling against the oncoming urge, she must have realized she could not escape the inevitable. Her stomach revolted, surged, convulsed and, with a squawking, gagging noise, she expelled its contents, largely a brownish-yellow stew of lumpy, partially-digested food, in a splattering, violent gush across the toilet bowl. Yet, at the same moment, she began to shake with the onset of a panic attack. Having now crossed the threshold and reached a stage of no return, each separate process, the panic and the vomiting, sped up, peaked. She continued to spew out her guts forcefully in increasing waves, and as her shaking and hyperventilating worsened, she started to cough and splutter . . .

It must have been hell for Sebastian watching his betrothed suffer thus, particularly now. "My God, she's choking!" It was an accurate, if not serious, clinical observation. We were faced with a medical emergency. *Hazel was aspirating.* Even after she'd completely emptied her stomach, she continued to retch, dry-heave, while hacking away, the sound of her laborious coughing mutating into high, shallow, agonal whoops as she struggled to breathe. "This was *your* idea! *Do something!*" Sebastian shrieked, aghast, with an accusatory look, panicking himself.

"Don't sweat the small stuff!" I told him sternly. "Maintain your professionalism, fulfil your oath as a doctor . . . Don't you think I anticipated this?" A good doctor foresees every eventuality and comes prepared. He advises, anticipates and acts whatever the complication.

Hazel was losing consciousness, her lips turning blue, her pulse becoming erratic and thready. She had stopped coughing and was making feeble, cawing sounds of respiratory distress—a bad sign. We had precious little time left to save her. Applying back blows or abdominal thrusts would have been useless in this particular instance since it wasn't a single foreign object that was lodged in her airways but aspirated fluid. Elvis Presley had died in a similar manner, but I would not let the same fate befall Hazel. Like I said, I came prepared.

While Sebastian placed Hazel on her back (as per my instruction), I went to the linen basket and pulled out the 17cm x 20cm blue box I had hidden there earlier amongst the dirty laundry, clicking it open. I placed it next to Hazel, making the necessary attachments and connections. Sebastian realized to his amazement it was a portable suction pump mini-aspirator. I activated the vacuum-operated machine, the suction pump chugging to life. No need to intubate just yet, I hoped, or deliver oxygen from the bag-and-mask I'd also tucked away in the laundry basket; the aspirant couldn't have gone too far down. As quickly and expertly as I could muster, I opened Hazel's mouth and manoeuvred the curved tip of the aspirator down her throat directly towards her trachea, careful to avoid triggering the gag reflex. Greenish-brown mucus and pieces of food debris were sucked up by the catheter, collecting in the suction bottle. We used the suction device for maybe ten minutes, clearing her upper airways, until no further gunk could be extracted.

I turned off the flow of the vacuum pump and checked Hazel's vital signs, listened to her chest with my stethoscope. Her pulse was 80/min and she was breathing a lot better. There were no additional, abnormal breath sounds in her lung-fields on auscultation, except for a mild wheeze, which a little salbutamol could easily resolve. Maybe a short course of antibiotics to prevent the potential chest infection that might arise from the little, inhaled aspirant. I assaulted her nostrils with the pungent smell of ammonia salts, and she groaned awake, bursting into a coughing fit. Her blue eyes peered up at us, perplexed. Her confusion soon cleared, and she sat up.

Sebastian immediately hugged her with unbounded relief. "How do you feel?"

"Terrible," she croaked, coughing again. "I feel as if I've run a marathon. I have a headache and my throat's raw."

"We almost lost you," explained Sebastian, holding Hazel's head tightly over his shoulder, stroking her blond hair, "until Marcus stepped up."

"Thank you, Marcus, I owe you," said Hazel, detaching herself from her future husband's affectionate embrace. "But I won't forgive you for the method you employed, what you put me through."

"I haven't finished yet," I stated with a crafty grin. I had to test the effectiveness of my therapy to prove she had overcome her phobia of vomiting. I deliberately shoved two fingers down my throat and vomited. I was tempted to throw up all over Hazel, maybe spew forth some projectile, pea-soup vomitus, *Exorcist*-style—now *that* would have been a real test! But I decided to refrain out of respect for Hazel and to protect her dignity. My dinner came up in an enormous rush, a stinking curdled vichyssoise of coffee, fish and spinach, splashing the sides of the toilet pan. I wiped bile from my mouth with a handkerchief when I'd ejected everything, belching. I glanced at Hazel, gauging her reaction. "Just for you . . ." I said in the manner of someone handing a close friend or loved one a gift.

She didn't vomit again or descend into panic. "That's disgusting . . ." she commented half-heartedly instead, with a weary sigh.

I grinned wider, sensing success, inwardly commending my well-coordinated operation, apparently rendering a deep-rooted phobia extinct. My therapeutic procedure had gone according to plan. I wondered what Pan, whom the Ancient Greeks also viewed as the god of theatrical criticism, would have made of all this. In keeping with my love of music, I thought of *Novocaine for the Soul* by the Eels as perfect accompaniment for the occasion. Like the man with the fear of wasps, Hazel was cured. "Welcome to the family, my dear!"

September 2011—October 2011

The Operators

"I'm a worrier, so the next logical step is paranoia."

Chris Carter
Creator of *The X-Files*

I suppose it all started with my interest in Clare Keating. We had both recently graduated as doctors from different universities and were working together at the same hospital, Fairview General.

Our contempt for our jobs, treated like dogsbodies on our respective wards, working ungodly hours, was what brought us together. It was fun being a medical student, but now fully qualified, the novelty had worn off within a fortnight. We were essentially glorified phlebotomists and clerking machines. Even the crash calls were led by the Anaesthetist-on-call and the Medical Registrar, ourselves little more than bystanders.

So we tried to make the most of our time outside our shifts. We'd spend most evenings together, smoking cigarettes and drinking champagne, not an easy thing to manage on a House Officer's salary. Sometimes, we'd go out to a restaurant or catch a movie. Other times, we'd drive up to the hills and take long walks.

We had a good time together, friends for life and all that. Except I wondered if I could move to the next level with my cute, adorable beauty from Belfast, whether we could be viewed as something of an item.

The roses I bought Clare went down well with her, and she kissed me.

We never slept together for she informed me she was not in

that place yet. It was all a moot point anyway because soon afterwards I came down with the shingles.

And that was when the really weird stuff started.

Having shingles is like being in quarantine. You really can't go anywhere because the condition is contagious and could spark off a case in someone else, and, of course, the rash itself—following the natural dermatomes of your body—looks distinctly unsettling. I couldn't go home, since home for me was Mauritius, and the flight attendants would not look kindly to a fellow who, post-7/7, appeared to be carrying a communicable disease, afraid that I might be some new breed of bioterrorist. So at the Doctors' Residence, I remained, in self-imposed isolation, applying analgesic cream to the affected areas, looking close to as unsightly as the Singing Detective—or like whom I perceived I looked.

Clare visited me less and less until one day she stopped visiting altogether. I tried talking to her on the phone, but she had always made plans that evening. It saddened me, yet who could blame her?

There is only so much TV you can watch or books you can read or music you can listen to, so I took to drinking. I'd order take-outs and a bottle of Glenfiddich by taxi and pay the driver when he arrived with my goods—the only time I ever ventured out of my room.

God bless alcohol and curse *Herpes zoster!*

On long-term sick, it wasn't long before I was consuming half a bottle a night usually to the point of keeling over.

Not a good omen for things to come.

Loneliness can do funny things to a person. You just have to remember the Sensory Deprivation experiments they conducted nearly half-a-century ago.

I didn't notice the voices at first. I thought they were simply background conversation drifting in from the hospital grounds. Then, they became more apparent, more intense.

I had just knocked back several glasses of scotch when I heard someone ask: *How you doing, old boy?* I lowered the volume of the *Horizon* documentary I was watching and listened intently.

It took next to no time for the voice to resurface. *So what's going down in Shingles Town?*

"What the—?" I muttered, perplexed.

Reading you loud and clear!

What was happening? Was my imagination playing tricks on me? Had my heavy drinking finally tipped me over the edge? Had I, Hitcham Gale, actually begun to hallucinate?

Except the voice was familiar. It sounded like it belonged to—"Is that you, Esmond?" I asked, astonished.

Esmond Cook was a fellow House Officer. *Perceptive as ever!* his voice mocked. *Looks like you've started talking to yourself. Doesn't bode well for the future. People are going to start to think you've gone strange.*

I shut the window and closed the curtains. I lit up another cigarette. "How are you doing this?"

I'm not doing anything. I'm coming to you from inside your head.

A statement like that can unnerve anyone. I admit I was scared, that maybe this second-person auditory hallucination was the result of Alcoholic Hallucinosis, but I was also intrigued. Most folk would have checked themselves into a Psychiatric ward on the strength of those words alone, but not me. I was so bored out of my skull and frankly quite drunk that I decided to let the conversation run its course. Besides, I needed the company. "What are you doing inside my head?"

Having a whale of a time, Esmond's voice replied. *Aren't you?*

"Difficult to tell."

How about now? emerged a second voice.

"Andrew?" I murmured in stark disbelief. "Andrew Trent?"

And Melanie and Tracy . . . went on Esmond, as smug as the day he was born. *The gang's all here!*

Hi there, Hitch! greeted Melanie Lieberman.

How's it hanging? Andrew Trent inquired jovially.

Then it was Tracy Gorman's turn: *Just thought we'd drop by and have a chat!*

Drs. Trent, Lieberman and Gorman were all colleagues, same rank, different serial numbers. I tried to keep it together. "You're all inside my head?"

Where else would we be? remarked Esmond with impish glee. *You're fucking possessed, man!*

You need the services of an exorcist, joked Andrew.

I am Legion, Tracy recited from the Bible. *For We are Many.*

Then all involved, except Yours Truly, burst out into gales of laughter.

"Why are you doing this to me?" I demanded, getting freaked.

To prove you're cracking up, commented Esmond, the smarmy bastard.

And where was Clare Keating in all of this?

As though having read my thoughts, Esmond growled with malice aforethought: *Clare doesn't want anything more to do with you! You're diseased, man! You've turned into an alkie and a waste of space, sponging off the NHS for sick pay! You're not fit to call yourself a doctor! You're a coon and a total fucking loser!*

Don't be so cruel, Esmond! intervened Melanie. *Can't you see the poor guy's got a crush on Clare?*

The guy doesn't deserve her, stated Esmond menacingly. *She's my girl and he'd better not go near her again or I'll break his fucking bones!*

"Fuck you, Esmond!" I shouted, hurt and humiliated and afraid. "I never liked you, anyway!"

The feeling's mutual, responded Esmond. *Let's see how long you can last.*

"Longer than you think, shithead!" I said, rising to the challenge. I stubbed out my cigarette and turned up the sound of the TV, drowning out the voices in my head. I poured myself more scotch and tried to focus on the documentary, which was curiously enough about the effects of isolation.

Wakey-wakey! somebody uttered cheerily from nearby.

My eyes drifted open. Dazed and confused, I looked around my room. There was no-one there. My tongue as rough as sandpaper, my stomach burbling with acid, I got up and used the en-suite facilities. My urine was almost as dark as the scotch I had drunk the night before. I checked my face in the mirror and barely recognized the person looking back. The rash around my cheeks and neck remained sore and tingly, but the stubble was a day older and my eyes bloodshot and sunken.

Still quite groggy, I came back to my room and dropped heavily on to the bed.

You look like shit, came the disembodied voice.

"I look how I feel," I groaned, my mind only just registering the initial observation. I bolted upright, suddenly alert and panicky. "Who said that?"

'Tis I, Lord Esmond, and his Merry Band of Followers. Together, we are your Psychosis.

Oh, God! I despaired. *Just when I thought I might have imagined the whole thing.* "I don't need this right now."

Why not? You're not getting away from us that easily.

"I have a five-alarm hangover," I remonstrated, "and it's still dark outside!" I checked my wrist-watch. "*It's half-three in the morning!* GO A-WAY!" I lay back down again, closed my eyes.

No can do, Esmond chirped. *We're not finished with you yet. We can't let you sleep,* Andrew added, just as chipper.

Nothing hypnagogic/hypnapompic about these babies, otherwise I might have considered myself vaguely normal. "I'm not sleeping, I'm just getting a little shuteye."

Can't allow that either, replied Esmond.

Out of nowhere, I felt a sharp pain in my chest. "*Jeee-zus!*" I roared, suddenly wide awake. The pain disappeared as quickly as it had struck. "You bastard, what did you do to me?"

Only playing with you, man, Esmond chortled.

In answer to your question, we did nothing, Andrew explained. *You eat crap, you lie on your bed all day long and you've been drinking like a fish for weeks. What do expect? Your body isn't what it used to be. You're experiencing the sedentary equivalent to weightlessness.*

"My own hallucinations giving me medical advice," I remarked wryly. "I'm touched."

We're not bothered what you do to yourself, declared Esmond with staid indifference. *We're just telling you like it is.*

"Thank you, but I really couldn't give a fuck. I'm going back to sleep."

We won't let you, Esmond warned darkly. *Over the last few days you've been running on high levels of adrenaline, dampened only by the depressant effects of the alcohol. The next time your adrenaline levels fall below a certain threshold, you'll suffer a cardiac arrest.*

Terror seeped through me. My hallucinations were warning me I might die if I slept. Should I believe them? Or were they screwing with me? Either way, it wasn't worth taking the risk. Instead of getting out of my stinky black clothes and taking a hot shower, I reached for the half-empty bottle of scotch. I tried not to take notice of the voices as they chattered away inside my head, talking amongst themselves and running a commentary on my behaviour. By eight that morning, I was steaming drunk.

The next few days—I'd lost track of time itself—I experienced all manner of exaggerated emotional states and weird bodily complaints. This was not so much *Groundhog Day* as the opening credits to *Apocalypse Now*. Insomnia gripped me like a vise, and I drank and cried and ranted and laughed like a loon. I could not open my bowels despite always being regular, and I seemed to have developed an overwhelming urge to vomit whenever I tried to eat. My heart trip-hammered every time I thought of a waterfall and slowed to a crawl if I envisaged a summer meadow.

My penis, too, was doing strange things.

I felt raunchier than a Rock Star, hornier than a bridegroom on his Stag Night anticipating the arrival of the token stripper. I cruised the *Playboy* website, and Shae Marks seemed as good as any.

Sleep deprivation, drunken stupor, mood disturbance and paranoia, impaired appetite and weight loss, palpations and various peculiar cardiac twinges, sweating profusely with minimal exertion, impacted bowels and an urgency to pee when I didn't need to pee—I suffered the freakiest, most undiagnosable list of symptoms ever encountered in a single patient and ultimately felt close to collapse . . . yet I was too petrified to admit myself into hospital in case I got committed.

And, all the while, no matter how much I tried to ignore them, the voices continued to pester and taunt and torment. Like some character in a cartoon, I felt the desire to rip my head off and throw it at them.

One man and his hallucinations, listening to me listening to them. I only had one thing to say: *Fuck you, too!*

He's falling apart at the seams, Melanie said, worried. *We have to do something. His heart can't take any more of the strain.*

Tracy wasn't so concerned. *Makes you wonder how long he can hold out.*

At this stage, partially sober, I was genuinely contemplating the possibility that I might actually be going mad. Floating in my head was the image of an inverted red triangle emblazoned with the words: LOSING MY MIND.

I ordered more scotch and a Big Mac and rested on the bed. I was finding it difficult to switch off, my thoughts speeding like a Grand Prix racer with inoperable brakes.

You need to stop drinking, Melanie implored, *and start cooperating with us.*

"I didn't know you cared so much," I muttered, disinterested.

I care, she replied. *So does Clare.*

The mention of Clare brought me back immediately.

You care about her, don't you? Melanie asked.

"Yes, I think I do," I answered, as honestly as I could muster.

Then, please, don't drink.

"What does it matter if I drink, or don't drink, if you're just figments of my imagination?"

That's the problem, Melanie said, sounding miserable. *We're not. We're real.*

"Oh, don't you dare!" I warned, getting angry. "Don't even go there!"

But I'm telling the truth, Melanie insisted.

Mel, why'd you have to go and tell him that? Tracy interjected. *You're giving the game away!*

He has a right to know!

"That's precisely what any hallucination would say," I tried reasoning, "Hallucinations are devils in disguise. They trick and tease, convince you they're as real as day, but in the end they're just symptoms of an illness. *I'm a fucking paranoid schizophrenic, for chrissakes!*"

You're part of a research project, began Melanie.

Enough, Melanie! Tracy nearly screamed. But Melanie would not be silenced. *Your room is bugged and there are a couple of implants in your body.*

Tracy could take no more. *That's it, I'm calling Esmond!*

Melanie continued: *We paid off your parents £45,000 so they could consent on your behalf and we could use you as a test subject. We needed someone unsuspecting, preferably a doctor, and you seemed like the perfect candidate.*

"Then if what you're saying is true, who's been running the wards?"

We've been cross-covering and using a lot of locums. It's costing the Trust a small fortune.

"Oh, you guys are good!" I exclaimed, feigning awe. "You do realize you're only feeding my delusions!"

If you don't believe me, ring the wards. Esmond has just left his ward and should be with us shortly.

Melanie, you're a stupid bitch! Tracy said angrily. *You've compromised the entire operation!*

"Shut up, Tracy, I want to hear her out!" I bellowed hotly. Quickly calming myself, I deliberated for a moment. "Okay, Melanie, what was the purpose of this experiment?"

To measure a person's tolerance to extreme stress, Melanie explained. *You've got two microchips in your body. The first is in your forebrain. It allows us to control your emotions, alter your mood, change your thought processes. We have direct access to* your brain chemistry so we can switch you from euphoric to paranoid to panicky in a matter of seconds. Andy's had a field day dialling up your serotonin, dopamine and noradrenaline levels. We can hear what you hear and see what you see by accessing your cochlear and optic nerves respectively. We have a direct com-link to your brain, which is why you're able to hear us.

"And the second chip?"

The second chip is in your heart. With it, we have control of your organs. We can speed up or slow down your heart rate, modify your blood pressure, paralyze your intestines, play around with your oesophageal sphincter and induce vomiting or squeeze your bladder muscles and make your dribble or—

"—Give me an erection just for the sake of it?"

That was my idea, Esmond spoke up, suddenly. Fiddled with your autonomic system and testosterone levels, you dirty tosser! I'll deal with you later, Melanie . . .! Now then, Hitch, what'll it be? Cerebral haemorrhage, cardiac insufficiency, aspirating on your stomach contents, swallowing your own tongue or dissection of the aorta?

I opened the newly-delivered bottle of scotch and swigged down half of the contents in one go. I coughed and spluttered as the alcohol burned my throat. I had accepted everything Melanie had told me. She had been the conscience of the outfit. Should I take to wearing a tin foil hat to block out the voices or would that only be a further sign of my craziness? "And whose brainchild was this brilliant piece of research?"

Dr. O'Neill authorized the experiment, Esmond replied. He put me in charge of the operation.

"The Medical Director?" I said thoughtfully. "Anyone else know?"

Not a soul. Dr. O'Neill stipulated, the less people who know, the better. You needed to hear voices whom you could relate to.

"When exactly did you install these implants?" I asked.

Esmond answered with a question. What date is it?

"The twenty-third."

No, it's the twenty-eighth. We decided not to correct the date on your watch.

Five whole missing days, I thought. "What if I blab?"

Who the hell's going to believe you? Auditory hallucinations, persecutory delusions, passivity phenomena, hospital conspiracies. This is State-of-the-Art Military Technology. Since it uses GPS, we can track you to anywhere on this planet and assassinate you then and there. Mossad designed it and tested it.

"These implants should be visible on a scan, right?"

I doubt it.

"Not even a radioisotope scan?"

Esmond went quiet.

"You do realize I've invalidated your whole experiment by drinking. Alcohol has a powerful depressant effect so no matter how much you tweak my adrenaline levels, you're not going to get an accurate reading."

I say, let's finish him! Esmond snarled. *Who's with me?*

No, you can't! said Melanie, horrified.

Isn't that a bit extreme, Es? Andrew observed, siding with Melanie.

Why don't we just disconnect him from the terminal, suggested Tracy. *He'll suffer a complete mental and physical collapse.*

He's expendable, Esmond informed them. Then directing his hostility towards me, he said: *Hitch, you still haven't told me how you'd like to die. Falling asleep at the wheel? Cerebral haemorrhage on the toilet? Making your heart explode? Losing control of your natural respiratory function so you just suffocate? Resetting your metabolic rate so your food consumption cannot keep up with the calories you're burning off and you waste away in a matter of hours? . . . What the fuck are you doing?*

"You make a very poor excuse for a doctor, Esmond," I remarked, picking up a chair. "See you in hell, you fucking Nazi scientist." I swung the chair at the TV screen in a fit of rage, shattering the set with an almighty explosion.

Oh, you're in deep shit now, warned Esmond. *Destruction of hospital property won't go down well with the Judge.*

"I'm not finished yet," I replied determinedly. I took my lighter and applied its flame to the curtains. The fabric of the curtain caught fire as easily as if it were made of silk, combusting upwards in a bright, billowing plume.

Flames licked the wallpaper, the fumes setting off the smoke detector.

I sat calmly on the bed, resigned to my fate, watching the flames rise higher. Expendable though I might be, my death would not be in vain. The more gruesome my end, the more high-profile the story. The firemen would surely find my body and a thorough post-mortem examination by a forensic pathologist would reveal the implants, implants capable of tampering with a man's sanity. The subsequent investigation would point the finger firmly towards certain members of the medical faculty at Fairview General. And I doubted any of the parties involved would be able to bribe a lie detector.

I finished off the rest of the scotch, letting the alcohol numb my senses and bring relief to my exhausted body, satisfied with my prompt solution to my problems. I waited for the moment when the smoke would overcome me and I would pass out.

That guy really is crazy! exclaimed Andrew, shocked. *He's going about everything the wrong way!*

Tracy interrupted him, trying to rescue the situation. *He doesn't know Clare's on her way to Fleet Street.*

What do you mean 'on her way'? Esmond said abruptly. It was news to me, too. I sensed alarm in his voice. Could it be possible that his masterplan was beginning to fall apart? *Is she planning to rat us out?*

What else? confessed Tracy, sounding worried and strangely afraid. *She loves him, and she's had enough of our mind games. She can't see him suffer any more.*

"Why the hell did no-one tell me this earlier?" I coughed, inhaling smoke. If Clare indeed loved me (which cheered me up greatly) and had decided to put an end to this madness (which I prayed for dearly), I could see only one way forward. Burning alive in a hospital dorm-room was not it. "I have to find her."

Esmond rounded on his female colleague. *Look what you've done! Now he knows!*

Sorry, Es, I didn't mean to—

Esmond's attention was quickly drawn back to me. *Shit, he's making a run for it!*

Sure enough, I hastily threw on some winter clothes, and as the flames spread to the ceiling, I made my getaway. I went down the smoke-filled hallway, trying to ignore the loud, interminable clanging of the fire-alarm. I pushed past my fellow doctors, who emerged from their respective rooms with high, panicky faces—chaos and confusion reigned everywhere I looked.

A fleet of fire engines was already arriving outside the Doctors' Residence, their screaming sirens adding to the pandemonium.

And, under cover of the compelling drama around me, I slipped out of the hospital grounds, relatively unnoticed.

Fairview railway station was less than a quarter-of-an-mile walk from the hospital. I strode briskly down the road, glad to be out in the open after weeks of solitary confinement. The air was crisp and chilly on my face, a refreshing anodyne to my racing thoughts.

I got to the station with time to spare and bought my one-way ticket to London. I only waited on the platform under a minute before my train arrived. I boarded, pleased that things were at last going my way.

The voices had gone quiet and I suspected evacuation of part of the hospital had something to do with it. My diversion had worked, for the time being at least. For once I could think without others tapping into my mind.

Clare was apparently in London, spilling the beans on the whole operation. It surprised me why I hadn't considered going to the newspapers myself—I suppose with everything that was happening, the idea never occurred to me. I even knew which newspaper she might be consulting with. Now I could follow her and provide the newspapermen with all the evidence they needed. This scoop—because it was a scoop—came close on the heels of the terrible death of that foreign journalist, Alexander Litvinenko, from Polonium-210 poisoning, sanctioned by the Russian state. So, without doubt, the whole world would be watching.

However, Clare didn't answer her mobile when I called.

The carriage wasn't particularly crowded, but the middle-aged couple sitting opposite me kept giving me suspicious glances. I tried my best to appear inconspicuous, but my general beat-up state and the curious rash on my face and the pall of madness that hung thickly over my head must have made grim viewing.

Outside, the lights of dusk twinkled away. November rain spattered the windows.

Then, just as we were passing through Oaks Fold—

—BOO—! came Esmond's voice with loud, wild merriment. I jumped in my seat, startled by the sound.

The couple looked at me again strangely.

I smiled back at them weakly. My attempt at reassuring them simply caused them to look away in disgust. I guess they must have thought I was drunk, considering I reeked of scotch.

Hi there, stranger, said Tracy playfully. *Just when you thought we'd forgotten about you . . .*

Leaving so soon? asked Andrew, amused.

Why can't you let him go? Melanie broke through, full of pity.

No chance, replied Esmond severely. *You're in this too, Mel, you accepted the deal. So I would be grateful if you could act like a team player or I may be forced to kick your fat ass off the field.*

Besides, added Tracy, *he's committed a serious crime.*

Esmond elaborated, in full support of his colleague. *Yes, nobody gets away with arson—not ever and certainly not on my watch.*

But we drove him to it! Melanie reminded him. *That won't hold up in a court of law,*

Esmond continued without a shred of mercy. *The voices made me do it—I mean what kind of defence is that? Nope, Hitch's up Shit's Creek, and there's no way back!*

And he's running away, Andrew observed, *a sure sign of guilt.*

Esmond spoke directly to me. *So how far are you exactly on the old road to London? Do us a favour and peek out the window, would you?*

Talk to us, man, Andrew urged, knowing full well I would be making an idiot of myself if I did.

I refused to engage, to fall for their bait.

Come on, Hitch, give us a clue, Tracy requested. *You know very well we have the capacity of haunting you indefinitely.*

Yes, Hitch, we can't let you make that journey, Esmond told me in a patronizing tone. *We think it's important we inform the nearest police station of your indiscretion so they can meet you at the next stop. How does that sound?*

I fished in my jacket pocket and pulled out a pair of foam ear-plugs. I shoved them in my ears and closed my eyes. The couple opposite I hoped would think I was napping, but my true intention was to block out the world around me, thus confusing my tormentors. I wished I'd brought along my MP3 Player to ward off my demons utterly and conclusively, but I supposed I could improvise. I began to mentally hum *The Great Escape* on a mad loop.

My ruse didn't go down well with my persecutors which pleased me no end.

Will you cut that out? Esmond demanded, irked. *You're blinding us. Give us something to work with.*

We don't need this aggravation, protested Andrew.

Tracy expressed her bit. *Yes, we only want to be your friend, help you through this difficult period.*

But I dared not relent. I ignored the voices rolling around in my head and continued blanket coverage of my jaunty tune. I soon lost track of them. All I remember was they started to argue and squabble amongst themselves and Melanie, it seemed, was on my side throughout.

Suddenly, someone was tapping me on the shoulder. I opened my eyes and realized it was the train conductor.

[*Andrew:* Guys, we have a visual!]

I removed my ear-plugs.

"Ticket, please," the conductor said whilst taking in my woeful appearance.

I obeyed, and he punched my ticket. He moved on but not before giving me a wary, mistrustful look.

A minute later I was blasted by a deep, crushing pain in the centre of my chest, so unexpected and excruciating I struggled for breath.

How does that feel? Esmond asked me, ice in his voice.

Within moments I suffered another awful cardiac assault. I clutched my chest, distressed.

I've set the machine to administer a hit every fifteen seconds, Esmond declared. *Let's see how much more your hyperpolarized ventricles can take!*

Stop it! Melanie screeched, horrified. *You're going to give him a heart attack!*

Will someone stop her whining? Esmond barked back. *If I wanted to finish him off, I would have done so by now! No, I want him to suffer—I'm going to make this so unpleasant he'll think twice about messing with me.*

"Mister, are you okay?" the middle-aged woman sitting opposite me asked. Her husband immediately warned his spouse not to get involved with a stern shake of his head.

"My heart," I gasped, my expression understandably contorted in agony, "they're squeezing my heart."

The pain eased off, and I braced myself for a further sally of chest-gripping pain.

But it never came . . .

Instead, Tracy cracked up into hysterics, apparently in relation to some inside joke. *I can't believe he fell for it!*

Andrew joined in the laughter. *How gullible is he?*

Then, addressing me directly, Tracy explained: *Just so you know, Clare never contacted the newspapers! We made it all up so we could see what your reaction would be!*

I reeled at the bombshell. The ground seemed to open up beneath me.

Boy, must you feel like a fine old fool? Esmond said, chuckling. *Tried to burn down the Doctors' Residence when there wasn't even a story.*

Could my humiliation be any more complete? Time, I supposed, to initiate Plan B—unfortunately there was no Plan B.

Do you really think Clare would go out of her way to expose us and the operation she helped develop? She doesn't give a flying fuck about you! You're nothing but a test subject! I repeat, EXPENDABLE!

And Esmond gave me another jolt of cardiac pain to emphasize his point. I let out a sharp, agonized whimper. So far, I had been keeping it together. But the danger—the very real danger—that my heart could arrest and I might actually drop dead pushed me into the highest stratosphere of panic and prompted me to take drastic action.

I rose up from my seat and glanced around the half-crowded carriage.

"People, please, I need you to listen to me," I announced, clapping my hands. When I had their attention, I told them what was ailing me. "I'm speaking to you all now because I don't know how long I can last. I discovered today I'm the subject of a medical experiment. I learned that colleagues of mine placed microchips in my body against my will. These devices allow them to control my internal organs and record whatever I see, hear or say. They mess with my mood and peer into my thoughts. As you might have gathered, I'm scared shitless because they've just threatened to kill me by stopping my heart. In case anything happens to me, the ringleader of this research project is Dr. Esmond Cook and, for your information, my name is Dr. Hitcham Gale..."

There descended a stunned silence, as the passengers decided what to make of this strange story from this strange foreign man with the strange, rash-covered face. I spotted a couple of amused faces amongst them, but the majority looked at me with incredulous, dismissive expressions. I might as well have told them extraterrestrials had abducted me and been probing me. I doubted they thought I was a real doctor, considering the dreadful condition I was in, and that my paranoid babblings might be the upshot of a mental illness or the fallout of abusing street drugs.

"I know how crazy it all sounds, but you *must* believe me," I entreated in clammy desperation.

"Shut up and sit down," derided the leader of a gang of shell-suited teenagers, "before we do you over."

"I've never heard anything more preposterous in my life," contended a stiff-necked businessman, who instantly went back to crunching numbers with a junior partner.

A pregnant woman sitting nearby gave me a sad, sympathetic smile—except I knew she didn't believe a single word I'd uttered.

Unconvinced, too, was the train conductor, who'd caught the tail-end of my disclosure. "I must ask you, sir, to leave at the next station," he pressed, stony-faced.

"But—" I began to protest.

"We don't want any trouble."

I nodded, feeling like a complete idiot.

I received no further bouts of chest pain—I guess things must have got interesting again for my persecutors.

Less than five minutes later, I disembarked at Chertsford Junction.

Outside the train station, I clambered straight into a taxi. "Take me to your local newspaper."

"That would be the *Chertsford Echo*," the driver, a bald, bespectacled gentleman, informed me. "Only a coupla blocks down, but it'll take forever in this traffic."

He drove me through the wet town centre, bustling with people going about their late-night shopping. Every so often he would cast an eye over me through the rear-view mirror.

I acknowledged his nervous glances. "I guess I must look rough."

"It's not my place to say," he replied, a little embarrassed— God bless him!

"If only you knew what I'm going through . . ."

"Try me," he suggested. "You look like someone who could use a friend."

"I suppose," I said, contemplating his offer. I decided to take him up on it. "First, if I suddenly drop dead in your cab, I want you to take my body to the nearest hospital and demand an urgent post-mortem."

The cabbie looked alarmed. "Why? Are you unwell? Is something going to happen to you?"

"Possibly," I told him . . . and summarized my story. "I've got a bug implanted in my brain and another in my heart. These bugs give the researchers control over my body and the power to kill me with the push of a button."

"My God!" the cabbie gasped, appalled. "That's despicable!"

"I haven't slept properly for weeks. They keep interfering with the chemicals in my brain. They've already broken my spirit and now they're trying to determine at what point my mind will unravel."

The cabbie had some time to reflect. "It sounds so incredible, like something out of a Robert Ludlum novel . . ."

"I need to go to the newspapers and tell the world about what's going on. I want my persecutors to suffer for what they've done."

He brought the car to a halt. "We're here . . ."

The *Chertsford Echo* was a modern glassine building down a narrow, dimly-lit side-street.

I exhaled hard. "I made it. Don't be surprised if I don't get to the newsdesk."

"I hear all sorts in my job, but nothing quite reaches the degree of what you've described."

"Thanks for being so understanding." I paid the fare and stepped out into the rain.

"Good luck!" the cabbie called back before driving off.

As I stumbled through the revolving doors of the *Chertsford Echo*, I heard Esmond curse from somewhere too close for comfort: *What a fucking sonofabitch! You'll pay for this!*

A security guard sat behind the desk in reception.

"Hold the Front Page!" I announced, confidently striding up to him. "Could you call down one of your senior news staff? I've a real corker of a tale to tell!"

The man summoned down to the lobby introduced himself. "I'm Morris Dailey, Assistant Editor."

"The name's Dr. Hitcham Gale," I said as professionally as I could manage.

For a brief moment, we sized each other up. The brown cardigan, blue jeans and the ragged woollen tie fixed to his white shirt gave Morris a harried look. His appraisal of my appearance—fashioned in black pullover, jacket and jeans— was slightly more discerning. Journalists are like Mental Health Specialists: they have an eerie way of seeing into your soul. The rash on my stubbled face must have seemed perturbing, even though he didn't mention it.

"Nice to meet you, Dr. Gale," said Morris, and quickly dispensed with the pleasantries. "You've got ten minutes. What can we do for you?"

"What I'm about to tell you may sound bizarre, but I really need you to hear it with an open mind. My very life is at stake."

"I'll do what I can," Morris assured me and gestured towards the faux-leather sofas in the lobby. "Won't you please sit down?"

We seated ourselves before I leapt into an abridged version of my ordeal. "I'm part of a cruel, unethical scientific experiment run by my former work colleagues. Mechanical devices were implanted in me without my prior knowledge. These people have been studying my response to extreme stress, accessing various aspects of my mental and physical functions. They have a stranglehold over me, afford me no peace. My last ten days have been sheer hell as I've had to deal with all kinds of symptoms that defy explanation and classification, not knowing why I was experiencing them. I've laughed and cried for no reason, I hear their mocking, insulting voices in my head all the time, they can track me anywhere in the world, they've violated and abused my body no end, nearly forced my heart to pack in completely. The problem is they've now told me they intend to kill me—the lunatics have broken loose and taken over the asylum!"

Morris was studying me closely. "Are their voices with you this minute?"

"I haven't heard them for a little while, but they're listening in on everything we're saying. They're certainly watching you through my eyes."

Morris shifted uncomfortably in his seat. "Come on, I've seen that movie."

"Excuse me?"

"You're saying they're doing a John Malkovich in your head?"

"I suppose," I said . . . and *farted*.

The unexpectedness of my loud, protracted gaseous emission caused all in the lobby to jump. The accompanying ripe odour made me want to gag. It was only then I felt the warm stickiness of human waste clinging to the seat of my boxers—I was Touching Cloth!

I tried recovering from my slight mishap. "See, *that* was them, making an arse out of me! Can you imagine what I've had to endure for the past fortnight?"

"I see your dilemma," Morris said, signalling to the security guard with a shrewd nod. "Either you suffer these devices in silence or you make an embarrassing spectacle of yourself in trying to convince others. Regrettably, I'm at a loss as to how we can help you."

"I could use some of your hard-hitting journalism in telling the world and bringing my conspirators to justice."

"Do you know what I think you need?" Morris suggested. "A hospital. Let them check you out, do all the tests to prove or disprove your claims."

The manner in which he had relayed his advice left no room for misinterpretation. "You're fobbing me off? You *don't* believe me?"

"I think you may be unwell . . . Nothing to be ashamed of . . . I've been a victim of burn-out myself."

I could feel my anger bubbling over, aided, no doubt, by my persecutors. "I'm not some whacko off the street!"

"We don't want this to get ugly," Morris admonished, trying to remain calm. The security guard had already risen from his desk, poised to intervene if the situation escalated.

"Why is it so difficult for you to accept? I know it's high concept and a hard sell. But you accept the scientific breakthroughs of Dolly the Sheep or the Human Genome Project? The surveillance technology I've described *exists* and it's inside me, killing me from within. Please, I *need* your help!"

"Dr. Gale, we'd like you to come with us," came a formidable voice from behind me.

I whirled my head round and saw two tall, unsmiling police officers standing in the lobby.

I rounded on the newspaperman. "You called the police?" I uttered in disbelief.

"Dr. Gale, these nice people are here to help you," Morris informed me, getting up and heading away. "I sincerely hope it all works out for you. Now you must excuse me—I've got the undesirable task of helping Angus put the newspaper to bed."

"Thanks a bunch!"

The huskier of the two policemen stepped in front of me. "I'm PC Watkins and this is PC Boyd. Are you prepared to go with us quietly?"

I didn't reply. I simply looked at him in mounting horror as I suffered the awful sensation of someone violently squeezing my stomach like a goatskin full of wine. Without warning, I doubled forward and vomited over his shoes.

PC Boyd slapped the handcuffs on me.

They bundled me into the back of the police car. I could see no benefit in resisting arrest.

"Where are you taking me?" I asked them as PC Boyd set the car in motion.

"We have suspicion to believe you set fire to your room at Fairview General," PC Watkins recapped. "However, the information we have in our possession suggests you may be of unsound mind. We're taking a trip to Chertsford Memorial Hospital so you can be examined by a Psychiatrist before we decide whether or not to press charges."

"Who told you I might be of unsound mind?" But I already knew his answer.

"Dr. Cook . . ."

Of course it was, I thought sardonically.

"I think you know him," PC Watkins continued. "He's been concerned about your health for some time."

"What about what he and his pals have been doing to me with their gadgets: invasion of privacy, mental rape and emotional cruelty, devising more and more ways of torturing me, abusing my body? Surely you can see the illegality of operating on someone without their consent? It is nothing less than psychological torture, pure and simple, unconscionable, *evil*."

"Dr. Cook warned us you might be harbouring some peculiar ideas. I suggest you tell the Psychiatrist."

And get myself locked up? You'd like that, wouldn't you?

Although we did not speak for the rest of the journey, PC Watkins kept an eye on me periodically through the grille partition.

I reflected on the events of the last hour. Things hadn't quite turned out the way they should have. Or maybe they had. I suppose I had handled it badly. Instead of blowing the lid off this conspiracy, I had got myself arrested and was well on the way to getting committed. The secret was out, but the newspapers didn't believe me. Perhaps it was the implausibility of the actual story that was the problem—I probably wouldn't believe it if someone else related it to me. Easier to believe I had suffered a psychotic break or I was jacked-up on something. I mean I was soaking wet, running on empty and smelling strongly of scotch... as well as being foreign. My plight, I assumed, was sealed.

You can't win, Esmond came chuckling through as though he had heard my thoughts. Which, of course, was closer to the truth than most people cared to think. At least, he had stopped tampering with my heart or wringing my guts.

You shouldn't have farted, let alone puked, teased Andrew, obviously sporting a smirk.

Thank you for your cringeworthy contribution to my impending incarceration in the nuthouse, I thought back wearily.

Always a pleasure, replied Andrew, *particularly when you're working with the best.*

Enter Tracy: *Your nightmare is only just beginning . . .*

You're not far wrong, I said inwardly. *Maybe I'll be granted parole after four weeks of good behaviour on the Psychiatric ward.*

No, you're not getting me, Tracy persisted. *Those aren't real policemen...!*

What the hell are you chatting about? I demanded from the mausoleum of my mind, cluttered with cognizant relics: fast-fading memories of a normal existence . . . and dwindling hope.

Didn't you wonder why the police came so quickly? Tracy asked me. *The real cops are waiting at the* Chertsford Echo *just as we speak.*

The pang of disquiet I experienced almost went unnoticed since my brain chemistry was spread all over the show. *If those men aren't whom they claim they are, what are they?*

Black Ops, Tracy claimed. *They're members of a covert military organization, who helped fund this experiment. You've developed into a serious security risk since you absconded from Fairview and they're taking you away to shut you up for good. It's probably the last we'll ever see of you.*

That didn't sound good. I could feel the anxiety blossoming up from the pit of my stomach. Being in easy reach of someone ought to have been a protective factor. The Bastards on the Bridge couldn't kill me if I was with a neutral outsider—like the police—as my sudden death after blurting out what I'd blurted out would look extremely suspicious. But this was brand new information.

These guys are vicious animals, no two ways about it, Tracy continued, *with no respect for ethics or the law. They specialize in torture techniques, delight in sadistic practices. They're going to hurt you, make you suffer until you beg for them to kill you. But they still won't do kill you. They will keep you alive and conscious for weeks, and when you become useless to their training needs, unable to fulfil their vast, sickening appetites . . . well, I daren't imagine what they'll do to you. Prepare to get raped and buggered three ways from Sunday!*

Yes, better start getting your arse into gear like the world's worst gang-banged queer! Esmond punctuated with ungracious rhyme, relishing my misery.

Tracy finished spelling out my fate. *The newscasters will announce your demise some day soon, when your body is found dumped in a field in the middle of nowhere at four in the morning, dead . . .*

So nice knowing you, old boy, went Esmond, hammering it right home.

Farewell, Hitch, said Andrew solemnly. *May God have mercy on your soul.*

Then, they signed off for I heard no more from them.

They had bailed out on me, leaving me to deal with the intelligence they had imparted. According to them, I was sitting in the back of a fake police car with a pair of deadly imposters on my way to certain death.

PC Watkins glanced back at me, and for a moment, I thought I saw a cruel knowingness in his expression.

Beleaguered, I found myself on the brink of a panic attack.

Rain splashed harder against the windows, obscuring the world outside, limiting the performance of the windscreen wipers. All that seemed visible in the dark night were the red taillights of the cars ahead, the dazzling headlights of oncoming traffic and the dim, watery lights of the shops, restaurants and bars along the sidewalks. We turned off the main road, negotiated a staggered series of narrow thoroughfares, passing what resembled deserted outhouses, until we arrived at the doors of a sinister Victorian building round the back of the estate.

Handcuffed in the back, I cowered, helpless, powerless, sick with fear.

"We've arrived . . ." announced PC Boyd, turning off the key in the ignition.

Their domain, I figured, of torture, rape and execution.

When I emerged from the police car, preparing to make a run for it, I realized we were not on some secluded paramilitary base but what appeared to be the grounds of a hospital. The sign above the entrance to the building we'd parked up to mysteriously read DEPARTMENT OF PSYCHIATRY.

Where exactly was I? I had never visited Chertsford Memorial—having worked solely at Fairview General—and my very first instinct suggested that these so-called coppers had succeeded in delivering me safely to that very establishment as they said they would. Was it possible that during the space of a single evening, I had travelled from one hospital to another?

Except there was no-one about and my persecutors had been so specific, so convincing and absolute in their pronouncement of my doom.

A disturbing thought popped into my head. *This is not Chertsford Memorial but a perfect replica of the real thing, a front to fool the public and lull the visitor into a false sense of security. Deep inside you'll discover the dungeons with each cell occupied by torture victims kept drugged and barely alive, awaiting the next round of unspeakable abuse inflicted with such nameless instruments of pain as devised by the most perverse, evil minds.*

"I can't go in," I murmured, filled with foreboding and the utmost dread.

The fearsome agents, who were in the act of impersonating ordinary police officers, grabbed my arms in a precautionary hold and began to drag me in the driving rain towards the building, which was disguised as a trusted place of healing. Psychiatrists had a name for it: reduplicative paramnesia, where a person holds a delusional belief that a familiar place has been duplicated or relocated to another site. But I knew better. I continued to struggle, but my two escorts were way too strong.

"I don't want to die...!" But my desperate pleas fell on deaf ears.

I was led through the main doors into a large, well-lit reception area. The walls were painted bright white with green borders, giving off a cold clinical feel.

Clever, I thought, reading between the lines. *The impression of a hospital. Very deceptive.*

PC Watkins informed the receptionist, an obese, frumpy cow, that they had brought me in on a Disposal Order for Psychiatric evaluation, and after taking down my personal details, she advised us to wait for the Duty Doctor in the waiting room.

We sat on plastic orange chairs, the police officers strategically positioned on either side of me.

Considering I had got no rest over the last couple of weeks, I longed to sleep, to doze off for a few moments, but I couldn't risk it. Tired though I felt, my mind was on high alert, spinning out dark thoughts and hideous scenarios. Primarily, I imagined PCs Watkins and Briggs jumping me when I least expected it, holding me down, ripping off my jeans and taking turns to thrust me.

I did not let my guard down for one instant. "You're not going to hurt me, are you?" I said in a small, childlike voice.

"Why on earth would we do that?" asked PC Watkins innocently enough.

I tested him. "Because you're part of a covert military organization . . ."

"I can assure you we're police officers," PC Watkins maintained, trying to allay my fears. "Our job is to stay with you until you're fully assessed. There is still the unfinished business with the arson." But I could see he was rattled. I had let the figurative cat out of the bag. Blacks Operatives were experts at deniability and relied heavily on the element of surprise. PC Watkins seemed unsure for a moment as if deciding whether he should give up the charade and go straight for the jugular. Then he said: "Just wait to be seen, hey doc. You'll see everything will be all right."

So I waited. I waited for the best part of half-an-hour in a hospital that wasn't a real hospital in the custody of two policemen who weren't genuine policemen. I waited for them to suddenly lunge at me.

It's coming . . . Any second . . . Any second now . . .

But attack me they did not.

The SHO-on-call was a short, slight slip of a girl called Dr. Tina Bedwell. Maybe she was a real doctor, but probably the kind who prescribed senseless pain instead of healing the sick. She could tell I was terrified, and I thought I detected pleasure in her face. She took us down a corridor to a plain interview room, past magnetically-sealed security doors supposedly leading to the wards.

From across the table, she asked for my story. The bogus police officers stood by the door, keeping watch.

I resolved to tell her about my headful of people, my ordeal. If she wanted to conduct a token interview, so be it. They could keep up their pretence if they so wished, but I was effectively being held captive, at the mercy of these monsters. I decided I would go along with their game—what did I have to lose? "Before you dismiss my story off-hand as the delusions of a paranoid schizophrenic, I want you to open your mind to the possibilities." I readied myself. "Here goes nothing . . ."

And I told her. I told her everything. I told her about my shingles, my isolation and drinking, of the unpredictable nature of my symptoms, how the internal voices of my medical colleagues kept reminding me I was the test subject of a unique scientific experiment. I told her of resorting to arson when at my lowest ebb, immediately countered by the hope of running to the newspapers. I described the humiliation I had suffered, the inhumane way I had been treated, how my persecutors had degraded me at every turn. I proposed she scan me for the biochips if she didn't believe me. I even told her I knew who she was and what I thought of the organization she represented.

When I had finished, I let out a long, weary sigh. I looked behind me, steeling myself for the onslaught. But the police constables hadn't left their posts.

"You know your symptoms can all be construed as an extreme reaction to stress," Dr. Bedwell speculated.

"That was allegedly the basis of the experiment." I glanced at the two men at the door again. "Okay, do your worst . . ."

The policemen did not move.

Dr. Bedwell got up from behind the table. "Can you uncuff him? I don't think he's dangerous." She headed for the door. "I'll be back. I just need to speak with the Duty Consultant, first."

PC Boyd did as instructed. I shrank away, expecting the inevitable, when he approached me. Yet, he made for my hands, and it astonished me when he actually removed the handcuffs. "Sorry for the inconvenience."

Dr. Bedwell wasn't gone long. She returned within minutes with a tall, silver-haired gentleman. "He's agitated and frightened..." she was telling him.

Her colleague gave me a quick once-over. "I'm Dr. Richard Stegeman. My junior doctor has filled me in on the basic details. I understand you've been through quite a gruelling ordeal. You claim to be the puppet in an elaborate, privately-funded experiment."

I repeated my entire statement.

Dr. Stegeman listened intently, stopping me at certain points and carefully questioning me on that particular aspect of my story in order to gain complete clarification. And as I related my experiences, my emotions proved unstable and erratic, and it was tough maintaining my train of thought. I couldn't stop fidgeting or sweating. However, despite my highly aroused state and my constant betrayal of an incongruous mood, I managed it.

In the end, he sat back in his chair, hands clasped together. He gestured to the police officers. "You can go now. Thank you for bringing Dr. Gale to our attention. I would suggest you drop the charge of arson against my patient since his behaviour was fuelled by a severe mental disorder."

PC Watkins nodded. "We'll need to make a report, but I suppose we can do that tomorrow."

When he and his partner had left, Dr. Stegeman turned back to me. "You do realize that most people would consider you to be suffering from an acute schizophreniform illness. You display all the relevant psychopathology. Stress would explain your physical symptoms."

"I know I come off sounding like an unmitigated madman—who'd believe such a fantastic tale? But all I ask of you is you do a thorough scan of my body." I bargained with him. "If you don't find those neural probes, then I'll happily spend the rest of my life on your locked ward."

"Although you give an account of your symptoms in a rational manner—probably because you're an educated fellow—it's a question of insight. Insight is a measure of how much a person recognizes they are unwell."

"I'm unwell, I know, but it's only because of these implants and the irresponsible bastards controlling them! They are in possession of a potentially lethal weapon with the capability of causing irreversible damage!"

"I believe you," Dr. Stegeman declared, all of a sudden.

"You believe me?" I said, bewildered. "Why?"

"You're describing what is known as a brain-computer interface," explained Dr. Stegeman. "The earliest research was done by Dr. José Delgado back at Yale University in the 1970s, working alongside the CIA, in his pursuit of a 'psychocivilized' society. It continued at John Hopkins predominantly on rhesus monkeys. We ran a similar programme at the London Institute of Neuroscience, using rats. We recognized the potential of this technology in the treatment of Parkinson's Disease and Alzheimer's, in speeding up the recovery of stroke victims and bringing hope to those deaf or visually-impaired, not forgetting its countless military and espionage applications. In the hands of the military and security forces, it would be theoretically possible for the operator to just tune into the human subject's specific radio frequency and do all manner of terrible things to them: cause a heart attack in the person, make them aspirate, release tiny doses of radiation leading to every conceivable tumour, even transmit their voice into the individual's head to give the illusion of paranoid schizophrenia if all they wanted to do was to discredit the individual, silence any political dissent. The work was only in its infancy when I left the project. I guess Mike O'Neill took the research into the next phase—it's mind-staggering how far it's advanced. Cognitive Recognition Imaging is the wave of the future, allowing the experimenter to map the test subject's unconscious thoughts using computer technology."

For the first time, I saw the promise of release from my nightmare. At last, here was someone who understood. I nearly wept.

He's only saying those things because it's what you want to hear before he sends in the troops to gang-fuck you, warned Esmond, out of the blue.

I could hold it in no more: "You bastards can put as many thoughts in my head as you want, but you can't make me verbalize the crap you're feeding me! *You will not take away my individuality!*"

Just wait and see what they do to you . . .

"You've got nothing!" I told my plague of whisperers and manipulators. "This is a real hospital, do you hear me, a *real* hospital!"

That's what they want you to think . . .

I thought my little outburst might have compromised my situation with Dr. Stegeman, but he did not deviate from his opinion. "Are they bothering you again?"

"Yes, they've started up again." I closed my eyes. "I really can't take any more of this grief. I think I might actually go mad."

He's looking directly at you, Es! Tracy exclaimed in a mixture of surprise and alarm.

How—? Esmond began.

My God, Tracy was right! With closed lids, I could vaguely make out a room and a group of spectral figures, Esmond and his cohort, hunched over what appeared to be a computer console. Not clearly, but like a faint, flickering wet-wired transmission. Whatever apparatus they were using, I concluded, it probably served as a two-way communication in the modalities of sight and sound.

The fuzzy form of Esmond rose up and walked across to my right. I followed his ghostly progress with my inner vision. It was a fascinating phenomenon to behold. In a perceptual sense, two separate rooms miles apart seemed to be occupying the same space at the same time, almost entering the realms of the Pauli Exclusion Principle.

My intrusiveness provoked an immediate response.

STOP LOOKING AT ME! Esmond roared, incensed. I'm sure he saw my mind's-eye image of himself on the monitor.

"Big Brother is watching . . . and I'm watching Big Brother—and I refer not to the reality show," I remarked, delighted.

You asked for it! he growled and rushed back to the com-station.

I opened my eyes when I felt a pleasant, electrical stirring in my jeans.

How's this for a fucking spectacle?

Drs. Stegeman, Bedwell and myself stared in shock horror as my penis enlarged of its own accord and pressed up against my zipper. Fair to say, I had developed a rock-hard erection from total flaccidity in less than ten seconds.

"Please don't say I'm sexually disinhibited," I lamented.

"I've seen enough!" said Dr. Stegeman, outraged. "I'm calling Dr. O'Neill! I'm bringing an end to this atrocity!"

The fuck he is...! pledged Esmond with a half-crazed laugh. *Time to terminate the subject . . .*

No, Esmond! screamed Melanie. *Don't do it!*

And my head suddenly exploded with pain. It felt as though someone had shoved a knife through my skull and was deliberately twisting and turning it, scraping against the bone. The pain was cataclysmic, all-consuming, as vast as the wide Universe. I cried in blinding agony, clutching my head, and collapsed to the floor.

I blacked-out.

I awoke in a side-room on the ward I used to work on. I recognized the song playing on the radio: *Extreme Ways* by Moby.

"Hi there," Clare Keating said, seated next to my bed. "How're you holding up?"

The sight of this blond, blue-eyed waif made my heart leap with joy. I mumbled some kind of inaudible greeting. Flinching in pain, I tried getting up, but Clare stopped me.

"Try not to overdo it," Clare said with a concerned expression. "You need to rest."

My speech returned as a dry whisper. "What happened?"

"We got you into theatre before you died from a brain haemorrhage. You suffered a seizure straight after Esmond popped an artery in your head. It was touch and go for a while. But we fixed you up and you'll be out of here in no time. No permanent damage."

"Explains why my head hurts," I said, rubbing my temple. "Why are you here?"

"I had to see you," Clare replied softly.

"Why would anyone want to see a lunatic like me?"

"You're not a lunatic, Hitch. The experiment was real."

"Believe me, there were moments when I had my doubts."

"We were stressing you out to see at what point you would snap. We even snuck into your room and sprayed your walls with beta-carbolines to heighten your sense of arousal."

"So you were part of this all along?"

Clare's face flushed with embarrassment. "I have a confession. It was me who suggested to Dr. O'Neill we recruit you. I'm sorry you had to go through all that."

"Don't be . . ." I gently reassured her. "If I'd been privy to the whole deal in the first place, knowing me I probably would have accepted the assignment."

"No, surprise was an essential requirement. Things had to happen to you for no apparent reason. Single-blind, you understand."

"So I needed to be an unwitting participant?"

"Exactly. It's always more stressful if you don't know."

"Did you remove the neural implants?"

"We neutralized them. They're no longer active."

"You know you guys were so mean to me, particularly Esmond."

"I can't condone what Esmond did to you," Clare said with a mixture of guilt and anger. "He was a nasty piece of work, an unapologetic racist. Power went to his head. Dr. O'Neill had him arrested for attempted murder. Esmond won't be working as a doctor again. Tracy's still got her job after a stern talking-to."

"So some good did come out of all this."

"You did great," Clare commended, honouring me with a loving smile. "You're famous now. Hitcham Gale—the doctor who lived through a groundbreaking experiment and survived with his mind intact." She smiled again, and I felt like kissing those sweet lips. "Dr. Mike O'Neill, the rest of the team and myself have already posed for the paparazzi. We're all waiting for you to get better so you can tell your side of the story."

"Makes me wonder if all schizophrenics have a device implanted in their brains by sinister government forces for the purposes of research."

"You mean that maybe this elite, shadowy group of scientists transplants thoughts and ideas and images into those susceptible brains is what actually forms the basis of madness?"

"You never know," I replied. "Lots of shadowy organizations out there." I asked her more personal question. "Why didn't you visit me?"

"My uncle insisted I didn't."

"Your uncle?"

"Mike O'Neill. Besides, I couldn't bring myself round to seeing what was happening to you."

"The mental torture I endured, the fact my mind was taken hostage, is going to stay with me for a long time to come," I reflected.

"Your ordeal helped us achieve something remarkable," Clare said excitedly. "We now have the ability to tap directly into the cortices of the brain and monitor and modify human behaviour. With your unique perspective on mental illness and the amazing amount of data we've collected, we're hoping you'll want to be part of any future research."

I gaped at her, dreading the worst.

"Relax," Clare assured me. "We could use you as the Chief Operator."

"No thanks. I have a new-found desire to continue my medical career. I was thinking Psychiatry." I gave Clare a deliberately spooky look. "Because I'm mad—I tell you—*mad!*"

February 2008—May 2008

Horns of a Cornute

"The poets and philosophers before me discovered the unconscious; what I discovered was the scientific method by which the unconscious can be studied."

Sigmund Freud (1926)

Mark Hopwood shifted a little in his seat as he prodded Jepson Quinn's subconscious. He maintained his steady, soporific voice, exploring the inner recesses of a troubled soul, the secrets buried within. "So what makes you think your girlfriend is being unfaithful to you?"

Quinn answered in soft, dreamy tones. "She arrives home well after seven, even though I know the nursery where she works closes its doors at half-four. I think back to all the times I have suspected something. Every Saturday she makes up some excuse—shopping, library, the gym, visiting her sister—and disappears for the afternoon. Little things that just don't add up, like losing the earrings I bought her as a Valentine's gift and miraculously finding them the next day, or a sudden change in the tone of her voice on a mysterious phone-call when I inadvertently enter the room. The conversation suddenly stops and picks up about the something unimportant like the weather. I study her face closely for any tell-tale signs, but she hides it well. She seems pleased to see me, claims she missed me—it's a performance worthy of an Oscar. She looks hot and bothered—an hour's work-out on the squash courts as she tries to convince me. Does she really think I'm going to fall for that crap? I hug her and, yes, in that moment, I catch the faint scent of cologne I don't own."

"Do you confront her with your suspicions?"

"I do that Tuesday evening, but her reply is always the same. Whenever I ask, she giggles innocently and tells me I'm being paranoid."

Hopwood stared at Quinn and his white linen suit, £13.50 from Primark as Quinn had proudly disclosed during the very first session some weeks back. "How is the sex?"

"The sex is fine, never been better. But I notice she seems eager to satisfy me in the bedroom at the expense of her own pleasure. It feels like she's trying to compensate for something, work through some kind of guilt trip."

Even after being a trained hypnotherapist of some ten years' good standing and now the owner of the single-therapist HYPNOTIQUE Clinic, Hopwood had to admit the mysteries of the mind never ceased to fascinate. Jepson Quinn was an interesting case in point. What had started out as a simple exercise in smoking cessation had snowballed into something more profound. Eight sessions later, and Hopwood had discovered that Quinn was a complete neurotic mess, who really needed the services of a good psychoanalyst rather than an ordinary hypnotist to tease out all those complex neuroses and bring the 'psychic pus' to the surface. Although Quinn's problems were well-beyond the hypnotherapist's range of expertise, Hopwood was proud of what he had achieved so far. Enough for him to understand what made his client who he was. And certainly enough material to present at the next hypnotherapy symposium.

Hopwood had hoped that if he could regress Quinn to a happier time, he could instill the same forgotten confidence into Quinn in the present. Except, remarkably, there really hadn't been a consistent enough happier time in the man's life. During the course of the sessions, Hopwood had learned that Jepson's mother had walked out on the family when he was only three years old after admitting to an affair with her tennis instructor, and little Jepson had been raised by a mean-tempered father, the tyrannical boss of a textile company, who would torture the growing boy emotionally without ever raising his hand against him because he saw the wife who had been unfaithful to him in the eyes of his only child. Fergus Quinn would put down Jepson at every turn, make him feel inferior and second-rate, an unnecessary burden on his hard-done-by father. Pointing out how he would 'amount to nothing' if his father felt Jepson had been 'up to monkeyshines' was a particular favourite, locking the poor boy in the old coal cellar for hours on end, in the cold and the dank and the dirt, without food or water, to reflect on his transgression. Jepson feared the cellar as much as he feared his father. He could not forget how his father had ripped up his teddy-bear after he had accidentally wet his bed or how his father would drum home the inherent stupidity, iniquity and mistrust of women with an almost evangelical fervour. Jepson had no friends at school and gained only mediocre final grades, falling far short of University entrance. Despite resoundingly vindicating his father's low expectations of him, Jepson went to work at QUINN TEXTILES as second personal assistant to his father because he was 'no good for anything else'. Quinn Sr. did not include his son in the big boardroom decisions, only openly demeaning him and pointing out his uselessness to the rest of the executives. As the years passed, Jepson did all the menial tasks his old man demanded, such as bringing coffee, doing the photocopying or chauffeuring him to and from work. Then, Fate intervened on the downtrodden son and his father dropped dead one morning at the breakfast table. Jepson vividly remembered how his father, now in his greying fifties, suddenly clutched his chest and, murmuring to his son, his expression twisted in contempt and sweaty agony, *You're the laziest person I have ever known, a disappointment to the family name and you should take full responsibility for what's happening to me*, keeled forward into his bowl of Corn Flakes. The Coroner ruled the cause of death as a heart seizure. Shock gave way to jubilation—Jepson was free at last to do as he wished! The old bastard was dead, hip, hip, hooray! Because the old bastard hadn't left a will, Jepson, as the only son and heir, inherited the family business. In the weeks that followed, he decided to get back at his father. He sold the company to the lowest bidder, closing a painful chapter in his life.

Jepson Quinn took a long vacation, embarking on a world cruise.

Then came Caroline.

Caroline Templeton was a phenomenon. She met Jepson Quinn in Luxor, Egypt. There was an immediate attraction. Even though his father had commanded he stay away from girls, Jepson could not resist his own natural curiosity. He thought Caroline utterly divine: blond, beautiful and strong-willed. He didn't know women could be like that when he had always been taught they were all scheming harlots. He wondered why someone like Caroline would be interested in him when she could get any man she chose. When she told him, he nearly wept. An author of children's books, she saw the child in him, the little boy who had been mistreated all his life by a spiteful, overbearing father and never been allowed to flourish. Extraordinarily still, Jepson found he could express himself better, actually be himself when he was with her.

They discovered each other at a secluded spot on the banks of the Nile. Afterwards, Jepson resolved to make up for everything he had missed.

Returning home, he asked her to live with him in his mansion. She did not refuse. Captivated by her intense beauty and unquestioning adoration, he dazzled her with his wealth in order to impress her and so would not lose her.

He proposed. She accepted. They married.

For a while, things were great. He worshipped her, she raised his ego. Then things took a turn for the worse. Jepson's insecurities got the better of him.

He began to suspect she might be seeing someone else. She was spending a lot of time down at the golf club, and the relationship between them seemed to wither. He remembered his mother who had deserted him. One day, she told him she was going to the golf club. He followed her to a hotel in town, where she was joined by her Australian golfing instructor. They went in together and came out two hours later, kissing on the steps. Undeniable proof that Caroline, who could have any man she so desired, *was* truly and utterly cheating on him . . . with her golfing instructor, of all people!

That weekend, at a garden party he was hosting, Jepson carried out Caroline's most expensive dresses and threw them on the barbecue. Jepson announced to all those gathered what he had seen outside the hotel. Jepson and Caroline rowed. The guests, gobsmacked by the turn of events, quietly excused themselves.

Caroline walked out, that day, and filed for divorce. Jepson never saw Caroline again. He signed the papers.

She wrote to him from Sydney, Australia, two years later, where she had emigrated to. She had remarried, apparently to the same golfing instructor, and they were in the middle of filming one of her books. She apologized for hurting him, telling him he was a sweet and gentle soul but much too needy and insecure. She had felt stifled by their relationship. She believed in finding love and eternal happiness; now that she had found it, could he forgive her for what she had done? She wondered if they could still be friends.

Jepson carefully considered the much-belated apology, her justification for her actions, her offer of friendship. He didn't write back.

Hopwood remained intrigued. Here was a man from a wealthy background, wearing a thirteen-pound-fifty Primark linen suit, who had failed to meet his potential. A difficult childhood with a barely-remembered mother and a father who took out his wife's betrayal on his son, the terror of the cellar, the violent loss of a transitional comfort object, low self-esteem and a lack of identity all the way through to adulthood, the father's famous last words, a belief that women were to be despised until one day along came a woman who seemed respectful and caring and understanding, but who later turned out to be no better than his mother. Yet, this man in this ridiculous linen suit had managed to snare himself another woman and was now, consciously or unconsciously, questioning her very integrity. Was history repeating itself? Could lightning strike twice? Or could Quinn be in the firm grip of a self-fulfilling prophecy?

The hypnotherapist had considered placing an earlier, healthier ego-state into Quinn's current dissociated state to allow him to regain his confidence, but where in his life story was it to be found? Hopwood might have opted for a more direct NLP approach, but he wanted to explore the mental terrain a little further before suggesting it.

Besides, Quinn claimed he was an English aristocrat in a past life.

Session seven was nothing short of a weird history lesson.

Hopwood regressed Quinn to his previous existence. The year was 1705, and Quinn in the shape of Roger Palmer, 1st Earl of Castlemayne, lay on his deathbed. Barbara Villiers-Castlemayne was there beside him, the wife who had been the bane of his existence. Quinn, as Roger Palmer, remembered his old life and his tempestuous relationship with his then-wife.

Quiet scholar, devout Roman Catholic and from a background of rich nobility, Palmer fell instantly in love with Barbara Villiers, 1st Duchess of Cleveland, the first moment he saw her at a banquet in honour of the King. He thought her a 'wild and sensuous' thing, one of God's flawless creations. She reciprocated his advances, drawing him into her private circle with seductive ease. Her title aside, her family was at the mercy of the creditors, and Barbara considered Palmer a sound marriage prospect. So beguiled was Palmer by her, he wed her in 1659, at the height of the Restoration, against his father's wishes and despite public knowledge that Barbara was already mistress to the Earl of Chesterfield. His father prophesized she would make him 'the most miserable man in the world'.

Barbara proved very accomplished in bed. However, her sexual olympics did not stop with her husband; she took in new lovers with a wanton breath. Within a year of her marriage, she became Lady of the Bedchamber and one of the most influential mistresses of King Charles II. He made Palmer 1st Earl of Castlemayne and a member of the Privy Council, a reward for his wife's services in the royal bed rather than his in the royal court. Due to his Catholic faith, Palmer could not divorce her, and he suffered humiliation after humiliation as his wife gave birth to a string of illegitimate children, 'a brood of Royal bastards' according to the noted diarist of the times, Samuel Pepys. When King Charles grew bored of her, she continued her Scarlet Manifesto in the arms of the Duke of Marlborough, who sired her sixth and final child. Palmer tried his best to raise the children as his own, but it was a dispiriting, uphill struggle—his heart just wasn't in it.

In 1679 Palmer was committed to the Tower of London on the grounds of High Treason after coming under suspicion during the fictitious Popish plot to assassinate King Charles. Palmer defended himself masterfully in Court, securing his own acquittal.

Appointed Ambassador to the Vatican in 1686, Palmer faced further ridicule as 'Europe's most famous cuckold'. The public compared him to the cuckoldry-fearing character Arnolphe in Molière's comedy, *The School for Wives*, who grooms his young ward, Agnes, with the intention of eventually marrying her, but ends up losing her to another, much younger man. Palmer's spell as ambassador, understandably, lasted only eight months. Mocked and shamed through no fault of his own, Palmer was forced to return to England.

During the Glorious Revolution of 1688, involving the overthrow of King James II by William of Orange, Palmer was again incarcerated in the Tower of London for a period of two years for refusing to recant his Catholicism. Barbara rarely visited him in prison, instead sharing a bed with men half her age.

After seventy years on this earth, Roger Palmer died in the country a broken man with an adulteress for a wife whose affairs were legendary and without a son he could call his rightful heir. Thus, the title of Earl of Castlemayne became extinct upon his death.

From his research, Quinn later learned that Barbara followed Palmer to the grave four years later, but not before marrying Major-General Robert Fielding, whose excesses eclipsed her own and whom she had no choice but to prosecute for the crime of bigamy.

Hopwood had helped cure a woman of her phobia of dogs, hypnotized another to endure the pain of childbirth and treated a compulsive gambler who would spend all his weekly wages at the races. But never before had he gone this far in his work. It was a highly bizarre yet fascinating exercise.

It would be nice to believe in the concept of reincarnation like those Hindus and Buddhists did in their pursuit of attaining a state of nirvana, but, to all and sundry, Past Life Regression was a controversial subject. There were various schools of thought. One theory postulated that, at best, it was the result of trace memories passed down over generations—a simple matter of genetics. Another, and the most popular, suggested it was a combination of cryptomnesia [a form of memory bias where the person unwittingly plagiarizes someone else's thoughts and ideas and believes them to be their own] and confabulation [delusional memories drawn from the person's experience, knowledge and imagination], guided on by hypnotic suggestion. Learning of Quinn's former incarnation as a beleaguered nobleman at the time of the Stuart monarchy could go some way in explaining his present hang-ups and neuroses. But, using the memories of past lives to address current problems was, in Hopwood's opinion, pseudoscience of the worst kind. He was a firm believer in evidence-based clinical practice. There was no room for karma.

Two things Hopwood had certainly picked up during this particular session. Firstly, Quinn's account was full of glaring historical inaccuracies as though he were relating his story from his own perceptions (and preconceptions) of the era. Secondly, the Quinns' manservant, Giles, who had been in many respects a surrogate father to the boy when he was growing up, had harboured a passion for biographies.

Mystery solved.

*****

Back in the present, Hopwood continued his line of questioning. "Why do you think Mandy took an interest in you?"

Quinn had first met Amanda Bowes less than six months ago at the local bookshop. He often visited the store in search of travel guides—Quinn was planning a trip to Prague in the near future. They collided into each other down one of the aisles, dropping their books. She apologized profusely. Quinn was immediately taken by her beauty. She reminded him of a younger, sweeter version of his ex-wife, probably on account of her being a Nursery Nurse and working with children. He asked her out and she said yes. They went to dinner several times after that. She joined him on his trip to the Czech Republic, where they hit it off famously. He told her he was a man of leisure. She told him she was looking for Mr. Right and that she might have actually found him. Quinn was thrilled. He spent lavishly on her, which she didn't protest to. Nor did she decline the offer of moving into his family mansion. All seemed to be going swimmingly for a while until Quinn began to have doubts, those same old doubts that had plagued his previous marriage, the suspicion that Mandy was cheating on him.

"She's exploiting me for my money," Quinn replied in the present. "I know I've frittered away the bulk of my fortune in recent years, but there is still a substantial amount left over to retire on." Rhetorically and with a weary sigh, he asked: "Whatever happened to the purity and chastity of women the Bible speaks of?"

It was a glorious Thursday afternoon. Slanting rays of sunlight streamed down through the Venetian blinds, illuminating the dancing dust-motes in eerie shades of blue. The air-conditioning hummed steadily, circulating cool air around the therapist's office, keeping the heat of day at bay outside. The noise of the traffic from the streets below was barely audible. Yes, a glorious day in May, thought Hopwood, shame to be stuck indoors. He turned his attention back to his hypnotized subject. Still a quarter-of-an-hour of the session to go.

Despite the emotional scars he carried, Quinn had got himself into another potentially wonderful relationship following the collapse of his marriage. As far as Hopwood was concerned, this constituted progress. Now it was down to him to prevent Quinn from making the same mistake twice. It seemed that Quinn was doing exactly what he had done before: pushing away the woman in his life through his own mistrust and insecurities. This relationship needed some serious saving. "Don't you think Mandy is with you because she loves you?"

"Once maybe, but her love for me has since dwindled and died."

Hopwood decided to approach the problem from a different angle, one that might involve a post-hypnotic suggestion. "I want to bring you forward from a week ago . . . Where are you now?"

"Saturday . . ." Quinn replied. Then, still held within his trance state, a look of agony convulsed his face as he suddenly yelled: "GOOD LORD!"

Hopwood jumped in his seat, startled. "Why? What's happening?"

"I see her!"

"Who?"

"Mandy, who else? I catch her being escorted into a restaurant by a man. I stop my car and watch them go in. The Maître D' leads them to a table not far from the window. I can still just about see them from where I'm parked. Mandy seems happy. She reminds me of a college girl in the spring of first love. I can tell from her look of pure adoration and because she's doing that thing with her hair. I can't see the man's features since his back is turned. I sit in my car for the best part of an hour, watching them have their meal, watching them chat and laugh and flirt. Meanwhile, I'm getting more and more worked-up. But I'm compelled to look . . . I wait for the right moment to strike. Finally, it arrives . . . Her date offers her a single red rose. She laughs and leans over and kisses him. I can't take it anymore. Something snaps in me and I feel a monstrous hatred rise up inside of me. It's like I'm another person watching myself lose control. I see myself getting out of my car and crossing the street. I see myself entering the restaurant and walking over to their table . . . *Just look at them sitting there, sipping champagne, listening to the sound of José González, with not a care in the world* . . . Mandy sees me, and her eyes widen in shock and horror. Her date, too, turns in my direction . . . *It can't be! I can't fucking believe it! Nor can he, it seems. After all the trust I placed in him, he betrays me like this?*... I reach into my pocket and pull out my father's old service revolver, which I keep fully loaded. Mandy screams, the cheating bitch. Her date pleads with me to reconsider. *I fire* . . ." Quinn broke down into tears, moaning: "Oh, my God, I *kill* them! I *kill them both in cold blood*!"

Perched on the edge of his seat, Hopwood was stunned, utterly flabbergasted. He didn't know what to say for a moment. Then, he took charge again. "What is the precise date?"

Quinn carried on sobbing. "Saturday the Sixteenth of August..."

The Sixteenth of August? Hopwood thought, astonished. *That's almost three months from now! That's got to be the absurdist thing I ever heard!* "Tell me about this particular Saturday. What's the weather like?"

"Twenty-nine degrees, clear blue skies."

"What's in the news that day?"

"Suicide of another soldier at Deepcut Barracks."

"Who's the man she's with?"

Quinn went berserk. Fury—the likes of which Hopwood had not seen in a very long time—caused Jepson's face to turn dark red. Eyes still closed, bound securely in his trance, he leapt out of his chair and lunged at Hopwood, his hands reaching for the therapist's throat. "*A REAL BACKSTABBING JUDAS! I DESPISE THE FUCKER! IF I EVER MEET THE BASTARD SONOFABITCH AGAIN, I WOULD SHOOT HIM!*" Hopwood reacted instantly, as though anticipating the attack. He jerked his body to the right just as Quinn's hands were closing round his neck. Quinn's hands snatched only air and, momentarily unbalanced, he toppled over. Hopwood decided to end it there.

"I'm going to count backwards from five to one . . . Five: your eyelids feel less heavy . . . Four: sensation is returning to your fingers and the tips of your toes . . . Three: you're beginning to drift awake . . . Two: you're becoming more aware of the sounds around you . . . One: you will wake up alert and refreshed with no recollection of what's been said . . ."

Hopwood clicked his fingers.

Quinn's eyes drifted open. He glanced around him, discovered he was sprawled on the floor. He looked up at Hopwood, bleary-eyed, bewildered. "What am I doing down here?"

Hopwood replied matter-of-factly, "There was an incident. You were acting out a fantasy. How do you feel?"

"Pretty good," Quinn said, rising to his feet.

"Remember anything?"

Quinn resumed his seat. "Not a jot . . . Did I make any progress?"

"Yes, I think so," Hopwood replied, pushing the STOP button on the Dictaphone. "A most interesting session." *Bordering on crazy, up there with that comedy film where the hypnotist dies from a heart attack before he can bring his over-relaxed subject out of his trance or watching the weird, stilted performances of the authentically-hypnotized cast in the most conceptual of Werner Herzog's movies or how a mad, hypnotically-gifted monk singlehandedly brought down the Romanov dynasty with his hard-drinking, whore-pursuing ways or those old news headlines involving that Indian doctor who would hypnotize his female patients and have sex with them, his crimes only coming to light when one of them gave birth to a brown baby.*

"What did you learn?" Quinn asked anxiously.

That you're one jalapeño short of a taco, amigo, concluded Hopwood, *a genuine passive-aggressive, close to dangerous—all you need to tip you over the edge is the slightest confirmation of your suspicions.* "I need to go over the session one more time before I can release my findings. As usual, I'll fax you a copy of the report early next week." *The sanitized version, of course.*

"What now?" Quinn said expectantly.

"Ask my secretary to book you in another appointment on the way out."

With a cheery farewell, Quinn took his leave. Hopwood watched this otherwise amusing little man, whose Primark suit grew more and more crumpled with each passing week, disappear out the door. He reflected on the session and the overwhelming distress of a man rejected by wife and parents alike, a man who, due to repeated blows to his self-esteem, seemed forever desperate to prove the inherent wickedness of women . . . a man who in a blind, expletive-choked rage had tried to strangle him. Hopwood was still shaking.

Hypnosis was not an exact science. In fact, no-one knew how it worked. The conscious only formed ten percent of the mind like the visible tip of an iceberg. The rest lay beneath and, if one was not careful, could sink the Titanic. The mind recorded all input from the senses, no matter how minute and insignificant, storing it in the subconscious. This information could be retrieved at any given time through focused attention and the power of suggestion. Whole days from the person's past, lost to the conscious mind, could be recounted in stunning detail through hypnosis. The Mesmerists had once believed the trance state resulted from the channelling of a mystical energy called 'animal magnetism'. The Scottish surgeon and Victorian pioneer of hypnotism, James Braid, looked to science for the answer and talked about the 'ideo-dynamic reflex', whereby if the conscious mind were aided in concentrating on a single dominant idea, it could produce an exaggerated psychophysiological response: a state of peaceful relaxation in the form of a waking sleep. Even Sigmund Freud, earlier on in his career, used hypnosis to regress clients to their childhood in order to 'abreact' [remember, confront and come to terms with] repressed traumatic memories. One of the most influential hypnotists of the twentieth century, Milton Erickson adopted complex communication patterns, both verbal and non-verbal, to improve the motivation and confidence of those suggestible, paving the way for Neurolinguistic Programming. Like God, the human mind moved in mysterious ways. The past life Quinn had recalled during an earlier session was a prime example. Could the same principles apply to these Memories of the Future he had just recounted? A false sense of subjective precognition derived from further confabulation and use of artistic licence, Hopwood speculated, working their magic through selection bias and a state of heightened suggestibility. To quote Betty Hill, famous UFO abductee and not exactly the most reliable of sources: medical hypnosis could be used to open up amnesia, but at the same time one could not testify under its influence since there was no way to test what was real or fantasy.

Or perhaps there was something more and the mind actually possessed metaphysical properties.

I mean what would happen if you hypnotized someone at the point of death? considered Hopwood. *What fascinating secrets would be revealed?*

Maybe we'll never know.

Trained to look at the world with a degree of clinical detachment, one thing he was certain of: he would not be undertaking any more sessions with this man, not after the events of today. He would cancel the next meeting. Period. He felt it his legal obligation to give Quinn the number of a reputable psychotherapist. Hopwood knew when to call it a day.

"That was close," he reflected, sighing with relief, "too damned close . . ."

When the time came to give Quinn the old heave-ho, Hopwood did it as gently as possible, without hurting the man's feelings. Quinn took it surprisingly well, showing no signs of dependence or disappointment. Quinn paid the final bill in full without protesting. In his private clinic, Hopwood went back to his usual range of clientele: heavy smokers wishing to quit, compulsive overeaters and run-of-the-mill phobics. He would occasionally think of Quinn, particularly during spells of tedium, and wonder how the man was getting on. Delving into the nooks and crannies of the man's unconscious had been an absolutely riveting experience and a genuine challenge. But in the weeks that followed, Hopwood thought of him less and less until, one day, Quinn became but a faded memory.

Besides, Hopwood had other things on his mind. He had just started seeing someone, a girl by the name of Amber Bunting. He had dated her only twice, and he had a sense that she might be The One. It was great being a player on the speed-dating circuit, but he believed he had reached an important crossroads in his life and considered it about time that he made a concerted attempt to settle down. If it didn't work out, so be it. But at least he could proudly say he had made the effort.

On the third date, Hopwood met Amber at Chistlewick Common, near to where she apparently rented an apartment. The drive up from Oaks Fold, where he lived, was an uneventful experience.

It was a sweltering summer's day with further soaring temperatures predicted, the sun a gold-gilded ball of fire at its zenith, not a hint of cloud in the bleached-blue sky. People lazed on the grass, soaking up the sun, reading or picnicking, keeping their dress-code to a modest minimum.

Like the other punters in the park, Hopwood and Amber were embracing the heat. Amber wore a fetching white dress which complimented the gorgeous tan she sported and gave her an altogether angelic appearance. Hopwood, dressed in an open-collared white shirt and blue pants, found himself pouring off sweat by the gallon. Amber seemed to be relishing the hot weather, whereas Hopwood felt uncomfortable and distinctly unattractive. However, he was able to distract himself from the prevailing heat by concentrating on the conversation between him and his date.

"I've just come out of a very difficult relationship," Amber was saying, lying on her back, looking up at the sky. "He was so possessive. When I left him, he started stalking me. I took out a restraining order against him."

"You sound as if you went through a tough time."

"I did. He was so sweet and sensitive when we started out. But he changed."

"Did he ever hit you?"

"Never. He was possessive but not violent. I thought about changing my name and moving far away, starting a new life elsewhere. Unfortunately, the restraining order doesn't seem to be holding him. I keep seeing him everywhere."

Feeling a smidgen of disquiet, Hopwood propelled himself up on his elbows. His eyes hunted the park, skimming across the people sunning themselves, wondering if one of them was the infamous ex-boyfriend Amber was referring to. Maybe the guy was hiding in one of the trees, watching them through a pair of binoculars. Despite the heat, he shivered. "Is he the jealous type?" Amber did not answer immediately. Then, on reflection, she decided: "Let's not spoil our time together by talking about *him*."

Hopwood tried to cheer her up. "Despair not, my fair lady. Your gentleman shall protect you."

Amber smiled. "Why don't we get a bite to eat? There's a great Italian place I know. I'm famished."

"Even in this heat?"

"More so when it's hot."

They got up from the grass, Amber putting on her white slip-ons, Hopwood picking up the jacket he had been sitting on and carrying it over his shoulder. They made their way towards the archway at the park entrance.

Joining the pedestrians on the busy main street, Hopwood checked his Rolex. "Just in time for lunch." He offered Amber his elbow and she took it. They walked arm-in-arm down the bustling pavement.

They mingled amongst various kinds of people, most out shopping or sitting under the café awnings, all making the most of the seasonably good weather. A bunch of half-naked blokes with man-boobs and hanging beer-bellies gathered outside THE TOBEY JUG, drinking and smoking, talking and laughing—three more hours before the football season officially kicked off. A busker and his faithful dancing terrier entertained a small group of onlookers with a crooning, guitar-driven rendition of a golden oldie which Hopwood couldn't quite place. Hopwood spotted some Japanese tourists, snapping pictures—what they were doing in Chistlewick was anybody's guess. The pace of the traffic had practically dropped to a crawl, and there seemed to be a lot of angry cursing and beeping horns.

The sun is shining, thought Hopwood pleasantly, *the birds are singing, a fine girl by my side. Life couldn't be sweeter.*

They encountered a newspaper vendor. "Read all about it!" the fellow-in-the-flat-cap cried, "Inquest into second suicide at Deepcut Barracks."

Hopwood felt another dash of unease, pausing for a moment.

Where have I heard that before?

"What is it?" asked Amber, wondering why he'd stopped, looking up at his puzzled expression.

"I'm not sure . . ." responded Hopwood ponderously. "*Déjà vu,* perhaps." The voice of reason interjected just then. *The news headlines should sound familiar. Deepcut Barracks has been in the news quite a bit lately, so why's that so strange?* He shrugged off the troubling sensation and continued walking.

They arrived at their destination: BELLISSIMO PIZZERIA & RISTORANTE. It had just opened for business. They went inside and were greeted by the Maître D', who, from the size of him, enjoyed his food.

"Table for two," requested Hopwood.

Beaming, the Maître D' sat them in the middle of the restaurant. Menus were offered.

Hopwood glanced around the place. No other customers apart from them. Nice décor: seamless red velvet. There was no escaping the sense of nostalgia. Old, framed black-and-white stills of street life in Naples adorned the walls. At intervals hung mugshots of possibly famous Neapolitan people, none of whom Hopwood recognized. The latest home and away kits of the Naples football team were proudly displayed above the door to the kitchen like the Shakespearean masks of comedy and tragedy. "I guess the owner has a soft spot for Naples."

"I come here quite often," said Amber. "Their peach Bellinis are to die for." Above her head was a route map of Naples, again framed.

They contemplated their menus before deciding to order. Their lunch arrived twenty minutes later by which time the restaurant had begun to fill up. Following their beef-carpaccio starters they tucked into their meals. Amber opted for a traditional Four

Seasons pizza—Parma ham, pepperoni, mushrooms and capers—while Hopwood decided to be adventurous and try their Festival of Seafood, which included half a lobster. He quickly acquired a taste for the Bellini cocktails. They ate and drank and talked. People continued to drift into the restaurant. Soft rock floated down from the speakers, ambiently-low, instead of popular Italian.

Since Amber refused to talk about her recent past, Hopwood kept the conversation gentlemanly and aboveboard. Even though he was a therapist and had the means of obtaining intimate information, he could wait until she trusted him enough to disclose details of her relationship with her Ex. Her manner, enigmatic and graceful, drew him in, and he could easily see himself falling for her. He listened to her talking about her family, her friends, her childhood, her hopes and dreams. The fact she got on well with children made her all the more appealing and elevated her up in his esteem. When the cappuccinos arrived, Hopwood was hooked. He decided not to let this delicate English rose slip through his fingers.

"What are you thinking?" Amber asked.

"I'm thinking I've had a fantastic time. Great food, wonderful atmosphere, perfect company. Well-recommended." Out of some canny urge, he turned his head to his left and saw the Maître D' approaching their table, carrying what looked like a bucket of red roses. Hopwood frowned, perturbed. Amber didn't notice.

"Would you like to buy a beautiful rose for your beautiful lady?" the Maître D' asked Hopwood hopefully.

"Uh, yes," Hopwood replied, suddenly unsure, filled with a sense of foreboding. Something was wrong. Hopwood caught the song playing quietly in the background—José González's sad cover of Teardrop—and realized what the busker had been attempting in his own unique folksy style earlier. The song had followed Hopwood all the way here. His stomach quivered, contracted, lurched. His heart skipped a beat. Gooseflesh erupted over his skin. Trying to keep calm, Hopwood handed Amber a single red rose. The gesture was almost involuntary, automatic. "For you," he murmured with a forcible smile.

Amber accepted it willingly, and with a dainty, romantic look of affection, she leaned forward and kissed him softly on the lips—their first kiss. "Oh, Mark . . ." she whispered from seemingly faraway.

And, as her face moved away from his, her attention caught on something just over his right shoulder. He saw her eyes expand and her mouth creak open in starkest fear. He saw all this in slow motion and felt the ides of March closing in on him.

"I should have fucking known you'd be out with another man!" snarled a voice from behind him.

Hopwood knew who it was even before he looked round. How could he have been so stupid, so complacent? How could he have missed that today was the Sixteenth of August? The signs were all there. They were living out that premonition of future events—the flashforward mined from the subconscious, an episode of chronosthesia tapped under hypnosis—that he had rather naively and stupidly put down to selection bias. *I can't believe I didn't see this coming.*

"You must be Mandy the Nursery Nurse," he said to Amber frankly. "You changed your name, didn't you?"

He encountered no guilt in her expression, only terror. He turned his head round.

And there stood Jepson Quinn as large as life. Except he looked dreadful. His once-white Primark suit was ripped and stained, and he hadn't showered or shaved in days. The wild, sweaty tangle of hair and the round, bulging eyes gave him the appearance of an escaped lunatic.

Now it was Quinn's turn to look shocked. His eyes bugged out even more, threatening to pop. "*You!* How can you do this to me? After all the trust I placed in you, you betray me like *this*?"

"I didn't know," Hopwood muttered. "Honest." Only the words came out tired and awkward and wouldn't have convinced a five-year-old.

"I won't be humiliated any more!" Quinn reached into his jacket pocket and pulled out a revolver.

Amber screamed. Most of the customers sat frozen, the reaction of the others was to duck under their tables. The Maître

D' dropped his bucketful of roses and ran panic-stricken and gabbling to the sanctuary of the kitchen.

Quinn waved the gun at Hopwood. "You backstabbing *Judas!*" spat Quinn, breaking down. "You fucking *bastard! You stole my girl!*"

There was so much hurt and rage on display, the result of years of repeated social insults, that Hopwood actually felt pity for the man. Was it any surprise it had come to this? Hopwood was amazed it hadn't happened sooner. So long overdue. "As far as we're concerned," Amber reminded Quinn defiantly, "we were over a long time ago."

Quinn wiped the tears from his grimy face, struggling with his emotions, cutting as much a tragic figure as King Menelaus. Then, his tortured, ruinous expression darkened, madness and jealous rage spilling over once more. "Just as well! You two make an excellent couple! Revenge is a dish best served cold!"

"There has to be another way," Mark Hopwood tried reasoning with him. "You really don't need to do this!" But he *knew* what would happen next. There could only be one outcome. He should let the scene play out as it was supposed to . . . for there was no fighting the inevitable. Far from the random coincidence it seemed to be, the actors in this mini-drama were surely part of a fixed cosmic plan. It was pure, unmerciful Determinism at work, colouring every conceivable situation in the Great Theatre of Life with design and purpose. Hopwood had unwittingly revealed in his last hypnotherapy session with Quinn that the future had already happened. Quinn had somehow demonstrated veridical dreaming, a prescient vision that amounted to *future recall*. Writer and broadcaster Colin Wilson couldn't have been wider off the mark; the mind did *not* have the power to change the destiny of men. It served only as a tool to record past, present and future events as renowned aeronautical engineer and parapsychologist, John William Dunne, had once postulated. Dunne theorized that all time existed simultaneously. All time was eternally present, with the past, present and future all happening together at the same instant, but our waking minds only allowed us to perceive time in a sequential, linear form. But, in the subconscious state, time ceased to be so concrete, and we would be capable of experiencing what we might call precognitive dreams as the mind ventured across the past, present and future unbounded.

Two shots rang out.

May 2010—August 2010

Reality Check

"By believing passionately in something that still does not exist, we create it. The nonexistent is whatever we have not sufficiently desired."

Franz Kafka

When Herschel Saxby woke up one morning from uneasy dreams, he realized that his wife and children were not his wife and children. As post-dawn sunlight slanted in through the gap between the drawn bedroom curtains, lighting up the dancing dust-motes in the air, he found himself on the same bed as a woman who resembled his wife, Maris, but who could not actually be his wife. He knew it was only a feeling, one that might be flawed, inaccurate, wide off the mark, but it was a strong feeling, a gut instinct, rather more tangible than a fancy or a mere inkling, one he was certain he could not be misreading. The sense that this woman sleeping next to him was an impostor, he was convinced was not some misconception—or misperception. Misconception or otherwise, such a revelation would have caused most people to jump out of bed as though the sheets were on fire, but not Herschel. Herschel Saxby was a fairly successful science-fiction writer who had the potential to entertain such far-out notions. He emerged from beneath the covers, crept silently across the room in the hunt for something that might put his mind at rest, a safety measure, before sneaking back into bed.

When Maris awoke and saw him staring strangely down at her in the early-morning light with a disconcerting intensity far from the dreamy, adoring look he had given her before they'd made love last night, a look of perturbation crossed her forehead and she sat up abruptly, fully alert, her mind instantly shaking away the remnants of sleep. "What is it, Hersch? What's wrong?"

"You're not my wife," he stated bluntly.

"What do you mean, Hersch?"

"You look like my wife, you sound like my wife, but you're not my wife. What have you done with her?"

The woman whom he knew was posing as Maris seemed to experience a moment of misplaced comprehension and a wicked smile slowly snuck across her lips as she leaned forward to kiss him. "Is this one of your kinky games?"

When Herschel pulled back from the kiss, his expression flinty and cold, the fear returned to her eyes. "Don't even think about it!" he warned her.

"What's going on?" she asked, suddenly afraid. "Don't you recognize me, Hersch?"

"You're not Maris! Where is my real wife?"

"But I *am* Maris . . ."

"That's what you want me to believe," he said, challenging her: "What are you? A doppelgänger? An automaton, an alien?"

"What's happened to you, Hersch?" Maris said and began to cry, gushing tears.

Crocodile tears, thought Herschel unsympathetically. *Nothing more.* "And I won't be going anywhere near the twins, either. I know they're not mine."

His rather indelicate remark, implying questionable parentage of his so-called offspring, pushed Maris to cry harder. "How can you say such a thing? Of course they're yours! Whose else would they be?"

Herschel thought of his two children supposedly sleeping soundly in the other room: Milo and Mila, both aged four years.

Herschel dismissed her. "No, you're not understanding me! They're not children at all, just 'creatures' made to look like my children! Changelings!"

"They're your children! Your own flesh-and-blood!"

"You're talking nonsense and I'm not listening to you any further! Anyway, you're not my wife!"

"Don't keep saying that!" Amidst her rolling tears, Maris looked perplexed, confused, gave the impression of someone wondering if their other half was suffering some kind of mental breakdown. Herschel worked hard, too hard sometimes, and maybe his stories had affected him in some terrible way, caused him to lose the plot. "I can't take this anymore. I'm calling the Emergency Services . . ."

"I insist you do just that," demanded Herschel in full agreement, "so we can clear up this unpleasant business once and for all. Find out who everybody *really* is?" He pulled out a small red hatchet from beneath his pillow, causing Maris's eyes to widen in alarm. "I thought I might need this for my own protection," he explained, trailing his thumb along the sharp, bladed edge of the hatchet. "Don't force me to use it. Not that you'll feel any pain because both of us know you're not real . . ."

"Why am I here?" Herschel moaned as he gradually arose from the depths of sedation. As his vision normalized, he discovered he was in a white, padded cell, arms locked in a straitjacket. He tried to shake himself free of the safety suit, but his arms were held tight with very little wiggle-room. The glare of the overhead light made him squint.

A tall, dapper gentleman, wearing a white coat, was seated on a chair in front of him, looking down at him. His shrewd eyes and hooked nose reminded Herschel of someone he knew, but he could not put his finger on it. Two burly orderlies stood either side of the doctor. "You know where 'here' is?"

"Yes, the loony bin!" Herschel remarked sharply, irritably, fighting against his restraint which afforded his arms only limited movement.

The doctor made the necessary introductions. "I'm afraid we don't use politically incorrect terms like that any more. You're at Greenacres Psychiatric Facility. I'm Dr. Cavortian and I'm in charge of your care. Can you tell me your name?"

Herschel was more awake now, though still feeling the vestiges of the sedative. "Herschel . . . Herschel Saxby."

"That's very good," said Dr. Cavortian, and Herschel immediately loathed the man's patronizing tone.

"Okay, but you still haven't told me why the hell I'm here?"

"The law dictates that you be admitted for a period of seventy-two hours' observation," Dr. Cavortian explained. "What happens afterwards will depend on our psych evaluation and your level of cooperation."

However, the original query remained unanswered. "Yes, but *why* was I admitted?"

"You don't remember?" Dr. Cavortian sounded surprised.

"Not quite . . ."

"This may come as a shock to you, but you tried to attack your family with an axe."

"Bullshit!" Herschel exploded incredulously. Then, the memories seemed to come flooding back like a tidal wave. It hadn't been a pretty sight. His so-called wife had leapt out of bed and done a runner the moment he showed her the axe and locked herself in the children's bedroom from where she apparently called the Emergency Services. He could hear two very frightened children, with Mila asking her mother, *What's wrong with Daddy?* And Maris telling her: *Daddy's not well.*

That's crap! he had yelled at the three of them through the bedroom door. *Open up, woman!*

He could hear them pretending to be terrified, probably huddled up together, encircled within Maris's arms. Yes, the operative word was 'pretending'. Indeed, operating under false pretences. When Maris refused to open the door, he tried kicking the door down, but it would not budge. So he did the only thing that seemed fitting at the time. He put the hatchet to good use, splitting the wood, ripping apart the door panels. Then, the EMTs arrived . . . but not before a large contingent of police officers smashed down the front door, spilling inside. The cops didn't shoot him, but their sheer numbers managed to wrestle him to the ground and grapple the axe out of his grasp while he comprehensively explained to them of his concerns over the imposters posing as his family. As he continued to struggle on the floor, resisting arrest as best he could, one of the EMTs injected him with a hypodermic needle and out he went like a light. Only to find himself in this place, presently. "You can believe what you like, Doc, but you know it's not true! I only threatened them. I never meant to harm them. They wouldn't talk to me. I wanted to get the truth out of them."

"Truth? And what is this truth that you speak of?"

"That my family are all impostors, plain and simple."

"Thank you for being honest with me, Mr. Saxby. Your wife mentioned you may not be well."

"She's not my wife," he told the psychiatrist. "And I'm as fit as a fiddle."

"Be as it may, there were children involved."

"They're not my children."

"That is yet to be debated. I think we should sit down in a more suitable forum and explore your concerns further."

Herschel indicated to the straitjacket with his head. "Is this absolutely necessary?"

"Only if you can guarantee that you won't jump up and attack me," Dr. Cavortian said warily.

Herschel nodded again. "You have my word as a scholar and a gentleman."

Dr. Cavortian seemed satisfied with the assurance. He gestured to the hulking orderlies, who moved in swiftly to remove his straitjacket. "Now that you're free of your shackles, freshen up, have a bite to eat and perhaps then we can sit down and find out what's what . . ."

"I shall await your invitation with candlestick and facepaint . . ."

"So what could possibly make a respected author of science fiction turn on his own family like that?" Dr. Cavortian began the interview from behind his desk in his private office at Greenacres. One wall housed a bookcase, laden with tomes and medical journals, the other a wall-mounted television set with all the equipment necessary for video conferencing. A black metallic filing cabinet rested in the corner. Behind Dr. Cavortian a double-glazed window afforded views of the arboreal environs of the mental health facility, the summer months bringing out the lush beauty of the grounds. Spick-and-span, Dr. Cavortian's office was a sanctuary to neatness, efficiency and, foremost, calm.

Freshly-showered and fed, dressed in a black jeans and T-shirt, Herschel sat in a comfy leather armchair opposite, eyes watchful, suspicious. Another attendant, as big, muscular and pug-faced as his colleagues, stood by the door impassively. *Just in case . . .* "I told you. My family's been replaced by duplicates."

"So you keep saying. If they're not your family, who are they?"

"I haven't yet figured that out and what their motive is but keeping me here won't help."

"You're here for a period of assessment," Dr. Cavortian reminded Herschel, asking: "Do you think they might be Pod People?"

"You make me sound as if I've started believing the stuff I write about."

"That is sincerely not my intention, not at all. Your physical examination and drug screen, like your EEG and brain scan, were normal with no suggestion of organic pathology or seizure activity. And there is no genetic loading for mental illness. I'm merely trying to understand how someone as highly-intelligent and widely-respected as you, not susceptible to mental health difficulties, could suddenly denounce his young family as 'impostors'. Did anything unusual happen last night?"

Herschel sat back more comfortably in his chair in preparation of the tale he was about to unfold. "Nothing out of the ordinary, if I recall correctly," he related. "We made love last night and went to sleep. I was briefly awoken by a flash of light, like lightning, suggesting the approach of a storm, but I drifted back to sleep, only to wake up in the morning absolutely sure that something wasn't right. I went to bed last night with my wife but woke up this morning with a total stranger."

Dr. Cavortian picked up on a potential point. "Flash of light, you say?"

"Nothing odd about it. We get electrical storms at this time of year."

"No, I would be thinking temporal lobe epilepsy—auras, strange lights, visions, hallucinations—if your EEG didn't turn out to be unremarkable."

"So what's your opinion, Doc?

"Let me be frank, this unhealthy fixation on your family . . . you're either in complete denial or you're quite deluded. Ever heard of Capgras syndrome?"

"Capgras?"

"Capgras syndrome is classified as a delusional misidentification disorder where the person holds the delusion that a friend, spouse or other close family member, or even a pet, has been replaced by an identical-looking impostor. Dr. Joseph Capgras, a French psychiatrist, first coined the term in 1923 when one of his patients, Madame M., claimed she had eighty husbands all with the same face. This 'illusion of doubles' is very rarely seen in its purest form, as it often tends to be part-and-parcel of a much more severe, wider illness, such as paranoid schizophrenia, dementia or organic brain injury, like a stroke."

"But I know my wife has been replaced by a lookalike."

Dr. Cavortian tried to reason with him. "That's the real definition of a delusion: a false, unshakable belief generally with bizarre content that is held with strong conviction, even in the presence of contrary evidence. I mean you are a science-fiction writer by trade, so you should be capable of considering all scenarios logically and rationally. Which is the more improbable: you're experiencing a delusional state brought on by stress or that your wife has been substituted by an exact double?"

It struck a chord. Herschel nodded at the two possible explanations, one cogent, the other completely outlandish.

"Believe me, this is a very common malady," Dr. Cavortian went on, "and I can understand how terrifying—*traumatizing*—existing in a perceived world of impersonators it can be for all concerned. Patients with the condition have been known to hack their loved one to pieces just because they believed their loved one was replaced by an exact copy of that person. But I'm going to let you in on a secret. There is a proven biological basis for the condition."

"How so?"

Dr. Cavortian did not wish to get too technical, but it might satisfy the curiosity of this high-functioning but very deluded man. "There is a significant disconnect between the facial recognition pathway of the temporal cortex and the limbic system, particularly the amygdala, which is meant to provide an emotional response to that face. In organic conditions like dementias or strokes, the neural transmission between this connecting circuit of the brain decays or is suddenly disrupted. In either case, the conscious ability to recognize faces is intact, but the individual with Capgras delusion does not necessarily feel the emotion that normally accompanies the sight of that person. Thus, when you see your wife's face, you recognize it—she looks and sounds and smells like her—but the emotions associated with her are missing, so you don't get the warm feeling that goes along with her, only a sense of emptiness, as though her essence—or soul—isn't there. Thus, you form the opinion that, although she is wearing your wife's clothes and acts like your wife, this cannot be my wife, ergo she must be an impostor.

"The funny thing is that if your wife spoke to you over the phone, the delusion would no longer exist; you would instantly recognize her voice. Yet, if she were to walk into this very room after that phone-call, you'd be convinced that she is an impostor. Just because of damage to the crucial link between visual recognition and that part of the brain that activates the emotions corresponding to physical appearance."

Herschel did not speak.

"So I ask you again," Dr. Cavortian challenged him, "do you think your wife has been replaced?"

Herschel remembered his wife's glistening tears from this morning, overwrought with fear and hurt, as she desperately implored him to see sense. "I see your point . . ." he conceded, mindful of his own conflicting emotions, torn between accepting that his wife was worried about him and believing she was something foreign, inhuman.

"There is hope for you yet, my good man, even if you don't entirely accept my explanation. At least we are already making some inroads into your recovery. Unfortunately, there is no overnight cure. The treatment involves reality testing and cognitive reframing with insight-orientated work, but that should not concern you at the present moment. Persistence is needed in reestablishing the connection between perception and emotion, redeveloping empathy for this person. Low-dose antipsychotic medication, alongside the therapy, can help to some degree."

"Capgras, hey?" said Herschel, mulling over the discussion. "What if I never recover?"

"Not all is lost. Some people adjust to this single, persistent delusion and lead perfectly normal lives. There're even people who find their Capgras delusion highly erotic and possibly the key to connubial bliss. One woman complained how awkward at lovemaking her husband was, but how his 'double' proved an absolute stud! Male sufferers of the condition actually believe they are being unfaithful to their wives with their wife's 'double' because every sexual encounter feels exciting and fresh, electrifyingly-new! So I grant you permission to cheat on your wife *with* your wife!"

But Herschel did not join in Dr. Cavortian's laughter, amusing though his anecdote sounded. He had much more to his argument against returning home and apologizing to his wife and family. "Maybe it didn't begin last night with that flash of lightning but started last week while I was watching the news. I was doing some serious thinking, some introspection, and it dawned on me how the world we live in is a pretty crappy place and our lives short, empty and meaningless."

Dr. Cavortian smiled. "You're not the first person to come to that conclusion. Philosophers like Sartre have been banging on about it for decades."

"I'm aware of Sartre and the existential crisis, and his theories may apply to some extent. But I was looking at this problem from a different angle. When I look closely at the world around me I see people who go to work so they can earn enough cash to buy food and put a roof over their heads so they have enough energy and security to go to work to earn enough cash to buy food and put a roof over their heads so they have enough energy and security to go to work to earn enough cash to buy food and put a roof over their heads so they have enough energy and security to go to work . . . until each day merges into one, and one day they just drop dead!"

"There is nothing to be ashamed of in making a living to feed ourselves and pay for our homes. And we humans all perish in the end—it is inevitable and our former lives open to celebration, hence the eulogy and the wake."

"But do you not see how futile and pointless life is?" Herschel emphasized. "We are born from nowhere, we go nowhere and we end up nowhere."

"And that depresses you?"

"It doesn't depress me, no. As you can see, I'm not pervasively depressed or psychotic in the least or experiencing hallucinations or persistent intrusive thoughts. No, rather than depressed, I feel frustrated. Frustrated at everyone telling me I should conform to the same inane norm: be born, grow up amidst a schoolroom full of cruel children until I'm old enough to waste my life toiling away to put food on the table and roof over my head before I eventually retire and live the rest of my days on the fringes of society with failing organs and receding mental acuity until I finally disappear from society altogether in a coffin."

"But there is more to life than that. Humans have values, ambitions, *sensibilities*."

"Scientists talk of humans being sophisticated animals whose purpose in life is to procreate, pass on their genes, provide for their children. If so, then the generations after us repeat the same irrelevant cycle. Do you not see there is nothing rational or logical to our lives on this earth? We have nothing to look forward to than work, food and shelter."

"But there's always religion. Billions of people believe we go to a better place after we die."

The observation did very little for Herschel, who remained skeptical to the core. "It's all nonsense," snorted Herschel. "To quote my favourite writer, Kafka: *One man's religion is another man's belly laugh*. One man's magic is another man's engineering. Religion is all about blind faith. It is even more pointless than life itself, flies against the face of logic, makes even less sense. Religion is like *searching in a dark cellar at midnight for a black cat that isn't there*. Priests aren't exactly the smartest people, behaving more like gullible saps, convincing themselves of anything—and *nothing*. Every religion believes that the other religion is flawed and only they can take you to this imaginary place after you die."

"You have a curiously bleak, very pessimistic outlook on life. What does this have to do with your view that your wife and children aren't who they seem?"

"You see the next logical step from my very pessimistic outlook on life, as you quite aptly put it, is that this world cannot be just a hollow, unimportant, nonsensical place for no discernible reason. It has, like the meaninglessness of our individual existences, to have been designed in such a way to fit a purpose." Herschel's eyes widened with triumph. "*And I think I have found that very purpose!*"

Dr. Cavortian wasn't all too impressed. He sounded as though Herschel's jubilation might be somewhat premature or greatly misplaced. "Have you indeed?"

Herschel decided to expatiate on his conjecturing, using ancient thought. "I compare human existence to the Allegory of the Cave."

"I am very familiar with Plato, but please go on."

"Let me refresh your memory. Deep inside a cave, a gathering of people has been chained to a wall since childhood. Not only are their limbs manacled but their heads are also immobilized so that their eyes are fixed on a blank wall opposite them upon which they see shadows projected. They give names to these shadows. These shadows are as close as these prisoners get to viewing reality. One of the prisoners starts questioning his existence and breaks his chains and escapes the darkness of the cave, whereupon he enters a world of sunlight and experiences enlightenment, realizing that previous 'truths' were falsely-held beliefs. However, when he returns to the cave to share his enlightenment with his peers, the other prisoners refuse to believe this newly-enlightened truth bearer. Plato provides a metaphor for the way we perceive things around us and the way we lead our lives as not actually being the 'truth'. We human beings are leading ignorant, incomplete lives, following a path of rules, norms and ethics set down by previous generations without questioning them. There is a need for our questioning spirit to break free of our chains and seek out enlightenment."

"You give a very good argument," admitted Dr. Cavortian. "But don't you think you are overthinking, overanalyzing, overreaching, trying to find meaning in nothing?"

"Not at all," replied Herschel, getting into his stride. "I can take it one step further and discuss Cartesian doubt."

"As in the work of René Descartes?"

"The one and the same," confirmed Herschel. "The process involves systematically doubting the truth of all one's beliefs, thereby reducing them to those few beliefs which are certain to be true, thus furthering one's knowledge. One should be skeptical of sensory experience in particular, our main mode of knowledge acquisition, since hallucinations themselves are a way our minds can deceive us, fool us, into having similar experiences when there is nothing there. The Dream Argument posits that the mere act of dreaming means that our senses cannot be trusted to distinguish reality from illusion because when we dream we are not usually aware we are dreaming, unless we're those few people who experience lucid dreams. Thus, if our minds can be tricked into believing that a mentally-generated world in a dream is the 'real world' in that moment, by the same token, could our waking reality be a simulation? Are we certain that we are truly awake or are our lives nothing more than a lucid dream? Enter the hypothetical concept of the 'evil demon', or *genius malignus*, a clever, cunning, deceitful and infinitely powerful being in this thought experiment, who may very well be controlling all of our experiences—our perceptions of the earth, the heavens, our bodily sensations, our understanding of the fundaments of logic and mathematics, all eternal truths—simulating an external world we may think we live in when there is no external world."

Dr. Cavortian interjected at this stage: "But you exist. I exist. *Cogito ergo sum: I think, therefore I am.* That is, Descartes tried to doubt his own existence, but found that even his doubting showed that he existed, since he would not be able to doubt if he did not exist."

Herschel nodded at that long-accepted dictum, but he had other, more pertinent ideas up his sleeve. "Accepted, but I think the world around me is an illusion, a distraction, a sleight of hand, an ingenious piece of misdirection, a ginormous, planet-wide stage-set with rigged lighting, populated by actors and stage managers immersed in a play intended to divert me from my true calling."

"So what do these 'actors' hope to achieve? And what is your 'true calling', if you don't mind me asking?"

There was triumph in Herschel's voice again. "This set-dressing, this counterfeit world, this great swindle—this *cheat*—is designed to prevent me from discovering the truth. These humans around me are unlike me. In fact, they are not humans at all, but creatures—*things*—that want me to believe they are human."

Dr. Cavortian's expression suggested he could not readily dismiss the glaring, head-scratching holes in his patient's logic. "And why would they want to do that? What makes you so special?"

"To make me believe I am human and keep me in the dark about what is really going on. The only way I can explain the irrelevance of this world is that there is a conspiracy afoot, a plot to pull the wool over my eyes."

Dr. Cavortian regarded Herschel soberly. "If you are not human, what are you?"

Herschel fumbled for the right words, found them. He went in for the kill. "I am at the centre of this world, and everything around me is an incredibly intricate dream. My dream, to be precise . . . To put it another way, I am *God*."

Dr. Cavortian had his own opinions on the matter, but he did not wish to antagonize the patient. This was getting interesting. The man was unloading his thoughts. "That's quite a leap. You've managed to stretch the Dream Argument to Solipsism in a couple of steps. Not a lot of people can do that so fluently. Only true philosophers can."

"Or science-fiction writers?"

"Perhaps. No wonder philosophers lead contented lives. They drop everything to explore the nature of Life, Reality and the Universe. Self-reflection only leads to self-discovery in the wider scheme of things. Always searching for that Eureka moment. You sound like you've found yours."

Herschel seemed to be enjoying himself. "The whole visible world is perhaps nothing more than the rationalization of a man who wants to find peace for a moment. Find those who have attempted to falsify the actuality of knowledge . . . regard knowledge as a goal still to be reached . . . Kafka, again."

"Kafka was more than just a fiction writer. He was a great thinker."

Herschel elaborated on the concept Dr. Cavortian had broached. "Solipsism holds the philosophical position that only one's own mind is sure to exist, and anything outside one's own mind . . . the external world and other minds do not really exist."

"You cannot refute the existence of my mind," Dr. Cavortian countered. "I can only assure you I am real."

"That's precisely what I expected you to say!" Herschel said, quite animatedly. "You can try and fool me with your words and actions, but you are nothing more than a 'philosophical zombie'. You only display aspects of consciousness, but I am the one who created you."

"I doubt that very much. Solipsism is only a school of intellectual thought, a metaphysical idea at best."

Herschel continued in full flow. "When a tree falls in a forest and nobody is around to hear it, does it make a sound? George Berkeley posited that physical objects do not exist independently unless the mind perceives them. Something only exists so long as it is observed—otherwise, it is nonexistent, because only the human mind and perception truly exist, a philosophical idea that eventually gave rise to a study of the subatomic realm and the idea of Schrödinger's cat. Open the box. What will you find? A kitten maybe, a skeleton, two cats—

one dead and one alive, to depict two counter-universes—or nothing but an empty box. In answer to the thought experiment—Does the tree make a sound if no-one hears it fall?—there is an omnipresent Mind who observes all. The observer and the observed are one."

"You're saying nothing exists but your consciousness?" Dr. Cavortian recapped. "You make this world exist? Because you are God?"

Herschel ignored him and shifted to another line of thought. "Immanuel Kant claimed: *All knowledge begins with the senses, proceeds then to understanding, and ends with reason. There is nothing higher than reason. Science is organized knowledge. Wisdom is organized life.* But where is the wisdom in our pointless society? Schopenhauer was a great critic of Kantian belief. He believed that Kant underestimated the Thing-in-Itself, which is defined as 'everyday reality as it is apart from experience', what remains to be postulated once the categories of space, time and causality are removed. Schopenhauer believed that knowledge and understanding can still be gained from the Thing-in-Itself, and it was the will to live through which mankind found all his suffering."

"This is getting a little too heavy for my liking," Dr. Cavortian said, sighing. "Are we doing a tour of Sophie's World? Kant claimed: *Metaphysics is a dark ocean without shores or lighthouse, strewn with many a philosophic wreck.*"

"Don't forget Kant also said: *God does not simply will that we should be happy, but rather that we should make ourselves happy.*"

The doctor's expression changed, became serious, grave. Time for him to enlighten his patient as to his professional evaluation. "Even if you come across as quite rational and knowledgeable on the surface, I might describe you as extremely delusional when you start talking of being some kind of god. There is a psychosis at work here which might have started from a prodromal state but has progressed to a pathological state. Insight into your illness is greatly impaired. Not only do you demonstrate the features of Capgras delusion, but these egocentric beliefs extend into paranoia and grandiosity. I could even throw Solipsism syndrome into the clinical equation."

"Solipsism syndrome? What do you mean?"

"Solipsism syndrome refers to a psychological condition in which a person feels that the outside world is not real and is not external from their mind. Such experiences of depersonalization/derealization are quite common in psychosis. Profound stress or extended periods of isolation, such as with hermits and astronauts, predisposes someone to this state of mind. The longer you leave any illness untreated, the longer it will take to treat."

The fact that Dr. Cavortian's formulation implied that Herschel had gone fruit-loop did not faze him. Herschel was convinced he was of sound mind. "*All truth passes through three stages,*" he waxed philosophical. "*First, it is ridiculed. Second, it is violently opposed. Third, it is accepted as being self-evident.*" He paused before he went in for the kill. "I think *you*, like my phony family, are part of this conspiracy, to keep me in a state of ignorance."

"You can't make accusations like that and consider yourself sane," Dr. Cavortian declared with a hard edge. Then, his voice softened with sympathy and compassion. "I can assure you I only have your best interests at heart. Your family loves you very much and misses you and only hopes you can get better soon."

Herschel wanted to believe the doctor, wanted to believe those kindly words, that his family cared deeply for him, for his mental wellbeing, but he could not get past his perception of the truth that they were not actual living, breathing entities, but only things that existed in his imagination. "No, you are as much a co-conspirator in this sham as the creature posing as my wife and those little ones masquerading as my children, but I have managed to see through your play-acting, rip through your flimflam. The Japanese speak of the contrast between *tatemae*—the surface of things, the façade—and *honne*—the honest truth and absolute integrity."

Dr. Cavortian swooped in, eyes lighting up. "Ah, it seems you have just defeated the object of your own argument! If I arise from you, if I am part of you, and all of us are nothing but your creations, why should you want to imagine yourself committed to a psychiatric hospital? If the real world is just an illusion, a dream, a *fraud*, should you not be able to wake up from it? *Escape*?"

But Herschel was a stubborn man and appeared to have an answer for that, too. "Perhaps my mind is rebelling, and you want me to believe that I'm mad and keep me locked-up, so you can exist for a little bit longer, maybe indefinitely. But if I'm right and you are a figment of my imagination, I should be able to wish you away quite easily." The small, residual lines of doubt smoothed out on his face, turned into a sly, knowing smile, which made the good doctor shift uncomfortably in his chair. Herschel thought he saw him shudder. "Shall we see?"

He closed his eyes and imagined that Dr. Cavortian wasn't there. Not there at all.

When he opened them again, the chair behind the desk was empty and Herschel was alone in the room.

He had been right on the money. Not only had he whisked Dr. Cavortian away, just as he said he would, as a bonus, the attendant, too, was gone.

So there was truth to what he had worked out in his head. If he had manufactured this world by will alone, he should be able to change it any way he chose through pure thought. Yes, if everything around him was merely a construct of a single consciousness, it therefore followed that this external world could be manipulated by the power of his will.

He flexed his will again, directed his focus on the huge bookcase in the office. It was up to him to ascribe permanence and a sense of reality to things that were effectively insubstantial, and vice versa. If he gave the world substance, imagined it into being, he could likewise take it away.

Before his very eyes, the bookcase dimmed, grew inconsistent, faded to nothingness.

Herschel concentrated on the wall behind the disappearing piece of shelved furniture.

He forced it to distort. Dissolve. *Disintegrate*.

Herschel concluded he possessed the godlike powers of a demiurge. Every object existed only as a phenomenon of his consciousness. He was an artisan capable of shaping reality, changing the foundations of this universe he had brought into existence.

Only he truly existed. An Immortal who could transcend Time. He was Absolute. The Source of All Things. His consciousness gave vitality to the non-being.

"I am God and there is no other God before me," he announced to no-one in particular.

He willed himself elsewhere.

He heard voices.

He instantly teleported himself into a large, high-ceilinged lobby, less a concealed inner sanctum, more the entrance to the hospital.

He heard them talking, discussing him. His willpower allowed him to maintain an invisible presence, to listen in without being detected.

Dr. Cavortian stood conversing with two short, bald, black-suited men, who possessed ethereal, androgynous looks, smooth, ivory skin and dark pitiless eyes, which made Herschel think of the twins. Were these the actual monsters his own children were? They were certainly not human.

"*He knows . . .*" Dr. Cavortian was saying.

"He is diseased," said the first of the small, bald men in a liquid-filled tone. "The infection will spread to the others."

"Justification enough to cease all operations on him," commanded the other egg-headed man, producing a cruel smile, a hellish sneer. "Terminate the subject."

Herschel crept closer, not liking what he was hearing.

Aloud, Dr. Cavortian said: "We know you have been listening, Mr Saxby . . ."

How was that possible? thought Herschel, taken aback. Surely, he had made himself invisible. And these creatures were meant to be the mere sum parts of his conscious reality, mere bit players in the ongoing drama of his inner mental workings.

Not so it seemed, on all counts. "You can't get rid of us that easily," added Dr. Cavortian. "We're *real*."

"No, you're in my head, my reality," insisted Herschel.

"Reality can be such a subjective term," replied Dr. Cavortian. "But let us bring in some objectivity. Show you where you really are."

The hospital lobby suddenly metamorphosed into white, sterile underground research facility, one that might be constructed for human experimentation, the first indication of alien technology.

Herschel had made it happen, surely. He was a writer of dystopian science fiction in another life.

The systematic distorting, twisting, collapsing of reality, like the re-organizing of holographic pixels. It was no longer a secret subterranean compound designed for experimenting on human subjects, but Herschel was now aboard the observation deck of an alien space habitat floating in the benighted depths of space.

Herschel had held his mind to be the only god and all beings were thought to be a result of his mind assuming infinite forms. But he knew he wasn't doing it this time. There was some kind of external control outside his conscious reality. He saw the random glitter of stars within the vast, sweeping vacuum gaping blackly beyond the observation window and tried rearranging the cosmos in his mind, couldn't. He wondered if he had reached the limits of his creation. Had he finally unmasked the hidden order underlying the fake appearances of reality? Was he offstage or still within the theatre of his mind?

Herschel and his captors stood on an artificial space station surrounded by starry blackness, possibly outside his consciousness-generated image of the outside world.

Were these characters in his head or was he a character in their universal landscape?

Dr. Cavortian was speaking directly to him, and Herschel realized he was no longer invisible. Dr. Cavortian answered the question for him, as though he could read his mind. "We know what you're thinking, but you can never access our thoughts because we have a psychic link to your brain. We exist independent of you."

"Who are you people? What do you want?"

"We are completely separate entities from your act of creation. We have surgically implanted ourselves in your simulated reality. As the Architect I helped you create this fantasy. These beings," Dr. Cavortian said, pointing to the strange, egg-skulled creatures, "are the Management. Together we are the Authority."

"But you're human?"

"No, your mind has fashioned me in the image of your old, childhood hero, Basil Rathbone, your favourite Sherlock Holmes. But I can assure you, you will never accept my true form if I were to reveal it."

Herschel recognized why the psychiatrist had seemed so familiar. "Try me."

"Alas, no. It will cause whatever sanity you have left to rapidly evaporate."

"What is this all about? What do you want with me?"

"You are a science-fiction writer of some merit," Dr. Cavortian explained, "which makes you an ideal candidate for our needs. Your superior vision we deem extremely useful and *potent* in the war against the Menos."

"The Menos?"

"The Menos Grex were once a distant civilization, whose bodies died out in an internal civil war, but who now live on as a race of psychic energy beings. They share a common consciousness and survive in a collective device called the Psychetron on Menos Prime. Our intergalactic war with them has been fought in various non-material realms over millions of your Earth years but is now being fought in the artificial reality of the human mind. A multiverse of countless mindscapes."

Revelation upon revelation. Each made Herschel's head spin as he tried to process the information. He thought of what the Dean of Science Fiction, Robert Heinlein, once said: *Everything is theoretically impossible, until it is done.* Or maybe pondering that quote by Andre Breton: *Wonderful thing about the fantastic. Everything is real.*

"As real as you want it to be, there are no laws or restraints in the imagined world." Dr. Cavortian paused before continuing, "We discovered your home world during our solar travels and abducted a few humans in order to breed our own version of the human race, fabricated a matrix of history and culture identical to your home planet's, but within the duration of a hundred years. Your minds were extremely malleable, easy to mould, the perfect terrain where the battle against the Menos could be fought and won."

Herschel took it all in, sought to understand. That brilliant coruscation, which he'd mistaken for lightning he supposed was probably of unearthly origin, signifying his own abduction, or was he in fact just one of this inferior species of human clones? Mind plundered, prepped for an aeon-old alien war. "Where is my real wife and children?"

Dr. Cavortian responded with further explanation: "They are in the same physical state as you. Female minds are tricky, emotional, child's minds are immature, barren. The conflict between logic and emotion, between heart and mind has plagued our subjects. Emotions cloud judgement, drag down logic. As the Menos thrive on emotion, we are eliminating emotion from the mindscape to make the Psychic War winnable. So we have been gradually purging your emotions from you. That is why you did not recognize your wife. Your imagination improvised the rest."

Herschel thought about Heinlein's words, again: *The universe never did make sense; I suspect it was built on a government contract.* In this case, the Authority. They were the real assembly of gods—*intellectualizing* gods—who had manipulated the human race for a higher, darker purpose. But it was a life dictated by protocol, free of emotion. Where was the humanity in all of this?

So, if all of this was a dream, a fiction of his consciousness, where was he exactly? Strapped to a gurney, attached to tubes and monitors and sinister mind probes?

But Dr. Cavortian decided to correct him, again reading his mind. "You may be the fashioner of this world, but you are not some super-existent, transcendent being. You are a fusion of human will and our advanced science. Let us bring you into the light. Let us show you the only part of you that proves valuable, if it were not for the unfortunate fact that your biological computer is heading towards a power failure . . . imminently so."

Herschel suddenly had a bad feeling about this. And, sure enough, he was now looking from the inside out. *Comfortably Numb* was fast-eclipsed by *Brain Damage*, so to speak. The dream fractured, splintered, dissipated; a nightmare took its place. His initial dread turned to stark horror. His mysterious, maddening head trip took him to the other side of perception. Herschel walked out of the allegorical cave of darkness/shadows and found himself in the wider field of reality, the *real* world. Greek tragedy sometimes relied on peripeteia to show that everything the hero knew was wrong.

On the observation screen, the starlit expanse of space was gone. Instead, Herschel saw the immediate footage of a medical lab with tables of transparent glass containers. The camera panned slowly across the room, stopping to focus on one of the receptacles. The label on the glass read: SAXBY, HERSCHEL.

It seemed he was not completely in the room. *Not completely there*. Indeed, they had scaled him down, made him infinitely smaller than he had first presumed. His body existed only as an idea in his mind, an echo. Of course, he could not physically speak, walk, or scream, but only *believed* he was speaking, walking, or *screaming*. Just as his mystical, psychokinetic powers only existed in his mind.

[*I am at the centre of this world . . . Reality can be such a subjective term. But let us bring in some objectivity. We will show you the only part of you that proves valuable . . . Your wife and children are in the same physical state as you . . . Your biological computer is heading towards a power failure . . . imminently so... Justification enough to cease all operations on him. Terminate the subject.*]

Because his thinking, conscious self was enclosed within the material form of his remaining humanity, projecting a complete illusion of his own body.

Of all the philosophical debates he had drawn upon to explain his condition, Herschel had deliberately shied away from the philosophical idea he had feared discussing the most. Maybe because he had been afraid for even one instant to ponder its nightmarish ramifications, the gravity of what he might have been ultimately reduced to.

The final, colossal, mind-shattering blow . . .

For Herschel realized he was nothing more than a disembodied but still-sentient brain suspended in a jar of bubbling life-sustaining fluid, removed from its skull by some mad scientist. The liquid was tinged yellow, slightly cloudy with pus, as the filters tried to clean the infection that had set in, the neurons of his discarnate brain connected by wires to a supercomputer which would provide it with the same electrical impulses as if it were still intact in its skull in order for it to generate perfectly normal conscious experiences, allow it to dwell with full awareness in an internally-constructed sphere of pseudo-reality.

To recite that old axiom: *it was all in the mind.*

October 2015—November 2015

Daubers of Dark Dreams

"You know I was curious—I was interested in all kinds of mystery or deeper meanings in the paintings . . . There is hope and a kind of beauty in there somewhere, if you look for it."

H.R. Giger

I: THE IMAGINARIUM

"This looks like fun," Monica Stilgoe declared, slowing down the car at the unexpected signpost on the lonely stretch of country lane. The lettering hand-painted in black read:

THIS WAY
TO
GRIMWOLDE'S IMAGINARIUM

An arrow pointed to the right and they soon arrived at a crossroads.

"Grimwolde's Imaginarium?" Dominic Hilling responded with similar enthusiasm. "Sounds like a mysterious and magical place. Why not give it a shot?"

"Right you are." Monica turned the midnight-blue Fiat 500—a rental—right at the junction, following the direction of the sign, and continued up the side-lane.

It appeared to be a road less travelled and afforded an

extremely bumpy ride, the tyres negotiating dirt and numerous potholes.

They didn't mind. They were in good spirits. Their road trip down south had so far proved an enjoyable experience and they had all day to roam the land before they crashed at their friends in Oaks Fold. They currently hovered somewhere between Netherton and Church Falls.

The afternoon sun was already beginning to set, the air unseasonably warm for the first day of Spring. Endless fields stretched off on either side of the lane, left to grow in wild profusion, offering the occasional glimpse of a derelict farmhouse, windows broken, roof caved in.

"I must say it's a bit off the beaten track," Dominic observed, jolting uncomfortably around in his seat, "I guess not a lot of people live in these parts."

"I suppose not," agreed Monica. "It's certainly out in the sticks. I wouldn't be surprised if it doesn't get a lot of visitors." They must have already travelled nearly half a mile on this lane, she calculated. "I wonder how much further to go . . ."

Suddenly, the wilderness opened up to a wooded area and the lane widened into a rudimentary carpark. The building in the middle of the woods loomed up ahead, single-storey and constructed mostly of heavily-tinted glass, with neogothic overtones to its overall architecture. More glass than brick, the windows seemed to soak up the daylight and gave the impression of a multitude of black, gleaming eyes like those of a colossal spider. *Come into my parlour*, it seemed to beckon.

Monica crawled to a stop and parked up in the carpark at the front, and she and her boyfriend stepped out of the car. Except for their presence, the carpark was completely deserted. She was right on that count. The place didn't get many visitors probably on account of its remote location, hidden from the world.

Dominic stared at the building, surrounded by leaning, hungry-looking trees. For some reason he had been expecting a big top, like a circus or a fairground. Again, he got the sense he was staring at a huge, mechanical spider already beginning to weave its web. He shivered momentarily, feeling the first pangs of doubt, of disquiet. "I don't think we should go in—"

But Monica cut him off. "Don't tell me you're getting the creeps? That's the whole point! You know I'm an artist and, as an artist, I love visiting these quaint, small-town galleries. What are the chances of us finding one in the middle of nowhere?"

His girlfriend's last comment didn't rest well with him. *Yes, what are the chances?* he considered, but kept the thought to himself. *Don't you get the feeling the place found us . . .?*

Instead, he surveyed the painted sign above the entrance:

GRIMWOLDE'S IMAGINARIUM
WELCOME TO THE 'HOUSE OF WEIRD' EXHIBITION
Extraordinaire. Excentrique. Fantastique

Monica was a woman full of positivity. Presently, she looked positively pleased, excited even. "I always have time for weird art."

"Hope it's worth it . . ." said Dominic, far from thrilled. He had lost all his initial enthusiasm.

"I'm sure it'll be worth the experience," Monica reassured him, "*honestly!*" She went on to remind him: "Besides, we've got a lot of time to kill."

She approached the open entrance. Dominic trailed nervously behind. He felt like they were Hansel and Gretel entering the witch's cottage in the enchanted forest.

But no witch greeted them. The girl in the ticket kiosk looked barely older than eighteen and was garbed like a goth, with multiple piercings and a black theme to her dress and makeup, including her eyeliner and glossy lipstick. Dominic thought he'd seen her before, but he couldn't quite put his finger on it. The girl, whose name-badge read WILLOW, surveyed the newcomers with a permanently-stoned expression. "Can I help you?" she asked, pulling out one earphone, the music blaring unhealthily loud into her ears. Monica recognized the tune the girl had been listening to, regardless of the low tininess of the exposed sound: *Still Life* by the Horrors.

"Two for your exhibition," requested Monica.

Willow printed out two tickets and handed them over to the visitors, along with a couple of brochures.

"How much?"

"Free admittance."

"Really?"

"It's out of season," the girl said matter-of-factly. "Few visitors this time of year."

Monica was delighted. "Oh, that's very kind of you. I promise to give you a good review."

"That would be most welcome," Willow invited, with a dull, disinterested air and returned to her music. "Enjoy . . ."

II: DRAKE LOCKHART

Monica Stilgoe was an artist of the purist kind. Although still relatively new to the Art world, she was a talented artist in her own right and her exhibitions up north attracted a good turnout and respectable sales. She also lived by the watchwords of some of the Old Masters. Van Gogh had once said: *If you hear a voice within you say you cannot paint, then by all means paint, and that voice will be silenced.* Jackson Pollock described painting as having a life of its own. Edgar Degas described Art as 'not what you see, but what you make others see'. Pablo Picasso philosophized: *The artist is a receptacle of emotions that come from all over the place: from the sky, from the earth, from a scrap of paper, from a passing shape, from a spider's web.* René Magritte supposed: *Art evokes the mystery without which the world would not exist.* Francis Bacon took it one step further: *The job of the artist is always to deepen the mystery.* Andy Warhol tested how far he could go: *Art is what you can get away with.*

Whether it was about sublimating one's own anxiety in one's art, like Munch, or exploring the anxieties of the age, as Dali did, Art was a journey of self-discovery, an expression of the soul, always awash with deeper meanings. Monica had an appreciation of all things 'Art'. More recently, she had even warmed to the gender-bending biopic of *The Danish Girl*, based on a real-life tale, full of tragedy and pathos. Weird art was a medium that made the impossible visually possible. It was a very specialist field, boasting very few such artists, old and new.

Walking into Grimwolde's Imaginarium, Monica discovered that this little gallery was hosting the works of a couple of much-neglected guest painters, Drake Lockhart and Kurt Hellier, collectively dubbed the 'Daubers of Dark Dreams'. Somewhere in there was also a painting by Haston Sant-Cassia, an artist much-maligned in his time for his fascination with the arcane mysteries of the occult. Even if it lacked the razzle-dazzle of a major gallery, the House of Weird exhibition promised something new. Something thought-provoking and hopefully something completely outlandish.

Inside, the lighting had been deliberately dimmed low, the walls the colour of gunmetal, the place decorated like a funfair at Halloween: rubber bats and plastic skeletons and Little Miss Muffet spiders, hanging down from the ceiling, punctuated the journey of the viewer. The first wall-space was understandably occupied by some dark pieces by Drake Lockhart in true Stalvart fashion, whose House of Horrors exhibition had once furnished the Modern Art Museum of Paris.

Fantastic art explores the space between the imagination and the dream state, the visions of the grotesque and the uncanny and the downright weird. Some critics regarded Hieronymus Bosch as the pioneer of fantasy art. They considered the highly-prolific William Blake in the same breath. They gave Goya, the Father of Shock, similar credentials. So, too, the surrealistic hallucinations of Dali and his contemporaries. Apparently, gothic art came under the same category as fantasy art, as Monica and Dominic were about to discover in the first instance.

Presently, a spotlight illuminated a scene set in cemetery at dusk and, in particular, an unearthed grave where the lid of a coffin was slowly rising open. Pale hands with grimy, unnaturally-long fingernails are emerging from the darkness within. Somewhere in the background, another such ghoulish creature in the shape of a buxom, scantily-clad maiden is partially-visible behind a tombstone, sinking her fangs into the neck of the unfortunate sexton, blood dripping down his throat. In the corner of the painting, on a barrow stands a regally-dressed, devilishly-handsome figure, with black, flowing hair and red, feral eyes, arms raised in magical invocation, orchestrating the summoning of the Undead. The piece was titled: *Vrolok & Strogoi*. A nod to Transylvanian folklore.

"Nothing to write home about," Dominic said, unimpressed. "Just your typical pulp horror painting. Beautiful women luring men to their deaths. What's new?"

"On the contrary," replied Monica, reaching for her extensive knowledge on the subject. "Lockhart has managed to distinguish between the different ranks in the hierarchy of vampires. Strogoi were vampiric spirits of the dead, able to take the form of lesser creatures, destined to haunt their grieving families and kill off their relatives one by one." She pointed to the cloaked, kingly demon on the knoll. "At the top of the pecking order is the Vrolok, the most powerful and malevolent of these monsters. The Vrolok, too, is a shapeshifter but capable of governing the weather and vermin as well as these Strogoi. He can even project himself into the astral plane and control the minds of men far, far away. A fanciful monster whose mythical status inarguably inspired Bram Stoker's timeless masterpiece."

"Who is this guy?" asked Dominic. "This Drake Lockhart?"

"Maybe I can enlighten you . . ." a deep voice spoke up from behind them.

The unexpectedness of the voice caused the couple to jump and swing round. They were met by a very tall, slim and bald man with distinct, acromegalic features who, like the goth girl in reception, wore black. Looming large, he resembled Lurch at first glance, the faithful Addams family retainer.

"Holy shit!" Dominic exclaimed, trying to bring his nerves in check. "You startled me!"

"That was not my intention," the gangling, bony-faced man replied in a slow, measured manservant monotone. "I leave that to the paintings."

Dominic demanded to know. "Who are you and what do you want?"

"Russ," the man replied simply, "your tour guide."

Makes sense, I suppose, thought Dominic, still put off by the man's huge, lumbering presence. *Nevertheless, exactly the kind of strange-looking fella you want to guide you through this creepshow, considering he looks like one of the damned exhibits.* Except, like the goth girl earlier, Dominic recognized his face from someplace else, someplace closer to home.

Monica introduced herself and her boyfriend as 'Mon' and 'Dom', respectively. Then, she said curiously, "These kinds of specialist galleries are like gold dust—so few of them about. Tell me about this place. So isolated and such a small space but allowing a certain intimacy to view paintings."

"Well, Mon and Dom, this gallery belongs to the Grimwolde estate," Russ explained in his slow, featureless tones. "They have a very dark history, the lineage dating as far back as the seventeenth century. Tales of smuggling and treason and blackmail and murder. Legend has it that Baelfire Grimwolde, the first Grimwolde, dabbled in witchcraft and sorcery and led the Devil into his soul, who cursed all future generations as recompense. Over the centuries, the family line has gradually dwindled away until the Grimwoldes have been left with only one living descendent, Unwin Grimwolde, and since he never married, the bloodline should die out with him."

"Fascinating . . ." murmured Monica, intrigued.

"Mr Grimwolde keeps the Imaginarium open as a reminder of his family's dark past and his own love of weird art. We hold special exhibitions, bringing together artists often overlooked by the public. We are currently showcasing a few paintings by Drake Lockhart and Kurt Hellier. The final painting is an original by Haston Sant-Cassia."

"The world's begging for more of these types of galleries. You are not doing the community a disservice, believe me."

Russ was grateful. "That is most kind of you to say . . ." He glanced at the painting on the wall in his immediacy. "Admiring Lockhart's vampire painting, I see."

"Yes," Monica affirmed. "Very Hammer House. Perfect material for horror-movie enthusiasts and those in search of macabre thrills."

"Horror's not my thing," Dominic informed them.

"Do not worry, sir," Russ assured him. "Even if Lockhart quietly specialized in themes of horror during the countercultural revolution of the 'Sixties, Hellier concentrated on more contemporary science-fiction concepts during his most productive period in the 'Nineties."

"That would be more up my street," Dominic replied, sounding slightly more interested.

"Onward and upward?" Monica suggested amicably.

They shuffled along to the second painting: *Scrawler from the Stars*. In the painting, a black-clad figure is beavering way on his old-fashioned typewriter, except the writer possesses the gills on either side of his throat and the laterally-placed, filmy moon-eyes of a fish, and the fingers doing the typing are in fact tiny tentacles. Through the study window, the observer can see the night sky filled with a crazy helter-skelter of stars. A 1930s airship floats by. The message scrawled on the side of the Zeppelin reads: DO YOU READ HASTUR MORTENSE?

Monica smiled. Her mind focused, volunteered information. "I think this painting borrows from the Cthulhu mythos. Something of the Virgil Finlay in it whose praises H.P. Lovecraft himself sang."

"But who is this Hastur Mortense?" asked Dominic, staring at the inhuman writer in the picture.

Russ explained: "A horror writer from these parts and former founder of Madworks publishing house. They say he's still alive and occasionally emerges from retirement to write."

"Creepy name for an author," noted Dominic with a shiver. "Perfect for a horror writer, I suppose."

"Yes," Russ elaborated, "named after a Lovecraftian god."

They went to the next painting. Russ shambled after them like Frankenstein's monster, minus sutures and scars. *The Spidery Man* depicted a hooded figure, face completely concealed by the cowl, standing in an actor's stance on a theatre stage, long-since abandoned and gathering dust and cobwebs, but the viewer already knows that there is more to this man than meets the eye, because the long shadow he casts onstage resembles the shadow of a huge spider. The picture was obsessively detailed despite its inky depths and one could have easily mistaken it for a charcoal instead of an oil.

Dominic was having a flashback from his days of childhood, the memory of an old creepy ad: of the Judder Man, haunting the woods when the moon was fat, mesmerizing the lonely traveller, tempting them to a bottle of Alcopop. "May I ask the significance of the Spidery Man?"

"A piece of fiction, whom some claim binds the Universe together in his web," Russ replied. "Pops up now and again."

"Never heard of him," dismissed Dominic.

Monica was thinking of Greek legend. "Mortals will get their comeuppance if they boast they are better than the gods. Arachne's hubris in a weaving contest and attempts to show up the goddess, Athena, led to her transformation into a spider."

On the wall across from them hung another oil painting: *The Axeman Cometh*. A hulking figure, dressed in a long, black coat and swinging an axe in menacing fashion, is slowly stepping out from a cinema screen to the sublime horror of the audience. One can almost hear the panic-stricken shrieks emanating around the dark movie theatre. Yet nobody can see the axe-wielding character's face properly, obscured by a sweaty, tangled curtain of hair. Once again, Lockhart's technique relied on a firm contrast between the light source (movie screen) and dark tonality (movie auditorium).

"Very inventive," opined Monica.

"This is a very interesting piece," Russ began, "from 1967. It's based on a faceless serial killer, dubbed 'Axel Hacker', who went on a murderous rampage in these parts in the late 1950s, beginning with the dismemberment of a bunch of cinema-goers in Oaks Fold. Like Jack the Ripper, the killer was never identified. Hollywood got a-hold of the story and turned it into a horror franchise."

"1967?" observed Monica. "That means—"

"—Howard Halliwell, the movie producer, made the first film in

1971. If you don't include Anthony Perkins' turn in *Psycho*, some movie critics say that the 'Axeman' franchise predates the emergence of the slasher genre—the all-too-familiar territory of American teens in peril stalked by a masked killer—by several years before it entered the mainstream with the likes of Leatherface, Jason Voorhees, Michael Myers and Freddy Krueger."

"You learn something new every day," Monica said, genuinely surprised.

"Worth a look, I suppose," added Dominic, lacking his girlfriend's natural enthusiasm. "Not my cup of tea, though."

The 'ghost train' trundled along to the subsequent painting, bringing a greater sense of strangeness to the proceedings, representing a much more disinhibited use of colour. *Borderlands Beheld* was composed in the true fantasy mould but without the dragons or the unicorns. A tall, crowned figure thrusts open the doors at the top of a tower to survey his vast kingdom. Even with his back turned, Monica and Dominic can see he is not human. He is extremely slender, almost as thin as a matchstick, and his hands are clawed. A mane of white hair flows down his frayed, black robes of state. The land he reigns over is forested with thick, gnarly trees, with weird, unearthly creatures creeping into the frame, painted in the finest detail. A cluster of pink toads, the size of beach balls, float in the moat surrounding the tower. In the forest yonder, a file of huge, spidery things, with the stinging tails of scorpions and as shiny as adamantine, scuttle down the distorted trunks of trees. In one section of the forest, a pack of six-legged wolves—no, six-legged *werewolves*—encircle a helpless, bipedal march hare, rendered with a degree of human anatomy. The sky is painted sunset-red, a richness to its texture, but congested with the presence of twin moons as a final flourish.

Monica was struck by the believability of this elaborate fantasy world. "It's like Lockhart dreamed it up from reality."

"Glad you said so," Russ replied, pleased. "The Borderlands are grounded in some sort of reality. There are stories of people claiming to have wandered into this fantastical realm. A few manage to return to our world, catatonic, deprived of their mental faculties, while most are never seen again."

Monica gestured to the figure opening up the bizarre, breathtaking vista from the balcony. "And this tatty, regal figure in the foreground?"

"That is supposedly the Spindle King, ruler of the Borderlands and sovereign to his army of Spindlers. Just as human travellers sometimes stray into his territory, they say Spindlers can cross over into ours if the conditions are right. You will know if a Spindler has ventured into our world because you will find the half-eaten carcasses of missing pets strewn across the neighbourhood."

"That's gross!" remarked Dominic. "No doubt the RSPCA would be appalled at the rate of dead pets and not being able to solve the mystery! *Now we know . . .*"

The sixth and final painting by Lockhart in the exhibition was a pictorial tableau of perversities. *Those Who Enter Here Will Be Damned* displayed the quest of a husband to save his wife from her personal hell after she commits suicide. Like every tortured suicide, she can never forgive herself and keeps punishing herself. She has forgotten she is dead and tries killing herself again and again but just won't die. Images of her simultaneously trying to hang herself or stab herself with a kitchen knife or throw herself off the top of the winding staircase do not yield the outcome she desires. She must have had a twisted mind in life, for her mind has conjured up her worst torments, forced to masochistically re-live them forever. Her house, now a gloomy, decrepit pit of despair, has more rooms than there should be, like the Winchester House, and crawls with the things she dreads the most, a cohort of huge, black spiders spinning a dense network of webs. In some of the rooms, aside from her acts of suicide, there are glimpses of the dead, possibly the souls of dead family members, copulating. In the master bedroom, a facsimile of her husband indulges in a disturbing mass orgy with her friends—or the illusion of her friends. Downstairs, her real husband has come to rescue her from her everlasting fate, crouching down before the weeping woman. The observer knows that, being an interloper in another's mental hell, the husband is at risk of losing his own mind altogether and being swallowed up by Hell itself once her reality becomes his. The light fades, the cold sinks in, and the darkness creeps closer. Soon he will forget who he is . . .

Monica was the first to speak. "That's dark. Dark, so dark."

"An idea probably borrowed from Richard Matheson," Dominic, Science Teacher, deduced. "A most remarkable and influential writer. Not only did he write about a love affair carried across oceans of Time, but he also wrote another love story across Heaven and Hell: *What Dreams May Come*."

"Maybe Hell is a real place—or all in the mind," Russ suggested in his usual monotone.

"Reminds me of Wally Wood," compared Monica, impressed by the picture's strong visual impact. "The idea for the painting, I mean."

"Wally Wood?" asked Dominic.

"A comic book writer and cartoonist, who caused all kinds of mayhem with his most controversial work, a group orgy of Disney characters engaging in sex, drugs and the sort of shocking behaviour that would make your mother blush."

"I can imagine the Disney faithful none too pleased by the desecration of their favourite characters," replied her boyfriend.

"Outraged . . ." Monica said, chuckling, "but give the man a round of applause for exposing Disney's hypocrisies and rampant greed as well as its ruthless exploitation of young minds." She referred back to Lockhart's work. "This, too, is a gem, even without the cartoon aspect, of course. His experiences of fear are staggering. Allusions to hell—and *depravity*."

"Give me *Looney Tunes*, any day!" remarked Dominic.

"Know what my favourite theme in fiction is?" Monica quizzed him.

Dominic shook his head.

"Art that drives you mad, let it be literature or a painting or a piece of music. Psychiatrists call it Stendhal Syndrome."

"I didn't know such a disorder existed."

"Psychiatrists have a disorder for everything."

"Alas, we have come to the end of the first set of exhibits," monotoned Russ. "But there is more to come, if you follow me."

"I have to admit I've been impressed by the expressiveness and powerful imagery of his artwork," Monica reflected. "His ability to almost carve colour into shape and transform his own inner pain into devastating beauty. I suppose I could quite comfortably classify him as a Fantastic Realist, like the Hausners and Fuchses of Austria, who came into conflict with the Surrealist movement for elevating the conscious mind to the status of the unconscious. They considered the waking life, the moment you opened your eyes, of equal significance as the dream world. René Magritte was somewhat kinder to the Fantastic Realists by suggesting that if the dream was a translation of waking life, then the waking life was also a translation of the dream." She looked back at the final Lockhart. "He died rather mysteriously, didn't he?"

"You're very well-versed, miss," said Russ, impressed. "Yes, Drake Lockhart died a strange death. He was not from around here, but he died right here in Church Falls. Village gossip accused him of being unbalanced of mind when he started claiming his paintings were real. They said he had started to believe the things he drew. Maybe he had tapped into something. He said there was more to the world than the eye could see, and he had looked into the dark, beyond the limits of our conventional reality, and begun to see what's really there. Incidentally, he was often found wasted on drugs. He was discovered dead one morning in a hotel. His hair had turned white and his face was frozen in pure shock, like he had been frightened to death. Personally, I think Drake Lockhart came to Church Falls to die. Church Falls does that to people. It lures those with talent and kills them. Only a fortunate few make it out alive—but mad."

"Some would say a rather fitting end to a purveyor of the macabre," Monica concluded.

III: KURT HELLIER

Following a moment's respite, Russ motioned them forward and latched onto the preliminary painting, from the next painter. A change in direction. "Might I interest you in a little Kurt Hellier?"

"Now this is more like it." declared Dominic, glad the baser horror themes had been dispensed with and they could now move on to science-fiction concepts. Whereas Lockhart's work explored violence and anti-intellectualism and the grotesque, Hellier's pictures were dominated by spectacle and a vision that appealed to Dominic's taste. With his scientific background, it was his turn to shine. "Kurt Hellier's earlier paintings had a distinctly graphical appearance and featured 1930s sci-fi serial heroes carrying rayguns, leather-suited space vixens and silly-looking aliens. His artwork would mature with time, become more focused and enterprising." Moving from one section of the gallery to the other caused the skin on his arms to tingle, the hairs to prick up, a peculiar sensation, as though touched by a strong electrostatic charge—or *fear*—which Dominic put down to the horror nonsense he had seen so far. But better things would follow. Hopefully.

Hellier possessed his own unique painterly style, as evidenced by the first painting, *The Clockwork Inventor*. It was a painting of an old man carefully fitting together the finer components of a clockwork bird at his desk in an inventor's workshop. Despite his Dickensian attire, the old man, like the creation he is working on, is himself clockwork, or at least in part, his left hand composed of steel and the left side of face, from the perspective of the viewer, is a series of cogs and delicate mechanisms. His workshop is filled with sketches and drawings, the designs of machines in the shape of animals. Behind the door, full-size and upright, stands a 'tin' man constructed of ironworks, forged from an assembly of steel plates and pulleys, the copper heart visible within the mesh of the chest cavity. Its eyes begin to glow as the self-activating automaton comes to life . . .

"Steampunk," explained Dominic, in his element. "Art of any medium that depicts an underground or alternate Victorian age where the technological advances are greater than historically recorded."

"You mean like *The League of Extraordinary Gentlemen*?" Monica said, recalling an old film.

"Similar tropes," agreed Dominic. "Takes a lesson from Da

Vinci's book. Da Vinci was the actual genius, an inventor ahead of his time, and we're going all the way back to the Renaissance."

"I suppose the Victorians were ahead of their time, too," decided Monica, "since we can cite the Industrial Revolution as the advent of modern civilization."

It Descended from Outer Space was set in the woods as a teenage couple making out suddenly encounters bright lights in the night sky. A flying saucer hovers above the clearing, emitting a dazzling cone of light to earth. A tall, humanoid silhouette is emerging from the downwardly funneling light. If that's not enough to scare the bejesus out of the young lovers, different figures—human figures—dressed in black suits and black homburg hats and resembling sinister Federal agents are disembarking from a long, black Lincoln on the other side of the nightly woods. They are obviously tasked with cleaning up the aftermath of the scene, perhaps hushing up the eyewitnesses, convince the frightened couple never to disclose their UFO encounter to the proper authorities and make them believe it's all in their heads . . .

Dominic told the others where Hellier had drawn his inspiration from. The Red Scare. The MacCarthy witch hunts. The all-pervasive paranoia of the Cold War. *The Body Snatchers. The Puppet Masters. The Father-Thing. Who Goes There?* Those spooky, nonsensical-talking Men in Black. Friend or foe? Genuine extraterrestrial beings or nothing more than government agents sent out as part of an ongoing conspiracy to misinform, confuse and distract the public, covering up a lie the government perpetuated, disguised as a truth to keep the UFO myth going, so the Military can continue its *Top Secret!* research projects and test out experimental stealth aircraft, plundered from Nazi technology. "Some say that even the Black Knight satellite which quietly watches the earth is in fact ultra-sophisticated military hardware, and any photos referencing its existence before time have been cleverly doctored to hide its earthly origins," Dominic was explaining. He stared at the Men in Black in the painting and said, grinning defiantly: "You may read my mind—you may even expunge my mind—but I will always have another way of remembering . . ."

Monica was happy for Dominic the Exhibition of the Weird had taken on a different, more cerebral turn. "Glad you're thoroughly enjoying yourself."

"You bet. Really liking it, thank you . . ."

Their guided tour took them to the next exhibit piece, titled *The Hum*. According to Monica, the style of the painting was reminiscent of the work of Roerich, except it was like he had turned his attention from the Himalayas to painting the baking, hot desert sands. It was a straight landscape, showing a small village nestled in the distance, with its own church and courthouse and clocktower, that appeared to be vibrating, slightly blurry in its rendering. But the most intriguing aspect about the painting is the presence of a man in the foreground who, having fled the village, has fallen on his knees in anguish, unable to escape the persistent, ubiquitous hum, head oscillating and slightly out of focus, hands clutching his ears to block out the sound around him, his mouth in an act of screaming like the tormented figure in Edvard Munch's famous painting. His local vicinity is littered with human skeletons, half-buried in the sand, picked clean by the vultures that circle the pale sky as the sun, a blazing chrome disk, beats down unmercifully. Like the oxidized white fibres that sprout upwards, needlelike, when drops of mercury are applied to aluminium foil, monolithic crystal spears of unknown origin project up from the sand, vibrating like tuning forks, suggesting they are the source of the Hum.

"What a cracker!" Dominic enthused appreciatively. "The Hum is one of the great unexplained mysteries of the world. The phenomenon has occurred in Taos, New Mexico, Kokomo, Indiana, West Seattle and even in Bristol, right here in England. Widespread reports of an endless humming sound or drone all around you, often at a low frequency of thirty-six hertz, equivalent to the sound an idling diesel engine makes."

Monica asked the obvious question. "What's the cause?"

"Nobody really knows. The vibrations caused by a nearby power station? A medical condition called tinnitus? Others claim it comes from outer space, as aliens probe the minds of the inhabitants they're studying. People have described the hypnotic, soporific quality of the hum, of it putting them to sleep. Reports of memory loss and missing time. Some people have fallen ill, others gone mad, a few have killed themselves."

Nobody spoke for a moment. They stared at the image, the pain and hopelessness and despair on the face of the man in the foreground of the picture, unable to take any more, as though his brain was about to explode.

Monica studied the brushstrokes. "The way it's been painted you can almost hear the hum yourself."

Joining her, Dominic put his ear to the painting and listened. Sure enough, his ears seemed to pick up a subtle, low-intensity hum. As though the colours in the painting were vibrating. Or could it just be his imagination? Suggestibility? "Eerie . . ."

They detached themselves from the painting and wandered over to the one that followed. Maybe the two paintings were related, shared the same dream. For just as you are about to fall asleep . . . *From Hypnagogia* captured the twilight state between the waking world and actual sleep. It could have been described as a Surrealist painting in its psychoanalytic interpretation, except it appeared more defined . . . if one could use the word 'defined'. Its ambiguity, however, could not be ignored. The scene is of an ordinary darkened bedroom with a little boy curled up in bed, eyes closed, trying to sleep, transitioning to another state of mind. But the look of fear on his face suggests he is teetering on the cusp of a nightmare. For, by the dull illumination cast by the bedside lamp, something is emerging from the carpet next to his bed, slowly rising up. The figure is not yet fully-formed, its left arm and leg, still quite flat, like a pool of melted plastic and recreating the terrifying biomechanical creature designs of Giger, but the rest of it is taking human shape, a two-dimensional being striving to become three-dimensional, gradually taking the form of the boy in the bed, mimicking him, maybe *replacing* him . . .

"Hellier reinventing sleep," Dominic critiqued. "That thing that is coming into existence, becoming alive, is more than just those

Shadow People scientists speak of, more than just a symptom of sleep paralysis."

"I'd be freaked out if I was that boy," commented Monica.

"The boy is freaked out," confirmed Dominic, studying the petrified expression of the kid tucked under the covers who knows what is happening yet is unable to open his eyes to witness the horror taking shape in his very room."

"What's it all mean?"

"Well, Hellier suggested that an ancient, superior race of interdimensional beings existed within our collective hypnogogic state, when our inner defences are at their most vulnerable, drawing upon our psychic energy, sometimes able to travel into the real world. They are an example of perfect evolution, the mind the perfect hiding place and using humans as conduits to enter our external reality. They are also supposedly the cause of some of the inexplicable events that occur in our everyday lives, objects that seem to move by themselves which we quickly put down to our own forgetfulness. Like the TV having switched channels suddenly when you come back to the room or misplacing your keys when you could have sworn you left them on the hallway table or a coffee cup that goes wandering from where you normally make a brew."

Monica shuddered. "That would be truly creepy if it were true."

Russ stated, "They say there is nothing more fertile than the minds of children."

Dominic quoted the seventeenth-century English poet, Andrew Marvell, who compared the mind to a garden: "*The Mind, that Ocean where each kind/Does streight its own resemblance find;/Yet it creates, transcending these,/Far other Worlds, and other Seas;/Annihilating all that's made/ To a green Thought in a green Shade.*"

Monica regarded the painting again, as believable as a trompe l'oeil, regarded the three-dimensional effect of the monster in the picture as it tested out its new body, its new arms and legs, tested out with its new eyes, a *child's* eyes, and as with any trompe l'oeil giving the illusion it was coming out of the painting, reaching out for the viewer . . . She shivered again.

Hellier's fourth, *Time Enough*, could have been a scene from *The Twilight Zone*. It explored the nature of Time with a plethora of visual paradoxes. Hellier had created a town that should never exist. Time has fractured and folded in on itself. There is no rational continuity between the different parts of the town, as the observer witnesses the fragments of the town square, the park, the cemetery, even the steel works on the outskirts, merge with Main Street, cobbled together like an ill-fitting jigsaw, a composite, their demarcations lost, making no geographical sense at all. The population of the town must surely have gone insane because everybody is the *same* person, a commuter, perhaps, who has got unexpectedly stranded in this place, forced to experience different stages of his life in no particular chronological order. He is the only inhabitant here, except he is *everywhere*—the bar, the hotel, the drugstore, the tenement block, even the old people's nursing home—all at once. He has lived his entire life in this town and met himself over and over again, further splintering the continuum, like a mirror, and creating more versions of himself and a conundrum of causal loops.

"Can you imagine the possibilities?" Dominic murmured in morbid fascination. "What Time has done to him, spending his entire existence trapped in this make-believe place, this microcosm. What could have been, what never was."

"It must utterly screw up his mind—his memories," postulated Monica. "The 'Un-persistence' of memory."

"Misremembering," concurred Dominic. "Remembering false or broken memories." He digressed, took a slight detour, "I sometimes wonder what would happen if the big corporations developed a device that could manipulate mass memories, make you remember what they wanted you to remember. Maybe make you forget their products are crap or kill people. In a sense, alter the past so as to control the future."

Referring back to the character in the painting, Monica said, "Memory relies on Time. If Time is no longer intact, has caved in, become non-sequential, so will the memories." She, too, wandered off on a side-note. "I suppose there are no time travellers?"

"Every so often we hear about people claiming to be time travellers from the future," explained Dominic. "They even beat lie detector tests, suggesting their claims might be authentic. Not to put a crimp on your day, but you don't need to be a scientist to know that if you're deluded enough, believe your own nonsense, you can beat any lie detector test. These so-called 'time travellers' often have underlying mental health problems, some turn out to be fantasists or nothing more than attention-seekers. Their common thread? Always unhappy with the world we live in."

Each painting told a story. The following painting told a story of the hybridization of man and machine, of beings more technologically superior than those in *The Clockwork Inventor*. Generations of science-fiction writers had been preoccupied with invisibility and miniaturization, alien encounters, alternate realities and time travel—and, of course, the *future*, let it be utopian or, in this case, dystopian. *Man is the Mother of All Machines* revolved around a world inhabited by both humans and synthetic humans—and humans with sophisticated, mechanical prosthetics. The painting took the shape of a stunning, futuristic cityscape, by way of *Blade Runner*, dark, polluted, rain-soaked and overcrowded and, judging by the landmarks, possibly London. The skyways are congested with flying vehicles and high-rise buildings punctuated by lofty, hologrammatic billboards advertising junk food and legalized drugs and cheap sex alongside new technological advancements in electrifying colours that, according to Monica, channelled the iconic French illustrator, Jean Giraud, aka Moebius, of whose extraordinary visionary imagination, the director Frederico Fellini once said: *Here is an artist, who has the ability to transport us into unknown worlds, where we encounter unsettling characters. My admiration for him is total. I consider him a great artist, as great as Picasso and Matisse.*

Blade Runner-esque or Moebiusienne, Dominic supposed the same praise could be bestowed on Kurt Hellier. Aside from the poetic and philosophical nature of the title or the trippy, architectural elegance of the skyline, the punkish figure on the nearest rooftop, unmercifully gunned down by a squad of armed police officers, Dominic knew was a machine, created by ANDROIDS INC. but gone rogue and authorized for recall and decommissioning as one of the fabulous, electric advertisements bespoke.

"I can imagine the androids being designed to be more human *than* human," Dominic was saying. "Impossible to distinguish from the real thing. The realism of these bioengineered beings may prove highly unnerving, too."

"I wonder what they have across the Pond," Monica contemplated.

"Amexica!" joked Dominic. Going back to his favourite writer, Philip K. Dick, he said on a more serious note. "If I had to write a screenplay and direct the film, it would have to be *Time Out of Joint*. I know, another phrase from *Hamlet*. If you thought *The Truman Show* was original, then think again . . ."

"I think you'd make a decent scriptwriter."

"Easier than full prose. Dick remains the quintessential writer of diverse, paranoid fiction. He's done things in his books that no other science-fiction writer could ever dream of. His tales should be a pleasure to translate. Mind-blowingly self-referential as reading your own work without knowing it and thinking this guy's pretty damned good."

Hellier's last painting at the Imaginarium was simply titled: *Dimensions*. It focused on another Main Street where the buildings seem to have warped in the midst of a mass panic gripping the streets. For good reason. Each of the townsfolk has begun to mutate and take on more arms and legs and heads in almost Siamese fashion. The cranium of the figure closest to the viewer bulges as though the skull is about to split open and he has somehow developed four eyes—*literally*—with eight half-irises. Two noses meld as one huge, misshapen lump in the middle of his face. As he hunkers down on his two pairs of legs and flails his four arms and screams through one ill-proportioned mouth, two sets of teeth are seen—sixty-four teeth—crooked, croggled, competing for the same space.

"Know what's happening here?" Dominic asked Monica, excited.

Monica looked at the grotesque humans with their multiple disfigurements. "Have they caught some kind of disease?"

"Not quite," Dominic said and went on to explain. "We're looking at the convergence of two realities. The humans of our reality have physically combined with their alternate selves from a parallel universe. Not only do the bizarre state of the buildings give it away, but don't you think it looks like there are two people in each person?"

"That's truly demented!"

"That means each person has a duplicate set of chromosomes, ninety-two instead of forty-six, hence double of practically everything. But what is the freakiest thing you cannot see in the painting regarding these gestalt entities? You can see the physical effects of merging with your other self from an alternate reality, but you cannot see the psychological implications outside of the panic and pandemonium in the streets."

It clicked. "You mean—?"

"Yes, not only have their brains fused together, but also their minds. Two consciousnesses in one person. Each person is forced to hold two sets of memories, one from this life and one from another version of themselves in the other dimension."

"That would be enough to drive anyone crazy!" Monica declared, suddenly feeling sorry for the painted characters.

"There's certainly more than a whiff of madness in the painting."

"How can two dimensions meet like this?"

"Lots of theories dating as far back as the ancient concept that energy derives from the vibration of the spheres, a primitive but intuitive model of 'string' theory, and tapping into this energy through specific mathematical formulae inputted into a quantum computer could unlock access to alternate dimensions as predicted by quantum theory. I like to call these doorways 'bilocation points'. Stephen Hawking was the real expert on this. He devised a mathematical theory, before he died, on how a spacecraft could detect a crack between two Universes, picking up the specific background residual energy of the dimensional leak."

Monica got sidetracked. "Didn't Stephen Hawking die in 1985, and the actor who replaced him just became the mouthpiece for the scientific community—or the Illuminati?"

"There have been numerous conspiracies about Stephen Hawking. That one ranks up there at the top. Another claims he was misdiagnosed in his early twenties, which is why he miraculously outlived the doctor's death sentence by half a century. Polio, perhaps, instead of Motor Neurone Disease. Still, he was the greatest scientific mind in living memory. God Rest His Soul."

On that sad note, Dominic went back to staring at Hellier's remarkable painting. Hellier certainly had evolved during his career, with the ever-grandiose flights of the imagination of a true visionary, tackling concepts like dimensionality, time travel, connecting conceptual threads shared by philosophers through the millennia and unorthodox theories about the cosmic origins of mankind and the history of life on Earth.

"Some say the last of the Daubers of Dark Dreams was an autistic savant," mentioned Russ.

"Figures . . ." Dominic murmured. "He's taken us up to date and forwards in time and beyond our known Universe." He asked a pertinent question. "What happened to him? Don't tell me he, too, was 'lured' by Church Falls . . ."

"Not at all," said Russ. "It would be quite a distance to lure an American. He is still alive but committed to a nursing home in New York. Dementia, the doctors say. Not the pleasantly confused kind, either. Quite out of it, reportedly. But on the rare days when he is lucid, he still firmly clings on to the belief that an extraterrestrial race contacts him in his dreams."

Dominic agreed. "We can watch the night skies as much as we want, but some scientists claim dreams are the safest place for extraterrestrial beings to make first contact with us."

"He's smart one!" Russ told Monica, referring to Dominic. "Hang on to him . . ."

"I fully intend to," replied Monica proudly and gave Dominic a gentle kiss on the cheek.

Dominic blushed, slightly embarrassed by the compliment and

the display of affection in front of a stranger. He stared at their tour guide, the vague, nagging familiarity of his face and frame. "I could have sworn I know you from somewhere . . ."

"Maybe you do," Russ replied, mysteriously. "It's a small world..."

Dominic went back to looking at the painting, searching his memory, and he lingered a little too long, the smirk barely fading from his lips. He didn't notice Monica disappear around the corner.

IV: HASTON SANT-CASSIA

"The collection concludes with a single painting by Haston Sant-Cassia," Russ reminded him, "painting one of his earliest, favourite models. The *pièce de résistance* . . ."

"Haston Sant-Cassia, hey?"

Russ enlightened him. "Sant-Cassia was an outsider artist, one of those artists who has little contact with the mainstream art world, in most cases their work often only discovered after their deaths. Interest in the art of the mentally-ill, such as insane-asylum inmates like Adolf Wölfli, began in the 1920s and gained the attention of the avant-garde artists of the time, including Paul Klee and Max Ernst. Like Wölfli's epic psychotic illustrations and imaginary life story, Haston Sant-Cassia methodically created an entire fictionalized world, combining imagery of our real world with the unnatural and unearthly, painting extreme mental states and very unconventional ideas, cosmic horrors and forbidden esoteric knowledge. A user of morphine and alcohol, he lived in relative poverty in Paris between the wars, despite the occasional sale of his pictures, which seemed to have a catastrophic effect on the viewer. He reportedly spent several days painting without eating or sleeping."

"The name does ring a bell . . . I don't suppose you've heard about this Haston fella?" he said, turning to Monica. He stopped in his tracks. Monica was nowhere to be seen. He asked Russ: "Did you see where Monica went?"

"Maybe she has run along ahead to see the final painting," Russ suggested.

Dominic relaxed. Where could she go anyway? The place wasn't big enough. "I don't particularly want to turn your lovely imaginarium upside down looking for her, although admittedly Monica has an awful tendency to go wandering off and get lost." It was at that moment he was suddenly distracted by the grey-haired man across from him, dressed in a black suit, back turned, facing a blank wall. He was surprised he hadn't spotted him before. "Who's that?" *A guest? Another visitor? We are not alone...*

"Oh, just a fibreglass mannequin. Belongs to the Imaginarium. Been in the Grimwolde family for decades."

"Why's he staring at the wall? Wouldn't it make more sense to stand him the other way round so he's facing the gallery visitors?"

"He's shy . . ." Russ said frankly.

His reply caused Dominic to look at Russ peculiarly. Yes, there was a certain lifelike quality to the Man in the Black Suit, even from behind, but he was still just a model created by somebody's hands and dressed up to look like a living person, nothing more than a statue in a museum.

"Okay, lead on, old chap . . ." Dominic said to Russ congenially. "Let's see some Haston Sant-Cassia."

Russ smiled. "But of course . . . Our final exhibit is just around the corner, sir."

Dominic followed his tour guide around the corner. As Dominic stepped forward, he felt another burst of static electricity prickle his skin. But that wasn't the weird thing. The room opened up into another gallery space devoted to only one painting. Except the room was fragmented, incomplete, as though reality had not been fully created, missing huge sections of the wall, revealing black space and the infinity of stars.

"What the heck is going on?"

"You've entered a higher substratum from the rest of the Imaginarium," Russ advised. Dominic remembered his prickling flesh, as though exposed to a field of static electricity. "This part of the Imaginarium has not yet been completely imagined, not fully *realized*."

It was a crazy notion, but Dominic knew his eyes were not deceiving him. Neither was he dreaming. The Haston Sant-Cassia hung on one section of wall. The rest of chamber had not been imagined yet. More importantly, he had expected to see Monica standing there, studying the painting. Except she wasn't. Instead, crazier still, Dominic realized where she had disappeared to. As he crept closer to the painting, horror dawned in his mind, accelerating with startling speed. His eyes grew large, threatening to pop. His mouth dropped open. His released a gasp.

The Changing Muse was a portrait. Except the portrait of the lady Haston Sant-Cassia had painted was the spitting image of Dominic's girlfriend along with slimy, alien tentacles crawling out of an ordinary vase, like obscene flowers, on a table in the background. There was no sign of fear on her face, Monica's expression as serene and enigmatic as the smile on the Mona Lisa. How she had managed to get herself into a painting Dominic could not conceive. All he knew he had somehow lost his girlfriend to this certifiable place, this imaginarium with its exhibition of weird paintings.

It explained the indeterminate fear he had experienced outside the building on arrival, a sense of premonition when he had stepped across the threshold, the foreshadowing that had followed him through the Imaginarium. To this very space, to this very moment. Culminating in an unthinkable event. Dominic stared at the painting of his girlfriend set against a backdrop of a half-imagined reality, a dimension of sight not yet fully-configured, continuing to slowly evolve. His heart pounding hard in his chest, he glanced desperately at Dominic for answers. "What is happening—?" he uttered incredulously, his words suspended in midair.

"She has come home . . ." Russ meditated, as though this was explanation enough.

Sant-Cassia has painted one of his earliest, dearest models, Dominic remembered Russ saying. He tried to make sense of it. The canvas must start as a blank. *Instruction to the artist: insert model's face, as desired.*

But Dominic could not proceed any further with this line of thought. A greater dread filled him at that instant, for he noticed, behind Russ, the Man in the Black Suit had moved.

The figure turned abruptly and walked with purposeful steps towards them, now visibly more flesh-and-blood than mannequin. His shoes clacked loudly on the polished floor.

Dominic watched him approach and nearly screamed. Although his general appearance was that of a middle-aged man, complete with a shock of grey hair, his face was horribly grotesque like one of the nightmare creations of the Chapman Brothers, wizened and almost animalistic, ferocious eyes above a wet, elongated snout, bearing the resemblance to a wolf or a coyote—or a jackal. When he opened his powerful jaws and spoke, Dominic saw long, pointy teeth, razor-sharp and lethal.

"Isn't she a work of art?" the Beast in the Black Suit growled. "She belongs to us now!"

Speechless, dripping with perspiration, feeling nauseated inside, Dominic stared at the abomination in the business suit.

Russ introduced the dread, wolfish figure reverentially. "Meet my boss, *Unwin Grimwolde*."

Dominic struggled to pull his eyes away from the miscreant, the supposed owner and curator of the gallery, monstrosified for his sins and granted unnaturally long life from his ancestor's pact with the Devil. Would it be any surprise if this wasn't Unwin Grimwolde after all, but Baelfire Grimwolde? Dominic managed to cast his glance back at the unfathomable portrait of his girlfriend, either freshly created or maybe actually painted one hundred years ago.

Of all the dark talent on display here, it was the last exhibit that ultimately defied sanity. Art that drives you mad, as Monica had divulged. The *pièce de résistance* Russ had boasted about, presently transposed with Monica's face, stolen by an artist who lived nearly a century ago. An impossible accomplishment.

In a sick, befuddled daze, Dominic said his peace to Monica, the woman he loved the utmost, an utterance of the noblest romantic sentiment. "You, to me, my darling, really are a work of art . . ."

V: THE UNFINISHED DREAM

He awoke. Bleary-eyed, he looked around him, slightly panicked. They were still in the Fiat 500, driving through open countryside. The sun had already begun to set.

Everything seemed normal.

Monica sat in the driver's seat, concentrating on the road ahead, looking as pretty as a picture—*pardon the pun*—and appearing completely real. Dominic's body sagged with relief. "Am I glad to see you?"

"You're awake," said Monica, glancing at him. "You just nodded off. Kept mumbling in your sleep about paintings. I didn't want to disturb you."

It had been a dream. A *dream*. Nothing but his brain working overtime.

Dominic remembered aspects of his dream. The spiderlike imaginarium, an exhibition of the Daubers of Dark Dreams set in different spatial substrata, the Beast in the Black Suit, the customized portrait of his girlfriend, his dearly-beloved Monica permanently sucked into a supernatural painting showcased in a room that had not yet fully manifested itself, using the engine of the imagination to dream the gallery into substantiality and close the boundary with the starry eternity of the cosmos . . .

"How are you?" Monica asked, sounding and looking as lovely as ever.

"All the better for seeing you . . ."

Monica was suddenly distracted. "This looks like fun . . ."

Outside the windscreen, Dominic saw the black-painted letters on the signpost along with an arrow pointing right at the approaching crossroads:

THIS WAY
TO
GRIMWOLDE'S IMAGINARIUM

A prescient horror stronger than mere déjà vu stirred his insides.

Threads of a dream strung together? Or a transmission from the future?

Could the future be changed? He thought they should give the rewound clock a wide berth, set the journey on a different course. "I think I'll pass . . ."

"As you wish . . ." Monica said, none-too-disappointed, and the car sped on, ignoring the crossroads altogether.

Dominic watched the side-lane leading to Griswolde's Imaginarium whizz by.

His relief would be short-lived, however. As the car somehow pulled up to the itsy, bitsy mechanical spider of the Imaginarium, as though space and time converged to this one single spot, Dominic was suddenly struck by a stabbing realization. Racing pulse. Forehead sweat. Fear spinning its dark web, spilling over into stark paranoia, his mind rapidly unravelling . . .

"We've arrived," Monica announced brightly, beside him. Except it wasn't Monica who occupied the driver's seat next to him, but the Beast in the Black Suit with his hideous, canine features speaking in Monica's voice, a deep, feral glow in his eyes. To confuse the picture, his coterie, Russ, the lumbering tour guide, and Willow, the stoner girl at reception, sat quietly in the back seat. It suddenly occurred to Dominic why they had both seemed strangely familiar. Russ reminded him of his eccentric, long-dead uncle and Willow his goth cousin, whom he hadn't seen since his early teens, alleged to have committed suicide. One minute they were there in the back seat, the next they were gone, as though they had evaporated into thin air. Dominic realized his mind had dreamed them up, mere figments, the ghosts of half-remembered faces. The only constant in all this was Unwin, aka Baelfire, Grimwolde, the Beast in the Black Suit, who refused to go away and whose deathless, nightmarish presence remained in the driver's seat, where Monica had been sitting only moments earlier. She must still be a part of the exhibition, victim to an occult artist and imprisoned in the final painting. Which meant the Daubers still needed the machinery of his mind and the burning fires of his imagination to bring a higher dimension into existence. He recalled Monica quoting Magritte: *If the dream is a translation of waking life, waking life is also a translation of the dream.*

Frenzied terror smashed over him like a tidal-wave.

For when he saw the flow of extra-cosmic blackness leak through a chink in the virtual, setting sky, like an unfinished painting, Dominic Hilling acknowledged his worst suspicions with a nerve-shredding, heart-stopping scream, horribly-aware he was still in the Imaginarium.

March 2018—April 2018

All Our Yesterdays

"The slave is doomed to worship time and fate and death, because they are greater than anything he finds in himself, and because all his thoughts are of things which they devour."

Bertrand Russell

There is a place nobody else knows about. Only I can make it exist...

"I need you to calm down," Carolyn Hayden told Chase Carver, the up-and-coming movie star, over the car cell. The panic in his voice was almost palpable. "I know it looks bad. I saw the pictures." Indeed, she'd seen the pictures. Splashed across the front pages of the gossip rags, photos of her client snapped sharing a hot-tub with three topless women when he should be at home with his heavily pregnant wife. What did he think would happen if he got caught? Didn't he realize the paparazzi circled like sharks around any prey they might find vaguely interesting, waiting for the right moment to attack and maul and feed? And Carver certainly made interesting prey, if not potentially big fish. Since he employed her as his publicist, he now expected her to perform miracles, automatically assumed she would pick up the pieces and make the whole thing magically disappear. "Take it from me, even bad publicity is good publicity. We can take advantage of this crisis and turn it around. We just need an angle." She paused, went in for casual reassurance. "Don't let it get you down, Chase. Leave it with me . . ."

Carolyn hung up.

As she took the next turnpike, she turned off the song on the radio, *Scarlet Sky* by 7Ray, and reflected on the likelihood of salvaging Carver's reputation.

Slim odds, predicted Carolyn, *a real long shot.*

The actual, unvarnished truth of the whole thing was Carver had damaged his popularity at a very crucial stage on the road to movie greatness. He was only just recently debuting with the major-leaguers, and first impressions mattered. If he'd been in the business a good few years and tomcatted around like Old Jack Nick, the fact he were firmly established would have yielded an entirely different response. And, besides, Hollywood, once the epitome of decadence, was undergoing some kind of puritanical revival. Carver had floundered spectacularly at the crossroads to fame. The scandal would probably destroy his career before it had begun, with the dirt dished out today sticking to him for years to come. All you had to do was to look back to what the media did to Rob Lowe and you would know the scale of the nightmare facing Carver.

Carolyn didn't like lying to him. He paid her well and trusted her implicitly.

Frankly, I think he's loused things up to the point of no return, she thought sadly. *Blame immaturity, shallowness, the conceit of turning twenty-one, getting too much too soon without any exclusive means of dealing with the pitfalls of overnight stardom. The lucky ones bounce back, most are never heard of again. Shame . . . because Chase showed such tremendous promise.*

Still, he was counting on her. Part of her job description involved damage control. She supposed she would pursue whatever course of action she felt necessary. She would do all she could to yank him out of whatever squalid hole he had dug himself into.

How's that for the fickleness of celebrity? From notability to notoriety, loveable to contemptible, saint to sinner all in the space of one day. Never underestimate the nature of the beast. Proof enough Hollywood—like a mob—can turn against you in the thud of a heartbeat. She thought no more of it . . . or chose not to.

When it came to her professional and personal life, she stood by the notion that never the twain shall meet. Her responsibility to Chase Carver, whether she ought to prepare him for the possibility that his future film projects could very well be straight-to-DVD releases, she would dwell on at a more suitable time.

Carolyn was now simply concerned with picking up her eight-year-old daughter from school. This unavoidable errand should have been straightforward enough (after all, she had done countless school runs as a full-time mother in the days of yore), but what happened that afternoon marked the starting point to a sequence of events in which the petulant gods of fate conspired against her. For Carolyn found herself in an altogether singular, perverse and apparently inescapable predicament.

And it would soon become painfully obvious that Time was not on her side.

Carolyn pulled up to the gates of BLOOMFIELD ELEMENTARY with plenty of time to spare and sat in the car, waiting for the end-of-school bell.

The day had got off to a bad start. Reading the gossip columns first thing in the morning, Carolyn had realized she was on the verge of losing her most expensive client. The fact Chase Carver kept ringing her every five minutes from a film-shoot off Madagascar in a vain and rather pathetic attempt to exculpate himself from the mess he had created didn't help matters. Then, Jeena Koznik, Isobel's usually-reliable nanny, had called her on her cell during lunchtime, informing her she could not collect her daughter due to ill-health. Matt, her ex-husband, rang moments later, apologizing to her because he couldn't take Isobel for the weekend. Add to that an afternoon spent providing further emotional support to an unmanly Carver while trying to convince the ruthless hacks that the business with the half-naked groupies had been an awful misunderstanding, Carolyn was genuinely contemplating quitting her day job. Still, there was one small consolation from this day of misery: it would come as a pleasant surprise to Isobel to find her mother waiting for her at the school gates. The school bell rang. Seconds later, children dressed in their neat, purple uniforms came spilling out of the main doors, blinking to the freedom of sunlight.

Carolyn needed time to de-stress. Tomorrow was a big day. Depending on the formal statement she composed tonight and released to the press tomorrow, it would be make-or-break for the Hollywood star. Seeing the look of happiness on her daughter's face would certainly cheer her up and set the mood for the evening ahead.

The children continued to emerge, some laughing and joking in small groups, others disclosing wicked secrets to close friends, a few preferring their own company. Most went their separate ways beyond the school gates, accepting the welcoming hands of their parents.

Just us girls tonight, sweetie, Carolyn thought, making plans. *Pizza, ice-cream and a Jim Carrey film.* Isobel loved Jim Carrey. Her absolute favourite was *Lemony Snicket's A Series of Unfortunate Events.* She could write up her speech after Isobel had gone to bed.

Something occurred to her, then. *Homework, you forgot about her homework.*

Now why should that bother her? *Because I never get a chance to see her do her homework. Since I'm home late every night, it's always done and dusted by the time I arrive. Tuck her into bed, kiss her goodnight, turn off the light.* There was a sense of sadness about this state of affairs because Carolyn felt she was missing out on an important part of her daughter's personal and social development. Oh, Isobel had everything she desired (money, friends, private schooling, a nanny who came highly recommended) . . . except for the complete, undivided attention of her mother. *We never get time to talk, I mean really talk . . .* Even Matt, who worked as an advertisement executive, did his best to spend time with her. *At least, I'll be there for her tonight. Should make a nice change.*

The steady stream of kids was now a trickle. Most had already gone off home. Yet, Isobel still hadn't appeared.

The last child, a little girl with a bright smile and brown pigtails, emerged from the school doors and Carolyn got out of the car and went to greet her. Then she saw it wasn't Isobel.

The girl's mother took her by the hand and, giving Carolyn a fleeting look of mistrust, hurried away with her daughter.

Carolyn stood on the deserted school grounds, mystified and slightly afraid. The rows of windows of the imposing red-bricked building seemed to mock her like a multitude of sneering eyes. The statue of a griffin stared back at her as though deciding if it should break free of its moorings and pounce. The sky grew overcast, the sun retreating behind a vanguard of bruised stormclouds. A cold wind sprang up from nowhere.

She headed towards the main building.

Something unforeseen had happened to Isobel. Had she been placed in detention? Had she hurt herself or got sick? Except her daughter wasn't the kind of pupil to be kept back after school for misbehaving since she was one of the most sensible and well-adjusted individuals Carolyn knew. And the school nurse would have obviously rung Carolyn if her daughter had fallen ill.

As she climbed the concrete steps leading up to the main entrance, she could feel the dread rising through her. Pulling open the main doors, she found herself at the end of a long corridor. Doors, concealing their respective classrooms, stretched away into the distance.

Two doors down, a severe-looking lady with horn-rimmed glasses was talking to a brown-suited gentleman with silver hair and a youngish appearance about the forthcoming school play.

Carolyn strode up to them, interrupting their conversation in mid-flow. "Where's my daughter?"

The fearful tone of her voice brought a perplexed, worried expression to their faces. "Your daughter?" said the silver-haired gentleman.

"Yes, Isobel."

"And you are?"

"Carolyn . . . Carolyn Hayden, her mother."

"I'm William Baxter, the Head, and this is—"

"—Miss McKindless, I know. We've met before."

The look of puzzlement deepened. "I don't think so," said Miss McKindless. "Otherwise, I would have remembered."

"Can you at least tell me where my daughter is? She's not sick, is she?"

"I'm afraid the name Isobel Hayden doesn't ring a bell."

Her comment, spoken with cold indifference, switched on a klaxon inside Carolyn's head. "What? How can you not know her? You're her *teacher*!"

The outburst was so sudden and unsettling that Miss McKindless stared at Carolyn as though she might be off her rocker. "I've been teaching here for over thirty years and I can assure you I have never met, let alone taught, a pupil by the name of Isobel Hayden."

"But I've dealt with you on several occasions," Carolyn said, almost pleadingly. "You must remember telling me on Parents' Night that Isobel has an aptitude for drama. You even went on to say she would make a very good Cassandra."

"I never said any such thing."

"Are you calling me a liar?" challenged Carolyn, overwrought.

"Are you saying I don't know my own students?"

"Edith, please," Mr. Baxter stepped in, gently chastising his colleague, "let me handle this." He turned immediately to Carolyn. "Look, Mrs. Hayden. As Principal of Bloomfield, it is my duty to get to know all the young people and their parents, and I can honestly say that Miss McKindless does not have a pupil by the name of Isobel in her class." However, on seeing the daggers in Carolyn's eyes, he continued, "Or maybe I'm overlooking something. Shall we proceed to my office, so we straighten this matter out once and for all?"

The Principal's Office was a plush, tidy, oak-panelled room towards the rear of the school building. Back turned, Mr. Baxter was perusing through the filing cabinets accommodating all the student records. Carolyn stood by the large desk, wringing her hands and watching him in nervous anticipation. Miss McKindless sat silently in one of the chairs, studying their visitor curiously.

Eventually, Mr. Baxter completed his search and turned sympathetically towards Carolyn. "I'm sorry, but we don't seem to have a record of an Isobel Hayden ever attending Bloomfield Elementary."

His words took a while to sink in. For a moment, she could produce no sounds. Then, her voice returned as a whisper, "There must be some mistake."

"No mistake, as you can check for yourself."

Carolyn did check. There was no confidential file marked ISOBEL HAYDEN.

Mr. Baxter closed the filing cabinet after her.

What if they'd misplaced her file? But, despite the panic gripping her, Carolyn knew they hadn't. Bloomfield Elementary, for all intents and purposes, had never heard of her daughter. Isobel, it seemed, had never set foot in this place. "Do you think I'm making this up? I dropped Isobel off on her first day at school. I pay her annual tuition fees. I've got all her report cards at home. I go to the PTA Meetings. For petessakes, I've even seen her perform at the Fourth of July celebrations with the rest of her class. So how can you tell me that my daughter has never been a pupil here?"

"That's just it. She *hasn't*."

Why weren't they helping her? Was it because they were hiding something? Was she in the midst of some cruel practical joke? Yet, the Principal's expression was one of genuine concern.

Tears, anger and confusion threatened to engulf her. But Carolyn stood her ground. "I came here to pick up my daughter and I'm not leaving without her!"

Miss McKindless said nothing, merely stared at her above her horn-rimmed glasses.

Hysterical women made Mr. Baxter uncomfortable and he seemed to realize the situation might turn ugly. He had to do something to defuse what could become a potentially explosive situation. Mrs. Hayden was, after all, a concerned parent, facing possibly the worst news any parent dreads. "What I suggest is you speak with the police. They might be able to assist you in finding your missing daughter." With that, he dialled 911.

This was possibly the worst situation any loving parent could find themselves in. As Carolyn sat in a drab interview room at the police department, she could already see tomorrow's newspaper headlines: PUBLICIST'S DAUGHTER GOES MISSING.

After questioning the Principal and Isobel's alleged teacher at Bloomfield, the detective in charge of the case, Braddock, had brought Carolyn down to the station. In her distraught, fragile state, the interview felt like an interrogation. "How do you explain the fact that the school has no record of her?" Braddock demanded. He was all six-foot-seven tall with a no-nonsense approach.

"How should I know?" Carolyn replied, distractedly. "Do you think I'm imagining this?"

"No, what I don't understand is why a reputable establishment such as Bloomfield Elementary would want to lie about your daughter not ever being there."

"Why don't you ask them?"

"We've got some preliminary statements, but we'll talk to them again in more detail and speak with the other staff members to see if the mention of your daughter jogs any memories." Detective Braddock looked at her hard. "You do realize you're talking about a conspiracy."

"It doesn't make any sense," Carolyn murmured.

"What I find even more bizarre is you're not carrying any pictures of your daughter on you. Most parents do."

There again, Braddock wasn't going to let it go. When she had reached into her diary to extract a photo of herself, Isobel and Matt from a happier time, she had been unable to find it. Her carelessness had surprised her, and she knew, at the same time, she may have sown a few seeds of doubt in Braddock's mind. He was making no qualms about treating her like a suspect. "I have a busy schedule. I probably lost it. Like I said earlier, you can check my house. There're hundreds of photos of Isobel there."

"Good, we'll do just that," said Braddock, shifting to another question. "Could your daughter have run away from home?"

"Don't be ridiculous!" exclaimed Carolyn, almost outraged at the sheer idea. "Isobel would never do that!"

Another line of questioning. "Anyone you know who might hold a grudge against you or your family? Want to harm your daughter?"

"No," was her answer. *Except* . . . Then it struck her. "Wait!" she blurted, the gloom lifting slightly, hope springing forth. "I employ a nanny to look after Isobel. Her name's Jeena Koznik. She claimed she was sick this morning. She may have something to do with my daughter's disappearance."

"We'll look into it immediately. Do you have her number?" Carolyn searched her diary and gave Braddock what he requested. "Please, you've got to find my daughter!" she pleaded with him. "She's *only* a little girl! Smart, innocent and oh, so sweet—she wouldn't hurt a blade of grass."

"We'll do all we can, Mrs. Hayden. And we'll keep you posted. Now Sergeant Warwick will take you home."

Another cup of revolting coffee and several hankies later, Carolyn was released, advised not to leave town and escorted home. She had never felt so helpless in her life. She blamed herself for not being there for her only child when Isobel had needed protecting the most, and her mind soon turned to darker thoughts: of child-snatchers, child-traffickers and evil-minded child molesters.

Just when she thought things could not get any bleaker, she arrived at her lake house to face an absolute heart-stopper.

No old report cards.

No school fee receipts.

No photographs of Isobel.

And nothing in her bedroom to remotely suggest she was ever there.

Sergeant Warwick suggested she sleep on it. Maybe he could bring more encouraging news for her in the morning. But, despite his gentle manner and efforts to make her feel better, Sergeant Warwick had left with a look of suspicion, the look of someone who's thinking that if there is no physical evidence of someone who's alleged to have disappeared, then maybe they never existed in the first place.

The not-knowing was worse than the guilt, helplessness and self-condemnation. Carolyn could not think, her mind a jumble of fractured conversations: Isobel's nanny calling in sick, Miss McKindless telling her she had never taught a pupil going by the name of Isobel, Detective Braddock wondering why she wasn't carrying a picture of her daughter, Sergeant Warwick's curious expression as he departed indicating he was seriously considering calling in some men with butterfly nets and a straitjacket.

The fact there was no trace of Isobel's things or belongings in the house complicated matters. It didn't make any sense at all.

Her sleep completely shot, in spite of the two Xanax she had taken earlier, Carolyn decided to call Matt. Matt would certainly share her grief, might be able to figure out what was going on and provide her with some modicum of comfort. Why she ever divorced him, she didn't know. He had been a pillar of strength throughout their life together and even after their separation during times of crises. She could always count on him to make things better.

He picked up the phone on the fifth ring. "Hello?"

Carolyn had been, so far, holding herself together, and on hearing his sleepy voice, her emotions gushed forth. She wept.

"Who is this?" he asked, then recognized the caller. "Carolyn? Is that you?"

"Yes, Matt . . ."

"What's wrong?" he asked, full of concern and perturbation.

"It's Isobel," she sobbed. "She's missing."

Carolyn didn't quite get the reaction she was expecting. "Isobel?" Matt said, sounding genuinely perplexed. "Who's Isobel?"

"*Isobel!*" Carolyn reminded him, not understanding his puzzlement. "*Our daughter!*"

Matt went quiet for a few moments. Then, he said something

that brought Carolyn out of her misery and set her directly on the warpath. "But we never had a daughter."

"How can you say that?" she wailed, shocked at the bluntness of his reply. "She has my eyes and your smile! She attends Third Grade at Bloomfield Elementary! She spends the weekends with you! How can you not remember her?"

Matt was thoughtful again. When he spoke, there was pity in his voice. "You were pregnant once, but you miscarried."

Carolyn couldn't believe what Matt was telling her. Yet, for the first time, his calm, sympathetic tone caused her to doubt herself. Had she manufactured the memory of her missing daughter?

Except, she remembered Isobel vividly. She remembered the sensation of new life growing inside her. She remembered the early morning sickness and the mood swings, verbally lashing out at people at the slightest provocation. She remembered the pica, the craving for peanut-butter-and-banana sandwiches. She remembered carrying her unborn child to term, and sure as heck remembered the seventeen-hour labour. The beautiful, healthy baby girl who emerged from her had been the culmination of her efforts. She even recalled her birth weight: 3.1 kgs.

Matt had been there the whole time, holding her hand and offering support and encouragement. Only, now, he had forgotten. "Isobel is our daughter," Carolyn repeated furiously, "and it's about time you start acknowledging her presence! Because she needs us both to be there for her when she's found!"

"Carolyn," Matt said wearily. "I think you've been under a lot of stress lately, what with this whole business involving Chase Carver. You need a break. I'm going to ask Dr. Wiley to drop by and see you—"

"Don't you dare!" she warned with real menace. "I'm not crazy, do you understand?"

"I'm not saying that you are," assured Matt. "I just think you've got too much on your plate at the moment. Now, please let Dr. Wiley attend to you. I'll be in later today to check on you and I want you in bed, resting. I'm going to have to cut short the conference. I'll tell them it's a family emergency."

The knowledge that Matt would be flying over from Denver settled Carolyn a little.

"Promise me you won't do anything foolish," Matt requested.

"I promise I won't."

"Good, I'll see you soon." With that, Matt hung up.

Carolyn checked the alarm clock on her bedside cabinet. Three-twenty in the morning. *Must rest,* she thought distractedly. *Should feel different when I get up.*

But Carolyn could not sleep. She was too keyed-up, unable to escape the obvious. Why was everyone, including her own ex-husband, trying to convince her she had no daughter? Why were they all denying Isobel's existence?

Carolyn's mind summoned up a disturbing thought. If you discounted everything she said and took into account what everyone else was telling her, then maybe what you were left with was the truth.

First to visit her that morning was Dr. Wiley, her white-haired, kindly-faced Family Practitioner. When she told him about her missing daughter, he was at a loss. He reiterated what her ex-husband had told her in the small hours: that she was childless, having suffered a terrible miscarriage a few years back. It caused her great distress, and when Matt Hayden arrived, Dr. Wiley was in the process of sedating her.

"How's she doing?" he asked the doctor.

"Not great, if you must know," Dr. Wiley said sadly, putting the syringe and the vial of Ativan back into his medical bag. "She has a fixed delusion that her daughter was kidnapped."

"I've not seen her like this before," Matt observed. "She's normally so resilient."

"Stress can do this to a person," responded Dr. Wiley. "She works such a high-pressured job that cracks can start to show if you're not careful."

Carolyn moaned, feeling the sedative circulate through her system. She opened her glazed eyes and caught her handsome ex-husband looking down at her. "Matt . . ."

"Yes, baby, it's me," Matt said, kneeling by her bed, taking her hand. "We all want you to take it easy."

"What about Isobel?" she mustered.

Matt exchanged worried glances with Dr. Wiley. "Unfortunately, I have to go," said Dr. Wiley. "I think it best if you keep a bedside vigil. Call me if you have any concerns. I'll see myself out."

Matt pulled up a chair and sat by Carolyn's bed, offering gentle reassurances. "I'm here now, baby. I won't leave you."

When Carolyn awoke at four in the afternoon, Matt's chair was empty with Matt himself nowhere to be seen.

The persistent ringing from the doorbell was what awakened Carolyn. Still groggy from the effects of the sedative, she made her way down to the front door. Detective Braddock and another plain-clothes officer stood outside.

"Mrs. Hayden," began Detective Braddock, "mind if we come in?"

Carolyn ushered them in. She took them to the kitchen. "Would you like some coffee? I'm making some for myself."

"No thanks," said Detective Braddock. "I thought we'd update you regarding the case."

"Have you found Isobel?" she asked.

"Not quite," said the other visitor, "I'm Agent Farrell of the FBI. We need to talk."

Carolyn poured herself a cup of black coffee from the percolator, took a sip. "Thank God you guys are finally taking this seriously. At least, now there's hope."

"That's just the problem," said Agent Farrell. "There is *no* Isobel Hayden. There never was."

Carolyn looked at him as though he were speaking in a foreign language. Anger and confusion and grief quickly welled up inside her. "What makes you so sure?"

"There is no record of her, anywhere," Agent Farrell replied sharply. "I mean, can you produce a birth certificate?"

"You know I can't," Carolyn responded in despair. "All her stuff has vanished."

"We haven't been idle all night," Detective Braddock said. "We checked the number you gave us for your nanny, even visited her apartment. There doesn't seem to be a Jeena Koznik."

"What do you mean 'doesn't seem to be'? Jeena kidnapped my daughter!"

"Look at it from our point of view," Agent Farrell tried to reason. "You claim your daughter disappeared and we put some of our top men on the case to locate her. However, the investigation has yielded absolutely nothing, not the slightest evidence to suggest your daughter is real. Even her nanny whom you allege kidnapped her doesn't exist. We went on to do a background check on you and we discovered you were neither married nor divorced."

"That's impossible," muttered Carolyn, disbelievingly. "I spoke to Matt last night and he came by this morning. I admit I was drugged-up, but I swear to you he kept me company until you arrived."

"Drugged-up, you say?" Agent Farrell said, staring at her intently.

"Dr. Wiley felt I needed a tranquilizer. He'll confirm I have a husband, or should I say, ex-husband. Speak with him."

"We will," said Detective Braddock, his demeanour growing prickly. "Lucky for you, you have quite a fierce reputation as a publicity agent. But I'm warning you: I'll book you for wasting police time if I find you're lying to us or this is some kind of unscrupulous publicity stunt."

"And I'll recommend," Agent Farrell added coldly, "you spend the next few weeks at Parkview, pending a Psychiatric evaluation, if I ever suspect you're unsound of mind."

"I'm not making this up!" Carolyn answered as emphatically as she could to their threats. "Isobel is not an invention! This has to be some crazy cover-up! Someone out there has it in for me! My life is being dismantled, piece by piece, and no-one else can see it!"

"That may be all good and well," said Agent Farrell, "but listen to how that sounds." He and Detective Braddock headed for the door. "We'll be in touch."

They left Carolyn deep in thought. *So much for the law—a fat lot of good they are!* But it was what she had uttered in the heat of the moment which she picked up on and was presently toying with. *My life is being dismantled, piece by piece, and no-one else can see it . . .*

Her thoughts turned to a few supernatural ideas. Was this the coming of the Rapture, as foretold in the New Testament, when the good are carried up to Heaven and the damned remain on Earth to face the dark days ahead? Couldn't be, because the events of the last twenty-four hours revolved specifically around her. Alien interference, then? Slightly more plausible, if not as weak and ridiculous as the whole Rapture explanation.

No, this was something more . . .

Carolyn tried Matt's cell and discovered it was a no-number. If she had no husband and no daughter, where did that leave her?

Nowhere.

On a sinister hunch, she went to the study and switched on her PC. She typed in: MADAGASCAR.

Like the hunt for her daughter, the search yielded nothing. She tried: UNITED KINGDOM.

Same non-result.

CANADA?

Still nothing.

She decided to narrow the field . . . COLORADO . . . TEXAS... NEW MEXICO . . .

None of the above existed on Google Earth. How about trying closer to home?

LAS VEGAS, NEVADA.

The place was still on the map.

So too was SAN FRANCISCO and the neighbouring towns of ARIZONA.

Filled with dread, Carolyn keyed in LAS VEGAS again and found it had suddenly disappeared off the face of the earth. She realized the rest of Nevada would follow suit as well as the outskirts of California.

Something strange and awful and unprecedented was

happening to the reality she knew. It was as though the Universe were contracting at an exponential rate. How something like this could be even remotely possible was beyond her understanding. This was the kind of weird stuff

[My life is being dismantled, piece by piece, and no-one else can see it] one might find on The Twilight Zone.

Carolyn switched on the TV, checked out the News Channel. "The fires sweeping through the Hollywood Hills," went the male anchor, "have already caused millions of dollars' worth of damage to the homes of the rich and famous. The Governor of California, Arnold Schwarzenegger, visited the scene and expressed his sadness at the destruction . . .

"In other World News, more riots in downtown Los Angeles, resulting in the deaths of six gang members, two police officers and one civilian . . ."

Carolyn sat calmly listening to the news as it became more inane and pettier and pointless.

"More breaking news: A surfer nearly drowned off the coast of Newport Beach . . .

"Three youths who can't be named were arrested for speeding and drinking at the wheel . . .

"Firemen were called in to retrieve a cat stuck in a tree by its very distraught owner . . .

"Many pupils around the city have missed school because they have been laid low with the 'flu . . .

"Some woman out there believes she may have dropped an earring at the local 7/11. . .

"And, finally, on a lighter note: despite being on a regular diet, my colleague has gained seven pounds since last week and come out of the closet . . ." The male anchor spoke to someone outside the range of the cameras. "Hey, is that the best news you got?" Hurriedly regaining his professionalism, the male anchor declared: "I'm Dick Brunswick. That was the late evening news. Good Night, and Good Luck . . ." Then there was just static on the TV screen.

Carolyn switched channels at random and received the same sizzle-pop. It seemed all the stations had stopped transmitting.

It's spreading fast, whatever it is, she thought. She looked out of the window of her study and saw a sight never before seen by the naked eye. She noticed there were no stars or cloud-cover. In fact, there was no sky, period. Only a creeping void of uninterrupted nothingness, absorbing the lake at an extraordinary rate, steadily wiping out the reality she was accustomed to.

The End of the World, Carolyn mused with quiet dignity.

No, the End of my World, she quickly corrected herself. *For I am at the Centre of this Universe . . . soon to fade into obscurity . . . into oblivion . . .*

Into Nothingness . . .

Suddenly her PC went blank, gave up the ghost.

No satellite coverage, she was sure, *because the satellites themselves have been* erased.

Had she died? Was she languishing in some purgatorial pitstop before resuming her passage to the Other Side?

As the Universe outside continued to shrink, *minimalize*, the lake continued to retreat towards her house.

What if Time were not laid out on a single continuum, but as a linear series of concrete blocks, each consisting of a day? What if, in her case, Old Father Time had taken a holiday and she was trapped in the Past? What if the world had moved on, and she was still here?

What happens to Yesterday when it is no longer Yesterday?

Carolyn was learning . . . oh, yes, was she learning!

She wondered what could have set off this chain of events, why the gods of fate had singled her out. If the Universe focuses on no-one, why had Time short-changed her. The answer would not come.

Time continued to spiral down. The Universe had shrunk to the dimensions of her room. Nothingness began to seep through the walls, making them as illusory as a mirage.

No Four Horsemen of the Apocalypse to greet her, no, soon she would literally fade away, be swallowed up by the Great Nowhere of Yesterday.

As parts of her study began to uniformly disappear, she thought of that quote from *Macbeth*: *And all our yesterdays have lighted fools/The way to dusty death. Out, out brief candle!/Life's but a walking shadow, a poor player/That struts and frets his hour upon the stage/And then is heard no more . . .*

Shakespeare had been more than just a playwright. He had been a seer and a prophet whose vision of the future far surpassed the ambiguous claims of Nostradamus.

The drifting, forever-hungered Nothingness swirled around her. It was a colourless, featureless, atom-less thing no words could describe or brush could paint. A paragon of weirdness, so utterly compelling and beautiful. Neither black nor white, alive nor dead, hot nor cold, here nor there, the Nothingness was as nothingness is, a liminal blankness, without essence, constant and uncompromising and all-consuming.

Her life had been whittled down to this. *I am at the Centre of the Universe and the Universe is about to fold in on itself and implode. I guess this is where we part, my friend.* As the Great Nowhere of Yesterday took her and Carolyn winked painlessly out of existence and was heard of no more, her last thoughts were for her daughter somewhere in the real world, whom she hoped would forgive her for not being there and live out the rest of her days as a Somebody, where Nothingness could not touch her.

While Matt Hayden and his daughter, Isobel, were still a day or two away from getting a visit from Detective Braddock regarding the mysterious disappearance of Carolyn, the respected publicist, Chase Carver sat brooding in a bar in Madagascar.

The film crew had stopped shooting for the day and were relaxing on the beach, swimming and drinking rum and making out with the natives to the rhythm of the stunning sunset.

Their leading man had decided not to join them, going instead to this obscure place in the jungle where he needed time alone, time to think. He had refused any company.

Chase was not a nice person and needed to think about what he had done.

"Hey, bartender!" he whistled, motioning to his empty glass. The bartender quickly poured him another shot of whisky. "Leave the bottle."

The bartender got out of his hair and went about serving another customer. Chase gulped down the shot and poured himself another one. Fame meant everything to Chase Carver. Born with good looks and plenty of talent and not without a striking resemblance to Leonardo DiCaprio, Chase knew the movie industry would bow to his stage presence. But you must live in the Zeitgeist, the Spirit of the Times. And the Zeitgeist is a perpetually changing animal, which will spit out your bones when it has had its fill. His excesses had caught up with him and Anonymity beckoned. There was one thing he was not going to do lying down and that was let his career sink into obscurity. Become a Has-Been, a part of Yesterday's Clique.

"What happens to Yesterday when it is no longer Yesterday?" he asked the passing bartender, philosophically. The bartender shrugged, unsure how to respond.

The witchdoctors had guided Chase, rescued him from his fate, reminded him who—and *what*—he was. He was a fallen god, whose prison-ship had crash-landed on Earth nearly one thousand years ago. And his malign essence had been reincarnated with every passing generation, with each of his lives through the centuries always forgetting the origin of his alien birth. Blame it on the primitive nature of the human brain.

This time, he remembered, though. The up-and-rising Hollywood actor was what he was in this particular incarnation. And he liked the fame, the attention, the women, the glamour.

Living amongst the humans, he came to remember the unique powers he possessed. Time was a worthy healer, capable of being exploited for whatever dark purpose he desired.

Why not grant Anonymity to another in the ways of Time?

Thus, Chase had chosen on whom to bestow this terrible gift, and by the sounds of it, it had worked a little too well.

"Not to fear," Chase muttered to himself, grinning. "Yesterday won't come a-knocking on my door in a hurry. I won't be eating Nothingness for some time to come." The solution had proved exceedingly simple. Carolyn Hayden had been the unwitting victim of his Time Engineering skills on this occasion; someone else would make the supreme sacrifice at a later date, if the worst came to the worst. Next time, the honour might belong to his pregnant wife, who had so far stood by the side of her husband instead of throwing up a fuss. Hurl them into the diminishing world of yesterday to propel his movie career into the future, likewise restoring the balance of the Universe before others of his otherworldly kind noticed any temporal discrepancy and came looking for him.

[*There is a place nobody else knows about. Only I can make it exist . . .*]

He wondered how many lives he had destroyed during his time on Earth—and smiled. For him, mediocrity would never be an option. Chase had expertly manipulated Time, those chronon particles which were the smallest quantized measure between two connected events, creating time eddies before unceremoniously discarding Carolyn into a time pocket where she would be cut adrift from the rest of the Universe and left to languish in isolation until old age took her.

Scarlet Sky by 7Ray played on the bar's stereo speakers at sunset, presently. In the time it took to finish the song, Carolyn's whole world would have unravelled, compressed, shrunk, and she would be gone. Such was the nature of time pockets.

After all, Carolyn had lost faith in him—*and that, ladies and gentlemen, is unacceptable.*

Always a good feeling to fuck over your agent! Chase acknowledged.

"Let's drink to your wake, Carolyn, my dear," Chase saluted, taking a gulp. "Shame . . . because you would have made an excellent fuck!"

Believe only *in me, Faust,* he thought, swaggering with self-importance, *because, compared to me, the Devil is nothing more than a dull simpleton, blundering around in the dark.*

May 2008—August 2008

Infection Will Travel

"The world, that understandable and lawful world, was slipping away."

Lord of the Flies (1954)
William Golding

1

Ashley Hines and the gang were gathered at Cygnet Cove that Sunday afternoon where they always gathered every God-given Sunday. It had been their favourite haunt since as far back as they could remember, a place where they could lounge around in the long grass, smoke weed, chat about anything under the sun, listen to music and chill, away from the prying eyes of their parents. *No Grown-Ups Allowed*, as Darius Craft, one of their number, would often boast. This was their secret place, just as the Famous Five or the Hardy Boys had their own, as exclusive as any Gentlemen's Club, a sacred place the adults were aware of but never dared trespass upon. Cygnet Cove was a small islet just off Swanney Haven, the little coastal village where they all lived, grew up, went to the same school together, upheld their friendship. Presently, all eight of the gang were assembled here, less one. They were at the height of summer, the sky an unclouded-blue, the vegetation lush and green. The sun beat fiercely down, tempered by the clear, clean sea breeze that kept the group of youngsters, who lay stretched out on the grass, relatively cool. The offshore landform of Cygnet Cove was accessible by water only, and Jonquil Buist-Wells spotted a rowing boat heading their way through his small, folding telescope. "Ship ahoy! Here he comes!"

Ashley—or 'Ash', as he preferred to be called—at age seventeen, was the oldest member of the gang, and therefore the designated 'leader'—or 'Chairman of the Bored', as he sometimes joked. Chewing on a blade of grass, he propped himself up on his elbows to take a casual gander. "I think we should give Darius a warm welcome when he gets here."

Ash was also only one month older than his soft-natured, blond girlfriend, Georgia Pearce. "He's been gone a long time. Hope he's doing okay."

"He's like a bad penny," Tyrone Braxton, two months younger than Ash, replied in mock-petulance, "which means the Craft's probably fine."

Jonquil (16), a good two-and-a-half-years older than his sister, Josie, and the intellect of the group, put his spyglass back into his pocket, replaced his round-rimmed spectacles on the bridge of his nose. Josie was half-dozing in the sun. "I wonder what tidings he brings from the mainland."

Piper Snaith was in the same class as Ash, Georgia and Tyrone and several months their junior. She was also a Plain-Jane, practising Christian. "News of God's wrath."

"Don't start on that religious crock, please," Tyrone warned her, albeit with gentle exasperation.

"Blasphemer!" muttered Piper, for which she received a Do-I-look-as-if-I-give-a-shit? glance from Tyrone.

'Oinky' Osgood Clemons, one month senior to Jonquil and the eighth member of the gang, could only grin.

All attention was focused on the boat's leisurely approach towards Cygnet Cove on the untroubled waters. They watched as Darius arrived on the shingled banks and tied-up the rowing boat. Darius climbed the steep trail and appeared in their midst. "Good afternoon, ladies and gentlemen!"

Ash and the others acknowledged his greeting with a wave or a nod of the head or a simple *Hi*.

"What kind of welcome is that?" Darius (17) the dosser, the joker, the class clown, the youngest of the 17-ers, the 'Craft', protested. His green T-shirt sported the slogan: THE NEED FOR WEED.

"In everyone's defence, it's just too hot and lovely up here to move," replied Ash.

"I can see things are very hectic. Not to mention, by your grins, half of you are stoned." He snatched the joint off Tyrone, who just grunted. Darius noticed music spilling out of the iPod speakers: *Rock with Me* by Inner Circle, the Swedish rockier edit. "You've even got the reggae out. The party began without me." He took a long, meaningful toke, and exhaled a huge cloud of smoke. "Been a while . . . Still plenty of time to make funny . . . *Miss me?*"

"We didn't hear from you and we got worried," Jonquil stated.

"All mobile communication networks are down. Besides, I've only been gone one week. I did say I'd be back today."

"So how is it out there?" Jonquil asked Darius.

"From our little reconnaissance up north, worse than ever. The world really has gone to hell."

"Are we still safe?" Ash asked the crucial question on everybody's lips.

Inner Circle's track segued into King Brillo's rock-reggae cover of T-Rex's *Children of the Revolution*. "Aren't we always?" Darius responded with a crafty smile. "Not a bad neck of woods we live in."

"The bubble's bound to burst sooner or later," Piper prophesized in typical doom-mongering fashion. "We all know the End draws near."

"You know the problem with you, Piper?" said Darius in typical Craftesque fashion. "You need to learn to chill out." He passed the joint over to her. "Here, have a drag! You might even meet God!"

As usual, she refused the joint, outraged. "Mocking God will only send you to the fiery pits of eternity. Neither does spending the Day of God in sinful reefer bliss bode well for your souls. God will always reside in my heart. Search for him in yours before it's too late."

Darius wanted to ask her that although she did not partake of any alcohol or drugs, why she always joined them every Sunday. Perhaps she was a girl who was subconsciously craving to break free of her religious tenets and would achieve her emancipation given time and the 'right' kind of nurturing. "This is the only god I need," joked Darius, puffing away on the reefer. His comment brought a look of disgust on Piper's face.

"Gimme-gimme-gimme . . ." Tyrone said, requesting the joint.

Darius obliged. "A million apologies for the Jew's Arse," he said, referring to the damp roach. He tugged affectionately at Osgood's fat cheeks. "How's Oinky?"

"Stop it!" protested Osgood.

"Not his fault he looks like Uncle Festor," Darius mock-confided in the others with his best Groucho Marx impression.

"Hey!" warned Osgood. "Not cool!"

Darius realized he might have overstepped the mark. "Don't take it personally, my old friend," he said, patting Osgood on the head. "You know I love you, man. But you really make it too easy for me." To everyone present, he added genuinely: "It's just great to see you all again."

"Good to have you back," said Ash warmly. "Glad to be back," reciprocated Darius.

And *coughed*.

The cough, although brief, fleeting, momentary, was *significant*. Yet, it did not raise suspicions. The others either did not notice or misconstrued it as a respiratory protest to the pot fumes Darius had abstained from for several weeks, not even receiving the bat of an eyelid from the normally-suspicious doomsayer, Piper, who went back to browsing through the Bible she personally carried with her. All moods had mellowed as the distinctive aroma of Mary Jane and the gentle tempo of the smooth Jamaican sound lingered sweetly in the June afternoon air. Failure to notice this early warning sign meant the teenagers did not yet know that this particular weekend would be different from every previous, catching them unprepared and unable to anticipate what it would entail. The End of the World had finally come to Swanney Haven but would not stop there, unleashing its full horror upon the small circle of teenage friends at Cygnet Cove.

2

So many writers have dreamed up ways of ending the world. All manner of formidable imaginations has concocted and inflicted plagues on Mankind: from the elementary zombie apocalypse, with the walking dead's insatiable desire for human flesh, to the more elaborate transmission of a vampiric virus, transforming the people into rampaging bloodsuckers, as conceptualized by Max Brooks and Richard Matheson, respectively. In Jonquil's intellectual opinion, the nightmarish, yet more believable infectious agents penned by Michael Crichton or Stephen King could not compare to the terrible beauty of Gabriel Garcia Marquez's Plague of Insomnia, or possibly the forerunner of them all, the devastating Scarlet Death as envisioned by Jack London.

When the End of the World did come, it did not come from the instructions of a bigoted, radical Islamic cleric or by the oft-dreaded onset of global thermonuclear war. It did not come from a lethal outbreak of Hanta or Ebola virus, SARS or Bird 'Flu, or the release of a nameless, indestructible and deadly high-tech virus engineered by military scientists for the purposes of germ warfare. None of the great thinkers could have predicted that the End of the World would be brought about by an outbreak of an apparently-innocuous virus four-fifths of humans didn't even know they carried.

This disastrous sequence of events began with the sharp rise of a new strain of Methicillin-resistant *Staphylococcus aureus* (MRSA) bacterium, despite the well-intentioned screening methods, extra sanitary measures, closing-off of entire wards and general quarantining of infected hospital patients. Hard-to-treat due to its absolute resistance to most conventional broad-spectrum antibiotics, this MRSA superbug spread uncontrollably through hospitals and nursing homes, military establishments and

~ 384 ~

prison communities, schools and gyms, as well as decimating the homeless. The pimples on the skin would progress to blisters and honey-coloured crusts, developing into pus-filled boils and foul-smelling abscesses, and if still left unchecked, eventually affecting the vital organs, resulting in severe pneumonia and infective endocarditis (vegetative growths on the valves of the heart), septicaemia and toxic shock syndrome and necrotizing fasciitis, the superbug rapidly eating away the flesh and burrowing through bone. The governments of the world were at a loss and looked desperately towards their greatest scientific minds for an answer. With the failure of every conceivable antibiotic, leading microbiologists considered their options, or lack of, and despaired. Until one bright spark suggested 'phage therapy'.

Bacteriophages, those viruses that infect and destroy bacteria, have always existed in Nature. People have known of the cleansing power of the Ganges River, even as far back as ancient times, how its holy waters seemed to cure such deadly diseases as cholera, dysentery and leprosy, but it wasn't until around the advent of the First World War that an infinitesimally-small, invisible bactericidal parasite was proposed which later became known as a 'bacteriophage' (eater of bacteria). The electron microscope turned speculation into fact decades later. The bacteriophage resembles a tiny moon-lander, far removed from the prion that causes CJD. Tail fibres flex and attach to the bacterium wall while the genetic material within the head capsid is injected in hypodermic-needle fashion through the base-plate directly into the host cell, disrupting all normal metabolism and reprogramming it into a huge-scale phage production factory, as it assembles virion upon virion until the host cell is ultimately overrun, bursting at the seams, a process called 'cell lysis', releasing the legion of offspring to go and infect other cells and perpetuate the life cycle. The beauty about the phage virus is that it attacks only a specific strain of bacterium, and for this reason, can be modified or designed to completely treat terminal pathogenic bacterial infections—and antibiotic resistance. Such phage therapy therefore had a potential application against, in this case, MRSA. The drawback with phage therapy is that, with its host cell-specificity, it is very expensive, not particularly cost-effective, which is why it wasn't authorized in the West, and only, albeit extensively, trialled and implemented in Soviet Russia from where the original clinical research sprang, going as far as treating gangrene in soldiers. Eastern Europe had long-since advocated the merits of phage therapy and the West listened closely and became wise. With the healthcare facilities overwhelmed by the rampant increase in MRSA infections and the complications incurred, Western governments paid their biotech labs billions to engineer and synthesize the phage to target this extremely dangerous hospital-acquired strain of the disease. Manufactured *en masse*, the phage proved a miracle in the making, mopping up the MRSA. Cases of MRSA fell dramatically, and the world breathed a massive sigh of relief and the scientific experts patted themselves on the back.

Yet, there was a snag. Despite the proven impact of phage therapy, the self-congratulatory boffins had not foreseen a different microorganism, present in up to eighty-percent of the population, normally harmless, awaken, inundate and crush the defences of its host in the most horrible way possible. Cytomegalovirus (CMV) is a virus which resides in a lot of people, infection from which largely goes unnoticed in healthy individuals and afterwards, like other herpes viruses, lies dormant in the body for the rest of the person's life unless they are severely immunocompromised (elderly, newborns, leukaemia sufferers, those undergoing dialysis or cancer treatment, organ-transplant recipients, etc.). In fact, a secondary infection from the normally-latent CMV almost defines the onset of AIDS in the unsuspecting HIV-positive patient as the T-cell count drops below the critical threshold. Whether asymptomatic or suffering the subacute clinical syndrome (sore throat, low-grade fever, enlarged salivary and cervical lymph glands and sometimes mild hepatitis) during the initial, primary infection, diagnosis is made through serologic testing or microscopically by the presence of 'owl's eyes' intranuclear inclusion bodies in the salivary glands.

CMV is transmitted through the intimate exchange of bodily fluids: blood, saliva, urine, tears, semen and breast milk. CMV is the commonest of the TORCH infections (together with Toxoplasmosis, Rubella and Herpes simplex) that can result in congenital abnormalities (40%). Infection during pregnancy can produce a condition called hydrops fetalis, an accumulation of fluid in the amniotic sac and hydrocephalus in the foetus, leading to miscarriage, whereas its postnatal complications include low birth weight, jaundice and neurological problems: seizures, deafness, visual impairment, motor coordination difficulties and mental handicap. In the immunosuppressed, CMV causes 'pizza-pie' retinitis, pneumonia, fulminant liver failure and encephalitis ('brain fever'). Dr. Jonas Riley, a freelance research scientist and statistical analyst, had already implicated CMV in the increasing incidence of emergency hospital admissions as well as noticing a curious trend in the rates of breast cancer, cardiovascular disease, diabetes, inflammatory/autoimmune conditions, neurodegenerative disorders and mental illness. He spoke of a hidden epidemic of a 'stealth' virus hiking up total healthcare costs. The scientific community ridiculed his findings, stating that a positive correlation did not necessarily mean 'cause-and-effect'. Proof, after all, can be an elusive mistress, and having dismissed his statistical data outright, no-one bothered exploring his claims and obtaining evidence either way. But Dr. Riley would soon be vindicated, as for once would the tramp wearing a sandwich board bearing the old legend THE END IS NIGH, because as MRSA admissions declined, cases of CMV infection soared. You see CMV is both a DNA and RNA virus and derives its name from the way it causes massive enlargement of the host cell it infects. In this case, the phage therapy reactivated the CMV, producing a severe, life-threatening infection. CMV was a microbe capable of incorporating the nuclear material of the phage virus and taking on its characteristics. In this extreme form, infection was rapid and lethal, associated with multi-system failure as it infected every organ in the body, including the brain. CMV was even able to extend its mode of communication through the air, hitching a ride on the once mutually-exclusive 'flu bug, adding the latter's genetic material to its own library of DNA.

As the emergency services of the world were bombarded by an accelerating epidemic, and the hospitals overflowed with new cases and were stretched to breaking point, the World Health Organization set up an Immunology, Infection and Inflammation Taskforce to address the worsening crisis. Isolate the sick, quarantine the exposed. Unfortunately, these high-ranking scientists could do little to contain the infection, with the preexisting anti-viral agents such as ganciclovir incapable of making even the tiniest dent on the numbers presenting with the CM-Phage or, as it came to be more commonly known, the Desolation Virus. There was no vaccine against CMV in existence since none of the clinicians had felt obliged to investigate Dr. Riley's observations, and their ignorance would be partly responsible for sealing the fate of Mankind. CMV's ubiquitous yet measurable pattern of involvement in hospitalizations, once recognized by this insightful statistician, would no longer be open to interpretation, now fully-realized and magnified to a catastrophe of Biblical proportions. Dr. Riley accepted a senior position in the newly-formed infection control subcommittee, but it was all too little, too late. The contagion ripped through the densely-populated cities with frightening speed, stretching its stinging tentacles, full of concentrated poison, outwards, contaminating and overpowering every aspect of normal biological functioning, death inevitable and unspeakable. Millions upon millions perished and the world came to a standstill. As with every viral contagion came the emotional contagion. The spiralling pandemic led to widespread panic and total pandemonium.

Law and order broke down, and anarchy reigned supreme. The social unrest was associated with looting and carnage and rape. Hazmat crews swept the streets with guns and flamethrowers. Governments collapsed and broadcast stations fell silent. All were left to fend for themselves, help never arriving. No person was immune: the monarch and the soldier, the priest and the prostitute, the banker and the pauper, the doctor and the invalid. The remaining humans fell victim to either the Desolation Virus or the savagery of the mobs, whose violence knew no bounds.

It turned into an unprecedented summer of death, as the grim streets, soon almost deserted of all life, piled up with rotting corpses, and the remaining human population subsisting in its post-apocalyptic ruins continued to dwindle. Ten thousand years of civilization and culture crumbled in less than twelve bleak months as the cities returned to the wilderness and its inhabitants turned to dust. Human existence on this planet, whether by evolution or intelligent design, had lasted an insignificant, ephemeral twinkling of an eye somewhere amidst the ungraspable infiniteness of far-reaching cosmic events.

The village of Swanney Haven, so-named because of its large, protected lake of Royal White Swans, had so far survived the highly-contagious plague sweeping the rest of the world. It was a rich and prosperous community, closed-off and, most of all, self-sufficient, forty miles from its nearest neighbour, rarely, if ever, requiring to smuggle resources from elsewhere since its forests frolicked with game, the coastal waters sustained an inexhaustible supply of fish and the pantries of the enormous mansions harboured all manner and quantity of exquisite things to eat and drink. Yes, thus far, Swanney Haven had got away with it, with business as usual, while the rest of society had been set back to a nomadic existence.

Ah, but remember, we should never underestimate Death, or believe we can cheat Death. We always live within the shadow of our own doom from the moment we draw in our first breath. Death is ever-present, condemning everyone of us, daring to claim us at any time, in umpteen different ways, no matter how much we lie to ourselves and deny its harsh reality or absolute authority. And Swanney Haven, like its children enjoying a fragrant afternoon in the sun, was living on borrowed time, overshadowed by a fatal, fast-moving pathogen that had already severely decimated the populations of the world and threatened to wipe out the human race.

Death does not discriminate. It judges us all to be equal.

3

Darius ran his tongue along another large Rizla as he finished rolling another elegant joint.

"I'm so happy you made it back safely," Josie said adoringly, now wide awake, appreciating his presence.

"Happy to see you too, kiddo," Darius replied absently, oblivious to the secret crush Josie harboured. He was focused on the fat, potent bomber he had expertly constructed. Even at seventeen, Darius was a veteran at the game. 'Builder's privilege' he reminded them and fired up the bad boy. He took several drags, held the smoke deep in his lungs to aid absorption and exhaled. The widening, contented smile on his lips spoke volumes. "Good quality shit!" he complimented, adding with his usual brand of loose but strangely plausible logic: "If Norman Bates had had a spliff personality instead of a split personality, he might not have gone psycho on everyone's ass."

Tyrone beckoned impatiently. "Here . . ."

Darius handed over the joint, and Tyrone went on to bogart it. "What's for lunch, guys?" Darius inquired.

"Munchies already?" asked Georgia, smiling.

Darius winked at Ash, nodding towards Georgia. "You tapping that?"

Georgia punched Darius's arm playfully while Ash just cleared his throat, perhaps embarrassed. "Behave!"

Darius chuckled, continuing the earlier conversation. "Come on, Georgia, you know I like my food."

Ash patted the Craft's lean stomach. "Doesn't show. Weedy as ever. Pardon the pun."

"Not as weedy as Jonquil."

"It's all about metabolism," explained Jonquil, always the budding scientist. They had it all at this party, even the obligatory rap-obsessed black boy as well as the fat oinky-oinker eating all the pie. All were loved, happy and well-fed, particularly Oinky

Osgood over there. More importantly, they were snug as a bug in their little, secluded-community rug even in this climate when the rest of the world was otherwise suffering the tortures of the damned, with food supplies scarce, and competing gangs of scavengers preying on the survivors, some resorting to cannibalism.

"The question still stands, addressed to the lady," repeated Darius. "Tell me about the grub."

Georgia went through the culinary inventory in the picnic basket. "One round of minute steak sandwiches with fried onions and horseradish, Kettle chips as an accompaniment and two boxes of individual apple pies for dessert, with lashings of ginger beer and OJ."

"Not forgetting the bottle of Grey Goose I smuggled out of my Dad's drinks' cabinet for a proper lash-up, of course," Ash added.

"Of course," Darius seconded. "Lubricate the old brain cells."

He tipped an imaginary hat to Georgia. "Thanks muchly."

"Keep everything away from Oinky," Jonquil ribbed, "or we'll all starve to death."

"You know I hate being called that!" moaned Osgood. "I prefer 'Oz'."

"Won't stick, I'm afraid. Besides, 'Oinky' is more amusing." Jonquil looked at Darius for goofy support and a witty follow-up, but Darius only returned a Don't-get-me-started glance.

Osgood did not attempt to defend himself or reply.

"Bottle of mineral water," Tyrone demanded. "Chop-chop!"

"Politeness doesn't cost anything," scolded Georgia gently.

"Yeah, and quit hogging," Darius mock-complained.

Tyrone glanced at them with bloodshot eyes, acknowledged the accusing looks, and protested his innocence: "What?" Suddenly grinning, he returned the doobie to the main, main man, even though Tyrone wished he bore that reputation. Darius passed it on to Ash.

"Ta, very much—" Ash accepted it with a cursory bow of his head, then stopped in mid-flow.

When Darius coughed on this occasion, his hacking was hard to miss, particularly since he sounded considerably chesty, verging on bubbly, and he spattered Georgia's face, who sat directly and lucklessly in front of him, with a fine, unintentional expulsion of blood and phlegm.

The unexpectedness of the episode produced a brief, eternal silence. The iPod came to a hissing halt.

Then, understanding gradually dawned on all their countenances, more so on Georgia's, whose expression twisted into one of revulsion and absolute horror. Someone seemed to have spray-painted her face scarlet. "Oh my God, *yuck!*—"

Darius was met by the others with wide-eyed expressions of apprehension and the starkest, realized fear.

"Why . . .?" Ash could only murmur. But he knew well enough what had transpired.

So did Darius. "I don't feel so well . . ."

Georgia was now panicking, her fingers working frantically but only managing to smear the full brunt of bloody mucus across her face. "I feel so *unclean!* Get it off me! *Get it off me! Why me, Darius, why ME?*"

Ash came to his girlfriend's rescue, carefully wiped her face with a clean napkin. She was shaking uncontrollably. Ash held her tightly, tried to comfort her.

"I didn't mean to . . ." Darius apologized ineffectually, suddenly appearing very ill and terrified.

Piper who hadn't uttered a word for a while suddenly raised the evil eye at him. "Get thee behind me, Satan!"

"Shut the hell up, woman!" Tyrone rounded on her, struggling to fight the effects of the pot and think clearly.

But Piper wasn't going to be intimidated by his tough, black boy act. He was the kind of imbecile who believed you could catch AIDS just by talking to someone with the disease. "Has it not occurred to you that you shared a joint with him?" she confronted him calmly.

Tyrone sobered up in a flash, his anger now directed at Darius. "*You goddamn asshole!*" His voice cracked, taking on the tones of a frightened, little girl, unbefitting for a self-styled bad ass who, like the rest of them, hailed from a privileged background, and despite never having stepped foot in any Hood, worshipped gangsta rap and often preached, in a rather juvenile, wishful manner, about the virtues of guns and bling, pimp mobiles and booty calls. "How could you do this to me?"

"I'm sorry . . ." came Darius's miserable whimper.

Ash, who hadn't yet taken a puff, dropped the offending joint as though it were a poisonous snake in a grimace of disgust and alarm. Pushing Georgia abruptly away, who fell backwards, still in shock, Ash rooted desperately through the picnic basket, found the hand-gel and splashed it across his palms, visibly overwhelmed by relief. Yet doubt lingered in his mind: *Kills 99.9% of germs, but what about the remaining 0.1%?*

He realized the others were looking at him for leadership and advice, despite his minor display of cowardly panic. He preferred to think of it as self-preservation, however. Nothing wrong with being cautious, thorough.

"What do we do about Darius?" Jonquil finally verbalized.

Ash took stock of the situation. The rate at which the good humour and friendship had evaporated was disturbing to say the least. Darius had contracted the Desolation Virus. There was no cure, and there was the ongoing risk of him infecting the others. As long as Georgia hadn't got any gunk into her mouth or eyes, she might just be okay—he prayed she was. He wasn't sure about Tyrone, either. "Someone needs to get back to the mainland and seek help."

Before anyone could volunteer, Darius heaved violently and barfed all over Tyrone's bad-ass Nikes. Splattered a thick, copious pool of greenish bile, streaked with blood, over those top-of-the-range Birthday kickers.

"Why you keep dissing me, man?" yelled Tyrone, after the initial startlement and revulsion had dissipated. He would have thumped Darius there and then—a first on his part—if it weren't for the fact the Craft was in a bad way. "You just can't leave me alone, can you?"

"You're doomed, I'm afraid . . ." Darius mumbled, a vague grin on his sweaty, sickly face.

"Don't say that! Oh shit, oh shit!"

Ash addressed the group. "I think we need to get moving now.

Row to the mainland, call for help, see what the grown-ups recommend . . . before it's too late . . ." But he knew it was already too late . . . at least for the Craft. But they had to try anyway. Hope was a powerful motivator.

Jonquil intervened, envisaging an even worse scenario. "We might infect the village."

"We have to do *something*," Ash replied adamantly. "I don't plan to die on this island."

That produced a tight hush. The reality, the bigger picture, was sinking in. It might be one of them next. Time was slipping by. Quickly, it seemed.

"I vote we make our way down to the beach," urged Piper in full agreement with Ash's suggestion.

Josie was crying. "You can't just leave him like this."

Ash looked sadly at the baby of the group, felt sorry for the poor little mite. He talked to her gently. "We have to. We've got no choice. He'll kill us all, otherwise. There might still be time to save his life."

Darius groaned, coughed up more blood. The linings of both his airways and gut were beginning to separate, break down. "Go, guys. Leave me be. I'll be okay."

Ash was grateful for Darius's blessing. It made the situation slightly more palatable, eased his conscience a little. "We won't be long, buddy. Promise. You stick in there."

"No, you're coming with us," Josie insisted to Darius. Her weeping eyes pleaded with him, with the others, who were treating one of their best, longest friends like a pariah, prepared to let him die.

"Don't be crazy, Josie!" Jonquil disapproved, putting an arm around his distraught sister's shoulders. "He's *infected*! We're supposed to minimize contact with the sick person and shouldn't even be in close proximity to them!"

Jonquil tried to reason with her, but she shrugged him off, resistive, determined. "I'm *staying* with him."

Jonquil couldn't believe his ears. He was at a loss for words, a look of dark alarm on his face.

"Fine, so it's decided then," Tyrone said, carefully removing his

Nikes and socks, discarding them, applying a little hand-gel across his feet and ankles. "What are we waiting for? Let's lock 'n' load!"

Jonquil was reluctant at first, afraid to leave his little sister behind like this in the company of someone—even if he was a friend—stricken with the plague, but Ash, along with Osgood's help, tugged fiercely at his arm. It surprised him that Jonquil had never suspected Josie was enamoured with Darius. Ash's long-held suspicions had been suddenly vindicated. "Come on. We don't have much time . . ." Jonquil started to move, wearing a dazed expression. As did Georgia, who was a little more responsive now, less bound by shock, but still equally robotically. Ash spoke to Josie in the friendliest fashion he could muster: "Please be sensible. Always keep in mind your own personal safety. Don't do anything risky or dangerous. We'll be back soon."

With that, the main party of teenagers departed, clambering down the steep rise for the beach and the single rowing boat on the shore. Josie stayed behind to nurse Darius, glancing up at the faded-blue sky, where screeching white gannets rode thermals, their stomachs full of fish. She shielded her eyes against the early afternoon sun, its scorching heat drying the tears on her cheeks. Hard to believe, she thought, how the unspoiled beauty of this peaceful idyll could lend a false, sinister sense of security to those who presumed, rather naively, that they had escaped the End of the World.

4

"How're you feeling?" asked Josie anxiously when Darius hadn't spoken or moved for a short while.

Darius stirred, opened his eyes, noticed her presence. "Hey kid," he murmured, the faint trace of a wearied smile on his countenance. "You chose to keep me company?"

Josie sounded critical and angry. "I didn't like the way the others abandoned you. I couldn't leave you like that."

"You know how much I cherish our friendship—and theirs— but they're right to shun me. You might catch something from an outcast like me if you stay."

"I don't care," Josie said stubbornly, applying a damp flannel to his burning forehead, wiping his runny nose with a napkin. Despite the heat of the afternoon, Darius was shivering from the high fever he had developed. "Someone must be with you in your hour of need."

"You mean my hour of doom?"

Josie began to sob.

Darius revised his comment. "My bad, kid—only joshing." He might be genuinely remorseful for torturing delicate little Josie with his distasteful attempt at gallows humour, but he knew he wasn't joshing about his impending doom.

Josie stopped crying. "Please, Darius, don't say such horrible things," she implored. Darius may have appeared seriously unwell, languishing on his deathbed *al fresco*, but it did not preclude him from detecting something peculiar in her tone and the way she had selflessly stayed behind to care for him. It suggested she did not just consider him as a friend, but it seemed as something more. Could it be—the girl had a *crush* on him? "I didn't mean to hurt your feelings."

"Then please behave yourself," Josie said primly.

"I shall indeed try to, Nurse," Darius responded.

Josie gazed lovingly down at him, dabbed his forehead again. Darius had another violent coughing fit, spitting more blood on the ground. He was gradually growing weaker, felt so inordinately tired. *The world is fucked*, he thought sadly. *Everybody's dead. Yet, I've somehow got exposed to the virus.* He decided to shut his eyes, blotting out the memory of the godforsaken, corpse-strewn cities he'd recently journeyed through.

"Darius, can you hear me? Are you okay?" Josie said, concerned, shaking him.

Darius's eyes flickered open, rheumy and puffy, picked her out, found their focus. "Hello, my dear, and who might you be?"

Josie gasped. The course of the illness was always the same. The respiratory symptoms, the vomiting and the diarrhoea, slowly bleeding from the inside-out, the memory problems . . . She remembered Jonquil had spoken about the CMV being 'neurotropic', that it had once even been implicated in Alzheimer's disease, that healthy elderly people had very low levels of CMV antibody titres in their systems. "Don't you know who I am?"

"No, my dear, I don't think we've ever had the pleasure . . ."

Josie was panicking now, but she had to come across as brave, in control, at least for Darius's sake. "Do you know where we are? What day it is?"

Darius thought about these questions with the profound look of someone who has just been asked to unlock life's greatest mysteries. "I couldn't tell you off the top of my head," he replied, the universal mathematical equation seemingly insoluble.

"Can you tell me your name?"

Darius considered, perplexed. "Now that's the funny thing . . ."

She was losing him. It wasn't simply a delirium state. Darius was dementing; there was no doubt in Josie's mind otherwise. The Desolation Virus had progressed to his brain, destroying his memories, obliterating his past. At this stage, the infected person would lose all knowledge of the world, unable to recognize people, even their own identity. There would be loss of language and motor skills, and ultimately, *oblivion*. But that wasn't the scary part. The scary part was the speed of the virus, a short four-hour incubation period, killing its victim in less than ninety minutes of them first showing the symptoms.

"So who are you again?" Darius whispered, scraping his sandpaper tongue drily across his cracked, scabby lips. His eyes were haemorrhaging internally as though he'd been throttled. His ears bled outwards as if his brain was leaking. "Too many questions making my head hurt . . . If I can just close my eyes for a few moments, rest, *sleep* . . ."

He shut his eyes and, this time, she knew he wouldn't wake up. He released a spent, terminal croak of breath.

The inevitability of his demise had somehow prepared her for his passing. Tears welled up in her eyes, spilled down her cheeks, but the intensity of her grief was somewhat diminished.

The Craft was dead.

Heartbroken, she looked down at his grey, flaccid body, peace instead of suffering written across his expression, and thought about kissing him, slowly leaning down. She just about stopped herself before her lips touched his pustule-encrusted mouth.

She recalled seeing the stream of news reports in those early days when the Desolation Virus was decimating whole communities and the world irrevocably changed, but *this* was— in this exact present spot—her first real-life exposure to death. Unless she had already contracted the bug—it didn't bother her if she had—she felt that witnessing the boy of her dreams suffer so unspeakably and succumb to the fatal sickness could only make her stronger.

5

Ash stood on the spit of shingle beach, staring out into the cerulean calm of the sea, figuring out how to proceed. His stomach growled, but lunch would have to wait. He couldn't eat now, anyway, not after the maddening afternoon heat he'd experienced and the awful predicament Darius was already in, knowing what must surely follow. Uncle Jim, who had dropped them all off in the morning in his powerboat, did not plan to collect them later since Darius and his very versatile and accommodating rowing boat had been tasked with this slight detail.

No mobile networks these days. One of them would have to go. Row solo. But who?

"I'll do it," Tyrone offered.

"Can't risk you going back just yet," Jonquil advised.

"And why not, may I ask?"

"You might be infected," said Jonquil flatly.

"Hey, doesn't inspire much confidence!" remarked Tyrone.

"Yes, you shouldn't go just yet," Ash seconded Jonquil, "at least not until you've been granted the all-clear."

"Hasn't it occurred to all of you," Piper suddenly interjected, "that our village might already be infected?"

"*What*—?" Tyrone exclaimed, incredulously.

"I mean we've been here since the morning, and who knows how many people Darius has infected on his return? There might not even be a village to go back to."

"Why would you want to say something like that, woman?" groaned Tyrone, getting agitated again.

"Yes, I have to side with Ty on this one," Ash instructed, "we need to start thinking positively." Yet, his attempt to convince the others that everything was still hunky-dory back home was met with a moment's troubled silence. Piper's chilling words lingered like a pestilence in the air. What if the village was really up shit's creek? Chances are they might actually be better off on this tiny, accursed rock. More to the point, what had become of their families? They daren't imagine . . .

Ash decided. "As the oldest, I think I should go . . ."

Tyrone stopped his whinging. "The hell you are! If it should be anyone, it ought to be me!"

"Okay, we could send Jonquil, then," suggested Ash.

"I'm not leaving my sister!" replied Jonquil.

"Someone has to go!" Ash insisted, "*Piper*?"

Piper dismissed his invitation to escape the island. "I'm safest here. Everyone in Swanney Haven might be *dead*."

"Will you quit it with that freaky shit, woman?" Tyrone demanded peevishly. "We don't need your kind of crock right now!"

Georgia, who hadn't uttered a single word, suddenly spoke up. "What about me?"

Ash grasped her arms, grateful his girlfriend was back in the land of the living, then on second thoughts, wiped his hands with more hand-gel, announcing full circle: "You stay here for now while I get some help."

Georgia nodded, as though only in partial understanding.

"What about me?" Osgood asked, annoyed at being ignored.

Ash began to head towards the rowing boat, only for Tyrone to swing him round and connect a clenched fist squarely with the jaw. "No way, mister! It's *me* who's going!"

Ash fell backwards, stunned for a few seconds. Then, as his vision was restored, and he realized what had happened, he lunged at Tyrone, rugby-tackling him to the ground. He climbed over Tyrone, trying to throw punches, albeit rather unsuccessfully. Tyrone tried to grab hold of Ash's wrists and they tussled furiously, the jagged shingles digging uncomfortably into their flesh.

"Stop it, guys!" Jonquil said, aghast, reluctant to physically intervene, separate them, in case he got thumped. After all, both boys were bigger and more familiar with schoolyard brawls than him. He looked at Osgood, whether the big guy might be able to dive in and stop this scrap, but Osgood did not catch his glance, only continued to stare dumbfoundedly at his scuffling friends. How the hell could this happen? Even when they'd moved from being 'big fish in a little pond' (in junior school) to 'little fish in a big pond' (high school), to quote Darius, they'd stuck together. "It doesn't help the situation! I'm sure we can resolve our differences in a more effective, civilized manner!"

Ash and Tyrone continued to roll around on the ground for several minutes, each as strong as the other, until the ferocity went out of their fight, and they surrendered to sheer exhaustion, leaving Ash propped up on top of a sprawled Tyrone. "*Get off me, asshole!*" Tyrone exclaimed, pushing Ash off, unable to contain the whiff of homophobia in his shrill voice.

Ash, too, got to his feet. "Arsehole yourself!" He consolidated his thoughts, regrouped, recharged. "What on earth are we doing? We're supposed to be *mates*!"

"I know, man," replied Tyrone, attending to his bare feet which had sustained cuts. "The situation is driving us crazy."

"Thank God you guys are back!" Jonquil said, immensely relieved.

"One of us has to go! And it's not you, Ty!"

Tyrone glared at Ash confrontationally. "Do you want to start again?"

"Guys, please, we need to resolve this now," Jonquil mediated.

"Hey, what about *me*?" Osgood reminded them again. "Am I invisible or something?"

"Nobody is going anywhere," Piper said suddenly, drawing the others' attention in her direction, and subsequently towards the rowing boat which they quickly realized she had set adrift during the commotion. It was already a faint, floating dot in the distance.

"What have you done, woman?" exclaimed Tyrone.

Piper justified her actions, quoting Scripture. "This is the Tribulation, a means to separate the wheat from the chaff, the righteous from the sinner."

"That was *not* cool!" Ash declared emphatically.

"What the fuck gives you the right?" Tyrone raged at Piper.

"I am only carrying out God's work," she replied, unflinchingly. "Your words will condemn you but only your works shall acquit you."

What on earth is that supposed to mean? Piper's puritanical tent revivalist nonsense was beginning to grate on Jonquil's nerves. Next, she'd be demanding a sacrifice to whatever cruel, wrathful, unforgiving god she prayed to. "Do you know what you've done? You've trapped us here!"

Ash was thinking fast. Unless someone could swim out and get the boat back, there would be no means of rescue or communicating with the coast. He knew they were all strong swimmers—it was part and parcel of living on the coast—but even if they got to the boat, retrieving it might be extremely difficult without the oars which still lay on the beach. He watched the speck of boat vanish into the distance, and he thought with dashed hopes, they were all now practically shipwrecked, cut off from all civilization. *"Tie her up!"*

"How dare you consider . . .?" Piper said, for once betraying a trace of emotion. But the boys moved quickly, surrounded her. "You can't do this."

"You're either with us or against us," Ash stated frankly. "And it sounds as if you're on the opposing team."

Jonquil deflected it back at her, cutting her down to size. "Only our works shall acquit us, remember?"

Before Piper could speak again, the boys stormed her with lightning speed, grabbing hold of her arms. They overpowered her, brought her to the ground. She struggled, protested, but they were too strong for her and it was a smooth, coordinated effort. Using the rope from the absent rowing boat, which had taken the single flare-gun away with it, they trussed up her wrists and ankles. When the unpleasant business was done and dusted, she furnished them with a glowering look. "God will smite you for preventing His devoted servant from delivering His divine message..."

"Woman, you really need to get laid," Tyrone remarked honestly.

"Why? Are you offering?" Piper sneered contemptuously. "Four big boys ganging up on a girl. How's that working for you?"

Ash was blunt with the boys. "I'm not going to mess around." He gestured to Osgood. "You stay with her. If she says another word, please slap her one."

Osgood nodded, and Piper shut up immediately, continued to glare up at them harshly.

The moments spun out in a much-needed silence. Yet in that brief moment's respite, Ash's mind was ticking over as he tried to figure out a way off this rock.

"Hey, guys . . .!" said Tyrone urgently, spotting something up the beach.

The others followed the direction in which he was pointing.

It was Josie, heading back towards the group. They beheld her with gawks of astonishment as though she were some kind of ghostly visitation, watched her slowly approach.

Jonquil was the first to react. Dropping his guard, he raced instinctively towards her and hugged her fiercely. "I'm so glad you're back."

"What the hell do you think you're doing?" Ash ejaculated.

"She's my *sister*!" Jonquil reminded him.

Ash backed away, as did Tyrone and Osgood. "She might be infected!"

But Jonquil was primarily—and, perhaps, understandably—concerned with reuniting with his baby sister. "We don't know that for sure!"

Ash addressed Josie warily. "How's Darius?"

Her tired, tear-streaked face should have said it all. But, in that sad, tortured expression, the boys discovered a new-found resilience, the look of someone who has seen too much suffering, like those unfortunate child soldiers of Africa, and developed a disturbing immunity to such horrors. "Darius didn't make it."

Jonquil notwithstanding, they no longer trusted her.

6

The party of teenagers sat on the isolated beach, gazing up at the westering sun, sensing the passage of the afternoon. It was bad enough their best friend had perished, but the fact that the wider world was encroaching deeper on their territory and threatening their very existence brought a new perspective on their current, dire circumstances and the concept of survival. They racked their brains, sought originality of thought, tried to devise a definitive means of fleeing this islet, but no workable solution presented itself. They kept returning to the option of one of them swimming to the mainland, but despite Osgood's optimistic offer to take on the task, Ash knew whoever chose to undertake this piece of strenuous exercise wouldn't stand a chance. The undertow would surely get them, pulling them beneath, and they'd also be at risk of the riptide repeatedly tossing them back. Ash wouldn't dare, let alone permit Osgood with his chubby frame to do anything so hazardous or suicidal.

As the boys took a mental step back and cogitated between them, Josie leaned her head against her older brother's shoulder, silent, preoccupied. Piper remained uncomfortably bound in knots and proverbially gagged, not daring to speak, lest the boys should honour their promise and strike out at her. Deliberately kept on the fringes of the group, head bowed, Georgia seemed to be its near-forgotten member until she started to unexpectedly and vigorously scratch her stomach as though infested with scabies. Now, though, the others took notice of her.

"You okay, Georgia?" asked Ash, suddenly suspicious.

Georgia glanced up at him, lifted up her summer dress, and

the others recoiled in stark abhorrence. Even Piper appeared somewhat startled, shuffling away in her tight restraints. Osgood who guarded her moved away, also. It wasn't so much the conjunctival haemorrhages, rendering Georgia's eyes vampire-red, or the widespread, excoriated rash on her belly, weeping blood, but her white panties that were no longer white. They were soaked crimson as though she had suffered a heavy menstrual bleed. She coughed, loosening the congestion in her chest, blood spilling down her chin, giving the others the impression she was wearing a Scotsman's ginger goatie. She mustered a hopeless, bone-weary moan. "I'm sick . . . I need help . . . *Help me . . .*"

"*No effing way!*" Tyrone shrieked in downright revulsion, scrabbling backwards.

"Let me deal with it," Ash said, rising slowly to his feet. He could not bear this anymore. He had to act . . . and *right now*. He walked meaningfully towards Georgia, stepped around her... and picked up a large rock as hefty as a bowling ball.

"What are you doing?" Jonquil began, catching a facial expression set in stone, as hard as the rock he was carrying.

Georgia must have known what he was about to do, for she murmured listlessly, her right hand reaching up towards him importunely: "I thought you loved me . . ." Ash looked down with a moment's pity at her once-lovely face, her chin now daubed in blood like some hungry cannibal, her grey, mottled skin the colour of rigor mortis, that juicy crotch he had 'tapped' haemorrhaging outwards with the flow of a leaky faucet. Doctors called it 'euthanasia', and before the coming of the plague, a debate had raged in Parliament over its legalization, a controversial subject successive governments and the medical profession constantly rejected, as they did with cannabis. But in a world where there were no longer any governments or police organizations to enforce the law, Ash had been forced to improvise, step up when no-one else would and commit an act that should humanely put his girlfriend out of her misery, spare her the full, hideous agony of her suffering as she sped imminently towards her death, like killing a severely-injured animal by the side of the road. Pushing aside the psychological constraints binding his conscience, he brought the rock down using every ounce of his strength, splintering her skull with the wet, crunching sound of a sledgehammer through a ripe marrow, Georgia's eyes rolling up into their sockets as she tumbled to the ground, motionless, very, very dead. Blood immediately seeped out of the shattered wound, staining the baking sand and pebbles with a carmine stickiness. Ash dropped the rock and, without uttering another word, walked off to reflect on the hardest decision he had ever made in his life. He supposed he had gained some appreciation of the term 'alpha male'.

The others watched the mercy-killing, speechless and appalled, but understanding the rationale underlying this grisly, morally-ambiguous act of violence. Because that's what it was meant to be: the *mercy-killing* of their infected friend by the said-girl's adoring boyfriend, who had already lost his best friend to the contagion. A horrendous deed but *necessary*. Some might even call it a 'kindness'.

Ash went up the beach, negotiated the slope and disappeared over the ridge. Tyrone didn't waste time. He followed him, even though he knew Ash needed some time to himself. Tyrone had his reasons, reasons that had nothing to do with being supportive or companionable.

Jonquil watched Tyrone chase after Ash, feeling a further nameless dread worm around his guts. Only six hours ago, they were all having a delightful time, drinking and smoking pot and basking in the hot sunshine. Then it had all gone downhill since the arrival of Darius, even though he should have been a welcome presence, the soul of the party, in fact, and Jonquil doubted the current downward slide would stop there. Jonquil suspected that something far more terrible was about to happen. He decided they had to move from this beach area. He did not fancy the idea of staying in the same vicinity as Georgia's corpse, seeing the damn thing decompose.

The shadows grew long, and despite the four of them migrating to a different location up the beach, one of their number securely-fastened, there could be no pretence that their overall situation remained unchanged and every living person on the islet remained firmly grounded between a rock and a hard place.

7

Ash needed time-out, to explore his dark and hollow headspace. The way in which he had murdered his first love sat uneasily with him. For the past twelve months, they had all been protected from the Desolation Virus by Swanney Haven's affluent, self-sustaining nature, and its hermitic location. Not any more, perhaps. Certainly not on this islet. The infection had killed two of the dearest people in his life in close succession, Ash forced to fast-track the second death. These weren't decisions any boy of his teenage years should be forced to face.

He did not want to go anywhere near Darius's corpse, see what had become of it—he knew from news reports it would not be a pretty sight. He wandered through the wooded hillside and found a fallen log upon which he plumped himself down. Sunbeams shone down through the chinks in the foliage, illuminating the dancing pollen like dust-motes. It was a glorious spot, the summer weather complimenting the greenery and the bustle of wildlife noticeably oblivious to the harrowing events of the day, but Ash remained somewhere else.

A man might be the sum of his memories, but it is the parents who maketh the man.

At this relatively tender age, your personality was still not fully-developed, and your sense of right-and-wrong was only as good as your parents'. Every growing child relied on their parents to guide them and instill whatever moral fibre they themselves had learned from their own parents. Ash and his gaggle of friends were still kids in need of adult supervision. And they needed it now, most of all. Ash felt he could have done with a verbal clipping from his Dad. Ash did not feel he was old enough or sufficiently mature to have made the moral decision he'd made. What he'd done to Georgia would plague his conscience just as the real plague stalked each and every one of them. Those discreet fumblings in the back of his father's car, one evening, had progressed to them mutually sharing the curiosity. He had come prematurely, as was often the case the first time, but both had appreciated that intimate moment, bringing them emotionally closer together. Yes, it was only the one time, but at least they had broken the taboo, with more such moments expected to follow. Now the girl who had passionately let him in, Ash had been compelled to bash her brains in.

Her tinkling laugh arose from the depths of his mind, reverberated inside his skull, faded like a forsaken ancient thing in the fog, and died. Ash wanted to cry, but the tears wouldn't flow. Besides, he didn't want the others to see him break down, show any visible sign of weakness. Not only did he have to come to terms with his violent actions, quieten his conscience, he had to work out a way off this uninhabited rock. So far, the weather was good.

We can't stay here till winter falls.

If we live that long, his other self responded bleakly.

Swanney Haven will send out a search party.

His inner pessimism shot him down again. *That's if Swanney Haven is still an active, thriving community, and its inhabitants haven't all snuffed it.*

The urge to cry was greater, but nothing happened.

We may need to build a shelter, hunt down a food source.

There could be no avoiding the truth, however. Their paradise of Cygnet Cove, once their Sunday sanctuary, had descended into a paranoid, every-man-for-himself living hell. *Not if the virus claims us sooner.*

But he couldn't tell the others that. They had to feel there was still hope, believe that he could lead them to safety. The sharp snap of a twig behind him disturbed the brooding silence, and as Ash began to turn, a white-hot agony flared up his back. Such was the blinding gravity of the pain, Ash fell forwards as his legs turned to jelly and gave way. He crawled briefly on his hands, dragging his body along, until the all-consuming pain sapped his strength, and he collapsed.

Somewhere nearby, he heard the perpetrator explode into a croup-like coughing fit—the coughing of someone in incurably poor health.

"You got rid of Georgia in a hurry, didn't you?" he heard Tyrone say. "You'd do that to me, too, would you?"

Ash tried to speak, and rolled onto his back, pushing the knife deeper into his body, exacerbating the already-unendurable pain to the point of blacking-out . . .

. . . He didn't know how long he was out. But he experienced the weirdest dreams in the world. He dreamed that Georgia was still alive, and he and she somehow got back to Swanney Haven to find the place deserted. In a sequence of delirious fragments, he learned they were the last people alive on earth . . . and started a family, mating like cats, to rebuild the human race. Generations down the line, they would be worshipped as the new Adam and Eve, until the genetic risks of inbreeding would devastate their small population of descendants . . .

As Ash drifted back up to consciousness, he caught the sweet scent of jasmine, the steady drone of insects . . . and it began to rain. He welcomed it. At full recall, he understood he was still on Cygnet Cove, during the last days of Man's domination of this planet. Someone had stabbed him, plunging and twisting the knife into his back. Hence the ongoing, searing, unfathomable pain shooting up his spine. It continued to rain. Then he noticed the rain was thicker and warmer than the usual summer showers that visited the land, syrupy in texture, with a distinct coppery scent, and rather salty on his tongue.

He slowly opened his eyes. The image before him swam but gradually steadied, and he finally attained full visual clarity.

Tyrone stood above him, combat shorts around his ankles, casually urinating over his face. But, it wasn't the yellow river, familiar to all men, which cascaded down. But a fountain of piss that appeared as ruddy as a good claret.

Grossed-out to the nth degree, Ash began to splutter in a prelude to upchucking, attempted to physically move, couldn't. Not on account of the utterly unbearable pain racking his body but because the knife had severed his spine and paralyzed him.

"What does it feel like being diseased?" Tyrone snarled, staring down at his friend, their eyes meeting. Ash's reflected mortal alarm. There was none of the old buddy love in Tyrone's eyes, either, only murder.

Unable to hold down a scream, Ash choked on the stream of frank blood that spattered into his mouth.

8

Tyrone pulled up his pants. His penis was inflamed and swollen and sore and raw. It was absolute agony to pee, like peeing through hard grit—or broken glass. But it had to be done. Ash had to learn. *Had to pay.* Tyrone had degraded him and left him either unconscious . . . or *dead.* He didn't care either way. The final outcome would still be the same.

Tyrone could admit he had acted beyond the pale. But so equally deplorably had Ash. Ash might think he was doing the girl a favour, but he had executed her with cold-blooded efficiency. There was something he knew that Ash didn't. Georgia had confidentially disclosed to Tyrone that she had missed her period. Apprehensive yet excited, she told him that a pregnancy test had proved positive. She was supposed to tell Ash, the father of the child, *today.* Ash had diddled her once and put a bun in the oven. Georgia might have added to the statistics for teenage pregnancies, but there was no official record-keeping these days. Nor would she be alive and well to reach full-term. It surprised Tyrone that unplanned pregnancies could even occur in smart, prosperous, well-informed communities like Swanney Haven.

Even if Ash wasn't yet aware that his girlfriend was in the family way, the cold-blooded manner in which he'd dispatched her and the spawn of his loins she carried was, in Tyrone's view, unforgivable. So Tyrone had dispatched Ash, cold-bloodedly stabbed him in the back with a table knife from the picnic basket, before the motherfucker could do likewise to him. *A breakdown of ego boundaries,* Jonquil would have nerdly diagnosed. Tyrone arrived back at the spot where they had all enjoyed a lovely morning. Before Darius had arrived. Where he had died. And where he still lay.

It was strangely intriguing to see what had become of Darius's corpse, knowing the same thing would happen to him, but Tyrone had now *accepted* his fate. It didn't bother him that he sat a couple of feet away from a rotten, disintegrating corpse, very likely breathing in its infectious miasma.

Tyrone's skin was flaking off, and he was coughing up his lungs and pissing blood. His memories were fragmenting, which had nothing to do with the lifetime of weed he had smoked. Might not be all that bad losing one's mind, being pleasantly confused. His fear was thankfully gone.

Tyrone sat down on a boulder and looked out across the water, contemplatively. The setting sun was bleeding the sky orange.

It seemed he would never see his family again or inherit his father's law firm. He picked up the contaminated joint Darius had built and shared earlier, sparked up and began puffing away. Surely for the last time.

And patiently awaited his death.

9

Ash's body was sprawled on the ground near the clearing in the woods. He neither moved nor breathed, eyes opened and glazed and unseeing. Staring down at his recently-deceased friend, Jonquil felt a bleak, overwhelming sense of loss, but he told himself he had to maintain his objectivity in what had turned out to be a seriously messed-up and tragic situation. It was no mystery that Tyrone had plunged a knife deep into Ash's back. Not that Jonquil dared to roll the body over; the blood pooled up and congealing on the ground provided confirmation enough. And then there was tacky mask of blood on Ash's face and the strange, ocean-trawled stench emanating from it . . . the smell of concentrated *urine*?

Jonquil recalled the book they had been studying in English Lit class, *Lord of the Flies*, a boy's own adventure gone terribly awry, the story of public schoolboys stranded in the South Pacific, as they slowly revert to a savage state, with painted faces, tribal dances and sacrificial gifts to the mythical beast they fear roams the island, which initially a downed, dead pilot is mistaken for, but soon becomes the metaphor for Man's intrinsic evil nature, the savagery that hides behind even the most civilized veneer. Here, on Cygnet Cove, the only things they were missing were the pig-hunts and the slaughtered sow's head on a spear.

Jonquil heard a rustling behind him, and he swung round. Josie had crept up on him and was silently surveying the scene.

"You shouldn't be here," advised Jonquil, the ever-protective brother. That meant Oinky was alone with Piper.

But Josie said nothing, continued to stare expressionlessly down at Ash. Jonquil tried to cover Josie's eyes, but she shook him off. "I'm not a baby . . ." she murmured.

Jonquil decided to check in on Tyrone. He wasn't keen to bump into him, but, judging from the splodges of bloody urine drying on Ash's face, Tyrone might not exactly be in the best of shape. He thought he knew where Tyrone might be.

He took Josie by the shoulder and they got going. It was only a short walk to where they had enjoyed a very entertaining and relaxing morning. Brother and sister arrived at the spot to find Tyrone still seated on a boulder. The stench of death hung heavy in the warm, dusky air.

As they approached him, he looked up and they saw that he was in the advanced stages of the disease. His eyes were the purest crimson, there was darkish blood smeared around his mouth and chin and on his T-shirt (which he had used to wipe his face with), and his once-mocha-coloured skin had greyed considerably, taking on a peculiar translucent tint. "Who goes there?" he asked, and suddenly the livid, liquefied flesh of his left arm separated from the bone, and dropped to the ground with a thick, mushy plopping sound. "I think I'm dying . . ."

The retch-worthy, yet almost comical, coming-apart of Tyrone's body might have amused some people, but Jonquil was staring at a close friend who was so incredibly close to death, the Desolation Virus consuming his body from the inside-out, his flesh losing its integrity, its cohesive properties. "I'm so sorry, old chum..." Jonquil managed to utter, knowing these sad, sympathetic words might be the last thing Tyrone ever heard. He couldn't believe Tyrone was still alive. Tyrone released the smile of a blind man, as serene as much as it displayed gratitude. More gelatinized flesh splashed wetly to the ground, this time detaching itself from his legs, so that now he sat on the boulder, propped up by the white gleam of the still-connected femur, tibia and fibula of each leg.

This is just way too crazy! thought Jonquil, fascination mixed with revulsion. Tyrone's face continued to melt of its own accord, liquefy and splatter on the grass with the sound of someone wringing a sodden towel, until at some point, he had lost a significant proportion of his bulk, and his heart stopped beating or perhaps his brain shut down, and he could now confidently be declared clinically dead.

His disintegrating corpse tumbled unceremoniously forwards. Several feet beyond were the carrion remains of their original Typhoid Mary. Darius's corpse had already been stripped to a near-skeleton, not by the foraging, egg-laying behaviour of the insect-life but rather through the end-stage liquefaction process of the condition. The crows, an unexpected presence on this rock, gathered to pick the human carcass clean. The few desiccated chunks of flesh that still clung to the bone attracted the first flies. Mealworm beetles crawled in the eye-sockets.

Josie raised a shaking hand to her mouth at the disturbing sight of Darius's meagre, fly-blown corpse. Nevertheless, she declined her brother's offer of a consoling shoulder. Such seemed the devastating effect of the Desolation Virus, driving its victims to the extremes of suffering and senility, rapidly reducing the person to a gruesome state of *living* putrescence.

Of the four surviving teenagers on Cygnet Cove, their ordeal was far from over. The midsummer sun long-since sunken below the horizon, the half-light of dusk surrendered to the approaching evening. Little did they suspect the inexorable horrors of the day would now spill over into the deepest, darkest hours of night.

10

Piper had been biding her time, plotting her escape and calculating her revenge. She wrestled with her bonds, but they could have been professionally-tied and would not budge. She thought she should use a different tact, spying Osgood sitting there, arms wrapped around his knees, silently staring out to sea.

Osgood wasn't the sharpest tool in the box, which must mean he was ripe for manipulating, open to suggestion. Unfortunately, God hadn't gifted him with the brains most people took for granted, the motive for which only He knew. Instead, Osgood's greatest asset was his stomach, rendering him a human dustbin, but also risking the sin of gluttony. Piper did not intend to question God's plan.

The sweltering day had given way to a clammy, stifling evening. The waves casually washed the shingled beach. Glittering pinpricks of starlight painted the clear, violet sky.

"Oz, how goes it?" Piper asked, deciding to strike up a conversation.

"Okay," Osgood responded, slightly surprised. "You called me Oz..."

"But of course," Piper explained. "I'm not like the others. I believe someone should carry the nickname they fancy, not one that has been forcibly and maliciously thrust upon them. I do not like humiliating others. I recognize everyone has a right to be treated with respect."

Ordinary surprise widened to stark astonishment.

Piper put forward emphatically, somewhat venomously: "Yet you and the others have humiliated me . . ."

She got the desired reaction. Osgood suddenly looked uneasy, perplexed—*God Bless the daft prat!*

Piper elaborated, citing the obvious. "You physically restrained me, tied and confined me, refused to let me go. That does not seem particularly respectful, don't you think?"

Osgood shook his head, evidently full of guilt.

"You must understand, Oz, it is very difficult being a Christian without receiving God's spirit, but I am privileged to be His instrument. You are either with God, who will reward you for your services, or against Him, in which case you will suffer His Absolute Wrath—and *believe* me, it will not be a pretty sight! Choose whose side you wish to be on."

"What about the others?"

"*They know not what they do . . .*" Piper testified, sharing some of her experiential insights with him. "They are too late to receive His salvation. They think they will be accepted by Him, but they have already condemned their unrighteous souls to the eternal fire. But there is still time for me to act as your minister and rescue your hellbound soul. *I* can promise *you* God's divine protection. We shall sit at God's table, reaping the bountiful fruits Heaven has to offer, when all of this is over."

"You're not going to trick me with your lies!" Osgood threatened, raising an open palm, getting ready to whack Piper.

"Oz, listen to me!" Piper impressed, continuing to steadily reason with him, quietly manipulate. "Who's deceiving whom here? Me, who studies the Good Book regularly with praise and conviction, or the others, who lounge around idly, smoking dope and getting wasted on the demon drink? I have faith in you, as you, too, should have in yourself. *The spirit is willing but the flesh is weak.* You are an intelligent, confident, sensible boy, no matter what the others think when they mock you and laugh in your face. I trust you will make the right decision. Tell me, Oz, are you with me?"

Osgood's expression softened. He nodded timidly.

Piper smiled inwardly, satisfied. "Wise choice, Oz. Now untie me..."

11

By the time Jonquil and Josie got back to the beach, Osgood and Piper were nowhere to be seen. Worse, Piper's bonds were discarded on the ground. Jonquil was at a loss, and afraid.

What do we do? Jonquil considered urgently. *We can't have Piper running amok on Cygnet Cove, spouting religious nonsense and acting on that very nonsense.*

Jonquil gazed out to sea as Osgood had done earlier, taking in the gentleness of the waves beneath a starry, midsummer night sky. Josie stood beside him, looking out, also.

"There they are," Piper's voice suddenly spoke up behind them, "back at the scene of the crime."

The two Buist-Wells kids swung round, startled. Piper and Osgood approached them slowly, ominously.

"What on earth are you doing, Oinky?" Jonquil demanded, staring nervously at the oar Osgood gripped in his chubby hands. "You're supposed to be watching Piper."

"Piper is going to save my soul," Osgood replied, as if this explained everything.

Jonquil was incredulous. "So you joined forces with her?"

"Piper promised to *save* my soul," Osgood reiterated.

"Think, Oinky!" Jonquil beseeched. "Nature has given you an amazing brain. Piper is deceiving you, *using* you!"

Osgood went berserk. "Don't call me Oinky!" With that final edict, Osgood swung the oar expertly in a half-arc, its paddle striking Jonquil forcibly on the left aspect of his skull. For a brief moment, Jonquil's head vibrated on his shoulders, and his vision blurred before gently filtering back. Josie threatened to lunge at Osgood but chose the better of it, opting against his substantial frame and aggressive posture. They had to move, get away. Josie instinctively grabbed her brother's hand and began to run, pulling Jonquil, who was gradually regaining his senses, along. Fortunately, Cygnet Cove, though not particularly big, was still large enough to conceal a few good hiding places, while Osgood would understandably slow down Piper's attempt to pursue them.

Josie led Jonquil hurriedly past the fly-infested skeletal remains of Darius and Tyrone on the rise (where the picnic basket full of cutlery had disappeared), through the clearing in the woods (where Ash's corpse was starting to disintegrate and stink), towards the farthest and the highest point on the islet. The land continued to get steeper and steeper, sweeping upwards to create a dangerous cliff-face. Here were also some sneaky hidey-holes where the fugitives could hide out.

Yet Josie knew neither of them could stay hidden forever and would at some point have to confront the Jesus freak and her goon. But not before she would learn her brother had contracted the virus, speeding towards a death as gracelessly as that of his erstwhile friends.

12

Jonquil didn't feel all that well. It was like he was coming down with a massive dose of 'flu, which might be a half-truth. His head hurt, he felt queasy and he was burning up and finding it harder to breathe. The Desolation Virus, capable of mimicking any viral strain, including the influenza virus, had got to him, and it was only a matter of time before it took him over. As he hugged his knees in the tiny cave-space they had snuck into, he reflected on the day so far. The unbeatable Great Outdoors and the priceless merriment and friendship of drunken, doped-up teenagers . . . and the ever-worsening nightmare that would follow. It was already past their bedtime. Had a rescue party been sent out to look for them—had he really expected rescue?—or were there only empty mansions back home, mass graves, the villagers now victims to the CM-Phage? He did not wish to speculate on the state of affairs at Swanney Haven since he did not believe he would be alive to find out.

Jonquil had always been fascinated by the microorganism coined the 'virus', the smallest living thing on this planet. Not surprising it did not conform to the characteristics of all other living organisms. Theories abounded about the virus having originated from outer space, with a historically documented positive correlation between meteor showers or the passage of comets close to Earth's atmosphere and influenza epidemics. Even more bizarre was how twenty-percent of the human genome contained left-over viral DNA, with the potential for epigenetic effects associated with this merger. The Desolation Virus had perfected the art of invasion, promptly expressing genes that progressively mutated and shut down the host's pristine biophysiological functions. Alien lifeform or not, the virus had dropped slap-bang in the middle of his immune system and commandeered his body at a cellular level, and no matter how much faith he had in his immune system, the disease was about to devastate all his defences, set to do its absolute worst. Jonquil thought about the poor excuse that was the human race and the foreseeable chance to give another species, no matter how infinitesimally small, mastery of this planet. Perhaps something useful might come out of the extinction of Man and displacing his one-hundred-and-sixty-thousand-year, self-conceited dominance of this world.

Josie sat a foot away, the whites of her eyes focused intently on him. "You're ill."

Jonquil could no longer hold back his cough. The cat was out of the bag. He hacked away. Even in the midnight dark of the shelter, he could see the faint drops of blood on his handkerchief. "Yes, I am." He did not know when or where he had got contaminated, but there was no point in crying over spilled milk. It had happened, he was already dead in many respects and it was now his responsibility for something constructive to come out of his death. He was a thinker, not a doer or a fighter, but he had to save his sister from the lunatics baying for their blood in the name of God. He coughed again, the loud, unhealthy, raucous sound echoing in the tight confines of the cubby hole. "I need to get you somewhere safe."

Josie continued to stare at him uncannily. "Don't worry about me. I can look after myself."

It wasn't the reply he was expecting, and he felt both fondness for his little sister . . . and fear. She sounded like someone who had been pushed too far until something snapped. "But I need to get you back to the mainland, out of harm's way."

"You should be more concerned about your own welfare. You should decide whether you die now or wait till the virus takes full control of you."

It was such a scary, grown-up thing to say that Jonquil realized that a part of Josie was prepared for him not to suffer any further. Someone had once said that life was a painful form of death. When we died, the pain should be over. Jonquil admittedly did not wish to experience the entirety of the illness, the absolute horribleness of the disease process: the rapid physical degeneration of the human body, flesh melting and falling off in chunks, and as the condition continued to deteriorate, the accompanying mental decrepitude and the complete loss of self-awareness, a closing signature of the condition, until the person expired and became carrion for the flies. Jonquil believed in intellectual nourishment, forever searching for the profound, and pride prevented him from hanging around until he lost his marbles. *Nobody wants to die of their own volition, even if bluster and bravado nudges them to. All humans possess an inbuilt sense of survival, which can sometimes be over-ridden: for family, for national pride during wartime, for a tender kiss from your sweetheart, or for the unconditional love of a newborn baby. When the end comes, we have no ownership over our deaths. Is that profound enough?* "Will you do the honours?" he wheezed, asking tentatively, filled by a soul-sucking sadness that threatened to spill over into tears. "I will always love you, little sis, you know that. Please make it quick—and painless!"

13

"Get out of there!" dictated Piper. "I know you're in there—I can see you!"

Josie had finally been found out. It had taken much of the night, but nobody could hide here without discovery forever. It was only a matter of time, even in the dark of the small hours. Josie wriggled out of her shelter.

The shapes of Piper and Osgood loomed over her. Josie rose to her feet several feet apart from the others, confronted Piper on equal terms, without any show of fear.

"Where's your brother?" Piper demanded to know, taking in the streaks of dirt and blood on Josie's face and clothes.

Josie gestured wordlessly to the shelter she had emerged from.

Piper motioned to Osgood. "Be careful. He might be armed."

Osgood cautiously peered down the rabbit-hole, but immediately withdrew his head, highly revulsed. It stank like the shits in there, and did he actually catch a glimpse of Jonquil— except Jonquil was practically unrecognizable, having gone the way of Darius and Tyrone, a mouldering skeleton? Which meant that Josie must have squeezed in with the corpse of her egghead brother all night? "He's totally dead."

"You certain?"

"He's already wasted away," Osgood reassured her. "Take a look for yourself."

"Not necessary," Piper accepted, presently gloating over Josie with undivided attention. "We must decide on the fate of this little one. I guess it didn't end well for your brother." She ordered Osgood. "Kill her, as Abraham once sacrificed his son."

Osgood adjusted his posture uncomfortably. He did not want to go anywhere near Josie. He could not believe she had been in such terribly close quarters to her brother, squashed up to his decaying corpse. *Did she really spend the night like that?* He did not want to catch anything from her.

Piper picked up on his hesitation, snarled: "Do as I command! Do you want to burn in the depths of hell? I am the Right Hand of God. Whatever God cannot handle He passes on to me."

It suddenly occurred to Josie that Piper, who like the others had attended Birthday parties, Christmases, christenings, the aromatic chill-out sessions every Sunday with the in-crowd on Cygnet Cove and the same school as her, once a dear virtuous friend, currently sounded well beyond any straightforward, religious fanatic. She sounded unhinged—and Josie couldn't even begin to guess how far gone Piper was. "Can you not hear her crazytalk, Oz?"

Osgood felt confused. "I don't know . . ."

Piper was furious. "Don't listen to her, Oz! She's *lying!* That's precisely what she would try and make you believe!"

"I can't hurt her," Oz whined, wrestling with himself. "She's got to be infected and she's only a little girl."

That was enough sedition for Piper to accept. "I seriously question your loyalty and commitment to our sacred mission." Piper shoved Osgood in the stomach, his peepers widening in surprise, tipped him over the edge of the vertical cliff. He did not scream. He possibly didn't have time to. Perhaps, he didn't even realize what had happened, by the unexpectedness of Piper's violent push or the pulse-pounding instantaneousness of his death. The only thing the girls heard was his considerable bulk impacting on the rocks below, the sound of a cricket bat striking a velvet bag full of fine bone china. Neither girl was curious to peer over the edge at the outcome. Both knew he could not have survived the fall and that he would be a heap of smashed bones on the rocks.

Then there were two . . .

"Wicked girl!" the religious nut continued. "Look what you made me do! God will not look kindly on you!"

"And nor you."

"What do you know of God?"

"More than you, it seems!"

"You dare—?"

"Why wear the cross if you're not going to respect it?"

"It appears I will have to deal with you myself!"

"You got *that* right, sister!"

Piper suddenly pulled out a table knife from behind her dress, the same table knife Tyrone had used to kill Ash. The blade glinted menacingly in the lightening sky, dawn approaching. "The Lord giveth and the Lord taketh away."

Josie remained unnaturally calm. She had witnessed her brother puke up like a firehose, doubly evacuate into his pants, cough up gungy fountains of blood. He did not wish to experience the same undignified exit as Darius, Tyrone or Georgia and asked her to kill him before the onset of dementia and its accompanying mindlessness. He was dying, and his brains, as any budding Professor of Logic will tell you, as well as his brotherly affection for her were what he proudly considered his most important assets. She had respected his wish, strangling him with her bare hands, surprised at her own strength. It had been a clumsy effort on her part, and Jonquil had struggled horribly, thrashing around, gasping for breath automatically, even if he had tried to consciously suppress his internal systems together with his inherent will to live. But Josie had fiercely maintained her grip throughout, focused fully on the task at hand. The horrific act itself had taken a moment's courage but a surplus of sincere compassion. Then, Josie had spent much of the night cuddled up next to him, entombed in a rock cavity that had, for all intents and purposes, become his final resting place, as his body decomposed to a putrid ickiness. It was the least she could have done for her wonderful loving brother. "Is that supposed to scare me? I killed my own brother—what the hell are you to me?"

The challenge and daring and downright moxy in her tone caused Piper to take a step back, not expecting anything so icy from anyone so young. Piper faltered for a second, staring into eyes that had lost all trace of humanity. Then, her expression grew as adamantine as Josie's, as she immediately lunged at her with the table knife. Josie anticipated the thrusting blow, stepping aside and elbowing Piper in the neck, unbalancing the older girl. Piper hit the dirt, facedown, and Josie took full advantage of her fall. Marshalling her resources, reacting like lightning, Josie dropped down hard and heavy on Piper's back. One hand viciously pulled back Piper's hair, producing a wild howl of pain, while the other managed to wrench free the table knife. Still kneeling on and pressing forcibly down on those shoulder-blades, Josie tormented Piper further with the starkest words her innocent age could ever have hissed, "So where is your god now?"

Two left, one possible victor, must have gone through both minds at some stage during this confrontation, and before a frustrated, infuriated and alarmed Piper could generate any breath of a comeback, Josie drove the relatively blunt table knife with exceedingly brutal force straight through her adversary's right eyeball, bursting open the white vitreous jelly, punching through the bridge of the nose with the clack of a nail-gun, before emerging from the other socket with its equally-exploded eye, spearing the head into the earth.

The damask blush of dawn cleared away the last, lugubrious dregs of darkness.

The thirteen-year-old girl, who had recently lost her brother and her teenage crush as well as all her closest friends, got up slowly, gaze fixed grimly on the senseless slaughter of her own doing, the table knife effectively skewering those eye-sockets into the ground. She recalled Jonquil debating between but ultimately choosing Ethics 101 over Religious Studies. Josie was abruptly overcome by an agonizing paroxysm of chesty coughing, her chin stained by crimson driblets.

The Desolation Virus had finally caught up with her. She didn't much care to consider its ramifications.

She remembered Jonquil had made no apology for the human race. He would not speculate on the motives of the faceless global corporations, whether they had funded, perfected and released a genetically-engineered plague, a weaponized virus for the purposes of selective population control and creating a New World Order. Or, maybe, Josie was really one of the last humans alive, at least until overpowered by the contagion, playing out the last act of a dying civilization, with perhaps a radio transmission from an extinct alien race echoing across cosmic gulfs and aeons of time . . . the obsolete alien species once known as Man.

As Josie hacked and sputtered out more blood, she took in the diffuse rufescent glow of summer sunrise and the gannets plunging into the sea in search of their morning feed. She had to admit it was going to be another beautiful day at the End of the World.

March 2013—June 2013

Hack Track Listing

The HACK TRACKS . . . for purely filking purposes, of course . . .

Journey to the Centre of the Mind	The Amboy Dukes
Train Kept A-Rollin'	The Yardbirds
Is That You Mo-Dean?	The B52s
Cutt Off	Kasabian
Weirdo	The Charlatans
Novocaine for the Soul	The Eels
Down in the Park	Foo Fighters
Dry The Rain	The Beta Band
Rock With You (Swedish Rock Edit)	Inner Circle
Children of the Revolution	King Brillo
Teardrop	José González
Brain Damage/Eclipse	Pink Floyd
Crazy	Alanis Morissette
Extreme Ways	Moby
Shut Up and Drive	Rihanna
Black Coffee	All Saints
Fantasy	Appleton
Freak Like Me	Sugababes
Still Life	The Horrors
Scarlet Sky	7Ray

Also by the Author

DAMNATION INN

www.ingramcontent.com/pod-product-compliance
Lightning Source LLC
Chambersburg PA
CBHW030930020726
47498CB00001B/191